BLACK
LIGHTNING

JOHN SAUL

BLACK LIGHTNING

FAWCETT COLUMBINE

NEW YORK

A Fawcett Columbine Book
Published by Ballantine Books

Copyright © 1995 by John Saul

Library of Congress Cataloging-in-Publication Data
Saul, John.
Black lightning / John Saul.
p.   cm.
ISBN 0-449-90864-X
I. Title.
PS3569.A787B53   1995
813'.54—dc20   95-7600
CIP

Text design by Fritz Metsch

Manufactured in the United States of America
First Edition: August 1995
10 9 8 7 6 5 4 3 2 1

For Michael

PROLOGUE

Five Years Ago—
Experiment Number Forty-Seven

It was a ballet the man had danced so many times before that the first steps had become familiar enough to be performed automatically, with little if any thought at all. If he'd been asked, he couldn't have said exactly what it was about this particular subject that first caught his attention, what particularly had piqued his interest in including her in his study. Certainly not age—he'd never been interested in the relative youth of any of his subjects.

Nor did sex matter. There were nearly as many men as women among his subjects; whatever gender imbalances existed in his study group were purely a matter of chance, and, he was certain, statistically insignificant. Not that his critics would ignore whatever imbalances existed when they began analyzing his work—he was all too aware that every possible nuance of his study would be minutely examined, that every possible interpretation, no matter how outlandish, would be applied to his choice of subjects.

But the fact was that he really hadn't come up with any standard criteria for selecting participants in the experiments. Neither race nor gender, age nor sexual orientation, had counted.

Nor had he ever been particularly concerned about whether he invited the subject to join his study, or whether the subject was the one to make the first contact.

His current subject had made the first contact herself, as it happened, and he had almost rejected her on the basis that she seemed somehow familiar to him, that he knew her from somewhere. Familiarity was the single grounds for automatic ineligibility for the project, for he could never be certain of his own objectivity if he had previously existing feelings for the subject, whether positive or negative.

He'd first become aware of the woman a couple of weeks ago, when he'd happened into a shop near the university for a cup of coffee. He'd briefly noticed her when he'd come in, sitting near the door alone, a copy of the *Seattle Herald* spread out on the table before her. He'd paid little attention to her until he bought his own coffee and settled into a chair several tables away.

Had he subconsciously known even then that he would include her in the project? He would have to consider that.

It had been she who first smiled at him, then come over and asked if she could join him. As he recalled it now, she said something she seemed to consider witty, about them not taking up any more room on the planet than they absolutely had to, and he produced the expected smile for her. But instead of inviting her to sit down, he pleaded work, and she left.

For the next ten minutes he'd tried to figure out why she looked familiar, but it hadn't finally come to him until he opened his own paper to the editorial section and his eye had been caught by one of the columns:

How Much Longer?
Police Fiddle While Seattle Dies

Another week has passed, and the Special Task Force set up by the Seattle Police Department in cooperation with the King County Sheriff's Office and the Washington State Patrol seems no closer than ever to an arrest in connection with the series of bodies that has turned up in the foothills of the Cascades over the past five years. Indeed, thus far all the police seem to have determined is that all the victims appear to have been killed by the same person, a conclusion anyone who has seen the bodies couldn't easily have missed.

Yet when I talked to several members of the task force this week . . .

It hadn't been the story that had caught the man's eye so much as the accompanying photograph of the column's author.

Anne Jeffers.

That was why the woman he'd spoken to a few minutes earlier had seemed familiar: she looked very much like the newswoman. He'd sat staring at the photograph for several seconds, considering.

The woman had been in her early forties, of medium height, with the same kind of even features reflected in the photograph. The woman's hair had appeared to be of a similar dark shade, too, though Anne Jeffers's was somewhat shorter.

Was it possible it had actually been Anne Jeffers he'd spoken to?

A patient man, he'd finished his coffee, refolded his paper, and gone on about his business. But he kept his eyes open, and a few days later, when he spotted the woman from the coffee shop, he realized that she was not Anne Jeffers, nor was she anyone else he knew.

Discreetly, he'd followed her.

She lived not far from the university, in an old Spanish-Moorish-style apartment building the man had always liked.

Afterward, he made a point of walking by the building every few days. He'd seen the woman several times, and nodded to her.

The dance had begun.

It had gone on for several weeks, the two of them circling around each other in a strange pavane that was almost like a courtship.

They began nodding to each other, then saying hello.

He had begun to absorb the routines of her life, and found her—as he found most people—to be pathetically predictable.

Today, for instance, being a bright and cheerful Sunday, he was almost certain the woman would take lunch in a bag and go to bask in the rare warmth on the lawn of the university, where she would pretend to be reading a book while actually watching for a man—nearly any man, he had discovered—to show interest in her.

Today he would be the man to show interest.

Today the dance would end.

He left his car at home that morning, taking the motor home he'd bought four years ago, when the study had commenced. Perfect for field trips, he often drove it into the mountains even on weekends when he wasn't working on his research, parking it near any one of hundreds of babbling streams while he indulged himself in his only passion outside of his project: fly-fishing.

Today he drove the motor home up to the university, parked it in the nearly deserted depths of the cavernous garage, and locked it. Taking his own lunch and two bottles of lemon-flavored sparkling water with him, he climbed the stairs to the surface and started across the lawn toward the spot that was the woman's favorite.

Half an hour later, after she'd consumed half the contents of the bottle of sparkling water he offered her, she frowned, then shook her head.

"Something wrong?" the man asked, his gentle voice freighted with benevolent concern.

"I—I'm not sure," the woman replied. "Suddenly I feel—" She hesitated, then stood up. "I'd better get home!"

The man scrambled to his feet and began gathering both their things. "Maybe I should drive you," he suggested.

The woman started to decline his offer, but a second later, changed her mind. He could see that the color had begun to fade from her lips.

"If you could . . ." she began, but then, feeling light-headed and dizzy, her voice faded.

Gratefully, she accepted the man's proffered arm and let him lead her down into the garage, where his motor home waited.

Even before he drove it out into the bright daylight, the woman had drifted into unconsciousness, and was now spread out on the sheet of plastic he'd placed on the floor.

He pulled out of the garage, went west two blocks, turned right up to N.E. 45th Street, and headed west to Interstate 5. Taking the highway south, he exited at Route 520, heading east toward Redmond.

After a while he wound up into the foothills, looking for the right spot.

Somewhere off the road.

Somewhere secluded.

Somewhere near a stream, so he could do a little fishing after his work was done.

Finally he found the spot: a narrow road, one he'd used before, but not for years. A half mile through the trees and he emerged into a clearing next to a fast-moving stream. He looked around.

He was alone.

Now he began his preparations.

First, he stripped naked, folding his clothes neatly and stowing them in the drawer beneath the queen-sized berth at the motor home's rear.

After pulling on a pair of rubber surgical gloves, he covered the bed with a sheet of plastic and moved the unconscious woman onto it.

He continued working with the sheets of plastic, methodically lining the entire interior of the motor home; one of his prime rules when carrying out an experiment was that nothing must be contaminated.

Finally he was ready.

Undressing the woman, he gazed at her naked body for a few moments, savoring the life that seemed to radiate from it even as she slept.

Her breasts moved rhythmically up and down as she breathed, and when he lay his fingers gently on her neck, he could feel the pounding of her pulse.

He laid out the tools he knew he would need, then picked up the instrument he'd purchased the day before for this specific experiment, and squeezed its trigger.

It squealed shrilly as its blade began to spin.

The man began his work.

The blade of the cordless saw sliced through skin and flesh, parting the woman's sternum in a single quick cut up the center of her chest.

Setting the saw aside, the man spread her ribs apart and closed off the largest of her severed blood vessels with some of the surgical clamps he'd bought years before, when the research was still in its planning stages.

The worst of her bleeding stanched, the man slipped his fingers into the cavity within. He felt the woman's lungs—still working strongly—and nodded in satisfaction. Once more he'd succeeded in making the primary cut so perfectly that the subject's diaphragm remained undamaged.

He slid his fingers deeper, working them around the lungs until both hands rested against the gently moving tissue. He paused, thrilling to the sensation of life pressing against his palms.

But now the woman's breathing was beginning to falter. Time was running short.

The experiment must begin.

His fingers probed deeper, until at last he felt the familiar contours of a human heart.

Time seemed to stand still. . . .

When he emerged from the motor home an hour later, the man's hands were covered with blood. More of the glimmering red fluid oozed from the body he carried in his arms, drizzling slowly down his torso and legs, dripping onto the ground he trod. He carried the body into a thicket of woods, waiting only until he was fully screened from the clearing before dropping it unceremoniously to the ground. He gazed angrily at the woman's remains.

Her organs were all there, but no longer in their original positions, for when he'd realized that once again the experiment had failed, a dark rage of frustration had come over him, a rage he'd released by plunging his fingers furiously into the woman's lifeless body, tearing her heart loose from its veins and arteries, then pulling more of her organs through the incision in her chest as he searched for the reason for his failure.

Now he glared down once more at the lifeless body, its chest torn open to offer the world an obscene view of the carnage within.

He turned his back and walked away, finally abandoning the subject for whom, only an hour ago, he'd had such wonderful hopes.

Emerging from the trees back into the clearing, he went to the river and plunged in, letting the rushing water wash the blood from his skin and cool the burning rage that failure always caused him. Only when he was certain no trace of the woman's blood remained did he emerge from the river and return to the motor home, where, still naked, he carefully began folding the sheets of plastic in upon themselves. Soon the vehicle's interior was again pristine, all evidence of his experiment wrapped in the sheets of plastic, which in turn he placed inside a large white plastic garbage bag.

The man went back to the river and washed once more, then dried himself, dressed, and drove the motor home out of the clearing. Leaving it on the edge of the pavement, he returned to the clearing, broke a branch from a tree and swept it methodically across the ground, obliterating every tire print the motor home had left.

The branch he'd used to whisk away his tracks joined the soiled plastic sheets in the large trash bag.

As he started back down the highway, the man glanced at his watch and was pleased: there was still plenty of time to stop for an hour or so of fishing before he went home.

And as he fished, he would begin thinking about the next experiment. . . .

The cracked white face of the clock stood in stark contrast to the institutional green of the wall upon which it hung.

Nine A.M.

Three hours before noon.

High noon.

As the phrase went through her mind, a scene from the movie she still vividly remembered from her childhood came into Anne Jeffers's mind, and she saw again the black-and-white image of two men facing each other on a dusty street. She'd sat riveted in her seat at the old Coliseum Theater in Seattle as Gary Cooper, photographed from a low angle to make him seem even taller than he really was, had faced down . . .

Who?

Who had Cooper executed at high noon that day?

Though she still remembered the scene almost as clearly as if she'd seen it last week instead of more than three decades ago, she could not remember who played the bad guy. In those days, back when she was a little girl, it was the sheriff everyone had cared about, not the villain.

The question wasn't whether the villain deserved to be shot, but whether Gary Cooper would get him before he got killed himself.

Justice, pure and simple. Good guy versus bad guy, with everyone rooting for the hero in the white hat.

But today, when high noon came, there would be a different kind of showdown. This was no movie; this execution was going to be real. Further, the state of Connecticut had decreed that its first execution in almost forty years be carried out in the middle of the day, rather than in the dead of night—a decree Anne suspected was deliberately intended to remind the people that though they had the right to execute one of their fellow citizens, they couldn't expect to have the action carried out clandestinely behind the dark cloak of midnight. Nor would there be a Gary Cooper for her to root for today. Instead, there would be only a nameless, faceless man throwing a switch.

Then another man—someone whom Anne felt she had known for a very long time—would be dead.

Anne shuddered, and felt instantly ashamed. At forty-two, after spending the last twenty years working for the *Seattle Herald* reporting on everything from fatal apartment fires to the AIDS epidemic, there shouldn't be much left to make her shudder. She'd seen people die before; her own mother had passed away five years ago while she had held her hand, and Anne could still feel that last surge of strength that ran through her mother's body, giving the dying woman just enough power in the last moments of her life to offer her a final smile and an encouraging squeeze of her fingers.

Anne hadn't shuddered that day; indeed, as her mother's last breath emerged from her crumpled lips in a soft sigh of relief, and her wasted body finally retired from its long battle against the cancer that had inevitably defeated her, Anne felt only a quiet sense of gratitude that her mother's pain had mercifully come to an end.

Nor was her mother the only person Anne had watched in the last moments of life. She had sat helplessly with friends as they succumbed to the plague of AIDS, and she'd stood by in mute horror as victims of gang shootings died in the emergency room of Harborview Hospital.

Once she'd even found herself cradling the broken body of a ten-year-old who had just been pulled from the wreckage of his father's car on I-5. Anne had stanched the flow of blood from his neck with her handkerchief as she prayed for the medics to arrive in time, and sobbed in frustrated fury when the ambulance lost the race for the boy's life to a crowd of rubber-necking onlookers who had choked traffic on the freeway to a standstill.

*The same kind of crowd who waited outside now, waited for the
stroke of noon and the announcement that justice had been served.*

Justice, or Anne Jeffers?

Was that why she was shuddering?

Suddenly wanting to be alone to examine her feelings, Anne rose
from the hard chair in the makeshift pressroom hastily set up for
the fifty-odd journalists who had descended upon the prison to cover
the execution of Richard Kraven. She made her way between two
rows of long tables whose surfaces were littered with notebook com-
puters and phones. She rapped once on the door of the single rest
room that served all the men and women in the pressroom, then
went inside, locking the door behind her. Stepping up to the cracked
sink that was bolted to the wall next to a stained toilet, she stared
at her reflection in the rectangle of polished metal screwed to the
wall above the worn basin.

At least her feelings weren't showing, she thought with some relief. Her reflection—the image of an oval face with deep brown eyes
and a straight nose—gazed steadily back at her, only slightly dis-
torted by the ripples and dents in the makeshift mirror.

She searched her features again, then turned away, annoyed with
herself. What had she expected to find? Some brilliant insight into
her conflicted feelings written across her forehead? The fact was, she
knew perfectly well why she had found herself shuddering as she
waited for Richard Kraven's execution.

She had shuddered because this time, when she watched someone
die, she would know that she was at least partly responsible for his
death.

"Not true!"

Anne spoke the words out loud, so sharply that they reverberated
in the tight confines of the rest room.

And it wasn't true that Richard Kraven was being executed because of her.

He was being executed because of what he had done.

He was dying as punishment for his sins, and his sins were great
enough that he should be executed ten times over.

How many people had Richard Kraven actually killed as he

roamed the country in pursuit of his "research," as he called it, selecting victims for his horrific experiments?

No one knew.

Kraven had steadfastly denied killing anyone, but that was nothing more than the typical insistence of a sociopath that he'd done nothing wrong.

Anne Jeffers knew better. In addition to the three people here in Connecticut, of whose murders Kraven had actually been convicted, she was certain there were scores more. The bodies of men and women, young and old, had been scattered across the country from Kraven's home in Seattle down the coast to San Francisco and Los Angeles, and across the continent through Denver, Minneapolis, and Kansas City to Atlanta. Sometimes it seemed as if there wasn't a major city in the country that Kraven's cold shadow hadn't fallen over; even now the list of crimes in which Richard Kraven was the prime suspect still grew.

Yet even as Richard Kraven's evil had spread, there had always been people to defend him, several of them among Anne's own colleagues in the press. Some suggested the evidence presented in court hadn't been strong enough to convict him; others sagely opined that Kraven should be kept alive to study. But every time someone had written a story advocating that Richard Kraven be allowed to live, Anne Jeffers answered it.

Instantly, and strongly.

In the end it was her view that prevailed. Richard Kraven had been sentenced to die.

Now, two years after the sentencing, all the appeals had been filed, all the motions for new trials had been considered and denied, and all the other states having claims against Richard Kraven had agreed to save themselves the not inconsiderable expense of trying him for crimes indistinguishable from those for which he had already been convicted. Yet, in the years since he'd been convicted and sentenced, Richard Kraven had become steadily more famous, and the clamor to save his life had grown ever louder.

Anne Jeffers had listened in amazement to the growing cacophony of protest. Were there really people who thought a man who had been convicted of murdering and dissecting a ten-year-old girl could be rehabilitated?

How could anyone insist that Kraven was innocent in the face of all the evidence against him?

Evidence that Anne Jeffers had recounted over and over again during the years she had covered this case.

Evidence that Richard Kraven coldly insisted had been concocted, constructed, manipulated, or planted for the sole purpose of convicting him of crimes of which he was totally innocent.

Not, of course, that Kraven had ever been able to present evidence of the nefarious plot that he insisted had made nearly a dozen separate states conspire to frame him. Anne was familiar enough with the paranoid mind to know that motive never entered into the certainty of persecution.

The persecution was simply there.

And Richard Kraven—to Anne's mind the personification of the handsome and charming sociopath—had been able to convince thousands of people that the persecution was real and he would be executed wrongly.

He's guilty. Beyond a shadow of a doubt, Anne told herself, consciously straightening her back as she turned once more to gaze at her reflection in the warped metal above the sink. Richard Kraven had been tried, convicted, and sentenced, and it was the wisdom not only of the judge who had heard the case, but also of the appeals court that had reviewed it, that Richard Kraven should die today.

And she would watch the execution, and she would not shudder as the executioner threw the switch. Yet even as she steeled herself for what was to come, her eyes burned and her vision blurred with tears.

As she pulled a rough paper towel from the dispenser on the wall to blot the dampness under her eyes, a rap sounded at the door, immediately followed by a voice Anne recognized as belonging to the warden's assistant.

"Mrs. Jeffers? He wants to see you."

Crumpling the paper towel and dropping it into the wastebasket, Anne brusquely ran her fingers through her hair, glanced briefly at her reflection, then opened the door.

"The warden?" she asked. "Why does he want to see me?"

The assistant hesitated for a second, looked confused, then shook her head. "It's not Mr. Rustin. It's Richard Kraven. You're on the list of people he wants to talk to this morning."

Anne felt a tightening in her belly as she entered the pressroom. Why would Richard Kraven want to talk to her today? What could he possibly have to say that he hadn't already said in the numerous interviews she'd already conducted with him over the years? Was it possible that finally, at the last minute, he was going to confess? As the questions tumbled through her mind she became aware that the sound of fingers tapping keyboards had ceased. Silence fell over the pressroom as all her colleagues turned to look at her.

Once again she steeled herself.

If she could watch him die, certainly she could also listen to whatever he wanted to tell her before it happened.

"All right," she said to the assistant, who had followed her. Immediately, she wondered whether she'd spoken the words too loudly in the silence of the room. "Now?"

The assistant shrugged. "I'm not sure. I was just told to bring you to the office. Mr. Rustin thought you might want to wait there."

Anne hesitated, then saw the other reporters already starting to formulate the questions they would ask her to relay to Richard Kraven. For a moment she felt a flash of annoyance, then realized that if someone else had been summoned to Kraven's presence, she too would be scribbling down a final question in the hope of getting one last exclusive out of the story.

But not now. Not this morning. As she walked through the room, she held up her hand against the proffered scraps of paper and the clamor of entreaties. At the door, she turned to face her colleagues. "I'm only going to listen to him," she told the crowd of reporters. "I'm not going to ask him any questions. And whatever he says, believe me, I'll give you every word of it. All I want is for this story to finally be over." Then, before anyone could try to talk her into relaying just one question—"Come on Anne, be a sport!"—she slipped quickly out of the room.

As she walked down the echoing corridor, she was already preparing herself to face Richard Kraven for the last time.

CHAPTER 2

On the opposite side of the country from his wife, Glen Jeffers lingered an extra five minutes in bed, wondering if maybe he shouldn't skip his morning jog just this once. It was the kind of Seattle morning he hated—overcast, with a drizzling rain that promised to go on all day; not heavy enough to warrant a raincoat and umbrella, but just heavy enough to be annoying. Especially today, when he was going to have to be out in it all morning, inspecting the framework of the first high-rise his company had designed solely within their own firm.

Jeffers and Cline, Architects.

No partners; no other architectural firms listed on the big sign on the last developable block of the downtown sector; no other architects with whom he would have to share the glory for the spectacular design he had created. Soaring up forty-five stories, the building would step back from Fourth Avenue in a series of terraces as it rose toward the sky. But the feature he loved most was the park he'd designed for the top of the skyscraper. Covering more than half the block, it would provide a spectacular view of the city, the Sound, and the Olympic Mountains for anyone who cared to use the glass elevator that would ascend the north end of the building, carrying passengers directly from the sidewalk to any of the terraced levels or the park on the roof. In his building, at least, the best views would be open to the public, rather than reserved for the high-powered attorneys who were already vying for office space in what was rapidly becoming known as the Jeffers Building. It was a source of quiet pride for Glen that his building would be named for its architect, rather than its prime tenant.

He lay in bed for another few minutes, savoring the feeling of well-being that warmed him this morning despite the rain, and listened to the creaking of the old house he and Anne had bought nearly twenty years before, when they'd first gotten married. The house had been bigger than they really needed, and in terrible condition, but Glen had talked Anne into it. After all, he was an architect; he would turn it into a showplace for next to nothing. What he hadn't told her was that his skills as a carpenter, plumber, electrician, plasterer, and roofer were nil. But Anne, of course, had known that all along, and was pretty good with a hammer herself. In the end, the crumbling wreck of a house they'd picked up for only forty thousand dollars was now worth the better part of a million, and the neighborhood had come back along with the house. Anne and Glen, and the two children they'd had along the way, were now smack in the middle of one of the better parts of Capitol Hill, only a block from Volunteer Park, on a tree-lined street filled with other houses that had also been restored over the years since the Jefferses had moved in.

Though Glen liked to think he'd been prescient enough to foresee the resurgence of the neighborhood, the truth was that the best he'd hoped for was to fix the old place up, make a few dollars selling it, and move on. But as they'd worked on the house, both he and Anne had fallen in love with it, and when first Heather had arrived, fifteen years ago, then Kevin, five years later, they'd decided simply to stay where they were. Though they got offers for the house every few months, it had been years now since either of them had thought of moving. Meanwhile, a calico cat named Kumquat, then a small black and white mutt named Boots, and finally an only somewhat raucous green parrot named Hector, had been added to the family, at which point the house no longer felt too big. Indeed, when Boots decided to tease Hector, the combined clamor of the dog and the bird sometimes made the house seem far smaller than it actually was.

Now, as the television downstairs went on—its earsplitting volume telling Glen that Kevin was in possession of the remote control—he reluctantly shoved the covers aside, swung his feet to the floor, and decided he felt just old and stiff enough that if he skipped jogging he'd suffer pangs of guilt all day. Pulling on some pants and a sweatshirt, he took the stairs two at a time, then paused to glance into the living room before heading out the front door.

Both his kids were sitting in front of the television set, glued to an image of the prison in Connecticut where Richard Kraven was scheduled to die three hours from now. "Don't you guys think you've seen enough of that?" he asked, remembering how he'd finally had to order them to shut off the television last night, when it seemed they might be ready to stay up until dawn watching the live coverage of the vigil going on in front of the prison.

"Maybe Mom will be on," Kevin said, using a gambit that had often worked in the past.

"Maybe she would, if this were a local station," Glen agreed. "But somehow I don't think even your mother is quite famous enough for CNN yet. Now why don't you turn off that deathwatch and fix yourselves some breakfast?"

"It's not a deathwatch," Heather objected, fixing her father with a scornful glare. "It's a protest. And I still don't see why you wouldn't let me go. I don't believe in capital punishment, and I should be there!"

Glen decided to ignore the bait, unwilling to let himself be dragged into yet another recitation of the importance of school over a protest in which neither he nor Anne believed. Pointing out one more time that the protest in question was taking place an entire continent away would, he knew, gain him nothing more than another of Heather's pronouncements that "right and wrong doesn't have anything to do with geography." Sometimes he wondered if it wouldn't be easier to have a daughter who was caught up in the music scene and spent most of her time hanging out on Broadway. Still, he and Anne had raised Heather to have a social conscience, and the fact was, he didn't believe in capital punishment, either.

Except for a couple of special cases.

Ted Bundy, for one, whose execution Glen had fully supported, being as certain as everyone else that had Bundy ever been given an opportunity, he would kill again and again and again.

And now Richard Kraven, who, like Ted Bundy, had apparently committed most of his crimes in Seattle, but had finally been caught, tried, and sentenced on the other side of the continent. This morning the state of Connecticut would free the country from Kraven in exactly the same way Florida had liberated it from Bundy. Anne, Glen suspected, was probably working on a final story about the strange parallels between the two killers even as he was thinking about them.

Heather, though, was still young enough not to let her ideals be tainted by any exceptions at all, and Glen didn't feel like arguing the point this morning. "All right," he sighed. "But do me a favor, okay? Put on some coffee, and make some orange juice? I'll be back in half an hour."

By the time he'd gone out the front door and started up the street toward the park, both kids had already shifted their attention back to the television set, and as he trotted into the park a few minutes later to join the other joggers making their regular laps around the reservoir across from the old Art Museum, he began marshaling all the arguments he would need to convince them that even this morning it was more important for them to go to school than to stay in front of the television "just in case Mom is on."

Which, of course, she would be, since it had already been announced by one of the Seattle independent channels that "crusading *Seattle Herald* journalist Anne Jeffers" would be interviewed immediately after the execution.

If he hurried, he could finish the inspection of the building in plenty of time to catch the broadcast at the office. Picking up his pace, he completed his usual six laps in five minutes less than his normal time, and felt a sense of aerobic virtue flood through him as his heart pounded during the final two-block sprint home.

By the time he arrived at the construction site an hour and a half later, though, Glen's feeling of well-being was fading. When he first began to feel an odd hollowness in the pit of his stomach as he gazed up at the skeleton of girders soaring above him, he attributed it to nothing more than excitement at the structure finally being topped out. But as he studied the network of beams, struts, and girders—and the open cage of the construction elevator that seemed to rise upward to nowhere, the hollowness in his belly congealed into a tight knot of pain, and he felt a clammy sheen of sweat break out over his whole body despite the cool of the morning.

Could he be coming down with some kind of bug?

But he'd felt fine just a couple of minutes earlier. Deciding to ignore the strange sensations in his body, he took a tour of the ground floor, talking rapidly to the contractor and the foreman as he inspected the building's structural framework. Though his stomach lurched as they took the elevator to the fifth level, he focused his mind tightly on the job at hand, and managed to put down the slight wave of dizziness that broke over him when he neared the precipitous edge of the subflooring, unguarded by even the most vestigial of safety railings. "Shouldn't there at least be warning tapes across here?" he asked the construction chief, trying not to let his voice betray the faint feelings of panic he was experiencing.

"Only gets in the crew's way," Jim Dover replied. "By the end of the first day, they'd all be torn out, and the whole street'd be littered with 'em." The foreman eyed the architect uncertainly. "You okay, Glen? You look kinda green around the gills."

"I'm okay," Glen said quickly, but as they progressed up the next twenty floors, he suddenly realized what was happening to him.

Acrophobia.

But where had it come from? He'd never had trouble with heights before—he'd always loved the sensation of shooting up the sides of buildings in glass elevators, watching the ground drop away from him. But this morning, unaccountably, he found himself growing increasingly reluctant to get back into the elevator after each of the incremental inspections had been completed. He told himself it was nothing serious, that all he was feeling was the natural insecurity brought on by having nothing solid between him and the abyss below. He decided to ignore the fear growing inside him, determined that whatever it took, he would make it to the top of the building, where he himself would crack open the bottle of champagne Alan Cline had brought to celebrate the building's topping out.

"Quite a view if you look straight down." As George Simmons, the chief engineer on the project, spoke the words, Glen had to steel himself from automatically glancing down through the heavy grate that was all that separated him from a twenty-story plunge to the concrete floor of the shaft.

"You sure you're okay?" Alan Cline asked as the elevator jerked to a stop and the contractor and foreman stepped off, leaving the two architects alone in the cage.

Up here, even the subflooring hadn't been installed yet, and all there was to support them was a series of thick wooden planks laid in what looked to Glen like a very precarious manner across the huge I-beams of which the building was constructed. "You sure those are safe?" Ignoring Alan's question, and struggling to control the terror that was now threatening to overwhelm him, he directed his question to Jim Dover.

Dover grinned. He was a ruddy-faced, six-foot-four-inch bear of a man who had worked his way up from a one-man odd-job operation to running one of Seattle's biggest construction firms. "They're fine, as long as they don't collapse under your feet." Then, seeing Glen's face pale, his smile faded. "You look kind of sick, Glen."

"I thought it was flu," Glen replied. "But now it's starting to feel a lot more like something else." He forced a grin, trying to make light of his ballooning terror. "A high-rise architect with acrophobia—kind of like someone who's scared of the water joining the navy, huh?"

"Want to go back down?" Dover offered. "Alan and I can finish the inspection."

"I'll be okay," Glen insisted. He moved toward one of the planks that would carry him out into the open network of girders, but as he neared the edge of the small platform around the elevator shaft, panic rose up in him again. He reached out to clamp his fingers onto one of the building's main supports. A terrible urge to stare down into the gaping void below gripped him, but he put it down, forcing himself to gaze straight outward, over the top of the building across the street and across Elliott Bay past West Seattle, toward Bainbridge Island and the Olympic Peninsula.

"Wait'll you see it from the top," Dover said, following Glen's gaze with his own eyes. "Gonna be the best view in the city. Not so high that it flattens everything out like Columbia Center does, but high enough so you can see damn near the whole town. Well, come on—if we're gonna do this, let's get it over with."

As Glen watched in growing terror, Jim Dover, followed by George Simmons and Alan Cline, set off along the planks. Dover moved swiftly, only steadying himself now and then by reaching out to one of the struts with one hand while he pointed out various features of the construction with the other. Glen, his stomach churning, his groin tingling, managed to follow only a few steps before he realized the acrophobia was going to win. Too terrified even to risk turning around, he gingerly crept backward until he regained the platform by the elevator. His knees trembling, both hands clutching the heavy mesh cage of the elevator, he struggled to control the paralyzing fear that was on the verge of overwhelming him. Slowly, taking one deep breath at a time, he got his breathing back to normal and felt a little strength come back into his muscles.

A few minutes later, when the rest of the group had completed the inspection of the twentieth level and returned to the elevator, Alan Cline gazed worriedly at his partner. "This is nuts, Glen," he said, reading the terror in the other man's face. "It's only a building. It's not worth scaring yourself to death over."

"And my problem is only a stupid phobia." Glen uttered the words through clenched teeth, then felt himself relax as the others surrounded him. "I'm not giving in to it, and the only way to get over it is to face it head on. Let's go up to the top." Standing to one side, he let the rest of the men precede him into the small cage, then stepped inside himself. Closing the mesh gate, he hit the up button, and instantly the metal contraption rattled to life.

As the cage ground upward, Glen felt the familiar terror surging inside him again.

He began to sweat once more, and then the worst part of the panic began: suddenly it felt as if metal bands were wrapped around his chest, and every second someone was screwing them tighter and tighter.

So tight, he could barely breathe.

Glen's heart began to pound, harder than it ever had before.

The building in which Richard Kraven had spent the last two
years was a simple rectangle of reinforced concrete, thirty feet
wide and sixty feet long, its foot-thick walls jutting out into the prison's enormous central yard from the otherwise blank facade of a
much larger structure at the annex's western end. Its roof was
sheathed in metal, and the only features that broke its drab monot-
ony were the two high rows of glass blocks whose function was to allow a certain amount of natural light to come into the cells during
the daytime hours, while at the same time preventing the inmates
from obtaining any view at all beyond the confines of the building.

Inside, the cell block seemed to have been specifically designed to
reflect the bleak connotations of the phrase "Death Row," for its interior was nearly as featureless as its exterior. There were two rows of
cells, six on each side, each cell ten feet square, the two rows facing
an eight-foot-wide corridor that ran the full length of the structure.
Though the one-man cells were barred in front and on top, they
were separated from each other by walls of solid steel plate, so although the prisoners could talk among themselves, they couldn't see
one another. Each cell was equipped with a bed, a chair, a table, a
toilet, and a sink. All the cells were harshly lit by long fluorescent fixtures hung from the high ceiling in three rows: one above each of
the rows of cells, and one above the passageway. Completely overwhelming the few glimmers of daylight that made it through the
glass blocks of the windows, the fluorescent fixtures threw a harsh
glare into every corner of every cell, creating a shadowless world that
totally confined without providing the slightest sense of shelter.

The cell in which Richard Kraven had lived for the last two years differed from the others in the block in only one way.

It was occupied.

The others, all eleven of them, sat empty and silent, for Richard Kraven was the only man Connecticut had deemed worthy of execution in nearly forty years. Indeed, until Richard Kraven's sentencing, the building had been scheduled for demolition, but when the warden, Wendell Rustin, was informed that Kraven would be delivered into his hands for safekeeping until such time as the legal processes finally and irrevocably approved the killer's sentence, Rustin stayed the cell block's own execution. Before the prisoner's arrival, Rustin himself spent a night in one of the cells, to emerge the next morning convinced that the harsh reality of living in the building would be nearly as terrible as the specter of death, for the warden had found that the cell block itself induced a feeling of abandonment and loneliness that nearly overwhelmed him during the eight silent, empty hours he had forced himself to endure.

Yet, if Richard Kraven had experienced any terror in his two years in the otherwise empty cell block, he had never given any sign or uttered any complaint. He had endured the waiting the way he had endured his trial, maintaining a silence that his guards found arrogant but which his supporters thought of as dignified, and granting interviews only in attempts to convert people to his cause.

"They may execute me," he would repeat over and over again, "but they cannot punish me, for it is impossible to punish an innocent man."

Now, on the day of his execution, Richard Kraven was—as always—sitting impassively in the chair in his cell. Today a book of Victorian poetry lay open in his lap, and to a casual observer it would have appeared as if this morning were no different from any other. When the heavy clang of the bar on the door at the far end of the corridor echoed through the cells, Kraven finished the poem he was reading, closed the book and looked up, his handsome face expressionless. His line of sight restricted by the cell's heavy steel side walls, he waited, motionless, staring straight ahead until he saw Anne Jeffers appear within his field of vision. Then, deliberately, he placed the book on the table and rose, moving toward the front of the cell and extending his hand through the bars.

Anne glanced at Kraven's hand for a moment, her eyes fixing on the long, strong fingers, the heavy tendons, and the thick veins starkly etched against Kraven's pale skin. An image rose in her mind of those hands sunk deep into the organs and entrails of his victims. Involuntarily, she took a step back.

Pulling her eyes away from Richard Kraven's hands, Anne forced herself to look directly into his face.

Though he was past forty, Kraven looked to be no more than thirty. The coal-black, wavy hair that had given his features a vaguely Byronic look had been shaved off the night before, but his face was exactly as Anne remembered it from his trial.

The softly curved, almost voluptuous lips; the straight, aquiline nose and wide-set eyes—movie star eyes, Anne had always called them—were the same as they had always been. No lines showed in his pale skin, no creases had formed around his eyes or mouth. When he spoke, it was as if he'd read her mind.

"If I were guilty, don't you think it would show in my face by now? Don't you think just the knowledge of what I'd done would have started to change me?"

Even his voice was the same, soft and reasonable.

"Did you ever hear of Dorian Gray?" Anne countered.

Kraven's lips tightened slightly, but the flatness in his eyes didn't change at all. It was that look that Anne remembered most, the cold flatness that had been the first thing she noticed about Kraven when she met him four years ago, after he'd been arrested in Bridgeport and it seemed as if every reporter in Seattle had gone to Connecticut on the same plane. It was those eyes that made his face a terrifying mask of almost alluring cruelty back then, and now, as he trained them fully on her, their effect hadn't changed.

"Shouldn't you be a bit more gracious?" he asked. "After all, you've finally convinced them to kill me."

Anne shook her head. "I wasn't on the jury, and I wasn't the judge. I wasn't even a witness. Neither at the trial nor to any of the things you did."

Richard Kraven offered Anne Jeffers the smile that had convinced so many people he was innocent. Had it not been for the flatness in his eyes, his expression would have looked almost wry. "Then how can you be so sure I did anything?"

"The evidence," Anne replied. Her eyes flicked toward the closed door at the end of the hall, and the guard, who was watching through a glass panel. How quickly could he open that door? Again it was as if Kraven could read her mind.

"Surely you don't think I'm any danger to you?" he asked, his voice taking on a warm concern that would have soothed Anne if it had come from anyone else.

How does he do it? Anne wondered. How does he make himself sound so normal? Except for the shaved head and the prison clothes, Richard Kraven still looked exactly like the popular young electronics professor he had once been, back when his star was still rising at the University of Washington. "I think if you had the chance, you would kill me right now," she said, keeping her voice level by sheer force of will. "I think if you weren't behind those bars, you would strangle me without so much as a second thought, and then take my body apart the way you did with all the others." As she stared into his expressionless eyes, Anne felt fury rising up in her. Why wouldn't he admit what he was, what he'd done? Her voice rose a notch. "How many were there, Kraven? Besides the three you were convicted of, how many? How many just in Seattle? Five? Seven?" There was still no reaction at all in Kraven's eyes, and Anne felt her rage building. There had to be some way to get through to this—this what? Man? But Richard Kraven wasn't a man. He was a monster. A cold, unfeeling monster who had never acknowledged what he'd done, let alone shown any remorse. "Have we even found all the bodies yet?" she demanded. "For God's sake, Kraven, at least tell me that it's all finally going to be over!"

His flat gaze fixed steadily on her, but when Richard Kraven finally spoke, his voice again belied that strange dead look his eyes projected. "How can I tell you what I don't know?" he asked in a tone that reminded Anne of an earnest child.

Her jaw set as the heat of her anger suddenly turned ice cold.

"Why did you want to see me?" she demanded. "What could you possibly have to say?"

Richard Kraven smiled again, but this time there was no warmth to his smile at all; the cold, unblinking eyes fixed on her, the jaw tightened, and in that hard, grim look Anne Jeffers was certain she was at last seeing the true face of the evil that dwelt within Richard Kraven. "Today won't end it. Killing me won't end it," he said, each word a chip of ice. "That's what I wanted to tell you, Anne. How will you feel, Anne? When I'm dead, and it all starts again, how will you feel?" Suddenly he laughed, a mirthless cackle that reverberated through the cell block, coming back to batter at her eardrums again and again. "You've always wanted me to express remorse, haven't you? Well, here's some remorse for you—I *am* sorry about something. I'm sorry I won't be here to see you suffer when you finally realize you were wrong about me." His eyes bored into her and his voice began to rise. "It's going to start again, Anne. Whoever really killed those people is just waiting until I'm dead. Then he'll start again."

As Richard Kraven's voice grew louder, Anne took a step backward, then turned and strode quickly down the corridor toward the exit. But even as the guard opened the door to let her out, the killer's words echoed in her ears: "What will you do, Anne?" he bellowed after her. "Who will you apologize to when you finally find out you were wrong? Will you have the guts to kill yourself the way you've killed me?" His shout bounced off the concrete and metal walls of the cell block, echoing harshly, and his bitter laughter reached a crescendo. "That's my regret, Anne," he howled after her. "That I won't get to watch you die the way you're going to watch me!"

Anne went through the doorway and slumped against the wall outside as the guard slammed the heavy metal door shut. She only wished she could close her mind to Kraven's words as easily as the guard had closed the door against his voice.

Straightening up, she started back toward Wendell Rustin's office, her eyes automatically going to the clock on the wall.

Eleven-thirty.

Another half hour and it would finally be over.

In her mind she began composing the first words of the piece she would write about Richard Kraven's execution. But even as she put the lead together, Kraven's words kept coming back, mingling with her own, worrying at her, creeping back into her consciousness no matter how hard she tried to shut them out.

Suddenly she wished this day were over, so she could go away from the prison, away from Connecticut, away from Richard Kraven.

Yes, that was what she needed.

She needed to go back home, go back to Seattle.

Go back to Glen.

Holding firmly to the comforting thought of her husband, Anne focused her mind on the story she would write after the execution, after Richard Kraven was finally dead.

After the horror was ended.

CHAPTER 4

The elevator jerked to a stop at the very summit of the iron skeleton of the Jeffers Building. For a single numbing second Glen was certain that the cage in which he felt claustrophobically confined was about to plunge downward, killing all of them as it smashed into the concrete bed forty-five stories below. For just that moment, the strange tingling in his left arm was gone and the queasiness in his belly and tightness in his groin forgotten. In the next second, though, as Jim Dover slid the elevator's gate open and stepped out onto the wooden platform that seemed to Glen to hover precariously in midair, all the terrors of his acrophobia came flooding back.

He steeled himself against the unreasoning fear that gripped him now, and tried once more to convince himself that his panic was irrational: this building was going to be the best engineered and best constructed in the city, and barring some unforeseen calamity, there was no chance at all that either the platform surrounding the elevator shaft, the shaft itself, or the girders that formed the skeleton of the building would collapse. He and George Simmons had gone over it countless times, the engineer arguing that the building was over-designed while Glen insisted on erring on the side of safety. Yet now, as he reviewed the specifications in his mind one more time, all the equations, all the coefficients of stress, all the statistics on tensile strength and rigidity suddenly became meaningless in the face of the terror that clasped him more tightly every second. A wave of dizziness swept over him, and he instinctively reached out to grip the mesh of the elevator cage with his right hand.

"You okay, Glen?"

Alan Cline's voice seemed to be coming from far away and had the hollow sound of someone speaking from the depths of a cave. But Glen could see Alan standing right there, only a few feet from him. His fingers tightened on the metal mesh and he forced the burgeoning panic back down. Determined, he looked up at the sky, and for a moment everything seemed normal again. The last traces of this morning's fog and drizzle were burning off, and nothing was left to mar the clear cerulean expanse overhead except for a few fluffy white wisps that seemed to evaporate even as he watched. He took a deep breath, and once more felt in control of himself. Finally easing his grip on the elevator cage, he shifted his gaze to his partner and managed a weak grin. "Great view from up here, huh?"

"For those of us who can look at it, yes," Alan Cline observed. By now only Glen was still in the elevator, and Jim Dover was already uncorking one of the bottles of champagne that had been waiting in the ice chest he'd brought up first thing this morning. "Are you going to join us, or shall we pass your glass into the elevator?"

Gingerly, Glen stepped out onto the platform, which was constructed of several lengths of four-by-twelve planking, secured to the I beams with heavy bolts, resulting in an open ten-by-twelve-foot deck.

Plenty of room, Glen silently assured himself, for four men to stand on perfectly safely.

But even as he tried to reassure himself, the dizziness crept over him and he reached back to grip the elevator door. He concentrated on breathing deeply and evenly until the dizziness subsided. As Jim Dover passed him a glass of champagne, he finally risked taking a good look around. It was, indeed, a great view. High enough now to see over the crests of First Hill and Capitol Hill to the east, he could see a narrow slice of Lake Washington and the skyline of Bellevue rising in the distance. To the south, the Kingdome squatted like a huge orange squeezer at the near end of the industrial expanse that stretched all the way down to Boeing Field, and the entire Olympic range was now clearly visible. In the far distance he could see Mount Baker to the north, and Mount Rainier to the south. Nearly overwhelmed by the beauty of the panorama, Glen unconsciously released his grip on the elevator and stepped forward, raising his glass. "To the most fabulous place for a park in the history of Seattle," he said. Raising his glass to his lips, he drained it, then tossed the plastic glass over the edge of the platform.

And moved closer to the edge to watch it drop through the skeleton of the building.

First he felt the instant tingling in his groin as his scrotum contracted to draw his testicles protectively upward. At the same time a black roiling pit seemed to open in his belly. Worst, though, was the terrible feeling of being drawn forward, pulled as if by some physical force over the edge to plunge into the abyss.

He struggled against the urge; took a step backward.

Then the bands tightened around his chest, his left arm began to tingle once again, and he felt that clammy sheen of sweat coat his body.

"Glen?" he heard someone ask, but now the voice sounded too far away even to be readily identifiable. "Jesus, Glen, what is it?"

Glen staggered backward, groping for something to steady himself with.

Found nothing.

His right hand moved wildly now, reached for the elevator.

Missed.

He staggered, his balance failing him, his knees buckling.

It was his heart.

Something had gone very wrong with his heart.

He could hear it pounding in his ears, feel it beating crazily in his chest.

Now the bands constricting his lungs tightened. He struggled for breath.

"He's having a heart attack," he heard someone say as he felt strong hands grip his shoulders, steadying him as he crumbled onto the thick planks of the platform. "You got your phone, Jim?"

Jim Dover was already punching 911 into the pad of his cellular phone, and as George Simmons and Alan Cline knelt next to Glen Jeffers's supine figure, Dover ordered an ambulance, then began barking orders into the walkie-talkie that allowed him to communicate with the crew below. A moment later, all his instructions issued, he slapped the phone shut, dropped it into his pocket, and took charge of the situation on the tiny platform. Suddenly, even to Jim Dover, the sturdy planking seemed to be no more than an insignificant speck suspended in the middle of nothing. "We have to get him into the elevator. George, you and I should lift him up. Alan, hold his head. Not real high—just enough to slide him into the cage."

As the three men raised Glen Jeffers a few inches off the planking and eased him through the open gate of the elevator, the semiconscious man's lips worked, and an incomprehensible sound came faintly from his lips.

"What did he say?" Alan Cline demanded. When no one replied, Alan bent over his partner. "It's okay, Glen," he said, trying to keep his voice steady and reassuring. "Soon as we get you down, you're going to be just fine."

The metal gate clanged shut and Jim Dover jabbed impatiently at the elevator's controls. After a second's hesitation, the cage jerked once, eliciting a barely audible grunt of pain from Glen Jeffers, then began inching its way downward at what seemed to be an impossibly slow pace.

"For Christ's sake," Alan Cline demanded of no one in particular, "can't you make this damned thing go any faster?" No one answered him, and he bent over his partner once more. "Take it easy, Glen. Just take it easy, okay?"

Above his head, Jim Dover and George Simmons glanced uneasily at each other. Glen's breathing was coming only in the shallowest of gasps, and his complexion had lost all its color, taking on a ghastly faint bluish pallor. "Either of you know CPR?" he asked. "I don't think he's going to make it."

Alan Cline glared up from his crouched position next to Glen. "Shut up, Jim, okay? Nobody's going to die." But as if to belie his partner's words, a terrible rattling sound issued from Glen Jeffers's lips, and now the blood drained from Alan Cline's face. Racking his brain to remember what he'd been taught in the cardiopulmonary resuscitation course he'd taken almost a year ago, he pulled Glen's mouth open, checked to make sure his tongue wasn't blocking his throat, then began pressing rhythmically on his chest. As the elevator continued its agonizingly slow descent, he bent over, closed Glen's nostrils with the fingers of his right hand, and began breathing directly into the unconscious man's lungs.

After three deep breaths he went back to work on Glen's chest.

They were only twenty feet above the building's floor when finally another small groan escaped Glen Jeffers's lips and his lungs began to work once again, though the most they appeared able to produce were spasmodic, gasping breaths that seemed incapable of sustaining life.

"Come on, damn it," Alan Cline whispered. "Breathe! For God's sake, breathe!"

As if in response to his partner's voice, Glen seemed to gain a little strength, and his chest heaved.

The elevator banged to a stop and Jim Dover threw the door open. "Where's the ambulance?" he demanded of the assistant foreman, who was waiting at the elevator's base.

The man's eyes fixed on Dover for a moment, then shifted to Glen Jeffers, whose ragged breathing had abruptly stopped again. "Not here yet," he said as Alan Cline went back to work on Glen. Then his gaze came back to the contractor and he shrugged helplessly. By the time the ambulance arrived, would it already be too late?

The crowd of demonstrators had begun gathering the day before, and every hour since the first arrivals had set up their makeshift camps, more of them had poured into the field across from the prison, until now the entire space was filled with tents, trailers, cars, and people. All night long a bonfire had burned, the demonstrators clustering around it as they sang songs of protest and chanted their conviction that the condemned man must not die, that somewhere some nameless lawyer was feverishly working in an ill-lit office, finding new grounds upon which to challenge Richard Kraven's sentence of death.

Perhaps there would be an error discovered in the court records, or some piece of evidence could be newly challenged.

Or perhaps the governor would have a change of heart and commute Kraven's sentence at the last minute.

But as night faded into morning and the bonfire burned lower, until all that was left of it were glowing coals smoldering angrily beneath a thick layer of ash, a watchful silence had descended on the crowd.

Anne Jeffers gazed down upon the scene from the window of Wendell Rustin's office on the top floor of the prison's administration building. A few curling wisps of smoke still rose from the last embers of the night's bonfires, and the demonstrators still stood facing the prison, waiting in bitter anticipation for the last moment of Richard Kraven's life.

How many were there—five hundred? A thousand?

And who was to say that their feelings about what was going to happen here today were any less valid than her own? An image of her daughter came to mind, and she saw once more the earnest expression on Heather's fifteen-year-old face a few nights before, when they had once more debated capital punishment over the dinner table. With the absolute certainty of her youth, Heather had insisted that there was not—could not—be any justification for a government executing anyone.

"Two wrongs don't make a right," she'd insisted. "And besides, aren't we always making a big deal about being a Christian nation? What about the ten commandments? The Bible says 'Thou shalt not kill.' Which means that capital punishment is just plain wrong!"

Now, her daughter's words ringing in her ears, Anne wondered just when it was that she'd lost her own innocence, had lost the ability to see the world in black and white. It had not, she reflected, been that many years since she'd agreed with Heather wholeheartedly.

Except that somewhere along the line she'd begun to believe that in some cases—cases like Richard Kraven's—there was no other real choice. To some extent, she supposed that her work had hardened her, that her many years of observing and reporting on man's cruelty to his own species had changed her.

As she gazed down at the demonstrators in front of the prison, scanning their faces, she saw among the crowd scores of people her own age, and just as many who were twenty years older. Even as she watched, an elderly woman sitting in a wheelchair, swathed in a long peasant skirt and a rainbow-colored shawl, proudly waved a sign that read CAPITAL PUNISHMENT IS MURDER.

I should talk to her, Anne thought. Before I go home, I should talk to that woman.

Her thoughts were interrupted by the jangling of a telephone. She turned away from the window just as Wendell Rustin picked up the receiver on the second ring, spoke for a moment, then hung up. "It's time," he said. Pushing himself heavily to his feet, the warden came around the desk, strode to the door, and held it open for Anne. When she made no move to go through it, he hesitated for a moment, then gently reclosed it. "Are you going to be all right?"

Anne frowned as she tried to formulate an answer to the question, and finally shrugged. "I don't know," she admitted. "I— Oh, God, I don't know what I feel right now. I thought I was absolutely clear on this, but now . . ." Her voice trailed off.

"You don't have to witness it," Rustin offered. "If you'd like, you can wait here."

For the slightest fraction of a second Anne felt tempted to take the warden up on the offer, but almost immediately shook her head. "This is something I have to do," she said. "What kind of a hypocrite would I be if I refused to watch what I've been arguing for all this time?"

Wendell Rustin's head bobbed slightly. "I know," he said. "But I have to tell you, Anne, believing in capital punishment and watching it are two different things. Take it from someone who knows."

In spite of herself, Anne hesitated. How much easier it would be simply to wait here in the relative comfort of the office until it was all over. Resolutely, she faced him and said, "I'll be all right." But even as she passed through the door into the hallway outside, she wondered if she'd spoken the truth. Conflicting emotions were still roiling inside her, but this time she reminded herself that she was here to do her job, and purposefully shifted her mind into work mode, a trick she'd learned years ago when she discovered that there were times when she simply had no choice but to separate herself from the task at hand.

Entering the gallery adjacent to the execution chamber, she was surprised at how many people had already gathered. Some of them she recognized: most of the lawyers who had been involved in Kraven's various appeals were there, as were a number of policemen she recognized from various states.

Mark Blakemoor, who had headed up Seattle's own task force when it became obvious that a serial killer was working in the city, sat in the front row, and as Anne came in, he nodded to her and gestured for her to take the seat next to him. Feeling an oddly incongruous sense of relief at seeing Blakemoor, she moved quickly down the aisle and slipped into the empty seat.

And found herself staring directly into the small chamber that held the electric chair.

Mutely, she stared at the executioner's toy.

It was wooden, constructed in what struck Anne as a cruelly simple design.

No cushioning, no even slightly relaxing angles.

Wide, flat arms equipped with heavy straps to hold the victim's arms in place.

More straps to hold the torso immobile, and still more to bind the legs and ankles.

Two electrodes, attached to thick cables.

All of it illuminated by the harsh white light of four powerful incandescent lamps suspended from the ceiling.

Anne stared at it wordlessly, her mouth going dry. Abruptly, the lights in the gallery dimmed, almost as if they were in a theater, and then a door to the left of the chair opened. A moment later Richard Kraven appeared in the doorway. He paused, his eyes fixing on the chair.

As Kraven stared at the instrument of death, Anne thought that a flicker of a smile crossed his lips, but if so, it was gone so quickly she couldn't be certain she'd seen it at all.

With two guards escorting him, Richard Kraven moved into the chamber and took his seat. He was barefoot, and wearing only a loose-fitting pair of pants and a short-sleeved shirt. Though she loathed this cold-blooded killer, the clothing struck Anne as unseemly, as if someone had decided it wasn't enough simply to execute him, but that he must be stripped of his last vestiges of dignity before being sent to his death.

The guards began strapping Richard Kraven to the heavy wooden chair.

His ankles were bound to the legs of the chair, his wrists to its arms, his torso to its back.

A priest came into the room and spoke to Kraven, but Anne could hear nothing through the heavy glass that separated the killing chamber from the viewing gallery. Whatever the clergyman said seemed not to affect Kraven in the slightest, and he made no reply.

After lingering for only a few more seconds, the priest left.

The guards dampened one of the electrodes with saltwater, and taped it securely to Richard Kraven's shaved scalp.

They attached the second electrode to the calf of his right leg.

After checking their work one last time, the two guards left the chamber, closing the door behind them.

It was only after the guards had left that Anne realized an eerie silence had fallen over the gallery.

She glanced up at the clock.

Thirty seconds before noon.

Now she found herself glancing around for a telephone, and realized she was half expecting that the event she was witnessing would suddenly be ended by a loud ringing, just as used to happen in the movies.

But there was no phone; if it existed at all, it was somewhere beyond her field of vision.

Beyond Richard Kraven's, too?

Was he, too, waiting for the last minute reprieve that would release him from the chair?

She made herself look once more at Kraven, and though she had been told that the glass was a one-way mirror and he wouldn't be able to see the execution's witnesses, she nonetheless had the sensation that his eyes were focused on her, and that he knew exactly at whom he was staring.

Those cold, expressionless eyes had lost their deathly flatness. In the last moments of Richard Kraven's life, his eyes had at last come alive and were projecting an emotion.

A strong, powerful emotion.

Hatred.

Anne could feel it burning out from him, searing through the thick glass of the window, snaking toward her—

She recoiled from Kraven's hate-filled gaze as from a striking cobra, and had to fight against a powerful impulse to abandon her chair and escape from the scene that was unfolding in front of her eyes. But before she could move at all, Richard Kraven jerked spasmodically as every muscle and nerve in his body reacted to the two thousand volts of electricity that shot through him.

Anne gasped, and then her whole body responded to the horror she beheld.

She stopped breathing as every fiber in her went momentarily rigid. Then an anguished moan escaped her throat as Kraven's body jerked again and again.

Next to Anne, Mark Blakemoor's eyes narrowed and his jaw clenched as he watched Richard Kraven die. Every muscle tensed, the detective silently counted the seconds, only relaxing when two full minutes had finally gone by and he was certain that Richard Kraven was dead. Then he spoke quietly to Anne Jeffers.

"That's it," he said. "Let's go home."

Anne shifted slightly in her seat, but made no move to get up. As the room slowly emptied, she stayed where she was, watching silently as the guards returned to the execution chamber, this time pushing a gurney and accompanied by a doctor. After the doctor confirmed that Richard Kraven was dead, the guards removed the electrodes from his leg and scalp, unfastened the straps that bound him, and lifted him onto the gurney.

But even after Richard Kraven's body had been taken away, Anne Jeffers remained where she was.

She knew that what she had just witnessed had changed her, but she didn't yet know quite how.

She knew she would never forget watching Richard Kraven die, nor ever get over the terrible feeling she had experienced as his final glare of pure hatred had burned through her.

Then she thought of Glen, and was instantly consumed by a desire to be held by him, to feel his arms around her, his lips on hers, his strength pulling her close to him.

She would be all right. In a few hours she would be with Glen again; in a few days, a few weeks, she would begin to forget the clinical precision of what she'd just seen.

But would she ever be able to forget the terrible hatred that had poured forth from Richard Kraven even as he'd died?

The wailing siren built to a deafening crescendo that was abruptly silenced as the ambulance braked to a stop in front of the construction site. Both doors flew open and two white-clad men leapt from the cab, one of them racing around to the back of the vehicle to pull out a stretcher, the other, carrying a small tank of oxygen and a face mask, breaking into a run toward the area where Glen Jeffers lay.

"Let me through," the paramedic commanded as he pushed his way through the crowd gathered around the fallen man. "Who's in charge here?" Without waiting for a reply, he knelt beside Glen's body, quickly felt for a pulse, then put the mask on Glen's face and turned the oxygen to high flow.

"We think he had a heart attack," Jim Dover said. "We were all up on top. All of a sudden Glen started looking weird. We thought it was just fear of heights, but—"

His words were cut off as the second paramedic pushed through the crowd, unrolled the portable stretcher and lay it next to the unconscious body. "Myocardial infarction?"

"Looks like it," the first medic said. "Let's get him on the stretcher and into the truck." Working together like a well-oiled machine, the two paramedics moved Glen onto the stretcher, then started back toward the ambulance. The construction crew fanned out ahead of the stretcher, clearing the way, while Alan Cline, together with George Simmons and Jim Dover, kept pace next to Glen.

"He's a member of Group Health," Alan Cline said, his voice

trembling as he saw the bluish cast his partner's face had taken on.
"If you can take him up there—"

The paramedics slid the stretcher into the back of the ambulance,
one of them climbing in to attach Glen to the waiting IV and heart
monitor. "You can go with him," the driver told Alan Cline. "There's
plenty of room, and if he wakes up—"

Alan Cline didn't wait to hear the medic finish what he was saying, but scrambled into the back of the ambulance. The driver
slammed the door shut, then dashed around to the driver's seat. The
ambulance started up the street, turned right up the steep slope of
the hill, and then the siren came on.

Muffled by the walls of the ambulance, its wail took on a mournful, keening note, and as Alan Cline gazed at his partner, he wondered if it would be possible for Glen to survive at all.

———————

*It was like slowly coming awake in a pitch-dark room. Except the first
thing that met him as he came into consciousness was pain.*

Pain such as he'd never experienced before.

Pain that consumed him.

Pain that threatened to tear his mind apart.

Away!

He had to get away from the pain before it destroyed him.

Where?

Where was he?

*His mind struggled against the blackness, and slowly it began to
recede.*

Now he could hear sound.

*It seemed to be coming from somewhere far in the distance, but in
a moment Glen was able to identify it.*

A siren, like a police car, or an ambulance.

*The dark receded further, and he was able to see. But it was odd—he
seemed to be floating in some dimension he didn't quite understand.
Far below him, he could see two men crouching near a figure on a
stretcher. They were confined by walls, as if perhaps they were in—*

An ambulance!

But why?

Even as the question came into his mind, he knew the answer, and looked down once more at the figure on the stretcher.

He was looking at himself.

His shirt was open, his chest bare, and his face looked as pale as death.

Death.

The word hung in his mind.

Was that what was happening to him? Was he dying?

But if he was dying, why didn't he feel anything?

Then he knew.

He was no longer in his body. Somehow, during that last terrible flash of blinding pain, he'd managed to escape, slipping away from the agony before it could break his mind.

Now, gazing back down at his body, he could see that the pain was still there, for his face was contorted into an anguished grimace.

He heard Alan Cline's voice drifting up:

"Jesus, what's happening? Can't you do something for him?"

Another voice, this one shouting, but somehow no louder than Alan's had been:

"We're losing him! I'm gonna need some help back here!"

As Glen floated far above, the scene continued to unfold. Though he felt nothing, he knew the ambulance had stopped, for now the driver had joined the man who crouched over him. As the first medic began pressing rhythmically on his chest, the second one removed a plastic object from a cabinet fastened to the ambulance's wall.

Almost disinterestedly, Glen Jeffers watched as his own mouth was opened and a plastic airway was thrust down his throat.

"Let's get some lidocaine into him," he heard the other medic order. As if no time at all had passed, he saw the other medic slide a needle into the IV tube and press the plunger. But even as the drug was going into Glen's system he heard the paramedic who was crouched over his body speak again.

"We're getting PVCs! Get the defibrillator ready!"

"What's happening?" he heard Alan Cline ask. "What's PVC mean?"

"Premature ventricular contractions," the paramedic snapped. But

when he spoke again, his tone had changed, now sounding almost pleading. "Come on," he crooned. "Come back to me!"

The words hovered in the space around Glen, but held little meaning for him. Darkness began closing around him until he seemed to be in the depths of a tunnel, with only a single speck of light visible in the distance. As the voice of the medic spoke again, Glen began moving toward the light, and now the light itself seemed to be beckoning to him.

He moved faster and faster through the landscape of his own life, watching himself as a baby in his crib, at home, and now his mother was picking him up, holding him, cuddling him. Then he was at school, and everyone he had ever known—everyone he thought he had long ago forgotten—was there.

On and on it went, his life spread out before him, and as he experienced it all, he grew ever closer to the welcoming beacon of brilliant white light at the end of the tunnel.

Now he could see figures in the lights.

His grandparents were there, and someone else, someone he recognized in an instant.

The baby.

The baby they'd lost twelve years ago, when Anne had gone into premature labor with their second child.

Alex, his name would have been.

And now here the baby was, waiting for him, his arms held out eagerly.

Glen moved faster now, racing toward the light, leaving even the memory of the pain far behind.

Then, from behind him, he heard a voice, pleading with him not to leave.

Not a single voice, but a plaintive chorus, a blend of tones in which he could hear not just Anne, but Heather and Kevin, too.

Calling out to him, pleading with him.

He paused, slowing his rush toward the light, and looked back.

All was darkness, a vast and forbidding expanse of black, which he knew was filled with pain.

Ahead, bathed in the sweet light, his grandparents and the child he'd never met awaited, reaching out to welcome him.

The voices from the darkness cried out again, though, and with a great wrenching pang of anguish, Glen knew that he had to turn away from the light, had to make his way back into the darkness.

Those who awaited in the light were eternal, and would be there to welcome him when the time was right.

But behind him there was still unfinished business, still things yet unaccomplished, still deeds left undone.

Turning finally away from the light, Glen Jeffers started back into the darkness.

———————

"Put it up to three hundred joules and hit him again," the paramedic who was struggling to revive Glen ordered. The driver adjusted the controls on the defibrillator, and a second later Glen's body jerked involuntarily as the flash of electricity shot through him. His heart stopped for a moment, then started up again. "That's the way," the medic murmured under his breath as he studied the display on the monitor. But a second later he saw his patient's heart run wild again, the first fluttering pulse turning into a useless vibration.

"Try again at three-sixty," he commanded, pressing the paddles against Glen's naked chest.

Once again the defibrillator fired. The paramedic held his breath as he watched the monitor, then ordered a milligram of epinephrine, and resumed applying CPR. As the seconds ticked by and Alan Cline unconsciously held his breath as he prayed helplessly for his partner to live, Glen's heart began to beat again, and a moment later he was once more breathing on his own.

Scrambling into the driver's seat, the second paramedic jammed the ambulance into gear and pressed on the accelerator.

The siren wailed its mournful plea, clearing the streets ahead.

The back doors of the ambulance were thrown open. Even before Alan Cline could scramble out, two orderlies pulled the stretcher bearing Glen Jeffers onto a gurney and wheeled it through the doors to the Group Health emergency entrance on Thomas Street. His mind only starting to recover from the shock of what had happened at the top of the skyscraper, Alan followed the stretcher inside, but as it turned left through another set of double doors, Alan went to the right, toward a counter behind which several people were struggling to cope with the barely controlled chaos of the emergency room.

On a worn Naugahyde sofa a large woman sat with her arm curled protectively around the shoulders of a sobbing child; in a chair nearby, a teenage girl with stringy blond hair and a vacant expression was attempting to nurse a baby whose screams made it sound as if it was in excruciating pain.

A man with eyes that smoldered with fury clutched at the makeshift bandage that had been wrapped around his upper right arm. When a woman with an already purpling bruise on her cheek tried to help him, he shoved her roughly away. "Ain't you already done enough, bitch?" he growled, and the woman instantly recoiled as if he'd struck her. A second later, as a policeman appeared, the injured man turned away from the woman, who immediately began insisting to the officer that nothing worthy of a police report had brought them to the emergency room.

The whole scene struck Alan Cline as coming from some alien planet he knew nothing about, and for a moment he felt completely disoriented. Then he remembered Glen, still unconscious—perhaps even dying—being rushed into the opposite wing.

"The man they just brought in," he said, injecting himself into the midst of a conversation one of the staff behind the counter was carrying on with a distraught woman. "Where is he?"

"Can't you wait your turn like everyone else?" the woman demanded, fixing Alan with a glare from her drug-dilated eyes. "You're not the only person here, you know."

"Just tell me where they took him," Alan demanded of the woman behind the counter, who had already moved closer to him, as though she welcomed even a momentary distraction from the angry patient's siege.

"The cardiac case?" the receiving nurse asked.

Alan Cline nodded, and the nurse immediately handed him a clipboard. "If you could just fill out as much of this as possible, I'll find

out where your ..." She paused expectantly, waiting for Alan to
identify himself as either a relative, a friend, or perhaps even the
lover of the patient.

"I'm his partner," Alan offered, then, remembering Seattle's do-
mestic partnership ordinance, whose passage had been a cause for
celebration among at least half a dozen of his employees, he spoke
again. "His *business* partner."

"Whatever," the nurse said. "All I really need is his name, if he's
a member of Group Health. I can pull the rest of it out of the
computer."

"Then why can't you pull my *prescription* out of the damn computer," the woman next to Alan complained as he wrote Glen's name
down for the nurse. When the nurse simply ignored her, the addict
swore under her breath, seemed to consider the odds of convincing
the nurse to give her whatever it was she wanted, then shambled
out, after mumbling that she would report the nurse to the co-op's
board.

"Do that," the nurse sighed, not even looking up from the computer screen she was studying. "See you tomorrow." As the woman
disappeared out onto the street, the nurse finally glanced up, shaking
her head sadly. "She thinks we're a methadone clinic," she explained.
"Comes in practically every day, asking for— Ah, here it is!" She
studied the computer screen, then smiled at Alan Cline. "Mr. Jeffers
is just being admitted to the cardiac care unit." Just then, Jim Dover
burst through the doors, spotted Alan and joined him at the counter.

"Where's Glen?" he asked. "Is he okay?"

Alan shrugged. "He's in cardiac care," he said. "Find out where it
is while I call the office."

Leaving Dover to get the information from the nurse, Alan
crossed to the pay phones that lined one wall of the emergency
room, found one that wasn't broken and dialed the number that
would bypass the switchboard and ring directly at the desk of Rita
Alvarez, Glen's secretary. As briefly as he could, he told her what had
happened.

Sitting at Glen's desk, where she had answered Alan Cline's call,
Rita Alvarez glanced at the small television her boss had told her
to set up in the office that morning in case his wife showed up on

CNN. Now, as she listened to Alan's disjointed account of Glen's heart attack, she found herself gazing at Anne, who, along with the warden and the rest of the witnesses to the execution, had just entered a room filled with reporters, cameras, and lights. "Go find out what's happening," she said. "Just stay with Glen, and let me know what's going on. I'll take care of everything else." Hanging up the phone, Rita Alvarez went to work, first making a list of the people who had to be notified immediately, starting with Anne and progressing quickly through clients who had appointments with Glen that day, the firm's attorney, and some of his closest friends. Less than a minute later she was speaking to the operator at the prison where Anne had just witnessed Richard Kraven's execution.

"It's an emergency," she explained. "I need to talk to Anne Jeffers right away. She's there at the prison. She was one of the witnesses—"

"Everyone wants to talk to everyone who witnessed the execution," the operator interjected. "And everyone says it's an emergency. If you'd like me to add your name to the list—"

"I'm secretary to Mrs. Jeffers's husband," Rita interrupted. "He's just had a very bad heart attack. He may be dying."

Anne hung up the phone but lingered over it, her hand unconsciously resting on the receiver as if maintaining physical contact with the instrument could somehow keep her connected to Seattle and whatever was happening there. A heart attack? Glen? But how was that possible? He wasn't even forty-five yet! And he jogged every day, watched his weight—both of them were the quintessential Seattleites, spending as much time as they could out-of-doors, skiing at Crystal Mountain and Snoqualmie in the winter, rowing on the lake and exploring the San Juan Islands in sea kayaks in the summer. People like Glen didn't have heart attacks!

Then she remembered the day almost ten years ago when she'd heard that Danny Branson had dropped dead while jogging, and Danny, only thirty-two at the time, had always been a major jock, running track all through their high school years. So what was life, anyway? Just a big lottery? Even if you did everything right, did you just drop dead?

The terrible feeling of fear and helplessness that had come over her as she listened to Rita Alvarez's report of Glen's heart attack began to transform into a calm determination: what had happened to Danny Branson would not happen to Glen. He would recover; together, they would learn everything there was to know about heart attacks, and they would see to it that he didn't have another one. As the last of the terror faded from her mind, her fingers finally left the phone and she turned around to find Mark Blakemoor watching her, his eyes betraying a concern he rarely allowed to be exposed, either on the job or off.

"Has something happened, Anne?" the detective asked.

"It's my husband," she replied. "He's had a heart attack. I have to get home right away. My flight's not till tomorrow." She felt panic rise. "I *have* to get home!"

Mark Blakemoor reached into the inside pocket of his rumpled gabardine jacket and handed her an envelope. "My flight leaves in a couple of hours," he told her. "If there isn't room for both of us, you fly, and I'll go home on your ticket tomorrow."

Anne's brows rose a fraction of an inch. "And in return?" she asked. There had to be a catch: in all her years of dealing with cops, Mark Blakemoor had been the single individual who refused to divulge anything unless he was promised a future favor as the price. Now, to her surprise, he shook his head.

"This isn't work," he said. "This is personal. With personal, everything's a freebie. Okay?"

"Let's go," Anne replied, instinctively knowing that he didn't want to be thanked for the offer.

Five minutes later they were out of the prison, being driven through the crowd of demonstrators and reporters in a car the warden had supplied.

At least, Anne reflected as she heard the muffled questions the press was shouting after the closed vehicle, I don't have to keep talking about the execution. One more article for the *Herald* and then, perhaps, she would take a leave of absence, and concentrate on Glen's recovery.

As the car sped away from the prison, the thought lingered in her mind, and the more she thought about it, the more it appealed to her.

After all, soon it would be summer, and school would be out, and the whole family would be together. Then her mood darkened: how much of the family would there still be?

What if Glen didn't make it? What would she do? How would she cope? How could she live without Glen?

Total silence hung over the tenth grade journalism class at Maples School, named for the grove of trees within which it had been constructed back in 1923. Heather Jeffers and her classmates gazed fixedly at the television set that had been brought into the room so they could watch and discuss the coverage of Richard Kraven's execution; the set had been on since eight-thirty, and until the stroke of nine—noon in Connecticut, where the execution was taking place—several of the students had been speculating on how close to the deadline it would get before the execution was stayed. Maude Brink, who had been leading the discussion of both the media coverage of the execution and capital punishment itself for the last week, had warned them that this time a stay was unlikely, but some of the kids clung to their hopes right up until the end. What struck Mrs. Brink as most interesting was that those students most strongly opposed to capital punishment were the most certain that the execution would inevitably be delayed, while those who were the execution's strongest supporters were convinced it would take place as scheduled.

Obviously, each faction believed that in the end the system would validate his or her own view.

Yet when the execution had taken place and the first word had come out of the prison that Richard Kraven was dead, the entire class had finally experienced the reality of it. This was not a television show, or a movie, or a book, in which the execution affected only a man who was the invention of a writer's mind. This time it was real, and a man who had only a few seconds ago been as much alive as each of them was now dead. As they all watched numbly, the news anchor on the screen began cutting to correspondents around the country, each of them interviewing someone whose life would be directly affected by the execution.

First there was Edna Kraven, being interviewed in her small home in the south end of Seattle, not far from Boeing Field.

As the camera's relentless eye zoomed in on the tearstained face of Richard Kraven's mother, Heather and her friends squirmed uncomfortably, watching the woman's most private emotions exposed for all the world to watch.

"He was always a good boy," Edna whispered, her fingers twisting a crumpled handkerchief with which she blotted at red-rimmed eyes every few seconds. "Smarter than all the other kids, always interested in everything, and always helping everyone. Everybody liked my Richard. How could they do this to him? Why did they want to? He never hurt anyone—never! It isn't right! It just isn't!" The camera held steady on the distraught woman as a fit of sobbing overcame her; then, in what seemed an almost reluctant retreat from her, so she could grieve in private, it cut away to Richard's brother Rory, who sat across a worn coffee table from his mother.

"It must be almost as hard for you as for your mother," the pretty blond correspondent said, her face carefully composed into an expression designed to tell the viewers that this job was not easy for her. "Tell us, what went through your mind as the clock at the prison struck noon?"

Rory Kraven, visibly nervous in front of the camera, glanced at his mother, then shrugged. "I—I guess I didn't really think anything," he stammered. "I mean, I know what my brother did, and—" But before he could continue, his mother cut him off.

"Nothing!" she flared. "My Richard did nothing, and you know it! How dare you speak ill of your brother? If you were half the man he was—"

As some invisible director at the network decided that Edna Kraven's furious outburst was less compelling than her grief, the image on the screen abruptly switched to an elegantly dressed and perfectly coiffed woman of perhaps sixty, who was being interviewed by another attractive young network correspondent.

"I'm with Arla Talmadge in Atlanta. Mrs. Talmadge, how do you feel today?"

Arla Talmadge touched the corner of one eye with a perfectly pressed handkerchief, then sighed and shook her head. "I'm not sure what I feel anymore. Ever since Richard Kraven killed my son, I—well, there's just an emptiness inside me. Did he say anything before they—well, before they did what they did?"

"Early indications are that he didn't," the reporter replied.

"Then we'll never know why he did it, will we?" Mrs. Talmadge asked. "And I can't help wondering, what was really accomplished today? After all, killing that man won't bring my son or any of the others back, will it? I keep wondering if maybe he wouldn't have—I don't know—*explained* it all someday, I suppose. But now . . ." She drew in a shaky breath, let it out, then shook her head again. "I just don't know," she went on. "I suppose there's nothing to do now except try to go on living."

For almost fifteen minutes it went on, the images on the screen shifting as the families and friends of the victims were interviewed, some of them expressing relief that at last this grim chapter in their lives was over; others barely able to contain their rage that Richard Kraven hadn't been tortured before he died; still others echoing Arla Talmadge's sad sense of resignation in the face of the inevitable.

It was in the midst of one of those interviews that the network anchor cut in to announce that the warden was ready to speak to the press, and the scene dissolved to a room painted in a sickly green in which lights had been set up and several microphones placed on the shiny surface of a gray metal table.

The classroom buzzed with anticipation, and then the students began nudging each other as they recognized Heather Jeffers's mother in the group of witnesses who followed Warden Wendall Rustin into the room. Her face pale, her expression strained, she hovered near the wall just inside the door.

"It's really *her*, Heather," someone said from the back of the room. "It's your mom! Cool!"

As the warden started to speak, Heather ignored her classmate's comment, her eyes fixing on the screen.

"At noon today, Richard Kraven was executed," Wendell Rustin began. "He entered the chamber at 11:55, and was strapped into the chair. The electrodes were applied, and at exactly noon he was exposed to a charge of two thousand volts. At two minutes past noon he was pronounced dead." The warden fell silent for a moment, then appeared to look directly into the camera. "Are there any questions?"

Instantly, a babble of voices emerged from the television speakers, but then Rustin pointed to someone, and the rest of the crowd subsided into a restless silence. "Did he say anything? Did he confess?"

The warden glanced toward Anne Jeffers, who shook her head and seemed about to speak when suddenly a door opened and a uniformed guard stepped inside and whispered into Anne's ear. A look of surprise crossed her face and she rushed from the room.

In the classroom, Heather Jeffers's schoolmates all turned to gaze curiously at her, as if by dint of being Anne Jeffers's daughter, she should be able to explain her mother's sudden departure. Maude Brink, seeing the look of worry that had now come over Heather's face, switched off the television. "All right," she began as she moved briskly to the front of the room and faced the class. "What do we think? Was the coverage fair? Was it justified? Was it responsible reporting of news, or was it sensationalism? Who wants to start?"

Three hands instantly went up, and Mrs. Brink nodded to Adam Steiner, who sat in the back row and rarely spoke in class.

"How come they always have to talk to the families?" he asked. "I mean, Mrs. Kraven didn't do anything—why couldn't they just leave her alone?"

"How do you know she didn't do anything?" someone else asked. "She must have done something to have raised a nut-case like Richard Kraven!"

"Maybe he had something wrong with his genes," a third voice suggested. "Nobody knows what causes people to do things like that."

"I heard he was a Satanist," someone else called out, and Mrs. Brink finally raised her hand to bring some order back into the discussion.

"For now, let's stick to the coverage, and not speculate on Richard Kraven's motives, all right? This is a class in current events and journalism, not criminology—" The teacher fell silent as the door to her classroom opened. One of the principal's secretaries came in, nodded curtly to her, and without any apology for disrupting the class, spoke directly to one of the students.

"Heather? Could you come with me, please? Mrs. Garrett would like to speak with you for a moment."

Maude Brink was about to object that whatever it might be could surely wait until her class was over, but then she remembered Heather's mother's mysterious disappearance from the press conference, and gave the teenager an encouraging smile as she left the classroom. Something, obviously, had gone very wrong.

As Heather entered Olivia Garrett's office, the principal gestured her onto the sofa, then sat in the wing-backed chair instead of returning to her desk.

"I'm afraid I have some bad news for you," she said, approaching the subject with the directness for which she was famous throughout the school. "Your father's secretary just called."

"Rita?" Heather breathed. "Rita Alvarez?"

Mrs. Garrett nodded. "Your father has apparently had a heart attack. He's been taken to the hospital, and your mother wants you to go there right away. Mrs. Alvarez is picking your brother up at his school, then she'll come—"

But Heather Jeffers was no longer listening to Olivia Garrett. Instead she was trying to absorb what she had just been told. Her father? In the hospital?

A heart attack?

If her mother wanted her to go to the hospital—and Kevin, too—it must be serious! But just this morning he'd been fine! He'd gone out jogging, and when he'd come back, he hadn't even been out of breath. So how could he have a heart attack?

Suddenly fifteen-year-old Heather felt far younger than she was, and far more vulnerable.

Was her father going to die?

They'd been in the air almost two hours, and if the uncomfortable silence between Anne Jeffers and him was going to go on for another three, Mark Blakemoor decided, he'd have a couple of drinks and then try to get some sleep.

He'd done far too much drinking lately, though, especially in the ten months since Patsy had left. Eighteen years and then the marriage had simply been over. All she'd said was that she couldn't take it anymore, that she couldn't deal with being a cop's wife any longer. But what else could he do? He couldn't change careers—didn't even want to. On the other hand, Patsy had complained about his drinking, too, and if he wanted to be really honest about it, she was right—he *had* been drinking too much. Besides, even one drink on an airplane always left him with a hangover. Better to spend the time finding out what, if anything, Richard Kraven had told Anne Jeffers before he'd died.

"Anything you want to talk about?" he asked, shifting his muscular six-foot-two, 210-pound frame a fraction of an inch in a futile effort to make himself more comfortable in the cramped seat.

Anne had been staring out the window at the endless expanse of clouds that lay in an unbroken blanket a few thousand feet below the plane, and at first the detective's words didn't register. Then she sighed, rubbed at her stiffening neck and glanced over at him. "About Glen?" she asked, deliberately pretending she couldn't read Blakemoor like a book. From what she'd gathered about his recent divorce, the man had barely paid any attention to his own wife when he'd been married to her; so why on earth would he now be inter-

ested in her husband, whom he didn't even know? Then she relented: after all, Blakemoor had been willing to give up his seat on
this flight, even though it hadn't come to that. "Or is it Richard
Kraven you want to talk about?"

"Either way," Blakemoor replied. "But I guess I'm not real good
with the sympathy thing. Patsy always used to say—" He cut his own
words short, reddening slightly. "Oh, the hell with what Patsy used to
say, right? So come on, give. What did Kraven say? I've got a lot of
open cases back home. If you can close even one of them for me, it'd
sure help."

Anne shook her head. "Believe me, Mark, if he'd said anything rel-
evant, I'd tell you. Even if I didn't use it in a story, I'd still tell you.
You've put too much effort into this for too many years. But it was
the same old thing: he didn't have anything to do with anything, he
was framed, there's a conspiracy, et cetera, et cetera, et cetera."

The detective's eyes narrowed darkly. "You'd think a man'd want
to go to his grave with a clean conscience, wouldn't you? But not
Kraven. Coldest son of bitch I ever saw." Silence fell between them
again as each retreated to his own thoughts. With Blakemoor's next
question, though, Anne knew at once that his mullings hadn't been
terribly different from her own. "What do you think? Any chance at
all that we were wrong?"

"Who are you asking?" Anne countered, a thin smile curling the
corners of her mouth. "Anne Jeffers, ace journalist, or Anne Jeffers,
private citizen?"

"How about we start with the private citizen?"

"He's guilty," Anne stated with no hesitation at all. "Guilty, guilty,
guilty, as charged. And guilty of all the others he was never charged
with, too."

"Okay," Blakemoor said. "Now, what about Anne Jeffers, ace reporter? What does she think?"

Anne spread her fingers wide and wiggled them as if she were typ-
ing at an invisible keyboard. "Show me a reporter who wouldn't like
to rip the cover off a conspiracy that sent an innocent man to the
electric chair. I mean, we're talking Pulitzer Prize here, Mark."

The detective eyed her speculatively, trying to gauge how much of
what she'd just said was meant seriously and how much was merely

intended to rile him. "Does that mean you're planning to keep chasing this one?" he asked.

Anne opened her mouth to answer, then realized she didn't know what she was going to do. Three hours earlier, before she'd heard from Rita Alvarez, it would have been an easy call: given what Kraven had said in their last conversation, she'd at least have to give it one more shot. Because if Kraven hadn't been lying, and she could prove it, there undoubtedly *would* be a Pulitzer in it for her. Not to mention a huge book contract, probably a movie, and a new job with a salary that would make her current paycheck look like a kid's allowance. Now, though, everything was different. In just those few minutes she'd talked to Rita, all her priorities had changed. "I don't know if I'll chase the story or not," she finally replied to the detective's question. "It's all going to depend on Glen's situation. It may be that I'll take a leave of absence."

An incredulous grin spread over the detective's face. "You? Give me a break, Anne—when it comes to working a story, you're no different from me when I have a tough case. The hell with hours, the hell with food, the hell with sleep, and the hell with the family, too."

Anne's first reaction to Blakemoor's words was to mount an immediate and aggressive counterattack: "Maybe that's why Patsy left you. At least my marriage is still very much intact, thank you." Blakemoor winced, and Anne immediately regretted her words. "I'm sorry," she said. "That really wasn't fair." As she thought about it, she realized just how unfair it truly was. After all, it wasn't she who had to hold dinner for Glen every night. Often it was exactly the opposite, or even worse—sometimes during the last few months it was Heather and Kevin waiting for both their parents, or eating alone while both adult Jefferses grabbed a bite in their offices. If she wanted to be completely honest about it, Blakemoor hadn't been far off the mark at all—she *did* tend to shut everything else out when she was working on a story. The one that had ended today had occupied nearly all her attention for most of the last five years.

Suddenly she had a chilling thought: If she hadn't been so consumed with the Kraven case, would she have seen Glen's heart attack coming? But how could she have? It had simply come out of the blue!

Or had it?

She cast her mind back over the last few days, then the last few weeks and months. How long had it been since she and Glen had simply taken an evening off together, let alone a whole weekend? Usually one or the other—if not both of them—were working. His birthday had gone uncelebrated, as had their anniversary three months ago. If she'd become too engrossed in her work even to celebrate some of the most important landmarks in her life, how could she expect to be aware of her husband's health?

Should she have seen the heart attack coming? Should she have found signs of it in Glen's face? Were there stress lines she hadn't even noticed, or a tiredness she'd ignored? A leaden weight of guilt began to settle over her as more and more questions formed in her mind, questions to which she had no easy answers.

"Hey, Jeffers, come on," Mark Blakemoor said as if reading her thoughts. "What happened to Glen wasn't your fault. You haven't treated him the way I treated Patsy. Jesus, there were times when she didn't see me for days at a time."

"And have I been in Seattle the last few days?" Anne asked, her voice edged with self-accusatory sarcasm. "Oh God, Mark, I keep thinking I should have seen it coming, that I should have realized he was working too hard and made him slow down."

"That would have been the pot calling the kettle black," Blakemoor remarked. But his face wore a smile.

For the rest of the flight, Mark Blakemoor managed to keep the subject of conversation off both Richard Kraven and Glen Jeffers's heart attack. The only subject left that came readily to mind was his own divorce, and to his surprise, he found himself telling Anne everything about it. What surprised him most was that by the time the plane landed in Seattle, he'd discovered two things: the divorce had been just as much Patsy's fault as his own, despite his ex-wife's insistence that she'd been a wronged woman; and that he could talk to Anne Jeffers about anything that came into his mind. He'd never felt that way about a woman before, and as he followed Anne off the plane at Sea-Tac airport, he wondered what it meant.

He also found himself wondering exactly how strong Anne's own marriage was. If she should ever be single—

Jerking his own reins up short, Mark Blakemoor tried to banish the thought from his mind. It was already planted, though, and he knew it wasn't going to go away. So what was he going to do now? Fall in love with another man's wife?

Swell! Just fucking *swell!*

The taxi pulled up in front of the Group Health Hospital entrance on Sixteenth East, and Anne, distracted, fished money out of her wallet to cover the fare and a tip.

"Thanks, ma'am," the driver said in an accent so thick she could barely understand him. "I hope whatever's wrong will be better real soon."

Nodding her own thanks, Anne lifted her suitcase, hurried through the main entrance, then asked for the Coronary Unit.

"You want Critical Care," a man in a red jacket replied. "Down the hall, first elevators on the right, then left on the third floor. You can't miss it."

As she stepped off the elevator into the third floor lobby, Anne found herself surrounded by a color she instantly recognized as "flesh," the long discontinued and totally unmissed hue the crayon people had apparently thought resembled the skin tone of some race of men that neither she nor anyone else had ever seen. The peculiar shade of the walls was set off by a faintly deco white trim, a depressingly institutional decor which Anne knew her husband would detest—if he were well enough even to notice it. Then she was in an anteroom outside the closed double doors to the Critical Care Unit, facing a sign instructing her to use the red phone in the waiting area. Before she could even look around for assistance, she heard Heather's voice: "Mom? In here!"

A second later Anne was hugged in a three-way embrace with both her children. "How is he?" she asked. "What have they told you?"

"He's going to be okay," Heather said. "They've got him hooked up to about a billion machines, but the doctor says it's mostly just to watch him."

As the pent-up tension in her body was suddenly released, Anne sank exhausted onto one of the chairs that sat next to the door. There, on a table a few feet from her, was the red phone the sign had mentioned. Now that she knew Glen was out of danger, she grinned at Kevin. "You asked for the President when you picked up that phone, didn't you?"

Kevin blushed as he nodded. "Couldn't help it," he admitted.

"I wanted to kill him," Heather said, glaring at her brother. "Daddy could have been dying in there, and he was making *jokes!*"

"He wasn't *dying*," Kevin protested. "Come on, Heather, gimme a break! It's not like . . ."

Leaving her children to settle the argument themselves, Anne picked up the red phone, identified herself, and was told to let herself through the double doors to the unit and come to the nurses's station.

"Your husband's in 308," the nurse said. "He's awake, but don't expect him to say much, and try not to stay too long, all right? He really needs to sleep."

The door to the room was open, but Anne hesitated for a moment before she went in, trying to prepare for what she might find inside. Then she took a deep breath, put on the best smile she could muster, and tried to think of something light to greet Glen with. Her words died on her lips as she crossed the threshold. The man who lay in the bed was barely recognizable as her husband.

His face was gray and his whole body appeared to have sunk in upon itself. And Heather was right—tubes and wires were everywhere. An IV needle was taped to one arm, his chest was nearly covered with electrodes, and on the wall around the bed, CRT displays seemed to be monitoring every function of his body. With just a cursory glance Anne could read her husband's pulse rate, his respiratory rate, and his temperature. There were myriad other data as well, indecipherable and worrisome to Anne: if he was truly out of danger, why were they watching him so carefully?

She moved closer to the bed, and his eyes flickered open, looked right through her as if she weren't there at all, then focused. His lips worked, then barely audible words emerged from them. "Maybe I better go back to houses," he whispered. "I guess high rises don't agree with me."

Anne's eyes flooded with tears of relief, and she moved close to the bed, leaned down and kissed Glen's forehead. "What are you doing? Do you have any idea of how badly you scared me?"

"You?" Glen complained. "What about me? There I was, having the worst attack of acrophobia in history, and then wham! Dropped like a rock!"

Anne stared at him. "Acrophobia?" she echoed. "Since when do you have acrophobia?"

"Since this morning, I guess," Glen told her. "It started on about the fifth floor, and just kept getting worse the higher I went."

Anne shook her head reprovingly. "Then why did you keep going up? Oh, never mind, I know—it's your building, and that's that. How do you feel?"

Glen made a move to shrug, gave it up, and managed a wan smile. "Like I got run over by a bus. One of those big ones, too. Not your ordinary bus, but one of those new double ones . . ." He groped for the word, couldn't find it in his drug-fogged mind, and gave up. "What do they call them?"

"Articulated."

Glen nodded weakly, and his eyes closed. Anne opened her mouth as if to speak, then changed her mind as the nurse appeared in the open door and gave her a look that clearly said she'd been there long enough.

Sighing, Anne bent over and gently kissed Glen's lips. "Go to sleep, darling," she whispered. "Just go to sleep, and get well. I'll be back in a little while." Straightening up, she followed the nurse out of the room. "Where can I find his doctor?"

The nurse glanced at her watch. "He should be coming in for rounds in half an hour, but I'll call him." Picking up the phone on her desk, she punched in four digits, spoke for a moment, then smiled at Anne. "If you'd like to take a seat in the family room, Dr. Farber will be up in five minutes."

Anne found her way out of the CCU, and as she came back into the waiting room, Heather and Kevin finally stopped their bickering. "What did Dad say?" Kevin demanded. "Did you see him?"

"He said if you don't do exactly as I tell you every second he's in the hospital, he'll have your hide when he gets out."

Kevin's eyes rolled scornfully as he turned to his sister. "He must've been asleep."

Anne sighed. "Well, you can't blame your old mother for trying." Then, as she remembered how Glen had looked when she went into his room, she felt her tears welling up. This time she didn't even try to hold them back. "He said he felt like he'd been hit by a bus," she told her children, her voice quavering. "He said—" Then she choked on her own words and dropped onto the sofa. "He's going to be all right," she said, making herself sound as positive as she possibly could. "He's going to be fine, and in a few days—"

"Mrs. Jeffers?" a voice interrupted her. Anne looked up to see a white-coated man with a stethoscope hanging around his neck standing in the doorway. He had dark hair, deep blue eyes, and wore a look of perfect confidence.

But he couldn't have been more than twenty-five years old.

"I'm thirty-seven," he told her as he crossed the room to offer her his hand. "And I'm really a doctor, too. I mean, a real doctor, not an intern. And the stethoscope is to keep at least a few people from mistaking me for an orderly. I'm Gordy Farber."

"Anne Jeffers," Anne replied automatically. "And these are—"

"I already met the kids," Farber told her. "Why don't we sit down so I can tell you what we're dealing with here. Unless you'd rather do it in my office?"

Anne shook her head, dropped back onto the sofa, and tried to follow the complicated medical terms that flowed from his tongue as easily as water from a tap. Finally, when he saw how confused Anne was, Farber turned and winked at Kevin. "Want to tell your mom what's wrong with your dad?"

"A myocardial infarction," Kevin promptly replied. "That's what the doctors call a heart attack."

"That's exactly right," Farber said, reaching into his pocket and pulling out a five dollar bill. "And since you got it right the first time, you get to take your sister to the cafeteria and buy a couple of milk shakes." Only when Heather had taken her brother out of the room did Farber turn back to Anne. "It was the kind of heart attack we used to call 'a real doozy' back in medical school," he said. "However, your husband has a lot going for him. Not only is he relatively young, but he's in excellent shape, he's very strong, and he had a very good team of paramedics working for him."

Anne suddenly had a feeling that Glen had had a much closer call than she'd been told about. "How bad was it?" she asked.

"About as bad as they come," Gordy Farber replied. Long ago he'd learned that most people could deal with pretty much anything, as long as they didn't think things were being hidden from them. "They almost lost him in the ambulance. It was touch and go for a few minutes, but they got him back."

Anne sucked in her breath in a sharp gasp. "Lost him?" she echoed. "You mean . . . ?" She left the question hanging, then steeled herself to learn as much as she could. She was a reporter, wasn't she? She'd never left a question hanging in her life. "How close was it?" she asked, and her tone told Gordy Farber that she wanted to hear all of it.

"He stopped breathing, and his heart stopped beating," he told her. "We got him back but it was a very close call."

Anne remembered Glen's inability to remember the word "articulated," and all the fear she'd felt that day came rushing back to her. "My God," she breathed. "Is he—is his brain . . . ?"

This time she couldn't bring herself to finish the question.

"Things look very good right now," Gordy Farber told her. "He's stable, and the next day or so will tell the tale. If there are no further incidents, I think his prognosis for a full recovery is excellent."

"And if there *is* another . . . incident?" Anne asked.

Gordy Farber spread his fingers noncommittally. "We'll cross that bridge if and when we come to it. For now, the important thing is that he's doing very well, given what happened to him, and in spite of how he looks, he's already a whole lot better than he was when they brought him in this morning." He stood up, handing her a pamphlet he'd produced from the pocket of his white coat. "I'll tell you what. Why don't you read this while I go check on my patients.

As soon as I finish my rounds, I'll do my best to answer any questions you may have."

Anne took the pamphlet, her eyes focusing only on the two major words in its title: Heart Attack. Nodding mutely, she sank back against the harsh material of the small sofa. She sat silently holding the pamphlet for a few minutes, trying to adjust herself to the fact of Glen's heart attack. Only two days ago—only this morning, really—he'd been so strong, so healthy, so . . . alive.

And today he'd nearly died.

Once again she thought of him lying in the hospital bed, his face ashen, his body connected to the monitors, looking weak and helpless. What if he didn't get better? What if he had another—what was it Dr. Farber had called it?

Incident.

But it wasn't any mere "incident"; it was a myocardial infarction—a heart attack—and another one would undoubtedly kill him.

What would she do if that happened? How would she cope with it? A terrible wave of loneliness and despair washed over her. She was afraid she might cry again, but steeled herself against it. Falling apart was the last thing she needed right now.

She opened the pamphlet, but the words made no sense to her. For right now, she couldn't deal with it. Right now she had to do something else, something that would take her mind off Glen, if only for a few minutes.

It was only then that she remembered the man who had not survived this terrible day.

Richard Kraven.

The man she had watched die in the electric chair only hours earlier. And about whom she should already have written and filed a story. Grasping at work as a way to keep the terrible fear of losing Glen at bay, Anne Jeffers concentrated on constructing a story in her head.

A story of death, but at least not of Glen's death.

By the time Gordy Farber returned to the waiting room, Anne had not only composed the story in her mind, but called the paper and dictated it into her voice mailbox.

Now, the story filed, she turned her attention back to her hus-

band and listened calmly as the doctor told her what she could
expect.

As she listened, her resolve took hold: she would deal with it.

No matter what it took, Glen would not die.

She wouldn't let him.

could share the joke with. Still, it wouldn't be long before the whole world understood his joke.

How long had it been since he had carried out the last experiment?

So long ago he had almost forgotten how it felt to see the look in his subjects' eyes when they began to feel sleepy and he assured them that they mustn't worry, that all was going to be well.

He could remember more clearly the keening whine of the saw as it cut through their sterna, and his fingers moved reflexively as he recalled the warm pleasure of sinking his hands deep within the thoracic cavity, slipping them between the two warm masses of the lungs, closing them around the strongly beating hearts. . . .

The Experimenter uttered an all but inaudible groan of remembered pleasure.

Now he could begin again.

Now he would prove to them that they'd executed the wrong man.

For more than two long years—ever since they'd finally made their arrest, finally acted on all the evidence he'd let pile up—he'd been waiting for this day.

This day, and the ones to come when he would begin his experiments anew, expanding his knowledge, exercising his power, proving to the mindless fools who had executed Richard Kraven that they'd made a mistake, that they had been wrong. Not for the first time, the Experimenter wished he could play the fly on the wall and watch their expressions as they examined his newest subjects.

They would recognize his work immediately—of that there was no question whatsoever. But there was also no question whatsoever that they would deny the truth. Instead they would search for inconsistencies, search for differences in technique, no matter how slight, search for anything that would allow them to keep their pride—and their reputations—intact.

It would be worst for Anne Jeffers, for she would not only be forced to retract everything she'd ever said about Richard Kraven, she would have to take the responsibility for his execution as well.

She'd hounded Kraven, hounded him to his execution, though neither she nor anyone else had ever heard him confess.

The Experimenter lay in near darkness, the walls of his room only faintly illuminated by the pale glow of the streetlamps outside. Though he lay still, he was not asleep, although he knew that soon he would have to sleep.

But not yet. Right now, he wanted to hear the report just one more time.

His fingers stroked the smooth plastic of the remote control, and he could almost imagine that the satiny texture was that of skin.

The skin of one of his subjects.

So long.

It had been so long since he'd dared let himself even think about conducting another experiment, but now it would be safe again.

Safe, at least for a while.

His forefinger pressed gently on one of the control buttons, and the volume on the television rose just enough so he could hear the anchorman's voice:

"Topping our stories today, Richard Kraven was executed yesterday at noon, Eastern Daylight Time, dying in the electric chair only hours after his final appeals for a new trial were denied. According to *Seattle Herald* reporter Anne Jeffers, the last person to talk with Kraven before he died, he expressed no remorse for what he'd done, even at the eleventh hour, continuing to proclaim his innocence despite the massive evidence presented in his trial. . . ."

The Experimenter, lying in the darkness, could barely suppress a gloating chuckle, and fleetingly wished there were someone he

Now he would pursue Anne Jeffers. He would toy with her for a while, let her think perhaps she'd been right all along.

Then he would plant the seeds of doubt in her mind, and in the end, after she knew the precise truth of what had happened, he would add her to his list, making her his final subject.

His fingers caressed the satiny texture of the remote control, and there was a soft click as the television screen went blank, the picture contracting into a tiny white dot in the center of the black screen, only to die away completely a moment later.

Die away as his subjects had died away.

But their deaths had not been in vain, for out of those deaths—no, not deaths, but merely failed experiments—had come knowledge. The Experimenter had long ago decided that knowledge was far more important even than life itself. Where Socrates had once observed that the unexamined life is not livable for a human being, the man in the darkened room knew better: for him, it was the examination of the very phenomenon of life that made his existence possible. Indeed, as he'd thought about it during the long hiatus during which the authorities—those pitiably small minds who were far too simple to understand his work—built their case against Richard Kraven, the Experimenter had come to understand that even the subjects who'd died during his investigations could not truly be considered failures. After all, even in their deaths they'd contributed to the body of knowledge he had been building as painstakingly as the authorities had been building their case against Richard Kraven.

Now—now that Richard Kraven had been executed—the time had come for him to begin again. The body of his knowledge would expand, and at the same time he would prove once and for all just how much smarter he was than those who sought to judge him.

Outside the window, a movement caught his eye. He glanced down at the street below.

A woman was walking along the sidewalk.

Going to work?

Returning home from a completed shift?

Did it matter? Not really. All that mattered was that the woman had caught his eye. Perhaps, now that the time was right and he could soon begin again, he would begin with her.

Or perhaps not.

Perhaps he would begin again with someone else entirely.

The Experimenter smiled to himself as he remembered how it had been the last time, when all the investigators—and the teams they'd put together to examine the scattered bodies—had carried out their fruitless searches of his subjects' backgrounds, looking for a common denominator that would tie them all together, tie the victims to the single person who had caused their deaths. Of course they had never found that common denominator, so now when it all began again, they would go running back to their records, searching yet again.

Searching for something they would never find.

The thought of the havoc his new experiments would cause brought a smile to his lips, and he finally turned away from the window. The day had been long, and filled with excitement, and now it was time for him to sleep.

Tomorrow he would begin designing the next series of experiments.

Unconsciously, the Experimenter flexed his fingers once more, this time in anticipation. . . .

A gray sky hovered low over Seattle the next morning, and as people all over the city huddled over their first cups of coffee, newspapers were opened to the editorial page. In kitchens, coffee shops, snack rooms, and offices, nearly everyone in the city began the day by reading the column that had been dictated from the Group Health Critical Care Unit on Capitol Hill the day before:

> ## Anne Jeffers . . .
> ### A Few Last Thoughts
> ### About Richard Kraven
>
> At noon yesterday, a reign of terror that spanned five years, as many states, and a dozen cities and towns came to an end when Richard Kraven was electrocuted. Though convicted of three slayings, Kraven was the prime suspect in many others, including at least seven still unsolved cases in his native city of Seattle. At the request of the condemned man, this reporter was among the last people to speak to him before his execution. During the course of that conversation . . .

"What the hell does this broad think she's doing?"

The booming voice that filled his office in the Public Safety Building was familiar enough that Mark Blakemoor didn't even have to look up from the report he was studying. From the moment he'd scanned Anne Jeffers's column in this morning's *Herald*, the detective had been expecting Jack McCarty to come barging into the office Blakemoor shared with Lois Ackerly. McCarty's own copy of the paper would be crushed in his huge fist, his normally ruddy face flushed to the point where anyone who didn't know him might suspect that the white-haired chief of detectives was about to suffer a terminal stroke. Sure enough, here he was. Mark smoothly moved his coffee cup aside just as the chief slammed the offending newspaper onto the desk.

" '*At least* seven unsolved cases'?" McCarty demanded. "What is this crap? And when did she write it? I thought you said her husband was in the fuckin' hospital!"

"He is," Blakemoor replied mildly, leaning back in his chair to savor his boss's rage. "I sent her some flowers this morning. Thought it might cheer her up." McCarty's face turned even redder, causing Mark to wonder if it could actually be possible for a human head to explode. Then, as a vein began to throb in McCarty's neck, he decided a little extra agitation might just be in order. "You know, if Ackerly heard you call Anne Jeffers a 'broad,' she'd have a sexism citation in your jacket before lunchtime."

The jab had the intended effect. Jack McCarty spun around, his eyes searching the area outside Blakemoor's office for any sign of Blakemoor's partner. But if Lois Ackerly had arrived at the unit yet, she was nowhere to be seen. "Jeez, Blakemoor, don't say things like that. I only got three more years to retirement, and the last thing I need is another chauvinist-pig chit." He dropped heavily into the battered wooden chair that sat in the corner of the detective's cubicle, his eyes fixing malevolently on the small picture of Anne Jeffers that accompanied the column. "You know she was going to do that?"

Blakemoor shrugged. "She had to write something, didn't she? She's a reporter, remember? Why else would she have gone to the execution?"

"The way she writes it, you'd think she got an engraved invite from that creep Kraven." His blue eyes took on a look of eagerness. "Did he suffer, Mark?" he asked. "Tell me he did, goddammit. Tell me the son of a bitch shit his pants before they whacked him." Mc-

Carty's right fist slammed into his left palm. "Christ, I wish I coulda done it to him myself!"

Mark Blakemoor shifted uneasily in his seat, wishing now he hadn't goaded his boss into an even more vindictive mood than the one Anne Jeffers had induced. On the other hand, there wasn't a man or woman in the department who hadn't wanted Richard Kraven to suffer after they'd seen the pictures of his victims. Even Mark, who after fifteen years on the homicide unit had thought he was inured to anything, had found his stomach heaving the first time he attended an autopsy of one of Kraven's victims. Actually, he'd been okay until the medical examiner had told him that it appeared the victim had still been alive when Kraven cut open his chest and began tearing him to pieces. At that point Mark had excused himself, hurried to the men's room, and deposited his lunch into one of the toilets. Still, Kraven had been executed, and Mark Blakemoor found himself strangely discomfited by McCarty's words. Then, as more members of the unit drifted into his office to complain about Anne's column, he remembered their conversation on the plane the day before. Was that what was worrying him? Some slight nagging doubt that everyone might have been wrong?

"Why's she want to kick a dead horse?" Frank Lovejoy asked, dolefully shaking his bald head. "She's been living off Kraven for five years now—can't she let it go?"

"Let her write whatever the hell she wants," McCarty groused. "Time for us to get on to other things. What about the DOA they took into Harborview last night, Frank? Anything I need to know about? The mayor gonna be calling me?"

Lovejoy shook his head. "Just another drive-by. Sometimes I think we ought to just let 'em all go at each other till they wipe themselves out. Fuckin' scumbags."

McCarty grunted his agreement, then turned his attention back to Mark Blakemoor. "So what are you on to now that Kraven's been burnt?"

Although it wasn't yet eight A.M., Blakemoor sighed tiredly as he gestured to the stack of open cases on his desk. In the corner, occupying half a dozen brown corrugated boxes, were his copies of every

scrap of information pertaining to every single case in which Richard
Kraven had been a suspect, not just in Seattle, but everywhere else
as well. It had been more than two years since he and Lois Ackerly
had spent all their time investigating the kind of killings that had
stopped with Kraven's arrest, but he still found himself going back to
the boxes over and over again, searching one folder after another for
something—anything—he might have missed that would tie at least
one of the local cases indisputably to Richard Kraven. The evidence
was there; he was certain of it. Buried somewhere in the depths of
one of those boxes there was something he hadn't yet spotted; some
insignificant fact that would let him at last put to rest the nagging
feeling he had that something was wrong, that there was something
about this case nobody yet understood. In the two-plus years that
Kraven had waited to die, Blakemoor hadn't found it. And maybe, he
had to admit on the days when the frustration of the case threatened
to overwhelm him, he hadn't found that little fact because it simply
wasn't there. Still, why did his gut consistently tell him that Richard
Kraven was as guilty as the courts had found him? Mark Blakemoor
had been operating on his guts every day for the last twenty years,
and they had never failed him yet. He sighed again. Maybe it was
finally time to let it all go, move the files down to the storeroom in
the bowels of the building, get them out of his sight, remove them
from the corner of his office, where they taunted him every day. He
looked up at McCarty, nodding toward the stack of boxes. "First, I
guess I'll get all that crap out of here."

Jack McCarty's head bobbed in gruff agreement. He started out of
Blakemoor's office, then wheeled around to glare once more at the
open newspaper that had started his day so badly. "You think that
Jeffers broad is going to keep harping on this?" he asked.

Mark Blakemoor, still remembering his conversation with Anne,
shrugged in a carefully calculated display of ignorance. No point putting the homicide chief in an even fouler mood. "How would I
know?" he asked. "I can't read her mind."

Grunting, McCarty turned and shambled out of Blakemoor's office, already feeling his ulcer start to act up. Another day of milk for
lunch, another day in which he would not dare eat one of the pas-

trami sandwiches he loved so much. Well, what the hell. Nobody ever said life was going to be a pastrami sandwich anyway.

As the chief made his exit, Lois Ackerly arrived, precariously balancing two Starbucks cups on top of what looked very much like a box of doughnuts. "What's wrong with McCarty?" she asked, putting the box down on Mark's desk. "The look he gave me would have killed a lesser woman." Then her eyes fell on the ruined newspaper protruding from beneath the doughnut box, and she understood. "Oh. Anne Jeffers." Her gaze shifted inquiringly to her partner. "Did you know this was coming?"

"Sort of," Mark replied. He pulled the top off one of the coffee cups and helped himself to a particularly sticky-looking, chocolate-covered pastry.

"And?" Lois Ackerly pressed when it became obvious that Mark wasn't going to tell her anything else.

"And what?"

Ackerly flopped into the chair behind the desk her partner always described as "compulsively neat" and fixed him with the look that meant he might as well tell her everything he knew or be prepared to subject himself to a day of nagging far worse than anything his ex-wife had ever dished out. Reading her expression perfectly, Mark closed the door to their office and recounted the events of the previous day.

"So what do you think?" Ackerly asked when he was through. "Is it over, or isn't it?"

Blakemoor hesitated, then decided to go with his gut feeling. He picked up the newspaper, tore it into shreds, and dropped the whole mess into the wastebasket. "It's over," he told her. "As far as I'm concerned, the case is closed." But as he reached for his cup of coffee, he found himself glancing down into the wastebasket, where Anne Jeffers's picture seemed to be staring back at him.

... Richard Kraven still insisted that he was innocent of all charges that have ever been brought against him. Even on his last morning, he still protested his innocence, and as I listened to him, I had to wonder what motive he could possibly have for lying, knowing that in only a few more hours he would surely be dead.

Did he expect a last-minute reprieve?

Surely not, for despite the hopes of the anti-capital-punishment forces gathered in front of the prison, both the courts and the governor of Connecticut had made it clear there would be no further intervention in the case.

What, then, would Richard Kraven have to gain by lying to me?

Perhaps it was simply his way of attempting to make me his last victim, by leaving me with questions in my mind, questions that remain unanswered ...

"How dare she write such filth?" Edna Kraven's voice quavered with anger and the newspaper rattled in her shaking hand. Finally, she had to set it down on the kitchen table. Really, it was simply too much to be borne! Richard—her wonderful, perfect Richard—dead not even twenty-four hours, and that awful Jeffers woman was already writing about him again, repeating yet again all the terrible things she'd written for the last five years.

It was bitterness, of course. Edna had long ago come to under-

stand that Anne Jeffers had fallen in love with Richard, and that
when Richard had spurned her, her love had turned to hatred. Why
else would she have pursued Richard the way she had, making up all
those terrible lies about him? For years Edna had written letter after
angry letter to the editor and the publisher of the *Seattle Herald*,
protesting that Anne Jeffers was slandering her son, but they had
never even responded to her. Once, though, they'd printed one of
her letters, but then they'd let Anne Jeffers write an article with the
disgusting insinuation that somehow the relationship between Edna
and her son might have led to the awful things she'd claimed Richard had done. When Edna read that particular article, she'd actually
felt faint—the very idea of what Anne Jeffers had implied fairly set
her skin to crawling. To sully the perfect love between a mother and
son that way . . .

Even now, just remembering that article made Edna Kraven's
blood boil, and she glared across the table at her other son, Rory.

Rory!

She'd named him after Rory Calhoun, who had been one of her
favorite movie stars. So handsome, so strong.

And so different from her own Rory.

Her Rory had taken after his father, that shiftless no-good with his
beady eyes and that weak chin, who had walked out on her right after Rory had been born, leaving her with no one to care for her except Richard. And Richard *had* cared for her, too. He'd helped her
with the baby, and done all the housework, and still managed to
have time to get perfect grades in school.

A genius, that's what Richard had been.

But Rory . . .

Her lips tightened with annoyance as she watched him eat the
cereal—*her* cereal, to which he'd simply helped himself—just as if
nothing had happened, just as if his brother hadn't been murdered
yesterday. Yes, murdered, she repeated to herself. That's what they
did to Richard, no matter what they called it in the newspapers or
in those terrible Star Chamber affairs they'd claimed were legal
hearings. They'd lynched Richard, and deep in her heart of hearts
Edna Kraven had a terrible feeling that Rory—his own *brother*—
didn't care.

Why else would he have brought the paper with that disgusting article into the house this morning? "Well?" she demanded, her lips pursing, her eyes glittering with fury.

Rory Kraven looked up from the sports pages he'd been perusing as he ate his cereal. Goddamn bitch was gonna start carping at him yet again. Nothing ever satisfied the bitch. Even after thirty goddamn years, nothing he ever did pleased her. Yesterday afternoon and last night had been the worst. He'd arranged to take the day off work to be with her, certain she would want his support when the time finally came for Richard to die, but by the time he'd gone to sleep on the Hide-A-Bed in the guest room that had once been his, he wondered why he'd come at all. All day long he'd had to listen to his mother rant on about Richard—how smart he was, how perfect he was, what a good son he'd always been. Rory had listened to it all, just the way he always listened to it, and he'd known what it really meant, because half the time she said it right out loud. Even now her words echoed in his ears:

Richard was smart—*not like you!*

Richard was perfect—*not like you!*

Richard was a good son—*not like you!*

All his life he'd known who she really loved. Even when he was a little boy, she'd always held Richard up to him as the ideal of perfection. *Why can't you get as good grades as Richard gets? Why can't you behave yourself, the way Richard always does?*

Richard could talk before he was eight months old!

Richard could walk when he was less than a year!

Richard is a genius!

Richard, Richard, Richard!

He'd heard it every day as he was growing up, even after Richard went to college, then moved into a house of his own. Rory himself moved out of the house as soon as he could, renting the little apartment on Capitol Hill where he still lived today, twelve years later. But moving out of his mother's house hadn't changed a thing. Edna had been glad to be rid of him, and she'd proved it by showing him his old room the first time he came back to visit her.

It hadn't been his room anymore. His bed was gone, and so was everything else that had been his. Now there was a Hide-A-Bed against one wall, a TV set against the other, and a big leather chair in the corner where his bureau had been. The words she'd uttered as he stood in the doorway, his stomach hollow as he stared at the room that had once been his, were burned into his mind forever: "Isn't it nicer now? Richard and I did it. His house is so small, you know, and we just thought it would be nice for him to have a special room here, all to himself. Someplace where he can come when he just needs to think."

Rory had wanted to hit her that day, wanted to put his face into hers and scream at her.

But he hadn't.

Instead he'd done as he'd always done.

He'd agreed that the room was nice and that Richard certainly did need it.

He'd kept his peace, hoping that if he didn't ask for anything, didn't demand any attention from her, didn't do anything she could criticize, maybe she would love him the way she loved Richard.

The years had gone by, and the pain had festered in Rory, but he stoically held it all in, certain that sooner or later his mother would love him, too. Then, when the murders started, and people started thinking Richard had committed them, he'd been sure his mother would start appreciating him.

Instead, she'd just given more and more of her attention to Richard, telling anyone who would listen that Richard couldn't have done what they said he did.

Richard was a good boy.

Richard was perfect.

Richard! Richard! Richard!

And now, even the day after Richard had finally been executed, it was going to be the same! Richard was perfect, and Rory was an idiot, and even with Richard dead, nothing was going to change at all.

Why?

Why couldn't she love him?

Why couldn't she defend him the way she defended Richard?

What had he done that was so terrible?

Instead of asking her the questions that were boiling in his brain, Rory only looked up from his paper, his eyes wary. "What, Mother? I was reading."

"The *sports* section?" Edna demanded. Her scathing voice made Rory wince, but she barely noticed it. "How can you care about sports after what's happened to your brother? Don't you even care what they did to him?" Now she picked up the newspaper and flung Anne Jeffers's column at him. "Don't you *care* what that woman is doing to your brother's memory?"

Rory picked up the paper, glanced at it, then stood up. "*They* didn't do anything to Richard, Mother," he said. "He did it himself. He killed those people, and they proved it, and they made him pay for it. That's what really happened, Mother." He started out of the kitchen.

Edna rose to her feet, clutching the collar of her favorite chenille bathrobe tight around her neck. Her black hair—hair he was pretty sure she dyed, since it didn't show even a trace of gray—hung lankly over her shoulders, and there were still traces in the wrinkles around her eyes of the makeup she'd fallen asleep in last night. Grabbing Rory's arm, she pulled him around so he couldn't avoid her glaring eyes. "Don't say that," she hissed, pushing her face close to his. "Don't ever talk about your brother that way! Never!"

Rory's mouth went dry and his stomach started to hurt the way it always did when she got really angry with him. Mutely, he nodded his head, and tried to pull away from her, but she wouldn't let him go.

"Say you're sorry," Edna demanded. "Say it!"

And Rory did.

After his apology, his mother released him and he left the house to go to the job he'd worked at ever since he finished high school, on the assembly line at Boeing.

And, as always, he wondered how he was ever going to get his mother to love him the way she'd loved Richard. He knew that was never going to happen, though, because no matter how hard he tried, he couldn't be Richard.

But maybe he could at least be *like* Richard.

CHAPTER 13

Richard Kraven is dead, but in the minds of the families of his victims, questions still linger, wounds still fester.

Richard Kraven's final challenge hangs like a dark cloud above us all. For if Kraven was telling the truth—which this reporter does not believe—then a killer may still be living among us.

This reporter therefore intends to take up Richard Kraven's final challenge, but not, as he hoped, with the intention of exonerating him.

This reporter intends to take one more look at the entire sequence of murders that have come to be known as the Kraven Killings.

This reporter intends to answer some of the questions that still remain:

Do we even know exactly how many died? Is it not possible that hidden away in the mountains and valleys that surround us, more victims are waiting to be discovered?

And might not one of those hidden victims provide the direct link to Richard Kraven that has always eluded the police, thus finally laying to rest all our doubts? Is it too much to ask that the police keep working on this grisly chapter in our civic history until the full truth is finally known?

This reporter thinks not. This reporter thinks the specter of Richard Kraven will hang over the city until . . .

"Talk to her. I gotta talk to her."

Though Sheila Harrar spoke the words out loud, there was no one to hear them. Not that anyone would have known what she meant anyway, for in the worn-out, wood-framed firetrap of a hotel into which Sheila had moved two months ago, no one knew his neighbors, and nobody *wanted* to know them. Most of the people in the building were just like Sheila—living from hand to mouth, telling themselves every morning when they got up that today they were going to get it together and find a job. But then the day just sort of closed in on them. Most days, Sheila didn't get much farther than the park in Pioneer Square, where someone would offer her a drink out of a bottle wrapped in a stained brown paper bag. And Sheila, just like all the rest of them, would tell herself it was only going to be one swallow, and then she'd get on with the day.

Somewhere there had to be someone who would hire her.

But after the first mouthful of whatever kind of fortified wine happened to be in whatever bottle was offered, Sheila would realize it was already too late. Anywhere she went, they'd smell the alcohol on her breath, then give her that look they always gave Indians.

"Not Indians, Ma. We're Native Americans. We've been here a lot longer than the whites, and they owe us! They murdered us, and stole our land, and they owe us!"

As she heard the voice of her son echo in her mind, Sheila Harrar's eyes flooded with tears. This morning, though, instead of giving in to them she wiped them away with the dirty sleeve of her best blouse and choked back the sob that rose in her throat. Taking a deep breath that rattled in her croupy lungs, she looked up from the paper she'd snitched from the lobby when she'd come home a few hours ago, and stared out the grimy window into the street outside. No point looking at the room itself; Sheila already knew every crack in the plaster, every curl in the peeling paint.

What would Danny think of her if he could see her now?

But he wasn't going to see her, because he wasn't ever going to come home.

So what did it matter where she lived? What did it matter if she didn't still live in the little apartment they used to share in Yesler Terrace, back when they still thought things were going to get better for them? Danny didn't know where she lived, because Danny was dead.

And Sheila knew who killed him.

Richard Kraven had killed her eighteen-year-old son, just like he'd killed all those others. Sheila knew it deep inside her guts, where the knowledge burned away at her, consuming her spirit just the way the wine she drank to try to quench the fire was consuming her body.

But without Danny, who cared?

Nobody.

Nobody had cared when she'd tried to get the police to do something about Danny. She'd done all the right things. Every day, she'd gone to the Public Safety Building, and filled out all the right forms, and talked to all the right people. But she could see that nobody cared, and she knew why.

Because she was an Indian.

Not a Native American. Not one of those proud people Danny had always talked about.

No, Sheila Harrar was just an Indian from the projects, and even though they didn't tell her right to her face, she knew what they were thinking. Her son was just like her—just another Indian. Probably got drunk and walked out, and didn't even bother to say good-bye to his own mother. When she shouted that it wasn't true, that Danny went to school, and worked, they hadn't believed her. If Danny had been white—if *she* had been white—it would have been different. Then they would have cared, they would have tried to find him. But she and Danny were Indians, and nobody gave a damn what happened to them.

After Danny didn't come home that day, Sheila stopped caring what happened, too. The ache of not having him anymore hurt so much that she started drinking just to dull the pain, and after a while she was drinking so much she couldn't make it to work sometimes. Then she'd gotten a job that only started in the afternoon, and that was okay for a while, until she started sitting up drinking all night, and sleeping all day. After that there'd been other jobs, but they didn't last very long, because Sheila's drinking was getting worse and worse. Finally she'd had to move out of the project, down here into the hotel in the International District. Since then, one day was just like another. She slept in her tiny room, promised herself that the next day she'd get it together, but every day turned out just like the one before.

Now, as she reread the article about the man who'd killed her son, she knew that today would be different. Today she really would get it together, and not drink, and maybe even find a job.

But most important, she would talk to Anne Jeffers, and Anne Jeffers would listen to her, and believe her, and even though it wouldn't bring Danny back, at least it might help.

If she knew someone else at least cared what had happened to Danny, maybe some of the pain would go away.

Leaving the paper lying on her unmade bed, Sheila went out into the hall and shuffled down to the pay phone at the far end. She fumbled with the tattered telephone book that hung from a chain beneath the phone, praying that the page she needed wouldn't be torn out. Then, when she found the number she was looking for, she reached into the pocket of her jeans and pulled out one of the quarters she'd cadged from someone the night before. As she held the quarter up to the slot, she hesitated, and for a moment thought of the wine it could buy her.

Danny was more important.

She dropped the coin into the slot, waited for the dial tone, then punched in the number of the *Seattle Herald*. Minutes later, after being moved from one extension to another, she came to the end of her search.

"To leave a message for Anne Jeffers, push 'one' now."

Sheila Harrar pushed the button on the phone and began to speak: "My name is Sheila Harrar, and Richard Kraven killed my son. If you care, you can come and see me."

Mumbling her address and the number of the pay phone, Sheila Harrar hung up the receiver and trudged back to her room. She would wait for a while, just to see what would happen.

Maybe Anne Jeffers would care.

Or maybe she was just like all the others.

CHAPTER 14

*H*e was hiding in the darkness, hoping nobody would find him, but from somewhere outside, out where it was light, he could hear the sound of footsteps. Heavy footsteps moving around not far away.

He held his breath, terrified that if he so much as let out the tiniest gasp of air, his father would hear it and know where he was. Not that it made any difference, really, because his father already knew where he was. He always knew, no matter where the little boy tried to hide. Always, sooner or later, he heard the sound of the approaching footsteps, and the closer they came, the more frightened he was.

Sometimes he was so frightened he felt like he was going to die, but he never did. And now, as he huddled in the darkness, making himself as small as he could, he was pretty sure he would never die, that it would just go on and on, and never end.

He knew what was going to happen next, although he didn't know why it was going to happen. He never knew why it was going to happen, because he could never relate it to something he had done. It wasn't like it was punishment for anything.

He guessed it was just something his father liked to do.

The little boy couldn't remember the first time it had happened, but neither could he remember any time in his short life when it hadn't happened. It was just always there, hanging over him.

As the thumping steps drew closer and closer, the little boy tried to make himself even smaller, wishing he could just disappear, so that when his father finally opened the door, he wouldn't be there at all. But he'd been praying for that to happen, too, and it never worked, even *when he held real still, and didn't breathe for so long his chest felt like it was going to explode.*

The footsteps grew yet louder, and now he knew the darkness was going to be torn away, and the light would flood over him. As if the thought had made it happen, the boy was blinded by a sudden flash of brilliance, and instinctively moved his hands to shield his eyes.

Was it the movement that betrayed him?

His father's hand—a huge hand—hovered over him, and the terrible fear that he was about to be squashed like a bug overwhelmed him. He began crying—tiny, sniffling sobs that he knew he had to control.

Had to, but couldn't.

The huge hand closed around him, picked him up, pulled him out into the terrible light. Then he was in the gloom of the basement, and his father had stretched him out on the cot that stood next to the wall and tied his arms and legs.

His father opened his shirt and pulled down his pants.

Then the worst part started, when his father started attaching the metal clips.

Some of them went on the boy's fingers and toes, and those didn't hurt so badly he couldn't stand it.

It was when his father put the ones on his nipples that he screamed out, but even as he screamed, he knew no one would hear him.

Then his father put the last clip on, and as the metal dug into his penis, he moaned in agony.

A moment later, when the first shock went through him, he screamed and tried to twist away from the pain.

But his scream was mute, and no matter how he twisted and thrashed, he couldn't escape the terrible pain.

The silence in Room 306 of the Critical Care Unit was broken by a low moan from Glen Jeffers's throat that quickly escalated into a terrified howl. Anne Jeffers, who had arrived only five minutes earlier to visit her husband before going on to her office, watched in stunned paralysis as her husband's body began to thrash in the bed. Before she quite realized what had happened, the wires attached to Glen's chest were torn loose and the monitors above the bed suddenly went flat. A second later the IV tube was ripped from the needle in his arm and clear liquid began dripping from the dangling hose as crimson blood oozed from the base of the needle. It was the sight of the blood—her husband's blood—that released Anne from her momentary paralysis. Jerking the door open, she called to the nurse, but at the station a few yards away alarms had already started to sound. One of the nurses was running toward the room even before Anne could call out to her.

Starting back toward the bed where Glen was still thrashing, Anne felt a sensation of helplessness such as she'd never experienced before in her life. She wanted to do something, to take some action that would help her husband. But she hadn't the slightest idea of what was happening to him, or how to help him. Instinctively, she reached out to him, but then stopped short, suddenly terrified that anything she did might make his condition worse than it already was. The split second of indecision stretched into an eternity of terror, then the door crashed open and the room filled with people. As the nurse and two orderlies brushed by her, Anne came back to life.

"He was sleeping," she began. "Everything seemed to be fine, and then . . ." Her voice trailed off as she realized nobody was listening to her. She moved closer to the foot of the bed.

The orderlies were holding Glen down now, and the nurse was struggling to cap the needle in his arm that was still oozing blood. Glen, though, was struggling harder than ever, and now she could see that he was awake. His jaw was working as grunts of either terror or anger—Anne couldn't be sure which—formed in his throat. He seemed to be trying to jerk his arms away from the two orderlies.

Suddenly Anne could stand it no more. "Glen!" she shouted. "For God's sake, Glen, they're trying to help you!" As the words exploded from Anne's lips, Glen froze, then collapsed back onto the bed. His breath came in great ragged gasps. Now that the orderlies no longer had to struggle with him, the nurse began issuing a series of orders. Almost as quickly as it had begun, the crisis was over.

"What was it?" Anne asked as the nurse reattached the last of the monitoring leads and began checking Glen's vital signs. The nurse said nothing until she was satisfied that her patient's pulse, respiration, and blood pressure were within acceptable parameters, then took his temperature. As she at last turned her attention to Anne, Glen himself spoke.

"Hey," he said, his voice weak but recognizable. The sound of his voice reassuring her far more than anything the nurse could have said, Anne suddenly felt shaky. Perching on the edge of the bed, she took his hand.

"Honey? What happened?"

Glen said nothing for several long seconds. The dream was still vivid in his mind, and even as he summoned up the memory, the terror of the nightmare threatened to close in on him once again. Shuddering slightly, he squeezed Anne's hand. "Just a dream," he told her. "And not a very nice one."

"A nightmare?" Anne asked. "You never have nightmares—"

"He never had a heart attack, either," the nurse interjected. "And from what his records say, he never had anywhere near the medication he has in him now."

Anne's attention shifted from Glen to the nurse. "You mean what he just went through was caused by the medication?"

"Maybe you should talk to the doctor about this," the nurse replied, wishing she hadn't said anything at all.

"Maybe I *should*," Anne said.

Now Glen, too, began to wish he hadn't mentioned the dream. Once Anne got hold of something, she wouldn't easily let it go. "Hey, take it easy, hon. It was just a dream, and it's over now." He glanced at the clock on his bed stand. "Aren't you going to be late to work?"

"If you had a reaction to one of the drugs—" Anne began, but this time Glen put his finger to her lips to stop her words. The effort of lifting his hand took much more energy than he would have thought possible just twenty-four hours ago.

"It was nothing," he lied. "Just a dream, and I can't even remember what it was about." His hand dropped back onto the bed, and now his eyelids began to feel heavy. "Just go on to work, okay? I'll be fine."

As his eyes began to close, Anne glanced worriedly at the nurse. "Is he all right?"

"I gave him a sedative," the nurse replied. "I know it looked pretty frightening, Mrs. Jeffers, but believe me, he's doing just fine. If you'd like, I can call the doctor. . . ."

Feeling as if she'd foolishly overreacted, Anne shook her head. "It's all right. I guess—well, I guess I'm just not used to seeing him like this." She got up from the bed and leaned over to kiss her husband. For a moment she got no response at all. Then Glen's fingers closed on her wrist and she felt his lips brush her cheek. His grip eased, and by the time she had straightened up, she was sure he'd fallen back into sleep. His eyes were closed and his breathing had quieted. Relieved, she moved quietly toward the door. His voice stopped her.

"Anne?"

She turned around to find him looking at her, his eyes barely open.

"What is it, honey?"

"Did you jog this morning?"

Anne blinked. Did she *jog* this morning? Why on earth would he be asking about that? "Of course I did," she replied. Then she added playfully, "Can't get out of shape, can I? Who'd take care of you when you come home?"

Glen smiled, but it was a smile that quickly faded away. "Just be careful, okay?"

"Careful?" Anne echoed. What was he talking about? "Careful of what?"

Glen was silent, and for a second she thought he'd finally fallen asleep. But just as she was passing through the door, she heard his voice once more.

"There're a lot of creeps out there."

She spun around to look at him once again, but this time his eyes were closed and his chest was rising and falling with the easy rhythm of sleep. She silently pulled the door to his room closed, nodded a good-bye to the nurse at the station and left the CCU, taking the elevator to the ground floor. As she left the hospital through the main doors on Sixteenth East and started toward her car, she turned, looking up at the window to Glen's room.

His last words still echoed in her mind.

"There're a lot of creeps out there."

Coming to her car, she happened to glance up at the shabby-looking brick building across the street. Someone was looking out

one of its windows, and for just a second their eyes met. He was a
man, perhaps sixty, perhaps much less. He was wearing an under-
shirt, his face unshaven and his hair uncombed, but none of those
details stayed in Anne's mind. It was the look in his eyes. He looked
beaten, as if the world had challenged him and he had lost. But it
wasn't just defeat Anne saw in his eyes.

There was anger, too.

The man turned away from the window, but Anne stayed where
she was for a moment, her eyes fixed on the building. It struck her
that the man looked very much like the apartment house he lived in:
worn-out, uncared for. Sad. Was the whole building filled with people like that, people for whom life had become one desperate day after another?

Probably it was.

Anne turned and looked back toward the hospital, where the window to Glen's room was clearly visible. Perhaps this was what he had
meant. Perhaps he had awakened early and seen someone—maybe
even the same man she herself had just seen—slipping back into the
structure's unwelcoming shelter as dawn washed away the protective
shadows of night.

Shivering in the chill of the morning, Anne hurried to her car and
drove quickly away.

CHAPTER 15

T he rain began as Anne turned into the parking lot of the building Glen had always called Seattle's ugliest. It wasn't a point
Anne was about to argue, for the building that housed the *Herald*
had been constructed in 1955, smack in the middle of one of the
dullest periods in modern architectural history. Utterly devoid of
any interesting features, it was a perfectly rectilinear, five-story
aluminum-and-glass box, its main facade punctured only by a pair
of glass doors. As if understanding that his building was architec-
turally unsalvageable, the designer had made no attempt to soften
the structure with lawns or gardens, and the concept of "one percent
for art" had still been years in the future. Anne, like the majority
of the *Herald*'s staff, had long stopped noticing the building at all,
and most people who passed it on the street weren't even aware that
it housed one of the city's major newspapers. If and when the park
that would be known as the Commons finally metamorphosed from
endless talk into a reality of trees, lawns, and pathways linking
Lake Union to the downtown area, the Herald Building would be
razed. No one—least of all the newspaper's employees—would
miss it.

Pulling into the only vacant space in the lot, Anne ducked her
head against the rain as she locked the car and threaded her way
across the parking area, then through the first of two sets of double
doors into a tiny foyer. Waving to the guard behind the scarred
blond-wood counter that was the inner lobby's single distinguishing
feature, Anne brushed a few drops of water off her jacket, then
pushed the second door open when the buzzer sounded. As if terror-

ists are just waiting to invade us, she thought as she nodded to the guard on her way to the bank of elevators opposite the doors. What makes anyone think we're that important?

She punched at the elevator button, prepared a sarcastic remark for the guard in the typical event that no car showed up within a minute, and was pleasantly surprised when one of the doors instantly slid open. The usual chaos reigned on the third floor, and it took Anne almost five more minutes just to get to her desk, what with half a dozen people commenting on her column in this morning's edition, and half a dozen more asking about Glen. When she finally crossed the newsroom to her desk, the monitor of her computer was flashing an accusatory beacon informing her that she had twenty-three unanswered internal messages, and forty-two more in her voice mail from outside.

Square in the center of her desk, where she couldn't possibly miss it, was a message from her editor. Scrawled in large black letters, the message was no-more-than-usually direct:

SEE ME
—VIV

Pausing only to put her purse in the bottom drawer of her desk and hang her damp jacket on the coat tree she shared with three other reporters, Anne strode into the editor's office, bypassing the sagging chair with the broken spring that her boss was gesturing her toward even while arguing with someone on the telephone, and helping herself to a cup of coffee. She scanned the papers scattered in front of the editor, her ability to read upside down and backward allowing her to assess that at least there were no formal complaints about her among the clutter on Vivian Andrews's desk.

"I know what you're doing, and I think it's at least rude, if not illegal," the editor said as she hung up the phone. "Are you going to read everything, or do you want to sit down?"

Anne eyed the rump-sprung chair with distaste, but answered neither question. "Got your newsy little epistle," she said. "What's up?"

Vivian Andrews burrowed into the mess on her desk and pulled out a copy of that morning's paper, neatly opened and folded to expose Anne's article. Tapping it meaningfully with one brightly polished fingernail, she gazed steadily at Anne. "As you can see, I passed this through exactly as you dictated it last night. Now, given that you're back from the execution, and given that 'dead men tell no tales,' as I believe the saying goes, just how much longer are you planning to chase this particular wild goose, and when may I expect you to begin working on something that might be considered news?" She leaned back in her chair and regarded Anne archly. "Oh, and by using the word 'news,' I'm suggesting you might want to find a story that occurred within, say, the last six months?" The questioning inflection at the end of her remark was always a clue that Vivian was not feeling particularly patient.

"How long will you give me?" Anne countered.

Vivian Andrews placed the tips of her fingers together, resting her chin on them as she thought it over. "Not much," she decided. "They're cutting budgets again, and we're stretched tight already." Then, as her own eyes caught a few of the words Anne had dictated last night, she relented slightly. "Do you really think something's missing? Something you can find, I mean?"

Anne dropped into the chair, wincing as the broken spring jabbed at her hip. "The execution is over, and there aren't going to be any more trials," she reminded her editor. "And Mark Blakemoor says they're closing the files, which means there's no reason for them not to let me see everything they've got."

Vivian Andrews weighed the pros and cons quickly. The loss of a few more days of Anne's time was far outweighed by the number of papers they'd sell if the reporter actually came up with something new. "Okay," she agreed. "A few days. But if you don't come up with something, it's over. Agreed?"

"Agreed."

Anne was already halfway out the door when Vivian Andrews spoke again. "Anne? How's Glen doing?"

Anne turned back. "Pretty well, I guess, all things considered."

"I heard they almost lost him."

Anne tried to put up a facade of bravado, but didn't quite succeed. "The important thing is that they didn't. He's going to be okay. It's just going to take some time."

Vivian nodded in sympathy. "If you need a leave—" she began, but Anne quickly shook her head.

"I don't think so. At least I don't right now. But I'll keep it in mind. When Glen comes home from the hospital, I might just take a few days. Okay?"

"Okay," Vivian agreed. "And keep me informed, Anne. About your story, and about Glen, too."

"Thanks, Viv," Anne replied. "I'll do that."

Back at her desk, Anne began going through the internal messages, most of which could safely be ignored. After she'd responded to the last of those requiring an answer, she picked up her phone and punched in the access to her voice mail.

Most of what she heard was just as inconsequential as the stuff that had been in her electronic mail—suggestions for stories, questions about things she'd written, pleas for her to give a mention to one cause or another, some of them good, some of them not so good.

Toward the end of the long series of recordings, there were several responses to her article this morning.

Again, some of them good, some not so good.

One, the last one, was disturbing.

It was a woman's voice, and it sounded strained.

"I got to talk to you," it said. "He killed my son! I know he did, but nobody listens! 'Cause we're Indians, no one listens!"

There was a name and a garbled address, but though she played it over and over, Anne couldn't quite make it out.

She spent the rest of the day at the police department, beginning her search through the boxes of files that Mark Blakemoor and Lois Ackerly brought to the storage rooms even while she worked.

To her surprise, Mark Blakemoor came downstairs in mid-morning to find out how she was doing, then showed up again at noon, this time with sandwiches and a couple of Cokes.

"Anything in particular you're looking for?" he asked as Anne tore the wrapper off a pastrami on rye and hungrily bit into the thick sandwich.

Chewing hard, Anne shrugged and signaled him to wait until she'd swallowed. "I don't know," she said. Then, remembering the garbled message on her voice mail that morning, she frowned again.

"Do you remember any reports of a Native American boy?" With the skills she'd honed in her years of reporting, she repeated the message verbatim.

Mark Blakemoor gazed at her. "That's all? Just 'He killed my son, but nobody listens'?"

"That's all."

A resigned sigh emerged from Mark Blakemoor's chest as he recalled the hundreds—thousands—of calls he'd fielded over the years of investigating the Richard Kraven murders. How was he supposed to remember just one? Still, if it would help Anne out . . . "Tell you what," he offered. "I've got some time this evening. Maybe if I go through the logs, something will jog my memory."

"You don't have to do that—" Anne began, but Mark silenced her with a gesture.

"If I don't do it, you will, and at least I know where the logs are and what to look for." Before Anne could respond, he spoke again: "Hell, at least it'll keep my beer intake down for a night, right?"

There was a plaintive ring to his voice that made the last of Anne's polite objections to his working overtime die on her lips. If he wanted to do it for her, why not? "I'd offer to give you a hand, but with Glen in the hospital—"

"It's okay," Blakemoor assured her. "In fact, why don't I get started right now?"

For the rest of the hour the two of them searched through boxes, Mark Blakemoor hunting for the telephone logs, Anne scanning the file folders for a name, a notation—whatever might catch her eye.

When he finally emerged from the storage area at one-thirty, covered with dust and sneezing more than he had since he'd left the Midwest twenty-two years before, Mark realized he'd enjoyed his sandwich in the basement with Anne Jeffers more than any other lunch he'd had in recent memory.

Anne, on the other hand, didn't give the lunch another thought. She hadn't noticed that all the time they were together, going through the boxes, the detective had kept glancing at her out of the corner of his eye, just like some high school kid with a crush on the prom queen.

CHAPTER 16

The long spring day was finally fading into night, and as dusk set-tled over the city beyond the hospital's windows, Glen Jeffers grew more anxious. All day he'd drifted between a fitful sleep that gave him no real rest, and a drowsy kind of wakefulness that never left his mind unfogged. As he gazed out the window, watching peo-ple move up and down the sidewalk two stories below, and lights come on in the apartment buildings across the street, he had the strange sensation that time had somehow twisted around: as the rest of the world drifted toward the end of the day, he was only now com-ing fully awake. Unless he could convince the nurse to give him something to send him back to sleep, he was certain he would lie awake all night.

Anne had come to visit him; so had the kids.

For some reason—a reason he couldn't quite figure out—he felt disconnected from them. It was the drugs, of course; once he was finished with them, he'd be back to himself. But today when the kids had come in after school, he found it hard to concentrate on what they were saying, hard to pretend interest in the fight Kevin had had with Justin Reynolds, or the new CD Heather had bought that after-noon. What was the name of the group? Crippled Chicken? Some-thing like that.

While he was pondering the possible hidden meanings of the names of rock bands and poking at the tray of food they'd brought in at exactly six o'clock, Anne arrived. He'd had to concentrate to follow her conversation, as his mind kept veering off to other places.

Or, more specifically, one other place.

The nightmare he'd had early this morning, when Anne had come in on her way to work.

The dream was still vivid in his memory, and had never been far from his consciousness all day. It kept reaching out to him whenever he drifted into the fringes of sleep, threatening to draw him once more into its dark terrors.

When Gordy Farber had come in an hour ago, Glen told him about the dream, and it hadn't taken the heart specialist long to come up with an explanation: "Well, I'm not a psychiatrist, but I've had a lot of experience with people in your situation. You've had a heart attack, which makes you feel helpless. And what could be a better symbol of helplessness than a little boy hiding in the dark from a threatening father?"

"But my father wasn't threatening," Glen objected. "In fact, my dad was so modern he never even spanked me! Said spanking was child abuse way back when everyone else was still using the belt every day!"

Farber's brows arched into an expression of exaggerated envy. "Wish *my* dad had thought that way—he was a big one for the 'spare the rod and spoil the child' routine, except his bark always turned out to be far worse than his bite." The doctor's features assumed a more serious mien. "But what your dad was like doesn't really make much difference, because we're not talking about reality here. We're talking about dreams and symbols." His gaze shifted to the array of tubes and wires attached to his patient. "As for the electrodes your father was hooking up to you, I don't know if you've noticed, but you're sprouting more wires and tubes than a high school science fair project." He'd grinned as another thought came to him. "Hey, maybe *I'm* the father figure in the dream. After all, who could be more fatherly to you than your doctor right now?"

Glen knew the explanation made a lot of sense. The nightmare's fear made sense, for what could be more terrifying than a heart attack? Even now he could remember the panic he'd felt as that band tightened around his chest, the pain shot up his arm, and the blackness closed around him. But although the explanation fit perfectly, Glen had a nagging feeling there was something else—that the terror he'd felt from the dream went beyond the fear he experienced when the "incident"—as Gordy Farber insisted on calling it—had occurred.

The incident. He kept going back over the whole experience. It wasn't a complete blackout, for he remembered being awake for a while in the ambulance. After all, if he wasn't awake at least part of the time, how had he been able to hear the paramedics talking? And he *had* heard them; even now he could clearly remember their voices.

"*Put it up to three hundred joules and hit him again.*"

"*That's the way.*"

"*Try again at three-sixty.*"

"Joules." That was an electrical term. Someone had said to "put it at three hundred joules and hit him again."

When it struck, the truth crashed into Glen's consciousness like surf hurling against a rocky cliff.

He hadn't been awake at all.

He'd been dead. He'd been dead, and the paramedics had been fighting to make his heart begin beating again, to make him start breathing again.

Glen felt an icy sweat break out on his skin, and for a moment he was afraid he might have a second heart attack. He reached for the buzzer to summon the nurse, but the wave of terror eased, and he let his hand drop back onto the thin blanket that covered him.

He hadn't died, and he wasn't going to.

But it had been close. A lot closer than he'd realized until just that moment.

Was that why he'd felt different today? Disconnected? Was that why he'd had a hard time concentrating on what Anne and his children had been saying?

He lay back on the pillows and turned to gaze out the window as he thought about it. Of course he felt different now—how could he not? When you come that close to dying—

His thought broke off as he spotted someone on the street below, the shadowy figure of a man moving along the rain-slicked sidewalk across the street, and for a moment had the feeling he knew him. But then, when the man looked up—almost as if he'd felt Glen watching him—his face was briefly illuminated by the yellow glow of a streetlight and Glen realized he'd been wrong.

The man was a stranger, someone he was certain he'd never seen before.

A moment later the man looked away again and quickly disappeared into the shadows of the street.

CHAPTER 17

All day long the fantasy had been growing inside the man, and all day long the pressure to act on the fantasy had been building. When it got to the point where he was starting to feel like he might explode, the man decided to go for a walk. At least he could breathe some fresh air, and in the dark he'd be by himself.

No one would recognize him.

No one would ask him questions.

But even going outside didn't work, for he wasn't on the sidewalk more than thirty seconds before he felt someone watching him.

When he looked around, sure enough, someone was staring at him out of one of the windows of the hospital.

Maybe he ought to just go up there and pull the guy's plug. Wouldn't that be something? Just to walk into the room, tell the guy off, then jerk the plugs out of the wall and watch him die?

Yes, just watch him die!

In the cool damp of the evening the man felt a shiver go through him, a chill that wasn't brought on by the weather at all.

It was brought on by the fantasy that had been growing in his mind until he finally knew he was going to act on it.

But not with the guy in the hospital room. Not where there would be lights, and people, and he would be caught so soon he wouldn't even get to enjoy what he'd done.

The man walked on up the sidewalk, finally cutting over a block, then zigzagged north and west until he finally came to Broadway. A lot of lights there, and a lot of people, but it didn't matter because he fit right in with the rest of the crowd. Broadway was humming with people tonight, but that was good, for it meant he would be only one more anonymous face in the crowd. He threaded his way along the sidewalk, ignoring the teenage panhandlers with their green hair, black lipstick, and pierced lips, brows, and ears.

When he saw the person he was looking for, he would know.

Two men holding hands came toward him. The man's eyes fixed angrily on them, but at the last second he stepped aside to let them pass, only to turn and glower at them once again when he heard them laughing as they walked away.

Laughing at him?

His fingers clenched with sudden fury, but when they didn't turn around to look back at him, he forced his anger down and continued on his way.

Covertly, his eyes searched the crowd.

He was almost up to the QFC supermarket when he saw her.

About thirty, with blond hair cut short, and a skirt that was even shorter than her hair.

She was on the other side of the street, going the same way he was, and it didn't look like anyone was with her. In fact, it looked like maybe she was doing the same thing he was doing.

Looking for someone.

The man crossed the street, increasing his pace until he was only a few yards behind her, then slowed, keeping the distance between himself and the girl steady.

She kept heading north, finally turning in at the DeLuxe Bar & Grill.

The man slowed, then loitered outside until he saw her all but disappear into the darkness at the back of the café. Only when he was certain she hadn't met anyone did he go inside himself.

She was sitting alone at one of the small tables for two.

The man, his heart suddenly pounding with anticipation, lowered himself into one of the chairs at the next table, choosing the one that would let him make eye contact with her.

His skin began to tingle and he felt a glowing ember of excitement ignite in his belly as he thought about what he was going to do.

His excitement growing, the man searched his memory, dredging up the minutiae of what the other victims had suffered, struggling to recapture all the details of what Richard Kraven had been accused of doing. . . .

An hour and a half later, when the woman finally got up to leave the DeLuxe, the man still hadn't spoken to her.

He had contented himself with watching her, with imagining what would happen later, when they were together, when he'd finally made himself known to her.

Now, as she passed through the front door, he dropped some money on the table to cover the cost of the single beer he'd nursed through the ninety minutes, and followed her out into the night. For a moment it seemed as if the woman had vanished into the darkness, but then the man caught sight of her walking west toward the Harvard Exit theater. Following her as he had earlier, keeping several yards between her and himself, the man tracked her two blocks west, then turned south to follow her down Boylston. When she finally turned to go into one of the anonymous two-story buildings that lined the block, she paused, looked back, then cocked her head and smiled at him.

She'd known.

Known he was watching her, known he was following her.

But she didn't know what he wanted, what he intended to do.

And when she spoke, the glowing ember of excitement in the man's belly flared into burning anticipation. "It's okay, fella. I'm kind of lonely, too." The man said nothing, but moved slowly toward the girl, whose smile widened as she nodded toward the building. "Want to come up for a while?"

Inside the woman's apartment, the man looked around to see a space not much different from the one he himself lived in a few blocks away. The once-white paint was dirty and starting to peel, and a few pieces of tired furniture stood on a worn carpet. The coffee table was piled with tabloid newspapers, and in the corner was a dying ficus tree, most of its leaves scattered on the floor around its pot.

"How come you didn't say hi at the DeLuxe?" the woman asked, going into the kitchen, pulling open the refrigerator and holding up a beer. "Want one? No extra charge!"

For a brief moment the man wasn't quite certain what she meant, but a second later she cleared up the confusion. "How's fifty for two hours?" she asked. "I usually get a lot more, but it's kinda slow to-night, and you seem like a nice guy."

The man glanced quickly at the windows. The curtains were drawn; not even a crack of light showed through from the streetlamp outside.

Perfect.

He rose to his feet and moved around into the kitchen. "That'll be fine, I guess," he said. He was standing right behind her now, looking over her shoulder as she pulled open a drawer to get a bottle opener.

The tool she was looking for sat in the midst of a jumble of other utensils, but the one that caught the man's eye was a knife.

A large butcher knife whose blade glinted hypnotically.

The man's fingers began to tingle once again, and the fire moved from his belly to his groin as he made the final decision. "But I don't think I'll really need two whole hours," he said softly.

Then, in a movement executed so swiftly that she had no time even to scream, let alone struggle away from his grip, the man's right arm slid around the woman's neck, catching her head in the crook of his elbow. As he jerked hard and twisted to one side, he felt the crunching of bones in the woman's neck as her spine was twisted beyond its limits. Then she went limp and the man lowered her to the floor.

He stared down at her.

Had he killed her?

He could hardly believe it—it had happened so fast he could barely remember what it felt like. Then, as he watched, the woman's lips suddenly began to work and a tiny sound bubbled up from her throat. Her eyes, wide open, stared up at him, and now he could see that she wasn't dead at all. He had broken her neck.

He had paralyzed her.

But he hadn't killed her.

He stared at her for a moment, anticipating what would come next, the fire now raging within him.

He reached for the knife.

At last, savoring the moment he'd been anticipating for what seemed an eternity, the man set to work.

The woman, utterly paralyzed from the moment the bones in her neck snapped, felt nothing.

And, blessedly, she died quickly, unaware of the carnage the man was inflicting on her body.

The Saturday morning that arrived two days later was one of the dull gray Seattle dawns that carried a chill far greater than the temperature warranted. It was on mornings like this that Anne Jeffers's dedication to retaining the body she'd graduated from college with was sorely tested, for getting up to join the parade of joggers in Volunteer Park was hard enough even when the weather was perfect. Actually, it wasn't even this hard in the depths of winter, when you knew each consecutive morning was going to be as clammy as the last. But Friday had produced one of those deceptively warm afternoons that promised—generally falsely—a long and sunny summer. Even the evening had stayed clear and warm, and when they'd walked home from visiting Glen in the hospital, she and the kids had cut over to Broadway to get ice cream cones and watch the passing parade. Now, as she lay in bed gazing glumly out the window, she realized she'd been suckered again. It wasn't summer yet; in fact even spring appeared to have decided the whole thing had been a mistake and invited the gloomy winter skies to take over again. Offered the opportunity, the clouds had quickly gathered, and were now occupied with drizzling their contents onto the city with, Anne suspected, the deliberate intention of drowning the good mood that had spread along Broadway last night.

Well, the hell with it, Anne decided. If it wasn't enough that Glen wouldn't be out of the hospital for another week, that she had so far turned up nothing at all in the files she'd been exploring in the basement of the Public Safety Building, and that Vivian Andrews had pointedly asked her yesterday how she was coming with a story, there was also the fact that she was finding sleeping alone in the big bed in the creaking old house a lot harder than she'd thought it would be. For this morning, her body could damn well take care of itself. She rolled over, snuggled deeper under the down comforter and closed her eyes. But instead of sleep, all that came to her was guilt.

She got up, pulled on her clothes, and went downstairs. Both the kids were already up, Heather on the telephone, Kevin staring at the television set. She went into the kitchen, poured a cup of coffee from the pot that had already been brewed—one of the less doubtful advantages of having a daughter old enough to start sopping up caffeine like a true Seattleite—and was just wandering back into the living room as the morning news came on. The face of Janalou Moorehead filled the screen, and since Anne had never been a fan of what she and the rest of the *Herald* staffers thought of as empty heads with nice voices, she picked up the morning paper. But today Janalou's seductive voice caught her attention: "Murder on Capitol Hill tops our report this morning," the woman said, putting a suitably serious expression over her normally smiling visage. "The body of a thirty-two-year-old woman has been found in an apartment on—"

Not waiting for Janalou Moorehead to finish her sentence, Anne sprang from the sofa, relieved Heather of the telephone, offered an unceremonious good-bye to the friend her daughter had been talking to, and pressed the button to end the call.

"Mother!" an outraged Heather exclaimed. "That was—"

"I don't care who it was," Anne told her. "That's why we gave you a phone of your own in your room. I have to—" But before she could finish what she was saying, the phone came alive and she instantly released the button. "Yes?"

"Who the hell have you been talking to?" Carl Waters, the weekend editor at the *Herald*, sounded even more annoyed than usual. "If you're going to sit on your phone all morning, at least turn on the cellular, okay?"

"I'm sorry, Carl," Anne said, knowing an explanation was neither expected nor wanted. "I just heard Janie-Lou Emptyhead. What's going on?"

"I don't know much more than she does," Carl replied. "We

caught the dispatch on the scanner half an hour ago, and I've been trying to get hold of you ever since."

"What's the address?" Anne asked. "And who's already there?"

Carl Waters gave her an address on Boylston, no more than ten blocks from where she was. "A photographer's on his way. If you head out now, you should be able to get there about the same time." Anne was about to hang up when Waters spoke again. "Anne, there's something funny about this one, which is why I kept trying to call you. The police dispatcher gave the address, then told the unit that maybe they sent Blakemoor and Ackerly home too soon."

Anne's fingers tightened on the phone. "Blakemoor?" she repeated. "They couldn't have been talking about the Kraven task force, could they?"

"They didn't take me into their confidence," Waters replied archly.

Anne was careful to betray nothing of the excitement she was suddenly feeling. "All right. I'm on my way." Hanging up the phone, she glanced around the room, but the big leather bag that was halfway between a grip and a satchel wasn't on the sofa where she was sure she'd left it. "Where's my gritchel?" she asked.

Kevin glanced up from the TV. "Under the coffee table," he told her. "You covering the murder?"

"Uh-huh."

"Can I go with you?" It was a request he always made, and his mother always denied. Still, he figured it was always worth a shot. Just once, he'd love to get in on the excitement, maybe even get a look at a real dead body . . .

"No, you can't," Anne told her son as she quickly rummaged through the jumble in her gritchel, checking for her tape recorder, notebook, and the camera she always carried, just in case. "And you can't go wandering over there on your own, either. Okay?" Kevin looked annoyed, but sighed his agreement. "You going to visit Dad this morning?"

"I don't know," Kevin began. "Me and Justin were gonna play ball in the park, but—"

"Tell you what," Anne interrupted. "I don't know how long I'm

going to be stuck on this story this morning, so if you'll visit Dad for me, I'll spring for a movie tonight. Okay?"

"Justin, too?" Kevin bargained.

"Why not?" Anne agreed. She dug into her large leather bag once more, produced a ten dollar bill and handed it to her son. "Call the hospital before you go, and find out if there's anything Dad wants."

As his mother disappeared out the front door, Kevin gazed at the ten dollar bill in his hand. If his father didn't want anything, was he going to be allowed to keep the ten?

By the time he walked into Room 308 at the hospital an hour later, though, most of the ten dollars was gone, spent on the magazines his father had asked for.

"So what's this big story your mother's working on?" Glen asked as his son handed him the copies of *Architectural Digest* and *Newsweek*, the two magazines that had nearly depleted the ten dollars. "I thought she was still rooting around in the basement down at the police department."

Kevin flopped into the chair at the foot of his father's bed, his eyes scanning the monitors on the wall above the bed. "It's a murder," he reported. "Something about the guy they electrocuted last week."

Glen's eyes clouded. What was Kevin talking about? What could a new murder have to do with someone who'd already been executed? "Richard Kraven?" he asked.

Kevin shrugged. "I guess. Mom said something about the Kraven task force, so I guess she must have been talking about that guy, huh?" When his father said nothing, Kevin shifted gears. "Hey, Dad? When are you coming home?"

Glen ignored his son's question, instead reaching over to pick up the remote control from his bedside stand and flip on the television, surfing through the channels, then stopping when he saw an image of an ugly three-story apartment building. The sidewalk in front of it was cut off by bright yellow police tape, and a crowd had gathered across the street. An off-camera reporter was trying to fill a lot of time with very few facts. "The victim is Shawnelle Davis, an unemployed woman who lived alone in an apartment on the second floor.

Early reports are that the body was mutilated in the same fashion as the victims of Richard Kraven, and that—"

Glen snapped the television off. "What the hell is going on?" he demanded, his voice so sharp that Kevin jumped in his chair.

"What do you mean?" the boy asked. "All I asked was—"

"Not that," Glen interrupted, cutting Kevin off. "That murder! What the hell is going on?"

Kevin's eyes darted around the room as if seeking some way of escape. What was going on with his dad? What was he so mad about? But before he could say anything else, his father spoke again, this time fixing on Kevin with a burning intensity the boy had never seen before.

"I want you to do something for me, Kevin. I want you to go home and get that file your mother's been keeping. You know the one I mean? The one with all the stuff about Kraven in it?"

Kevin shifted nervously. He knew where the file was, but he also knew he wasn't supposed to go into his mother's desk. "I thought you didn't care about that stuff," he said. "You said it was—" Kevin hesitated, trying to remember the word his father had used when his mother started talking about going to the execution. Before he could think of his word, his father fixed him with that stare again, like he was angry.

"Maybe I changed my mind," he said. Then he chuckled, but even the laugh didn't sound right to Kevin. "Dr. Farber says I'm going to have to take at least a couple of months off work, and that I'm going to have to take up a hobby. So maybe I'll just make your mother's fixation on Richard Kraven my new hobby." Once again his eyes bored into Kevin. "What do you think? Sound interesting?"

Kevin said nothing. What was going on? His father didn't have hobbies—he didn't even like hobbies! And then he remembered the word his father had used whenever his mom started talking about Richard Kraven.

Morbid.

That was the word. His father had always called it morbid.

So why was he suddenly so interested in Richard Kraven?

But then Kevin remembered what his mother had told him the

day before yesterday, when she'd come home from talking to Dr. Farber: "It's going to be rough for a while, kids. Your dad's going to have to change his whole lifestyle. He's going to have to work a lot less, and rest a lot more. And that means it's going to be different for all of us, too. So what do you think? Can you make some adjustments? Get used to some changes around here?"

The day before yesterday, when he and Heather and his mother had all talked about it, it didn't seem like a big deal at all. But now that he was all alone in the hospital room with his father, Kevin began to wonder. Suddenly his father didn't seem like his father anymore. His mom had said his dad was going to be different, but if it meant his father would be mad all the time, and sounding weird, Kevin wasn't sure how easy things were going to be after all.

"Well, how about it?" Glen asked as Kevin's silence stretched on. "Does my new hobby sound interesting, or not?"

Kevin rose to his feet and edged toward the door. "Yeah, Dad," he said, his eyes avoiding his father's. "It sounds fine. And I'll get the file for you, okay? I'll be back in a while."

As he left the hospital he wondered what would happen if he just sort of forgot about the file and didn't come back at all. A couple of weeks ago he would have known exactly what would happen: his dad—the one he'd known all his life—would get mad at him for a minute, and then it would be all over. But now everything was different—since the heart attack, anything might happen.

He decided he'd better do as he'd been told.

"I mean, like, Jeez, it's not like she was committing a crime, you know? Like, so she was turning a few tricks—so who doesn't? This is Capitol Hill, you know? If she got paid, like, good for her, know what I mean?"

Anne Jeffers was on the sidewalk across from the building where Shawnelle Davis had both lived and conducted her business. Though she had been talking to the man of the laissez-faire sexual-economic theories for nearly twenty minutes, she still wasn't quite certain if he'd even known Shawnelle, let alone held the bosom-buddy status to which he'd laid claim. Still, she'd let the photographer snap some pictures of him. If nothing else, they'd at least wind up decorating the bulletin boards at the *Herald*, complete with appropriately off-color captions. Certainly he was one of the more flamboyant of the crowd that had gathered on Boylston Street, and he'd managed to pierce parts of his body that made Anne wince simply by thinking about the pain he must have undergone. In fact, as she talked to the young man, she wondered for the first time if perhaps she and Glen might want to think about moving a little farther from the Broadway area, at least until Heather and Kevin were safely past their teen years.

When a small eddy of whispered conversation rippled through the crowd, Anne cut the rambling interview short. Working her way to the front of the crowd, she saw that the door to Shawnelle Davis's apartment had opened and a gurney was being wheeled out, its attendants taking as much care with it as they would have had its occupant been critically ill, rather than dead for more than two days.

Glad for the excuse to cut the interview short, she stepped off the curb and crossed the street, unconsciously taking on the confident manner that often got her into crime scenes long before they'd been opened to the press. This morning, though, her jogging clothes undercut the act, along with the fact that Lois Ackerly was accompanying the gurney as the attendants bore it carefully down the stairs to the street level, then wheeled it toward the waiting panel truck that would convey it to the morgue.

As the wheeled stretcher neared her, Anne was, as always, stricken by the peculiar anonymity of the body bag that hid the corpse from the eyes of the public. Rather than delicately concealing the victim's wounds from the public, the bag had the effect of instantly making everyone who saw it wonder what it covered. Though Anne knew the modern plastic bags were far more efficient for their purpose, she still couldn't help thinking the old-fashioned blanket had been far more humane, at least offering a kind of comfort to the victim, rather than advertising the violence of death; even after a decade of seeing them, she had never gotten used to them. Still, she had her job to do.

"Any chance of getting a quick look?" she asked the detective, who was almost as casually dressed as Anne herself.

Lois Ackerly shook her head. "Once they're in the bag, they stay there until the M.E. takes them out." As Anne started toward the stairs to the second floor, Ackerly stepped in front to block her way. "And the apartment is still a crime scene," she added firmly.

"Can't blame a girl for trying," Anne observed, grinning, and a flicker of humor glinted in the detective's eye.

"And you can't blame a girl for stopping you, either. Come on, Jeffers—you know the rules."

Anne cast a wistful eye at the second floor, but knew better than to push. In the four years she'd known Lois Ackerly—since the first day Ackerly was assigned to the Kraven killings—Anne had rarely known the detective to bend a rule, let alone break one. And letting her or anyone else not connected directly with the Seattle Police Department enter a crime scene was a rule Ackerly never even dented. "So how about answering a few questions?" Anne ventured.

Ackerly shook her head. "No time." Turning her back, she started back up the stairs. Anne briefly considered trying to grab a few words with the detective on the stairs, but her attention was diverted as the engine of the vehicle that would take Shawnelle Davis to the morgue roared to life. Maybe she should follow it downtown and see if she could weasel her way into the autopsy. Then, from behind and above, she heard a familiar voice teasing her.

"Don't even think about it. Reporters still can't get into medical examinations."

Feeling herself flush, Anne swung around and looked up to see Mark Blakemoor grinning down at her from the long gallery that provided access to all the apartments on the building's second floor.

"So they *did* call out the A team," Anne deadpanned.

"No rest for the wicked, to coin a cliché," Blakemoor said. "Did the paper call you, or were you listening to your own trusty scanner?"

"The paper," Anne confessed. "I gave up on the scanner after they convicted Kraven. So what's the story? I assume there's no connection."

"How about a cup of coffee?" Blakemoor countered. "We're about done here for now, and Ackerly can baby-sit the lab guys. Want to see what you can pry out of me?"

"You're on," Anne said. "Dutch treat, though. The press can't be bought."

Blakemoor made an exaggeratedly sour face. "And cops can't even take doughnuts anymore."

Five minutes later they went through the back door of Charlie's, barely even glanced at the three people already nursing drinks although it wasn't yet ten A.M., and went to the front of the restaurant to take one of the tables next to the windows facing Broadway. "I love this place," Anne sighed, glancing around at the vaguely Victorian decor decorated with an eclectic collection of posters, pictures, and objects. It was a restaurant style that had both come and gone twenty years earlier.

Charlie's, though, had remained, slowly evolving from its original celebrity as Broadway's newest-and-nicest restaurant into its current status as a nostalgic relic from a long-ago past when something called "Three-Steak Charlie" wasn't considered politically incorrect.

"Double-tall, no foam?" Blakemoor asked Anne as the waitress came over. When Anne nodded, he held up two fingers. As they waited for the lattes, Anne reached into her gritchel, fishing out her tape recorder.

"Uh-uh," Blakemoor grunted, shaking his head. "You might be able to pry something out of me, but it won't be in my voice, on tape. No interviews until we know a lot more than we do so far. Okay?"

Anne dropped the recorder back into the depths of the leather bag. "You know me—I take whatever I can get. So, what's going on? The rumor is that the task force may have been broken up prematurely."

Mark Blakemoor's eyes rolled scornfully. "Don't believe everything you hear from the dispatcher, okay?"

"Not a problem," Anne replied. "On the other hand, I wouldn't be doing my job if I didn't ask why the dispatcher would say something like that. What's the scoop? Copycat?"

The detective hesitated, and Anne could almost see him going over the crime scene in his head. Finally he shrugged. "If it's a copycat, it's the worst one I ever saw. And copycats usually start up right away. Richard Kraven's been out of circulation for two years, and even when he was working, we didn't have any copycats."

"You're sure?" Anne asked, eyeing the detective suspiciously.

"I'm sure," Blakemoor told her. "There are still things no one knows about Kraven's M.O., and that includes you." He fell silent as the waitress arrived and set two steaming glasses of mocha-colored liquid in front of them. Without even tasting it, the detective added two spoonfuls of sugar to the latte, stirred it and took a sip. "The bitch of it is, there *were* certain resemblances between this one and Kraven's work."

Anne's reportorial antenna began to quiver. "Such as?" she prompted, trying not to let her eagerness creep into her voice.

Once again Blakemoor's face took on a look of intense concentration, and then he began slowly ticking several points off on his fingers: "First, there was no sign of a struggle. Remember how Kraven's victims used to just disappear, as if they'd gone with him voluntarily? Well, it was the same way with Davis. 'Course, she was a whore, so she probably thought she'd picked up a john." He moved on to the next finger. "Her chest was opened up, and her organs were torn out."

Anne's jaw tightened, and, as always, she felt sickened by the carnage man was capable of inflicting on his fellows. "Exactly like Richard Kraven."

"Except that compared to Kraven, this guy is an amateur," Blakemoor went on. "Also, he broke her neck first."

Anne frowned. "That's nothing Richard Kraven ever did. He never killed them until after he opened them up, did he?"

"Not as far as we know," Blakemoor agreed. He glanced around as if to see if anyone was listening, then leaned forward. "The thing is," he added, his voice dropping, "from the amount of blood that came out of the wounds, it looks like this guy opened Davis up before she died, too."

Anne's unblinking eyes fixed on the detective. "So what are you saying?" she asked. "*Is* it a copycat, or isn't it?"

Blakemoor fingered the rim of his coffee cup, thinking hard. He knew he really shouldn't be talking to a reporter at all, at least not this early in the investigation, but he was confident that Anne Jeffers wouldn't print anything that would get him into trouble. Besides, during all the years he'd been on the trail of Richard Kraven, he'd always found her to be a good sounding board. And, of course, he just plain liked her. "I don't know," he finally said. "If he hadn't cut open the chest and spread her organs all over the kitchen, I'd say it was someone Davis knew, who was pissed off at her. No sign of a struggle, no sign of a forced entry. But with that kind of killing, the creep usually just makes the hit and takes off."

"What about a john?" Anne asked.

Blakemoor shook his head. "No sign of any sex at all, kinky or otherwise." He sighed. "And that's what worries me. If it wasn't sex, and it wasn't a fight with someone she knew, what was it?"

Anne hesitated, knowing what she was about to say was heresy among the press. On the other hand, she'd come to trust Blakemoor as much as he trusted her. "There's been a lot of coverage on Kraven lately," she began carefully. "With me right up there with the best of them. I suppose it's possible we pushed someone over the brink."

Blakemoor's eyes met hers. "That's exactly the thought that occurred to me," he told her. "I have a real bad feeling about this one, Anne. It's almost like now that Kraven's dead, someone's decided to emulate him, just to mess up our heads."

"And if that's true?" Anne asked, though she already knew the answer.

Blakemoor's lips tightened into a hard line. "Then there will be more." He sighed, then uttered a disgusted grunt. "Sometimes I just don't get it, Jeffers. It's like now that we've gotten rid of one wacko, we're just going to have to deal with another."

"Maybe it won't happen," Anne suggested.

Blakemoor listlessly stirred his latte. "Maybe it won't."

Neither of them believed it.

CHAPTER 20

*T*hough he saw nothing, the boy knew the cat was there. This was where it always hid, skulking behind the house, doing its best to conceal itself in the thick foliage of the rhododendrons his mother had planted along the fence. The boy didn't know why the cat never actually left the backyard, but since it never did, he guessed there must be something outside the yard that terrified the creature even more than he did himself.

Or possibly—and the boy was becoming more and more certain that this was the real truth—the cat enjoyed the game as much as he did.

The boy crouched low, settling down on his haunches, balancing perfectly so he was almost as still as the cat when it was stalking one of the birds that occasionally ventured into its domain. Only the boy's eyes moved now, and even they moved so slowly the motion was all but imperceptible, scanning the shadowy interior of the rhododendrons, searching for the slightest movement that would betray the cat's presence.

Then he saw it—no more than a twitch of the animal's tail, but enough to betray its hiding place.

Taking on the same grace as the cat itself, the boy began moving, first rocking forward until his hands touched the lawn, the sensitive skin of his palms feeling every blade of grass just as he imagined the cat's paws experienced whatever surface they trod. His confidence growing as the cat remained crouched where it was—not yet certain it had been spotted—the boy began to inch his way forward. Now he felt as if he had become the cat, felt all the muscles in his lithe body tense,

felt time stretch out as he crept forward, each movement slow and liq-
uid, so he felt as if he was oozing across the lawn toward the bushes.

Now he could see the cat tense—but it was more than seeing; it was
as if it were happening to him. He and the cat were becoming as one;
he was experiencing what the cat felt, while the cat, in its turn, lived
the boy's life as well as its own.

Was that why the cat never tried to escape the yard? For the same
reason the boy hadn't, either?

The cat tensed as the boy crept closer, and now he could see not only
the end of its tail twitching nervously, but its whiskers as well. As if
in sympathy, the boy's own face began to tingle, and he felt the down
on his jaw stand up.

He edged closer, and saw the cat draw back. "Nice kitty," the boy
breathed, so softly only he and the cat could hear the soothing words.
Reaching into his pocket, he drew out a pair of thin black leather
gloves and carefully pulled them on. "That's a good cat," he crooned.
"Nice, nice, kitty."

As though mesmerized by the caressing whisper, the cat calmed
slightly, and its ruffling coat began to flatten.

The boy slipped closer to the shrubs.

His right hand reached out, winding through the foliage as silently
as a serpent. Once more the cat tensed, this time rising to its feet, its
back arching as every hair on its body stood on end. A thrill—like a
light charge of electricity—ran through the boy, and now, like black
lightning, his hand struck, his fingers closing on the cat long before it
could spring away to safety. Drawing his prize from the shelter of the
rhododendrons, the boy held it at eye level.

The cat's eyes met his own, and it hissed. Then one of its forepaws
shot out, claws extended, as it tried to slash his face. The boy's other
leather-clad hand closed on the paw, and the cat, as if finally truly as-
sessing the precariousness of its position, didn't even try to struggle.

Just as the boy had never tried to struggle.

Holding the cat, the boy stood up and started toward the house,
which today was empty.

Empty, save for himself.

And the cat.

Inside the back door the boy paused. He knew he was alone, but the house still held terrors for him. Today, though, fear subsided in the face of what he was about to do.

He moved quickly now, and a moment later was in the basement. His heart pounding, he approached the workbench.

Pounding from fear, or from anticipation?

He knew the workbench well. It was as much a part of him as life itself. Always, it had been there.

Now it was his to use.

Putting the cat into a cage, the boy set to work.

Everything he needed was there, carefully prepared, as everything had always been carefully prepared for him.

The rag, the ether.

The boy felt good, knowing he would show kindness to the creature.

He soaked the rag with ether, then opened the cage and reached inside. The cat struck out again with its forepaw. This time its talons slashed through the leather of the gloves, digging deeply into the boy's skin, but the boy felt nothing.

Inured from every pain, of every kind?

His fingers closed on the cat; his other hand pressed the ethered rag against the cat's face. The cat struggled, but soon its struggles flagged. Then it went limp, and the boy knew it was time to begin.

Laying the cat on the workbench, he set to work, splaying its legs out, tying them down much the way the Lilliputians bound Gulliver. But if the cat was Gulliver, the boy was not of Lilliput.

He was of Brobdingnag.

He began attaching electrodes to the cat, just as his father attached electrodes to him.

He waited then, waited for the cat to wake up.

Only when it was fully awake, only when it would be able to fully experience the effects of what would happen, did the boy's finger reach for the button that would activate the electrodes. . . .

Glen's whole body jerked spasmodically and his eyes snapped open.

A heart attack—he was having another heart attack! He reached out, groping for the buzzer that would summon the nurse, but even as his thumb was pressing it down, his mind cleared and he realized his mistake. It wasn't a heart attack at all—it was simply a bad dream.

But a dream of what?

A second ago it had been so vivid.

A cat.

Something to do with a cat.

Kumquat?

He tried to remember what the cat had looked like, but the details of the dream vanished like ephemera, fading from his mind even as he tried to retrieve them. A second later the door to his room opened and one of the nurses stepped in. It was Annette Brady, whom Glen had liked from the minute he was conscious enough to know who she was, but this morning her normally cheerful smile was nowhere to be seen.

"Yes?" she asked with a curtness that was as unusual as her scowl.

Suddenly Glen understood—Annette worked the swing shift, so she must have been called in early today. "Sorry about the ring," he said. "I just had a nightmare, and when I woke up I thought I was having a heart attack."

The nurse scanned the monitors above the bed. "Well, it all looks normal now." She started out of the room.

"Gonna be a long one, huh?" Glen asked.

Annette Brady turned back. "No longer than usual."

Frowning, Glen shifted his gaze to the clock. Seven-thirty?

How could it be seven-thirty? He hadn't even awakened until—
No longer than usual?

His gaze shifted to the window. The streetlights were already on outside, and the last evening light was rapidly fading away. Had he been sleeping all day?

Why hadn't they awakened him for dinner? This was a hospital—a couple of times they'd even awakened him to give him a sleeping pill! He was about to ask about it when he realized he wasn't hungry. Now he began to feel totally disoriented. Had he forgotten the whole day? But maybe he was wrong—maybe they really had let him sleep. "I was just thinking, maybe if I could get something to eat—"

Annette Brady's eyes widened. "After what you had for dinner, you're hungry again?" She shook her head in resignation. "Okay, let me see what I can do. But if I can find something this late, I expect you to be polite about it, at least. Okay?"

As the nurse left the room, Glen tried to make sense of it. Obviously he'd eaten, and equally obviously he'd complained about the food. But he had no memory of the meal, any more than he could remember the rest of the day.

He glanced around the room as if hoping to find some clue, and the first thing his eyes fell on was a thick file folder lying on the table next to the bed. Picking it up, he opened it, and frowned. Anne's file on Richard Kraven? What was it doing here?

She must have been here while he was asleep, and left it. Picking up the phone, he dialed the number, but even as Anne answered, he suddenly had a thought.

He was supposed to go home in a few days—if he'd had a memory loss, would they still discharge him?

Not a chance. They'd keep him here until they were certain they knew exactly what had caused it. So when Anne answered the phone, he hesitated. And while he hesitated, she spoke.

"So you decided to call and apologize, huh?" she asked, her voice only half bantering. "Where would you like to start? With me, or Kevin?"

Glen searched his mind. He couldn't remember having talked to Anne at all that day, but he did recall talking to Kevin on the phone that morning, and asking him to bring some magazines to the hospital. His eyes flicked back to the bed table; the magazines lay under the file.

So at least Kevin had been there, and probably Anne, too.

"I guess it was just a bad day for me," he said, uttering the total truth, but still not admitting his memory loss. "I'm really sorry, okay?" A minute later, after he'd repeated the apology to Kevin, Anne came back on the line.

"How long do you want my file?" she asked, her voice sounding almost amused now.

His eyes went back to the thick file. So he'd asked for it. Why?

"I don't know," he replied, still not lying, but still not admitting that he seemed to have lost most of the day. But why had he even wanted it? He'd always thought Anne's fascination with the Kraven case bordered on the morbid, which she well knew. "I guess I just thought as long as I was lying here, I might as well try to figure out what you found so interesting about him," he improvised. "Maybe I'll stay up all night reading it."

A few minutes later, after he'd said good night to Anne, he picked up the file, not really intending to read it but half thinking that the motion would jar his memory. He paused, the thick folder in his lap, then, instead of putting the file aside, opened it.

He began paging through it, and as he scanned the articles, he experienced an odd sense of déjà vu.

All the material seemed very familiar, though he had no memory of having read it before. Then, as he turned one of the pages, he froze. He was staring at a photocopy of an article that he knew Anne must have written, though it had no byline:

Richard Kraven: Animal Abuser?

Former neighbors of Richard Kraven report that the suspected serial killer was a habitual torturer of small animals, even when he was as young as twelve years old.

Martha Demming, 76, who lived for nearly

two decades in the house next door to the
South Seattle residence still occupied by Edna
Kraven, reports that on at least two occasions
she witnessed Richard Kraven—then in his
very early adolescence—stalking his mother's
pet cat.

"I don't want to say he was torturing it,"
Miss Demming stated in a telephone interview, "but [the cat] always seemed to be afraid
of him."

Later in the same interview, Miss Demming
reported that there were rumors the body of the
cat had been found by another neighbor who
"thought it had been electrocuted, or something." The neighbor who reputedly found the
cat, Wilbur Fankenburg, died three years ago
at the age of 56, and could not confirm Miss
Demming's report.

Glen Jeffers read the article through twice, small bits and pieces
of the nightmare that had awakened him at last coming back. Closing the file and setting it on the bed table, he leaned back into the
pillows.

The origin of the nightmare, at least, was now apparent. Obviously
he'd read at least part of Anne's file during the day.

Why, then, didn't he remember it?

He was still pondering that question as he sank into a deep sleep
a few minutes later.

While the night brought a deep and peaceful sleep to Glen Jeffers, to Anne it brought only tortured wakefulness. Glen's call had come just as she'd finally convinced herself that his peculiar behavior when she'd visited him at the hospital that afternoon hadn't meant anything at all.

After all, Dr. Farber had warned her the day after Glen's heart attack that nothing would be the same. For some people, he'd said, a heart attack such as Glen's brought on a complete personality change. One of his patients who had been a Type-A personality his entire life suddenly became a Type-B practically overnight. Impatient people often found themselves no longer bothered by things that had driven them crazy before the attack, and easygoing people could just as easily turn cranky. It was the latter that Anne discovered late that afternoon when she'd gone to visit Glen before coming home to fix the kids' dinner. Her normally sunny husband had been propped up in bed, a file—one of *her* files, it turned out—spread out around him, and when she leaned over to kiss him, he barely responded at all. When she asked him why he had suddenly become interested in Richard Kraven, he replied that he'd just become curious about her own fascination with the case. "And you know what?" he asked, finally looking up from the file. "He was an interesting guy. You always made him out to be some kind of monster, but—"

Anne had stared at Glen in shock, barely able to believe her ears. Only last week he'd said the only legitimate reason for her to go to the execution was to "make sure the bastard's really dead." Now he was an "interesting guy"?

"He was a monster," she'd interjected. "God only knows how many people he killed. And he didn't just kill them, Glen. He dissected them!" When Glen had glanced up from the story he was reading—one she herself had written, though the way he was talking it was as if she knew nothing about Richard Kraven!—he almost looked angry. She'd dropped the subject right then and there, knowing the last thing Glen needed was to get upset. But for the rest of the visit, she'd felt as though he was barely putting up with her. Finally, she cut the visit short, since Glen hadn't even acknowledged her presence for almost ten minutes.

On the way out she'd stopped and spoken to the nurse, who assured her that patients often preferred not to have visitors at all, that so much of their energy was taken up with getting better that they simply had none left to entertain anyone. Anne had tried to let it go at that, but still found herself worrying all evening, especially after hearing what had happened when Kevin visited his father that morning. And when Glen finally called, though he'd sounded more like himself, she'd been able to tell that something was wrong. Despite his apology for the way he'd treated both her and Kevin, she had the strange sense that he hadn't really known why she was upset with him. And ever since the call, the sense of nervousness she'd only just managed to assuage had come flooding back.

Now, setting aside the stack of notes she'd been working on— notes gleaned from hours of work in the storerooms of the Public Safety Building—she abandoned her desk, knowing there was no chance of getting any more work done that evening. Leaving the small study that Glen had carved out of one end of the cavernous living room, she glanced at Kevin, who was sprawled out on the sofa, reading a book while the TV droned unheeded in the background. "If you're not watching the TV, you might turn it off," she commented.

"I *am* watching it," Kevin replied, not even looking up from his book.

Anne decided not to bother arguing with Kevin. If pressed, he would be perfectly capable of telling her all the details of a plot he had seemed to be ignoring. It was a talent he'd inherited from her own father, whom she knew for a fact had been able to read a book, follow a conversation going on in the same room, and still catch any errors she made while practicing the piano in another room. It was a trait that had both impressed and annoyed her in her father. In Kevin she often found it totally confounding, since she knew the ability undermined all her reasons for him not to watch TV while he did his homework. "I'm going over to the hospital to see your father."

Kevin finally glanced up from his book, and Anne knew her voice had betrayed her worry.

"Is something wrong?"

Anne shook her head. "I just feel like taking a walk, so I thought I'd look in on him."

"Okay."

"Tell Heather not to go out."

Kevin rolled his eyes. "Jeez, Mom, I'm not a baby. I'm here by myself all the time."

But not at night, Anne thought silently. Rather than voice the thought and expose herself to another of her son's scornful looks, she leaned over and kissed him on the forehead. "Be back in an hour. Stay out of trouble, okay?"

The night air had grown chilly, and as she headed down Sixteenth East, Anne shoved her hands deep in her pockets. When she came to Mercer Street, where the neighborhood started to deteriorate, she turned right, cut over to Fifteenth, then went south again to Thomas Street, entering the Group Health complex through the emergency entrance, then threading her way through the corridors until she finally came to the elevators that would take her up to the Critical Care Unit on the third floor. Using the red phone in the family room, she identified herself, and a moment later Annette Brady appeared.

"Your husband's asleep, but I don't see how it could be a problem if you want to look in on him for a minute."

"How's he doing?" Anne asked as the nurse escorted her into the CCU.

"Actually, a lot better tonight. I think he fell asleep after dinner, and when he woke up, he was a human being again. But frankly, if

I were you, I don't think I'd wake him up right now. The best thing for him is just to let him sleep."

The nurse quietly pulled Glen's door open, and Anne peered inside. A soft glow of light from the street beyond the window bathed his face. Though he was still attached to the heart monitors, he was starting to look once more like the man she'd married. The last vestiges of the anger she'd felt toward him that afternoon and evening evaporated, as did the worry his uncharacteristic behavior had caused. Feeling much better, she stepped back from the door and let Annette Brady close it again. "Suddenly I feel kind of silly," Anne confessed as the two of them walked back toward the unit's main doors. "I suppose I should have just called, but suddenly I feel about Glen the way I used to feel about my kids when they were babies. Being told they're okay is one thing, but you don't really believe it until you see it for yourself."

"Not a problem," the nurse assured her. "Believe me, we have wives coming in here every night, at all hours. On the other hand, husbands," she continued, "hardly ever show up at odd hours. Amazing how weak the maternal instinct is in the American heterosexual male." Anne started toward the elevators, waving a final good-bye as the nurse warned her to be careful if she was going to walk home. "That woman who got killed the other night was only a few blocks from here, you know."

And she was a hooker who picked up the wrong john, Anne thought as she rode the elevator back to the ground floor, instantly reminding herself that all Shawnelle Davis had been trying to do was earn a living, something for which she certainly hadn't deserved to die. In almost conscious defiance of Annette Brady's warning, Anne left the hospital through the main doors and started up Sixteenth East. As she strode up the sidewalk, moving from pools of light into dark shadows, then emerging into the light again a few seconds later as she neared the next streetlamp, she suddenly had a feeling that she was being watched. Pausing, she scanned the street ahead of her, then turned around.

She was alone.

Gazing up and down the street once more, finally satisfied there was no one lurking in the shadows ahead, Anne walked on until, reaching the corner of Thomas Street, her nerve deserted her and she turned left, quickening her step as the brighter lights and heavy traffic of Fifteenth beckoned. By the time she reached the corner, the prickly sensation on the back of her neck had eased, and as she started northward, she began to feel as if she'd just played the fool.

The Experimenter stepped back from the window as Anne Jeffers turned the corner and disappeared from his view. She'd felt him watching her, of that he was absolutely certain. She'd sensed a presence, though she had no idea it was his presence. He'd seen her scan the streets, hesitate, then scan them again, the way he himself always did, watching warily to be certain no one was paying too much attention when he began focusing on a new subject for his experiments.

Soon it would be time to begin again, time to take up the work once more. His fingers twitched with eagerness in the dimness of the room as he anticipated the feel of plunging his hands once more into the very center of life, experiencing again the thrill of holding a living, throbbing organ in his palms, exhilarating once more to the towering sensation of holding the power of life and death within his very grasp.

He'd already decided that Anne Jeffers would be the subject of one of his experiments this time. He would toy with her first, of course, just as he'd been toying with her for years. But when her time finally came, and it was finally her body he opened up, her life force he experienced, he might even keep her awake, so that she could share the exhilaration with him.

There were ways to do that, ways he'd learned about in the years during which he suspended his work. He would have to experiment with the needles, but he was looking forward to that, as he looked forward to all his experiments.

Not so long now. Soon it would all happen. Soon he would hold Anne Jeffers in the palms of his hands. Soon . . . soon . . .

"All right, here are the rules." Gordy Farber leaned forward in his chair and pointed a pencil at Glen as if he were a recalcitrant ten-year-old rather than a forty-three-year-old architect. "You can go home today, but that doesn't mean you can go back to the kind of life you were living before, understand?"

Glen rolled his eyes toward the ceiling and began parroting the instructions Farber had already laid out in such great detail that Glen felt as if they were branded onto his eyelids. "No going to the office, get plenty of rest, eat healthy meals, and get plenty of exercise." As Farber reddened slightly, Glen grinned. "Shall I also take Geritol every day?"

"It wouldn't hurt," Farber groused as he shifted his attention to Anne, who had taken the day off to get Glen settled back into the house after almost two weeks in the hospital. "I'm counting on you to make sure he doesn't cheat. If he behaves himself, I don't see any reason to worry about a repeat of this little incident." He swung back to Glen and once more assumed the stern demeanor of a schoolmaster. "On the other hand, if you go back to sitting at a drawing table all day, eating nothing but hamburgers and french fries for lunch, and sucking up twenty-five cups of coffee a day, I can almost guarantee you'll be back here within a year. Or less. Assuming they even get you this far next time."

"What about the stairs?" Anne asked. "Should he really be going up and down them all the time?"

"If you didn't have them in the house, I'd make him go buy a stair-climbing machine," Farber replied. "I don't want him out running right off the bat, but there's no problem with stairs, and I want him to start walking at least a mile a day." Glen uttered an exaggerated groan, which Farber ignored, forging ahead with the lecture he'd given heart patients so often he could do it in his sleep. "And as for sex," he finished, finally touching on the subject most of his patients wanted to know about first, "as far as I'm concerned, it's one of the healthier forms of exercise available, so feel free. Any questions?"

Glen hesitated. Should he mention the memory lapse he'd had last Saturday? Even as he formulated the question in his mind, he knew he wouldn't. After all, it had only happened the one time, and he was sure it was nothing more than a brief side effect of one of the drugs they'd been stuffing into him. All he really needed was to get out of here, get home, and start living his life again. "How could there be?" he asked, standing up. "Is that it?"

Farber came around from behind his desk, accompanying the Jefferses to the door. "Just keep an eye on yourself. If anything seems strange, or not right, let me know. And if you experience any pains in your chest or arms, don't write it off to heartburn. Get over here right away. And, most important, don't either of you start feeling like Glen's some kind of invalid. He's not. Just go home and get on with your lives."

A few minutes later, when Anne slid her car into the parking space she was lucky enough to find right in front of their house, Glen got out and automatically opened the back door to begin transferring his suitcase, and the box full of the clutter that had migrated into his hospital room over the last ten days, back into his home.

Just as automatically, Anne started to tell him to let her do it, that he should go inside and take it easy. But even as her lips parted to utter the words, Glen seemed to sense them coming. Their eyes met, they were both silent for a split second, then they began to laugh.

"Tell you what," Glen offered. "You take the suitcase, and I'll take the box. Deal?"

"Deal," Anne agreed.

As he stepped through the front door a minute later and set the box on the table in the foyer, Glen uttered a contented sigh. No more hospital bed, no more monitors, no more nurses waking him up to give him sleeping pills. Then Boots came hurtling down the stairs like a little black and white missile to throw himself at Glen's legs, his high-pitched yap instantly eliciting a jungle scream from Hector, who was at least still confined to his cage in Kevin's room. Kumquat, of course, wasn't interested enough in his arrival even to wander through the foyer. As he tried to calm the excited dog, Glen smiled almost ruefully at Anne. "Maybe I should have stayed in the hospital after all. Didn't Farber say something about getting a lot of rest?"

"Want me to take you back?" Anne countered.

By way of an answer, Glen picked up the suitcase Anne had set at the foot of the stairs and started up to the second floor. Halfway up, as the parrot stopped squalling, he turned back, eyeing Anne speculatively. "How often," he asked, "do we have the house to ourselves in the middle of the day?"

Anne's brow knit worriedly as she instantly read his meaning. "Do you really think we ought to?"

"Didn't Gordy say it was the healthiest form of exercise he knows?"

"He said it was *one* of the healthiest," Anne corrected. But she was already starting up the stairs.

Dropping the suitcase to the floor as they entered the master bedroom, Glen put his arms around Anne, drawing her close. Her familiar aroma filled his nostrils as he nuzzled her neck, and he felt her shudder with anticipation as his lips began nibbling toward her own. A moment later they were on the bed, his fingers working feverishly at the single row of buttons that ran up the back of her dress. Then he was pulling it off her shoulders, and she was helping him slide it down over her hips. As his fingers touched her bare skin, a sensation went though him he'd never felt before. Her skin seemed to tingle under his touch, as if somehow an electrical charge were running through her.

Now she was undressing him, too, and wherever her fingers touched his flesh, the same tingling sensation coursed through him, making his whole body hum in a way he couldn't remember ever experiencing.

He groaned softly as he slipped her bra loose and his palm covered her naked breast. Her flesh seemed almost to vibrate under his touch, and when her hand slid beneath his boxer shorts to close on his already hardened flesh, he had to struggle to control himself in the face of the climax that threatened to overwhelm him.

Had it been that long since they'd made love, that every touch seemed new and different?

Or was it the drugs they'd given him?

Suddenly he remembered years ago, when he and Anne had smoked a joint before making love. Everything felt different that night, and he'd had the unnerving sensation that he was making love to a stranger, to a woman he'd never met before. The feeling had frightened him. After that night he'd given up the drug, and since then he'd always felt a comforting familiarity in their lovemaking, so that beyond the excitement and exhilaration of the act itself, he'd also felt a sense of safety—almost of coming home—as their bodies enveloped one another.

Today, though, there was an electricity running from her body into his own that made not only his flesh tingle, but his very being throb with excitement.

He pulled her closer to him, pressing his flesh against hers, feeling his skin thrill to the touch of her own. It was as if every fiber of his being was suddenly tuned to her, every nerve in his body vibrating under the energy she exuded.

It was as though her very life force were flowing into him, and he felt he was absorbing it through his fingers, his palms, every part of him that touched any part of her.

He began moving, his hands roaming over her, his limbs writhing around her until finally he was inside her, feeling as if he were searching for her very soul. He thrust deep, straining to touch some part of her that still remained just beyond his reach. He pulled her still closer, feeling the life force within her, struggling to clutch to himself the source of that tingling energy that flowed from her body into his. Their bodies moved together then, the rhythm building, the tempo increasing. Glen could feel her arms tightening around his neck, her legs twisting around his thighs, pulling him closer, deeper, as if she wanted to draw him inside of her to the point where their very lives merged into one.

He felt his groin tighten, felt the electricity between them build once more, and this time he made no attempt to postpone the climax that quickly engulfed him. Gasping, he felt himself surging into her, and as the heat in his groin poured into her body, he felt the strange electrical charge on her skin begin to fade. He drew her even closer, trying to prolong the sensation, desperate to keep her energy flowing toward him, but it was too late.

As his climax faded, so also did the tingling of her skin, and at last the urgency of his grip on her began to relax. His breath escaped him in an explosive gasp, and first one of his arms fell away from her, then the other. His breathing, which had come in great heaving pants only moments before, eased slowly into its normal rhythm, and he felt himself begin to sink into the soft gray depths of sleep.

As she heard Glen's breathing drift into the gentle whisper of sleep, Anne lay still, part of her wishing merely not to waken him, but another of part of her not wanting to move until she understood what had just happened between them.

Glen's lovemaking today had contained an element she'd never experienced before, and though part of her had been excited by it—even thrilled by it—another part of her had been almost frightened. There was something different about him just now; a desperation. It was almost as if he were trying to reach within her, to grasp something, to draw something from her that she wasn't giving him.

Finally leaving the bed, she moved into the bathroom and stared at herself in the mirror. Faint red marks were beginning to show on her body where Glen's fingers had dug into her flesh.

Involuntarily, she shuddered.

She took a shower, dried herself off, and began dressing.

On the bed, Glen lay naked, his arms spread, his legs akimbo, his eyes closed in sleep.

He was thinner than he'd been before he went into the hospital, and there was an unhealthy pallor to his face.

That would change. Within a week or two he would be back to his normal 180 pounds, and a few hours in the sun would bring the color back to his skin.

But what about inside?

What about that desperation she felt from him when they'd made love?

Would that go away, too?

She leaned over and kissed him gently on the forehead, but he didn't stir. Before she left the room, she covered him with a blanket, but even as she started out the door she turned to look back at him.

He was still Glen, still her husband.

But he was different.

The heart attack had not only damaged his body; it seemed to have altered his spirit as well.

As she left the house and started toward her office at the *Herald*, Anne told herself that as his body recovered from the trauma it had undergone, Glen's personality would heal as well.

The next time they made love, everything would be as it had once been.

But what if nothing between them was ever quite the same again?

To that question, she had no answer.

On the morning after his release from the hospital, Glen Jeffers came awake slowly, just for a moment feeling the same cloudy disorientation he'd experienced so often during those first few days after the heart attack, when his mind, fogged with drugs, had refused to recognize his surroundings. But this morning his mind cleared quickly, and he luxuriated in the feeling of awakening in his own pajamas, in his own bed, in his own house. And it had been his wife who had awakened him briefly a while ago to kiss him good-bye, rather than one of the nurses arriving abruptly to strap a sphygmomanometer around his arm, insert a thermometer under his tongue, or stick a clip on his finger to check his oxygen absorption.

Home.

He was home, and he was alone.

He stretched languorously, listening to the silence of the house. How long had it been since he'd enjoyed this kind of quiet?

He could barely even remember.

Of course, it had been quiet in the hospital, but it was a different kind of quiet: the hospital held the sepulchral silence of illness, rather than the peaceful quiet of home. In the hospital he had always been aware of someone coughing or moaning in the adjoining rooms. This morning he could only hear Hector muttering to himself from the perch in his cage in Kevin's room. And from beyond the house Glen heard only the chirping of more birds, a distinct improvement over the steady drone of traffic that had laid a continual noisy siege to the hospital.

Feeling at peace, he got up, slipped into his bathrobe, shoved his feet into his comfortably dilapidated slippers, and went downstairs, following the heavenly scent of fresh-brewed coffee into the kitchen, where a note in Anne's handwriting was propped up against the coffee maker:

You shouldn't drink this at all, so try to hold it down to one cup.

It was at the very moment that his eyes fell on the note that he first had the strange sensation that he wasn't alone in the house after all. It was as if he were being watched: the hairs on the back of his neck stood on end, and he felt himself tensing. But when he turned around, the kitchen was empty; not even Boots was there. The odd feeling passed, and he reached into the cupboard, took out the largest mug he could find, and filled it to the rim. Moving to the kitchen table, he sat down. A moment later Kumquat, obviously assuming he held no ill will against her disinterest at his homecoming yesterday, darted in from the dining room and leapt into his lap. Stroking the cat with one hand, he pulled the front section of the morning's *Herald* over and gazed at the article prominently displayed at the top of the page to which the paper had been opened.

Police Report No Progress
in Capitol Hill Slaying

Nearly a week after the discovery of the body of Shawnelle Davis in her Capitol Hill apartment, Seattle police report that there are still no suspects in the slaying of the thirty-two-year-old prostitute.

Although police investigators admit that the killing bears certain resemblances to those attributed to Richard Kraven, they are currently ruling out the possibility that this may be a copy-cat crime, despite suggestions that the execution of Kraven himself might have inspired the killing. According to Detective Mark Blakemoor . . .

Glen pushed the paper aside, not bothering to finish the story even though he was absolutely certain his wife had written it. Why was Anne still harping on Richard Kraven? The man was dead, for God's sake! Picking up the sports section, he scanned the headlines, then turned to the business section. Buried in a lower corner of the second page he found a small story noting that not only had work on the Jeffers Building continued to progress during his illness, but they were actually two days ahead of schedule. He reread the short article, wondering if the implication that the work was progressing better with him out of the picture was intended or inadvertent, then decided that it wasn't there at all, that he was just being oversensitive. Still, a call to the office after he'd had a shower couldn't really be considered work, could it?

Abandoning both the paper and the mug of coffee, he started toward the stairs, but once again the peculiar feeling that someone else was in the house came over him. This time he went through the downstairs rooms, feeling more and more foolish as each one proved to be as empty as it should have been. Still, even when he finally went upstairs to the bathroom, he found himself glancing through the open doors to the kids' rooms, just to be sure.

Nothing.

He stripped off his robe and pajamas in the master bedroom and went into the bathroom. Turning on the shower, he waited until steam was pouring out of the stall, then adjusted the temperature so it was just off the scalding point. With a sigh of pleasure he stepped into the stinging spray, lathered himself luxuriantly, then let the steaming water sluice over him, relaxing his muscles as it washed the last of the hospital odor from his skin. Only when he felt the water beginning to cool and realized he'd nearly exhausted the heater's supply did he shut off the faucets, step out onto the cold marble tiles of the bathroom floor and begin toweling himself dry. After taking a swipe at the steamy mirror on the bathroom door, he tossed the soggy towel toward the hamper that stood next to the sink, missed, but let it lay where it fell as he caught a smeared glimpse of himself in the still mostly fogged mirror.

He'd lost at least ten pounds while he was in the hospital, and it wasn't a ten pounds he was happy to have gone. In fact, he'd spent months gaining those pounds, exercising, running, doing all the right things. Now they were gone, and he was nearly back to the skinny frame he'd hated so much during the first thirty years of his life, before he'd discovered working out.

Well, he'd just have to start over, regain the weight, and retone the muscles that had gone flaccid while he lay in the hospital bed.

Turning away from the full-length mirror, he moved to the sink, brushed his teeth, then used his hand to wipe a small patch of the mirror above the sink. Bending close, he examined his reflection.

Christ! He looked like a homeless person: his cheeks had hollowed, his eyes were sunken, and the laugh lines around them were threatening to turn into genuine wrinkles. Worst of all, the stubble on his cheeks and jowls had taken on a gray cast he'd never noticed before.

That, at least, he could fix right now.

Opening the medicine cabinet, he picked up the shaver Heather and Kevin had given him for his last birthday and switched it on.

Suddenly, the sensation that he was no longer alone—that someone else was not only in the house, but in the bathroom itself—became overpowering. Every muscle in his body tensing, Glen readied himself to whirl around to confront whoever was there. But even as he turned, the shock struck him, and he tumbled once more into the kind of blackness that had yawned beneath him on the day of his heart attack. In less than a second he was unconscious.

The Experimenter gazed at the razor that had dropped into the sink as Glen Jeffers had fallen into unconsciousness.

Tentatively, he reached out and touched it lightly with a single finger. Then he picked it up, turning it over in his hand, examining it the way he liked to examine everything he came in contact with. It seemed perfectly all right—no cracks in its case; its hard plastic shell hadn't even chipped when it struck the porcelain of the sink. Satisfied, he held the appliance to his face and gently rubbed it over his right cheek.

And instantly dropped it as millions of tiny electric needles seemed to shoot from the shaving head into his skin.

Picking the shaver up again, the Experimenter turned it over in his hand once more.

There was a flaw in it—there had to be.

There were flaws in everything, if you looked closely enough. He'd found that out from all the examinations he'd conducted. In even the most perfect of the specimens he'd observed, he'd always been able to find a flaw. So now he turned his full concentration to the shaver, focusing his mind, searching for the cause of the shocks he'd just felt. Yet no matter how hard he looked, he could find no sign of damage.

The object sat in his hand, purring and vibrating almost like a living thing.

The Experimenter's mind began to work once more, and his yearning to understand the force he'd felt grew stronger.

Had it truly been electricity he'd felt?

He pressed the shaver against his skin, and felt again the prickling tingle.

This time, though, it felt slightly different.

Different, and familiar.

He moved the appliance over the skin of his face, and now he imagined it was something else.

The touch of a finger, stroking him gently, exciting him.

The stroke of a woman.

Yes, that was it. It felt like the stroke of a woman, and he'd felt it before. The same erotically caressing sensation, as if an electrical charge were flowing out of her.

But how could it be flowing out of the thing in his hand?

It wasn't alive, it held no blood, carried no spirit, no energy of its own.

It was only an object, totally inanimate.

Yet the tingling . . . the tingling . . .

He had to know.

Had to experiment, as he always had before.

Clutching the shaver with the same grip he'd used on all his subjects—tight enough for security, but not so tightly as to harm— the Experimenter carried it to the basement below the house.

Excitement was growing in him—the same excitement he'd always felt before one of his experiments—and it was good to feel it again.

He'd been idle too long.

He pulled the string of the fluorescent light suspended above the three two-by-twelve planks that formed a rough workbench. Laying the shaver down, he glanced around the area, finding a toolbox at the end of the bench, exactly where it should be. Rummaging through it, he found a set of miniature tools. Choosing a tiny Phillips screwdriver, he set to work.

As always, he worked in the nude.

Twenty minutes later the shaver lay in pieces, the major section of its black case broken into three fragments. Its motor and battery sat next to the case, the wires of the motor torn away from their connections to the battery. The gears that connected the three blades were scattered on the bench, and the Experimenter knew they would never be fitted together again.

Like all his previous researches, this one, too, had ultimately failed.

The Experimenter stood trembling in the basement, glowering at the ruined shaver, his frustration and anger growing by the second.

Why hadn't he been able to find what he'd been searching for?

Why hadn't he been able to determine from where the energy in the shaver had been leaking?

He knew he'd felt it—even now he could almost feel the tingling on his face!

It should have been perfectly simple. An idiot should have been able to take the machine apart, find the flaw, fix it, and reassemble it!

After all, it wasn't a living thing. It was only an object!

And now it was broken beyond repair, or at least beyond his ability to repair it. Seized suddenly by a desire to be rid of the offending object—a desire that was at least as strong as had been his urge to disassemble it—the Experimenter picked up the pieces of the shaver, mounted the stairs, and left the house through the back door. Crossing the yard, he strode past the garage, toward the back fence where the four recycling barrels were lined up.

Lifting the lid of the first one that came to hand, he threw the broken shaver inside, slammed the lid back onto the can, and started back toward the house.

He was halfway across the yard when he heard a faint gasp.

Stopping short, the Experimenter glanced around, his attention immediately caught by a flicker of movement from the house next door.

He was being watched.

A blowzy-looking woman had been about to step out onto her back porch. The Experimenter gazed coldly at her, and for a brief moment their eyes locked. Then, as if frightened by what she was seeing, the woman's face turned scarlet and she backed away, disappearing into her house as suddenly as she'd come. Her back door slammed sharply behind her.

Only when she was gone did the Experimenter finally turn away and start once more back toward the house from which he'd emerged only a few moments ago.

The razor was already forgotten.

Now he was thinking about the woman next door, and an idea was beginning to form in his mind.

But was it really time to begin again?

And was the woman truly a proper subject?

He would have to think about it.

Think about it, and make preparations.

... the police are "satisfied" that Richard
Kraven was solely responsible for the series of
murders that seemingly came to a halt when he
was arrested and charged in another state. But
the detective also pointedly repeated that "it
has yet to be fully proven that all the victims
attributed to Kraven have been discovered."
Nor would Blakemoor go so far as to absolutely rule out the possibility that Kraven did
not act alone in the crimes attributed to him.

Sheila Harrar gazed at the paragraph through bleary eyes, the
hangover from last night's party making her feel as if someone
were pounding spikes through her skull. Squinting even against the
gray daylight in Pioneer Square, Sheila tried to concentrate on the
rest of the words in the stained piece of the morning paper she'd
found abandoned on the bench along with almost half a cup of not-
quite-cold coffee. But it didn't matter if she finished the article or
not—she'd already read enough.

There was at least one body they hadn't found yet—Danny's. And
now it wasn't just the police who didn't care—it was the paper, too.
Sheila had waited all day for that woman to call back. What was
her name? Then she remembered that she'd saved the other article, stuffing it into the canvas bag with the rest of her important papers. Still clutching the remainder of the cup of tepid coffee in one
hand, Sheila burrowed deep into the tote bag with the other, feeling

around until her fingers finally closed on the crumpled scrap of newspaper. Spreading it out flat on the wooden bench, she forced her eyes to focus on the print.

Anne Jeffers. Yeah, that was the name of the woman she'd left a message for. When had it been? Sheila wasn't sure, but she knew she'd waited all day long for the woman to call back, only going out when she had to scrounge up something to eat. But the woman had never called back, and Sheila knew why.

It was because she was an Indian.

A drunken Indian.

Sheila's fist closed on the paper cup, crumpling it. She hadn't felt very good that morning when she called the newspaper. Not as bad as this morning, but not good, either. Maybe the woman had tried to call her back, but she hadn't been there to answer the pay phone in the hall. And if someone else had answered it, they sure wouldn't have bothered to give her the message.

Nobody who lived in the hotel gave a damn about anybody else.

Suddenly Sheila wanted a drink. She heaved herself to her feet and immediately a wave of dizziness and nausea struck her. Gripping the back of the bench with both hands, she bent over and retched onto the bricks of the square.

Not much came up, and she was left feeling just as bad as she had before, except now her mouth was filled with the sour taste of vomit. Wishing she could sink through the bricks and disappear into the ground, but knowing it wouldn't happen, Sheila Harrar shuffled over to the drinking fountain at the corner and filled her mouth with water, swirled it around, then spit it out. This time, though, she spit carefully into the catch basin around the fountain's mouthpiece rather than spew more of her expectoration onto the sidewalk.

What the hell good was she like this? If she was ever going to find out what had happened to Danny, she had to pull herself together.

She burrowed into her tote bag again, this time finding a few stray coins hidden among the odds and ends that had gathered in its corners. She gazed at the money, automatically calculating how much wine she could buy with it.

An image of Danny came into her mind, and she determinedly ignored her body's craving for alcohol. Making her way down to First
Avenue, she went into one of the cafés that catered to the neighborhood derelicts as long as they had the price of one of its cheap
meals, and ordered a cup of coffee and a doughnut. Though her
stomach threatened to rebel once again at the unaccustomed intru-
sion of food so early in the day, she consumed the entire pastry,
washing it down with two cups of coffee. As she ate she had a long
talk with Danny, even though he wasn't really there to talk to her:

Maybe she never got the message, Danny's voice suggested. *Or
maybe you didn't wait by the phone as long as you think.*

"I waited," Sheila muttered, then made herself stop talking out
loud, as the person two stools away glanced at her.

*Maybe you only waited a couple of minutes, then went out and got
drunk,* Danny's implacable voice went on.

Sheila didn't try to argue with him—she knew he was right. In
fact, she might not even have left the right number for Anne Jeffers
to call her at.

Better call her again. She got off the stool and started toward the
rest rooms at the back of the café, where she knew there was a pay
phone. Leafing through the phone book in search of the number of
the *Herald,* she suddenly had an idea.

What if Anne Jeffers had never even gotten her message at all?
What if it had just gone into one of those machines, and no one had
ever listened to it? Dropping the yellow pages, Sheila picked up the
white pages and began thumbing through them. A minute later she
found it. "Jeffers, Glen & Anne," were listed, up at the fancy end of
Capitol Hill.

Dropping a quarter into the slot, Sheila dialed the number. On
the eighth ring, just as she was about to hang up, someone answered.

"Hello?"

"Is Anne Jeffers there? The one who works for the paper?"

"This is her residence, but she's at work now. May I take a
message?"

Sheila hesitated, but then made up her mind. At least this time she
was talking to a real person, and if it was Anne Jeffers's house, then
she'd probably get the message. "I left a message at the paper, but she

didn't call me back," Sheila said, pronouncing each word very carefully in the hope that whoever she was talking to wouldn't know how drunk she'd been last night. "Are you her husband?"

Sheila didn't notice the slight hesitation before the voice replied with a single terse word: "Yes."

"It's my son," Sheila went on. "Danny Harrar. That man Richard Kraven killed him, but the police didn't do anything. They said he was just a drunken Indian, but that isn't true. Danny was a good boy. He worked, and he went to school, and he never drank at all." Sheila felt her eyes sting with tears, but she wiped them away with her sleeve, determined not to let her emotions get the better of her. Not this time. "All I want is to find my boy. All I want is to find my son so I can bury him."

Sheila heard a silence. Then the man spoke again. "And you want Anne to help you find him?"

Sheila's breath caught in her throat. He hadn't hung up! "Do you think she would?" she asked, her voice trembling with anxiety. It had been so long since anyone had even listened to her that she could barely believe this man's wife might actually be willing to help her.

"Why don't you tell me about it?" the man asked. "Just tell me what you think happened to your son, and how my wife can get in touch with you."

Suddenly, Sheila Harrar's hands were shaking and a sheen of sweat covered her skin. Where should she start? What should she say? "He was going fishing," she began. "With that man, Richard Kraven. I told the police, but they didn't believe me, because I'm an In—" She hesitated, then took a deep breath. "The police never believe Native Americans," she went on. "They say we're all drunks, but that isn't true. Danny wasn't a drunk, and neither was I, not back then. But they didn't believe me anyway."

"Just tell me what happened," the man said. "Tell me everything you know and everything you think."

Speaking slowly and carefully, Sheila Harrar began to relate what she suspected had happened on the day Danny disappeared.

And the man at the other end of the line listened.

Listened, and remembered. . . .

* * *

The sound of his own heartbeat throbbed so loudly in his ears that the Experimenter could barely believe it was audible to no one but himself. But who else would hear it?

He was by himself, sealed alone into his private world.

A mobile world made of metal and glass in which he was in total command, in utter control of his environment.

Free to do anything he wanted, free to roam wherever his mood took him, free of all the distractions of the larger world beyond, in which he had little control at all.

It was good to be alone.

But soon he would be alone no longer, for through the windshield he saw what he'd been looking for.

A boy—perhaps seventeen or eighteen—standing on the corner half a block ahead.

A boy holding a fishing rod.

Waiting for him.

At the same time he began to slow the motor home to a gentle stop, the Experimenter also tried to slow his heartbeat. But it was impossible: the thrill of anticipation was too much.

But the boy wouldn't notice—none of his subjects ever noticed.

The vehicle came to a smooth and silent stop, and the door opened.

The boy smiled at him, showing a double row of even teeth whose whiteness was accentuated by his bronze skin.

The Experimenter smiled back, waving the boy into the motor home.

"Where we going?" the boy asked.

"The mountains," the Experimenter replied. "I know a great spot along the Snoqualmie River." Automatically he glanced around, but the streets were empty.

No one had seen the motor home.

No one had seen him.

If anyone had seen the boy standing on the corner by himself, it wouldn't matter.

He drove the van carefully, seldom changing lanes, never exceeding the speed limit.

In the seat beside him, the boy talked, just as all the other subjects had talked. But he found the boy much more interesting than most of the rest of them, for the boy was a Native American, though of what tribe the man wasn't sure.

"Did you know our people believe the first woman came from a fish?"

The Experimenter shook his head.

"It was a salmon," the boy said. "And it must have been a big one, because when the man who caught it pulled it out of the river and tore it open, there was a woman inside."

"Tore it open?" the Experimenter asked, his heartbeat once more quickening as a thrill of excitement went through him.

"Its belly," the boy explained. "The man sliced the fish's belly open to clean it, but instead of its guts coming out, the first woman came out. That's why our people revere the salmon. Because it was from them that our own ancient mother came."

"And the man who cut the fish's belly open?" the Experimenter asked, his voice betraying nothing of the excitement that stirred in his own belly. "What happened to him?"

The dark-skinned boy shrugged. "I don't know," he said. "In the legend, the only important thing is that the first woman emerged from the belly of a salmon. Sort of like Eve being created out of Adam's rib, you know?"

"But it wasn't a man who opened Adam," the Experimenter said. "It was God."

Again the boy shrugged.

The Experimenter's excitement grew.

The city was behind him now, and the motor home was making its way up into the foothills. Fog closed in around them, fading the morning's light to a colorless gray, and the world inside the van grew smaller, more private.

The boy seemed to sense it. "It's weird. It's like there's no one left in the whole world but us."

"Maybe there's not," the Experimenter suggested. "Maybe there's never been anyone but us."

"Or maybe one of us doesn't exist?" the boy asked, grinning as he picked up the thread of the postulation. "But which one of us is the figment of the other's imagination?"

The Experimenter said nothing, knowing that for himself, at least, the boy's question had long ago been answered.

Only he existed.

All others were nothing more than subject matter for his experimentation.

He slowed the motor home, scanning the fog-shrouded forest for the gap in the trees that marked the entrance to one of his favorite fishing holes. Finally he found what he was looking for, and turned into the narrow lane with the easy expertise born of repetition.

The same easy expertise with which he now carried out his experiments.

The vehicle bumped along the dirt track, and the Experimenter gently applied the brakes against the acceleration generated by the downhill slope. As the road leveled out, the trees gave way to a small clearing next to the river, which was, as he had known it would be, deserted.

"I'll make coffee," the Experimenter told the boy. "By the time we're done, the fog will have burned off and the fish will be feeding."

As he switched the generator on, its droning hum finally drowned out the beating of his heart, and the Experimenter relaxed a little. Filling a teakettle with water, he put it onto one of the three burners in the motor home's small galley.

Twenty minutes later, as the fog finally began to burn off and the morning sun cast its golden light through the towering treetops, the boy's head dropped to his chest and his breathing took on the steady rhythm of a deeply narcotized sleep.

The Experimenter lowered the blinds over the windows of the motor home and switched on its interior lights. Opening one of the cupboards below the galley counter, he took out a roll of transparent plastic sheeting. Working slowly and methodically—so practiced now that he barely had to think about what he was doing at all—the Experimenter began lining the interior of the motor home with plastic.

First the floor, running the edges of the plastic a few inches up the walls.

Then the walls themselves, letting the plastic hang down so it overlapped the coverings on the floor.

Finally the bed. Two sheets here, folded together twice where they joined, and carefully taped so they couldn't come apart.

The Experimenter began to disrobe, removing one garment at a time, carefully folding each item and storing it in one of the drawers beneath the bed.

When he was finally naked, he at last turned his attention to the boy who was slumped in the passenger seat at the front of the vehicle.

He undressed the unconscious boy almost as easily as he had peeled the clothing from his own body.

This time, though, each garment was methodically put into a plastic bag before he removed the next.

When the boy was as nude as he was himself, the Experimenter lifted him in his arms and carried him to the plastic-shrouded bed.

Working with all the skill he had developed over the years, he made the initial incisions, using a new scalpel that he would dispose of as soon as this morning's research was concluded. The razor-sharp blade sliced through the skin of the boy's chest, and as blood began to ooze from the open wound, the Experimenter stanched it with beeswax.

A moment later the thrumming of the generator was drowned out by the high-pitched keening of the electric saw. As his practiced hand held the saw steady above the boy's incised and naked chest, the Experimenter felt the same thrill of anticipation he always experienced before making the first deep cut into the interior of a new subject.

His heartbeat increased, as did the rate of his respiration.

He could feel a sheen of sweat covering his skin, oozing down between his shoulder blades just as a thin trickle of blood was making its way down the boy's belly.

Gently—reverently—he lowered the whirling blade, reveling in the change of its pitch as it bit into the gristle and bone of the boy's sternum.

Soon . . . soon . . .

Soon he would be deep inside the boy, discovering the secret of his existence.

Soon he would feel the energy of the boy's body with his fingertips, feel the heat of it enveloping his hands.

Feel the tingling energy of the youth's life force—

Soon . . . soon . . .

But then it was over, and he was standing naked in the morning sun, the boy's lifeless body clutched in his arms, his own body trembling with the frustration of his failure.

Angrily, he dropped the corpse to the ground and began covering it with rocks, working steadily until the body had entirely disappeared beneath the rough construction of a rocky cairn that could as easily have been built by the river in flood as by the hands of the Experimenter in his fury.

Then he was in the forest, dousing the clothes with gasoline and setting fire to them, prodding and stirring them with a stick until they were consumed by the flames.

Finally he returned to the river, plunging naked into the icy water to wash himself clean of all traces of the latest of his experiments. And as the icy water sluiced over his skin, he screamed out loud, partly from shock, but even more from the frustration of having failed yet again.

CHAPTER 26

Anne Jeffers ducked through the front door of the Red Robin on Fourth Avenue just before the rain that had been threatening all morning finally began to fall in earnest. If it didn't let up within the hour—and she was pretty sure it wouldn't—she'd have the devil of a time getting a cab back to the paper. Well, maybe she could beg a ride with Mark Blakemoor, unless he'd gotten chewed out over letting himself be quoted in this morning's paper. But when Mark himself hurried through the door a second later, peeled off his raincoat, and proceeded to shake water not only all over her, but onto a couple of complete strangers as well, she knew his mood wouldn't matter.

"Did you drive?" he asked, confirming her certainty that he'd left his car in the garage. " 'Cause if you didn't, I'm going to get completely soaked going back to the office."

"We'll split a cab if we can find one," Anne told him, relieved that he hadn't mentioned the story in the *Herald*. Moving deeper into the restaurant, she asked the hostess for a table for two. As she threaded her way through the restaurant behind the waitress, she decided that maybe Mark wasn't going to chew her out over this morning's story after all. Surely he couldn't think she'd happily give him a ride back to his office if he spent an hour ragging on her for suggesting that the department might not be doing its job quite perfectly. On the other hand, there was another possibility, which might be even worse than getting chewed out.

Mark Blakemoor, she'd noticed, had been giving her a little more help with her search of the Kraven files than she would have expected. In fact, he'd been giving her a *lot* more help, especially given that anything she found that might be worth a story would almost by definition be critical of the department. After all, if she unearthed something that was news, it would have to be something the department had overlooked.

So why was Mark Blakemoor helping her, and why had he asked her to have lunch with him?

Obviously, he'd developed some kind of crush on her. She already knew what the proof of it would be—if he didn't give her a hard time over the story, he was definitely getting the hots for her.

As she seated herself at the table, she realized that the idea of his infatuation with her didn't offend her at all. Indeed, it was flattering, especially since she knew she would never admit to him that she was aware of his feelings, let alone doing anything to encourage them. What's more, the detective wasn't bad-looking, and it was nice to know that Glen wasn't the only man in the world who found her attractive. As Mark Blakemoor dropped into the seat opposite her, Anne had to check a sudden urge to flirt with him, and felt herself starting to blush.

"Don't worry," Blakemoor assured her, misreading her blush. "I'm not going to ride you about the story. I'm not saying Ackerly and some of the others aren't pissed—not to mention McCarty—but what the hell. You're only doing your job, right?"

Suspicions confirmed, Anne thought. So now what do I do? "Well, if you're not going to chew me out, to what do I owe this lunch? What was it you couldn't just tell me over the phone?"

Blakemoor didn't answer until they'd both given their orders. Then: "Sheila Harrar."

Anne pursed her lips. The name was familiar, but she couldn't quite . . . Then it came to her. "The woman who called me, whose number was all garbled."

Blakemoor nodded. "It took a while, but I finally found it in my case notes. Except there wasn't much to find. She's an Indian— pardon me, a Native American—and she made a lot of calls to the task force a few years ago. Claimed Kraven killed her son, and wanted us to go right out and arrest him."

"Which you obviously didn't do," Anne observed dryly, though her words apparently had no effect on Blakemoor.

"No reason to," the detective replied. "No body, no signs of foul play, not much of anything."

"But her son is really gone?"

"Depends on what you mean by gone," Blakemoor countered. "If you mean is he still around Seattle, the answer is no. Or if he is, there doesn't seem to be any record of him being here. On the other hand, that doesn't mean much. The boy was eighteen when he disappeared, which means he could have simply taken off, and it really isn't a police matter. Despite what you hear to the contrary, adults in this country still have the right to go where they please, and tell or not tell whoever they want, even including their mothers."

"*Whom*ever," Anne said.

Mark gazed at her sourly and shrugged. "Whatever."

"So the police did nothing?" Anne asked in the journalist's tone she'd carefully honed over the years until she could make even the simplest question sound like an accusation.

Blakemoor's big hands spread in a dismissive gesture. "What was there to do? The kid went to school at the university—Kraven taught there. Big deal. He was never a specialist in students—in fact, it seems to me he generally steered pretty clear of them. And it turned out Danny Harrar was one of Kraven's very own students, and as far as I'm concerned, that almost eliminates him. His pattern was strangers."

"His pattern was to have no pattern," Anne observed, her brows arching with skepticism. "Which means he could have done one of his students, and it would have fit in just fine. What's the deal on the mother?"

"A drunk," Blakemoor sighed. "For all I know, she could have been one all along. Who knows? Maybe that's why the kid split." Quickly, he sketched out Sheila Harrar's recent history, which hadn't taken him more than a few minutes of asking questions, first in the Yesler Terrace projects up at the foot of Broadway, then down in the bars around Pioneer Square. Pulling his notebook out of his jacket pocket, he copied an address onto a clean page, tore it out and handed it to Anne. As she took the page, their fingers touched, and Mark's face instantly flushed a bright red. "Sorry it took so long," he mumbled, obviously flustered by his reaction to their contact.

"I'd almost forgotten it," Anne admitted, tucking the sheet of notepaper into her gritchel and deliberately taking enough time to let Mark recompose himself. For the rest of the lunch, both of them were careful to see that their hands stayed well away from each other, and that the conversation never veered toward a personal level. And although it was still raining when they left the restaurant an hour later, neither of them suggested sharing a cab. Mark turned and hurried off in one direction, while Anne hurried just as quickly in the other. A brief flirtation was one thing, she told herself as she searched the street for an empty taxi, but from now on she would keep that particular relationship on a strictly professional level. The next time she needed help with the Kraven files, she would ask Lois Ackerly.

Who, Anne was fairly certain, would turn her down flat.

Well, what the hell—she'd just do it all herself. The last thing she needed in her life right now was a Seattle detective mooning over her.

Still, it *was* flattering. . . .

The first thing Glen felt as he began to wake up was the cold. Not the bone-chilling cold the Arctic Express brings when it occasionally comes barreling down from the north in the middle of winter and freezes Seattle solid for a week or so, but the nightmare-bearing cold that comes from kicking the blankets off too long before morning. Except that Glen wasn't in bed, and it wasn't nighttime.

As his mind slowly cleared, he realized he was lying naked on the bathroom floor. He felt disoriented, but then began to remember what had happened. And with memory came fear.

He lay still, trying to assess how he felt, trying to decide whether it was safe even to move. Had he had another heart attack? He struggled to remember how he'd felt when he woke up in the hospital two weeks earlier. Had his chest hurt? He couldn't remember.

Not that it mattered, because his chest didn't hurt now. He focused his mind on his breathing, and pressed the fingers of his right hand against his left wrist. Both the rhythm of his breath and the beating of his heart seemed normal, at least to himself.

Then he remembered the feeling he'd had of not being alone in the house. The feeling that had grown when he'd gotten out of the shower. He'd been about to shave, and sensed something—someone?—in the bathroom with him. He'd been about to turn around when . . .

Had he been hit? Knocked out?

Sitting up, he rubbed his head and neck. His neck felt a little stiff, but that could be from lying on the floor.

Lying on the floor for how long?

He got to his feet, bracing himself against the sink, half expecting to feel dizzy. In the basin was his shaver, lying where it must have fallen.

Leaving his face still unshaven, Glen left the bathroom, starting across the bedroom toward his closet. He was halfway across the room when his gaze fell on the clock radio that sat by his side of the bed.

Two P.M.? Could he have been unconscious for five hours? He glanced across the bed at Anne's alarm clock, which confirmed the time: two o'clock.

The fear that had begun to abate when he'd decided that he hadn't had a heart attack suddenly came flooding back. Going to the dresser, he found his wallet where he'd left it last night, and pulled out the card with Gordon Farber's phone number on it. Sitting on the edge of the bed, he punched the number into the phone, his fingers now trembling so badly he didn't get the number right until the third try. "This is Glen Jeffers," he said when someone finally answered in the heart specialist's office. "I know I'm not due until tomorrow, but I need to come in today. In fact, I need to come in right now."

"Well, whatever happened, you're all right now."

It was almost an hour later, and Glen wasn't certain whether or not the words Gordy Farber had just uttered were good news or bad. His pulse had been taken, his blood pressure measured, and an electrocardiogram had been administered. And as each test showed normal results, his fear had eased a little more. Except that he still didn't know what had caused him to wind up unconscious on the bathroom floor. "Then what happened?" he asked. "Did I faint, or did someone knock me out?"

"Were there any signs of someone being in the house?" Farber countered.

Glen felt himself flush. "I didn't really look. It seemed more important to get down here."

"Well, you didn't get hit over the head," the doctor assured him. "If you had, there'd be swelling, contusions, probably even concussion."

"So I just passed out?"

"I didn't say that. Someone who knows what he's doing can knock you out in a matter of a second or two, just by pressing the right nerves. But you said you didn't see anyone."

"Everything was so steamed over, I could barely see myself."

"Did you hear the door open?"

Glen shook his head. "But it wasn't even all the way closed."

Farber shrugged. "Well, if you want my opinion, I'd say you just passed out. Which, frankly, doesn't really surprise me all that much. You've been in bed for two weeks, you're still recovering from a major heart incident, and you were in a very hot shower. Add it all together, and what happened isn't all that surprising."

"But five *hours*?" Glen pressed.

Farber cocked his head. "You want me to readmit you to the hospital?" he asked. "If you're really that worried, I can order up some more tests."

"But you just said I was okay, didn't you?"

"An opinion you seem disinclined to accept," Farber observed. "I think you just fainted from overheating yourself in the shower, had a good nap, and woke up on the floor. You were right to call, and right to come in, and I'm now satisfied that whatever happened, it wasn't serious. All I'm saying now is that if you're really worried, I can put you back in the hospital for a few more days."

Glen remembered the room filled with equipment, the tasteless food, and the nurses who had come and gone at all hours, taking his temperature and giving him pills. Suddenly, sleeping on the bathroom floor for a few hours didn't seem all that bad. "Forget it," he said. "If you say I'm okay, that's good enough for me." A few minutes later though, as he was leaving the doctor's office, he had another thought. "Do me a favor, Gordy," he said. "Let's just keep this between us, okay? I mean, this is just the kind of thing that would scare the hell out of Anne, and if nothing's wrong, what's the sense, right?"

"No problem," Gordy Farber replied. "Now get out of here and stop worrying. Go do something totally useless."

"Like what?" Glen asked, wondering just what a heart specialist's idea of "something useless" might be.

Farber thought a second, then: "Go over to Broadway Market, get a magazine at the kiosk and a decaf latte at one of the stands. Then sit, read, and watch the passing parade. I'll see you in a couple of days."

Dismissed from the doctor's office, Glen left the Group Health complex, got into his car, and was about to start back up Sixteenth toward home when he changed his mind.

Why not just follow his doctor's orders? Abandoning the idea of going right home, he turned left on Thomas and headed toward Broadway and the big brick building that housed the market.

For years the structure had contained only an enormous Fred Meyer's store, with food at one end and a cavernous variety and pharmacy section at the other. It had squatted quietly on its block of Broadway for decades, serving the equally quiet middle-class citizens who had lived on Capitol Hill in the middle of the century. But through the second half of the century, a change came over Capitol Hill. Its middle-class neighborhoods slid into a downward spiral, and as families moved across the lake to Bellevue, the big old houses began to get chopped up into smaller and smaller apartments. And as the neighborhood slid downhill, so also did the shopping district along Broadway, until, by the early seventies, most of it was fairly well decimated. But then, inevitably, change came. First the gay population discovered the cheap rents and bargain houses to be found on Capitol Hill, and the process of gentrification began. Then, as the suburbs east of Lake Washington became more crowded and less appealing, the children of the families who had fled eastward twenty years earlier began migrating back toward the city. As the neighborhood came back to life, so did Broadway, evolving from a strip of dying shops whose custom consisted primarily of elderly women pulling shopping carts, into an eclectic collection of small restaurants and boutiques, each of them catering to one or another of the new groups who now strolled the street. And Fred Meyer, seeing the graffiti on the wall, changed, too. Moving the pharmacy into a trailer in the parking lot, they gutted their building, kept the old facade, and rebuilt the interior into a vaguely European-feeling shopping structure, complete with a multiplex theater upstairs, a huge subterranean garage, and a few apartments for those who could never live quite close enough to the action. Resigning the food business, Fred Meyer concentrated on the variety store and drug operations, and the rest of the space was rented out to all the entrepreneurial types who had a business dream and enough cash to rent one of the carts with which the main floor of the new building was lined.

Some grew.

Some failed.

Some simply stagnated, their owners scratching out a living selling everything from crystals to condoms. Inevitably, the Broadway Market became the center of the suddenly bustling neighborhood.

And that afternoon, as Glen wandered from shop to shop and finally settled down to watch the wildly diverse crowd that swirled and eddied around him, he found himself far more fascinated by it all than he would have thought possible.

So fascinated, indeed, that when he finally got home and turned on the television, the local news was just beginning.

Could he really have sat at the market for almost two hours?

It hadn't seemed like more than an hour.

In fact, it had seemed like even less.

Switching the television off, Glen started up the stairs. Though he'd already slept five extra hours that day, he suddenly felt the need for a nap.

Or at least an escape from the confusion in his mind.

O dds and ends.

It had been an afternoon of odds and ends, just the sort of afternoon Anne Jeffers hated. First, she realized that the most important question she'd intended to ask Mark Blakemoor at lunch had completely slipped her mind when she realized that the detective's emotions toward her were no longer based purely on business. Then, she wasted twenty minutes vacillating over what message he might get if she called him so soon after their meeting. Finally, she decided to put it off for a while, and went on to other things.

With the rain apparently over for the day, she'd gone in search of Sheila Harrar. At the address Mark Blakemoor had given her, she was told that "Harrar's on the fourth floor. In the front." So she trekked up to the fourth floor and found the room, but no trace of Sheila Harrar.

Downstairs, the man behind the desk looked bored when Anne asked if he knew where Sheila Harrar might be. "Look in the square. That's where they all hang out," he told her. "She's an Indian broad," he added, rolling his eyes, as if his identification of her as a Native American should be enough to explain everything about her.

Saying nothing, Anne left the hotel and walked the two blocks to Pioneer Square, searching for someone who might be Sheila Harrar. Almost to her own surprise, she found Sheila on the second try. Though it was obvious the woman was an alcoholic, it was equally obvious that today she hadn't been drinking.

"I read your article this morning," Sheila told her, seeming unsurprised when Anne introduced herself and sat down on the bench next to her. "That's why I called your house."

"My house?" Anne asked blankly, wondering if maybe she'd been mistaken and that Sheila Harrar was drunk after all.

Sheila appeared puzzled. "Didn't your husband tell you?" she asked. "Isn't that why you came looking for me?"

Anne shook her head, explained about the garbled message on her voice mail and how she'd finally tracked Sheila down.

Sheila Harrar's expression clouded at mention of the police, and her eyes narrowed to suspicious slits. "The police got no reason to be looking for me," she said. "I didn't do nothing wrong."

"They weren't looking for you," Anne reassured her quickly, sensing that the woman was about to bolt. "The detective is a friend of mine, and he was just doing me a favor."

" 'Cause you're white," Sheila Harrar grunted.

"I beg your pardon?" Anne asked.

Cynical eyes fixed on her. "He did you a favor 'cause you're white. When I wanted them to look for Danny, they didn't do nothin'."

Anne knew there was no point in trying to explain to Mrs. Harrar about how many tips had come in on the Kraven killings, how many phone calls there had been from anonymous sources, how many mothers just like Sheila had called the police to report that their children had been murdered by Richard Kraven. There had also been husbands, wives, boyfriends, girlfriends, lovers of all sorts, even children calling to report that they were certain Richard Kraven had killed their parents.

"Why do you think Richard Kraven killed your son?" Anne asked instead. At worst, it would give the woman an opportunity finally to tell her story; at best, Sheila Harrar might actually know something that could directly connect Richard Kraven to at least one local murder.

Sheila took Anne back to her room, where she pulled out a worn photo album—one of the last things she still possessed from better days. In the album were yellowing pictures of herself as a girl, then some of her former husband, Manny Harrar. At the end were the pictures of Danny, all of them smudged with fingerprints from the many times Sheila had pulled the album out late at night when she was far into a bottle of fortified wine, and paged through the pictures, touching Danny's image with as much gentleness as if she were actually stroking his cheek.

What Anne saw was a handsome boy who was always neatly dressed, although the clothes he wore looked nearly worn-out. His hair was always combed, his lips smiling, his eyes sparkling.

Even in the snapshots, Anne could sense the boy's intelligence. And he didn't look like the sort who would get involved in drugs or simply take off. Indeed, in the few photographs showing Sheila and Danny together, it was clear that before Danny disappeared, his mother had been a different person. Though they obviously hadn't had much money, nothing in the photos betrayed anything other than a devoted mother and loving son.

The snapshots alone were enough to convince Anne that Danny Harrar had not run away from home.

"What can you tell me?" she asked. "What happened the last day you saw Danny?"

"He was going fishing," Sheila told her. "He was going to go fishing with Richard Kraven."

Fishing.

It was one of Richard Kraven's passions. He'd had a motor home, and often used it to go up into the mountains, where, according to him, he liked to spend a day in solitude, casting for trout in the roaring streams that poured out of the Cascades. Anne was well aware of how thoroughly that motor home had been searched, for after Kraven had been arrested and charged in Connecticut, the Seattle police had seized the vehicle and nearly torn it apart in a search for evidence that might link Kraven to the long list of murders in which he was the prime suspect.

No trace of any of his known victims had been discovered. What little detritus had been found—a few hairs and traces of lint—had never been matched to anyone. Richard Kraven had either been very lucky or an absolute perfectionist.

Or innocent?

"Did the police ever question Kraven about your son?"

Sheila's lips tightened into a hard, resentful line. "I don't think so. They said Danny ran away."

"Tell me about him," Anne asked.

For most of the afternoon, Sheila talked. Anne listened. What she heard was the story of an ambitious boy, determined to get ahead in the world, determined to right the wrongs that he perceived had been done to his people.

And then one morning he'd gotten up early, taken his fishing pole, and gone to wait for Richard Kraven at a corner near the university where Kraven taught and Danny went to school.

Sheila had never seen him again.

Richard Kraven, when she'd called him, had told her that he knew Danny, that he had indeed had a date to go fishing with Danny, but that when he arrived at the corner to pick Danny up, Danny wasn't there.

Kraven told her he'd waited a few minutes, but when Danny didn't show up, he decided the boy must have slept in, and he'd gone on to fish by himself. Sheila Harrar hadn't believed him then, and when the stories about him—Anne's stories—started appearing in the *Herald*, she'd been sure that Kraven had killed Danny. But no one ever listened to her. Not until today, anyway.

"I don't know what to tell you," Anne said when Sheila Harrar finally fell silent. "It's been how long since Danny disappeared? Four years?" Sheila nodded miserably. "Do you remember what he was wearing that day?"

Sheila nodded. "What he always wore. Blue jeans. A plaid shirt. Tennis shoes—not the fancy kind. Danny wouldn't waste money on those. Just Keds, like when we were kids, you know?"

Anne smiled. "Twenty dollars, ten if they were on sale?"

"Like that, yeah. And he had his fishing rod with him, and his knife."

"His knife?" Anne echoed.

"A pocketknife, with a turquoise handle," Sheila told her. "It was something his daddy gave him, before he left. Danny always had it in his pocket."

Anne glanced around the shabby room that was all Sheila Harrar had left in life. "I wish I could tell you I think you're wrong about Danny," she said finally, deciding the one thing Sheila Harrar didn't need right now was false hope. "But I suspect you're probably right. The thing about Kraven that no one ever understood was how he picked his victims. There was never a pattern, never a common denominator. Mostly, it just seemed random. And I suppose it really was random, and if he had a chance, there's no reason why Kraven wouldn't have killed someone he knew once or twice. In fact, it might even fit with the *lack* of a pattern." She reached out and laid her hand on Sheila's. "But that doesn't help, does it?"

Sheila shook her head and sighed, but then a faint, rueful smile curved her lips. "You listened," she said. "That helps. No one else listened—they didn't even care. It's better, just knowing someone else knows what happened to Danny, too."

Wishing there were something she could do for Sheila Harrar, but knowing there wasn't, Anne went back to her office and continued with the odds and ends of the day.

She called Mark Blakemoor and got the answer to the question she hadn't asked at lunch.

"Why would there be any progress on Shawnelle Davis?" he asked, his tone clearly implying that he expected better of Anne. "She was a hooker. You know how it is around here when hookers get killed— nobody cares. If nobody cares, I can't get very far. No time, no cooperation, hardly even any interest. I don't like it, but I can't change it."

And though Anne didn't like it, either, she understood it. It was just the way of the city, and it wasn't Mark Blakemoor's fault.

Still, the killing of Shawnelle Davis bothered her. Though it lacked some of the distinctive features of what Kraven had done, the similarities were still there, whether anyone in the police department wanted to admit it or not. Maybe she should write another follow-up story. If the department wouldn't pressure itself, maybe she could pressure them.

She was just beginning the outlines of the story when the phone on her desk jangled. Picking it up, she was surprised to hear Joyce Cottrell's voice.

Joyce was her slightly over-the-hill—and perhaps not completely sane, as far as Anne was concerned—next door neighbor.

"I've been trying to get you all afternoon," Joyce told her. "And I didn't want to leave a message because—well, you'll understand when I tell you."

Anne listened in silence, barely able to believe what she was hearing, as Joyce Cottrell described what she'd seen in the backyard that morning.

"I only saw him for a split second, and he hardly even looked like Glen at all! But who else could it have been? And it wasn't just that he was naked," Joyce finished. "It was the way he looked at me. Anne, I can't tell you how strange it was. It was—well, I don't know—I've always liked Glen, you know that. But the way he looked at me just scared me." She was silent for a second, then her voice dropped almost to a whisper. "Anne, it *was* just a heart attack, wasn't it? I mean—well, Glen's *all right*, isn't he?"

Though she assured Joyce that Glen had suffered only a heart attack and hadn't secretly been in the psycho ward at Harborview, when Anne hung up the phone, she felt a lot more frightened than she'd let Joyce know.

The house no longer felt the same. Yet as she let herself in the front door late that afternoon, Anne Jeffers couldn't have said exactly how it felt different. All her journalistic training told her that the sudden frisson she felt as she turned the key, the surge of anxiety that chilled her as she stepped into the hallway's silence, was ridiculous: it wasn't the house that felt different at all—it was *she* who felt different. It had started yesterday, when Glen made love to her and she'd felt as if a stranger had been touching her.

An exciting stranger, granted, but still a stranger. It had disturbed her, although by this afternoon she had all but assured herself that if anything truly strange had occurred, it had been mostly in her own mind. She had been worried about Glen, uncertain whether they should be making love, despite what Gordy Farber told them, and so the sheer energy Glen had shown struck her as being—well, *disturbing*.

Even more disturbing had been the phone call from Joyce Cottrell. From the moment she'd hung up the phone, Anne was telling herself that whatever Joyce might think she'd seen, she must be mistaken.

Assuming she'd seen *anything*. After all, hadn't she and Glen been speculating for years that Joyce was a secret drinker, sitting alone in the big old house next door where both her parents had died, tippling gin in the false and empty comfort of a darkened room? It had only been speculation, of course, but if it turned out they were right, it would certainly explain the peculiar phone call Joyce had made to her. Probably nothing had happened at all. Or maybe, taking advantage of Glen's presence at home in the middle of the day, Joyce made a pass at him, was rebuffed, and had been trying to extract some kind of warped revenge.

Now, though, all Anne's rationales were crumbling around her in the too-silent foyer. *Something* had changed in this house. "Hello?" she called out. "Anyone home?"

"I'm up here." Heather's voice echoed from the second floor, muffled by the closed door to her room.

Dropping her gritchel onto the table by the foot of the stairs, Anne took the steps two at a time, knocked once on Heather's door, and pushed it open at almost the same second she heard her daughter telling her to come in.

Heather was sitting at her desk, a math book open in front of her, a badly gnawed pencil clutched in her fingers.

"I thought you promised to quit chewing those things," Anne said, sliding automatically into mother mode, and knowing even as she did that mostly it was a way to put off her half-formed anxieties for at least a minute or two.

"I'm trying," Heather sighed. "I just don't think about it. It's hard to stop doing something you don't even know you're doing."

"I know," Anne agreed. "But it's still going to ruin your teeth." She moved farther into the room, lifting the window to let some fresh air in. "Where's your dad?" Anne hoped the question sounded casual, and when Heather spoke without looking up from the equation she was laboring over, she thought she'd succeeded.

"Taking a nap, I guess. The door to your room was closed when I got home, and I didn't even knock." Finally she glanced up, her eyes falling on the clock on her nightstand. "Is it really six already?"

"It's six." Anne sighed. "I better go wake your father up. I assume no one's started figuring out anything for dinner yet?" Heather shook her head. "And where's Kevin?"

"He said he was going over to Justin's, and he promised to be home by five-thirty." Reading the look in her mother's eye, which clearly said, Do I have to do everything around here? Heather got up from her desk. "I'll call the Reynoldses and find out where he is. And why don't I call Dino's and order pizza for dinner? That way you don't have to worry about it."

Anne hesitated. It was tempting, but then she remembered Gordy Farber's admonition about Glen's diet. Was pizza on the recommended list for heart attack patients? Somehow she doubted it. "Let me go wake up your dad, then we'll see," Anne temporized, telling herself it wasn't too late to run down to the Safeway and pick up something healthy, but suspecting that in the end they'd probably all wind up going out somewhere instead. As Heather went downstairs to call Justin Reynolds, Anne went to the closed door of the master bedroom and found herself hesitating before going inside.

But what was she expecting?

It was *Glen*, for God's sake!

Abruptly feeling foolish, Anne pushed open the door and went inside. The shades were drawn and the room was stuffy, and when she switched on the lamp on Glen's side of the bed, he immediately came awake, sat up, and shielded his eyes against the glare. For a second—no more than an instant, really—Anne had the unsettling sense that she was looking into the eyes of a stranger. Then it was over. Glen's eyes cleared and he smiled at her—the same smile she'd known for years, the smile that had always reassured her that everything in her world was intact.

"Hey," he said. "Come here and give me a hug, okay?"

Flopping onto the bed next to her husband, Anne slipped her arms around him, gave him a kiss, then lay her head on his chest.

"You'll never guess who called me at the office today," she said, suddenly certain that Joyce's crazy tale could only have been a figment of the woman's imagination. "Joyce Cottrell."

"Joyce?" Glen echoed. "You're kidding. What did she want?"

As Anne began relating the conversation she'd had with their next-door neighbor, she felt Glen's body stiffen. All the fears that had been allayed by his smile only a few moments earlier came flooding back to her. Still, she tried not to let her voice or her body betray the questions that were ricocheting in her brain. "Crazy, huh?" she asked as she finished.

"Maybe we've been right all along," Glen suggested, but his bantering tone didn't quite cover the instant's hesitation before he answered. "Maybe she really *has* been drinking over there all these years."

Anne sat up and looked into Glen's eyes, now openly searching for that look she'd barely glimpsed a few minutes earlier. "Then it didn't happen?" she asked.

"How could it have?" Glen countered. With a quick hug that Anne read as an evasion, he stood and crossed to the bathroom.

Glen's mind raced as he tried to figure out how to answer Anne's question. He didn't want to lie to her, but he didn't want to worry her, either. Surely, if he'd been wandering around the backyard stark naked, he'd remember it, wouldn't he?

But the last thing he remembered of the morning was being in the bathroom, naked. He'd showered, and was about to shave, and then—

The black hole in the day, as if lightning had come out of nowhere and struck him unconscious.

Glen's mind was churning. Why was he even thinking of lying to Anne? Why not just tell her he was missing part of the day?

The answer came to him as quickly as the question: because she would insist he go right back to the hospital, despite what Gordy Farber had told him this afternoon. Besides, nothing had happened anyway.

Or had it? What if he really *had* gone outside, and Joyce Cottrell had seen him? Why on earth would he have done something like that? He'd been asleep on the bathroom floor.

Then he spotted his razor, still lying in the sink, exactly where he'd left it this morning. Except now he could see that it wasn't his razor at all; his had been five years old, its plastic case scratched and stained.

The Norelco he was staring at now was brand-new.

Where could it have come from?

Could he have been sleepwalking? Could he have actually gone out and bought a new one? But surely he couldn't have done that naked, could he? He would have wound up in jail! So he must have gotten dressed, gone out, and bought a new razor. But that was nuts, too! He'd been naked when he woke up!

A sharp terror closed in on him. He was losing his mind! Maybe he should call Gordy Farber again. But there wasn't anything wrong with him—the doctor had already told him so!

"Glen?"

Anne was at the door now; he could feel her watching him, and when he glanced into the mirror, he could see the worry in her eyes. Making up his mind, he picked up the gleaming new shaver and turned around.

"I'll bet Joyce has been fantasizing about me for years," he began, improvising a story even as he spoke. "I suspect she saw me out there chucking my razor, poured herself another gin, and mentally stripped me naked. The wish is often father to the thought, isn't it?"

"Your razor?" Anne asked, confused. "What on earth are you talking about?"

Now the words came more quickly. "I dropped mine. So I took it out and threw it in the garbage." He held up the new shaver. "And I went out and bought myself a new one."

"Stark naked?" Anne demanded. "You took it out stark naked and threw it in the trash? Then what did you do, head out shopping with no clothes on?"

"I was wearing a bathrobe," Glen insisted. What the hell was happening? How had he gotten himself into this? And what if she went out and looked in the trash barrel? "I mean, I was wearing a bathrobe out in the yard. I was dressed when I went down to Freddy Meyer's." At least that part wasn't made up! He *had* been dressed when he'd gone to the Broadway Market that afternoon. As Anne continued to stare at him as if he were speaking in some strange, incomprehensible tongue, he offered her the shaver. "See? New shaver."

Anne felt totally disoriented. When she'd first told him about Joyce's call, she knew something was wrong, and the story he'd just told sounded totally far-fetched! In the years she and Glen had been married, plenty of electric shavers had given out on Glen. And she knew what Glen did with them.

He dropped them in the wastebasket. He did not take them out to the backyard and throw them directly into one of the garbage barrels!

Saying nothing, Anne went down the back stairs of the house, out the back door, and across the yard to the trash containers. Lifting the lid of the first one, she peered down into the depths of the barrel. And there it was.

Shattered—broken into a dozen pieces—but unmistakably the remains of a ruined electric shaver. A shaver that could not possibly have been that badly broken simply from having been dropped into a sink. What was going on?

She headed back to the house, entering the kitchen just in time to hear her son's excited voice.

"Hey, Dad," Kevin was shouting up the front stairs. "Where'd this come from? Is it for me?"

Moving quickly through the kitchen and dining room, she found Kevin standing in the foyer, holding a fishing pole in his hand.

"Where did that come from?" she asked.

Kevin grinned mischievously. "Down in the basement," he said. "I was stickin' my gym clothes in the wash and I found it. Where'd it come from?"

Anne was still gazing at the fishing pole when she heard Glen speak from the head of the stairs.

"I bought it," he said.

Anne turned to stare up at him. There was something strange in his voice, just as there had been when he told her about the razor. "*You* bought a fishing rod? But you—"

Glen started down the stairs, determined not to let Anne see his confusion, the panic that was creeping up on him as he searched his memory for some clue as to where the fishing rod might have come from. But there was nothing—no more memory of the new fishing rod than of the new shaver. It will come back to me, he told himself. Sooner or later, it will come back to me. Forcing a grin as he came to the bottom of the stairs, he slipped an arm around his wife and held her close. "Don't you remember?" he asked. "Gordy Farber said I have to get a hobby. So I chose one today. I'm going to go fishing."

Fishing. The word echoed eerily in Anne's mind. Only a few hours ago Sheila Harrar had been telling her how her son had disappeared after setting out to go fishing.

Fishing with Richard Kraven.

And now here was Glen, saying he was taking it up as a hobby. Of course, it was nothing more than a coincidence, but even so, the thought made her shudder. It would probably be only a passing fancy, something Glen would lose interest in within a week or so.

And if he didn't, so what? Despite her perfectly rational arguments, she knew that her first instinct when she came into the house a few minutes ago had been right.

Something in this house *was* different.

Her *husband* was different.

Joyce Cottrell's life had not gone exactly as she planned it. By the time she was looking at her fiftieth birthday from the wrong direction, she had given up all hope of a lasting marriage and a family of her own. Her few relatives were all gone. Her phone almost never rang, and she rarely spoke to anyone save the people she worked with at Group Health on Capitol Hill. Her parents had left her the house she'd grown up in, but not quite enough money to get by on, and a career beyond making a home for the husband and children she'd expected to have had never been among the few plans she'd laid out for herself. She'd been married briefly but when she'd come home to her parents after Jim Cottrell left her six months after the wedding, a job hadn't been high on Joyce's priority list.

She had returned home to lick her wounds and pick up the broken pieces of her emotional life.

Now, almost thirty years later, she was still at it. Her parents, who had provided refuge during the long months when she was too ashamed of her failure even to leave the house, had finally died. Joyce's few friends had long ago tired of her woeful tale of betrayal, and stopped calling her.

The years had stretched into decades, and though she eventually secured a job as a receptionist on the swing shift at Group Health, she had also turned slowly into a strange kind of recluse. While she rarely left her house except to go to work, trash did not build up in Joyce Cottrell's house as it did in those of older recluses, nor did paint begin to peel, or furniture grow stained and threadbare. Joyce Cottrell kept her house meticulously clean, immediately redecorating any room in which paint began to fade, choosing colors and fabrics from catalogs, finally venturing forth to make her purchases only when the newly redecorated room was complete in her mind down to the last detail.

Over the years, she had become expert in stripping paint from old wood, paper from old plaster, and worn fabric from the excellent frames with which her parents had furnished the house. She had become even more expert in applying the new materials she bought on her rare shopping expeditions, and in time the house had evolved into an eclectic assortment of rooms, each of them reflecting whatever fashion had been in vogue at the precise moment Joyce had most recently decided to redo it.

No one, though, had seen the interior of the house in years, for whenever one of her neighbors—the only people who saw her with any regularity at all—asked if they might see what she was doing, Joyce would always protest that the house wasn't done yet. Nor was it a lie: one or more of the house's ten rooms was always in some stage of redecoration.

Joyce herself was in a steady state of redecoration, too, as she dreamed and planned for the glittering party she would throw when the house was finally ready, a Martha Stewart–perfect party to celebrate the completion of the redecorating and mark her reemergence into the social world. She spent hours and days imagining herself as the beautiful, charming hostess, throwing open the doors to her elegant home to hordes of admiring friends.

Unfortunately, Joyce had not developed the same knack with herself that she had with the house. Her figure could best be described as "full," a circumstance that Joyce concealed as well as she could by wearing loose-fitting clothing in bright colors, and her hair was, at age fifty-three, even blonder than it had been half a century earlier. Joyce's taste in makeup hadn't changed since she was a teenager, running to the same bright lipsticks and eye shadows—a riot of reds and oranges, blues and greens—that she loved in both her clothes and her interior decoration.

People who chose to be charitable might have said Joyce Cottrell looked a little blowzy.

Those who chose not to be charitable could have said she looked like an over-the-hill hooker.

It was precisely what attracted the man to her.

That, and the fact that she lived next door to Anne Jeffers.

CHAPTER 31

Sources within the police department will neither confirm nor deny that they are investigating the possibility that Richard Kraven did not act alone, and that his execution may have triggered the beginning of a new wave of murders, with Kraven's accomplice now acting by himself. The same sources also refused to discuss rumors that in light of Miss Davis's career as a prostitute, the long-disbanded task force investigating the Green River murders might be reconstituted. Police are, for the moment, treating the Capitol Hill slaying as an isolated event, and are so far refusing to entertain the possibility that it could mark the first incident in a new wave of serial killings. In the meantime . . .

The man felt utter rage when he read Anne Jeffers's article in the paper that morning. For one thing, it had been buried deep in the second section, when it clearly belonged on the front page. After all, it was a murder *he* had committed, and it had been every bit as gruesome as any that Richard Kraven had ever performed.

Hadn't he done it the very same way?

Hadn't he cut open the girl's chest and hacked out her heart and lungs?

But the other murders made the front page, while his had barely shown up at all.

And he knew why. It was the reporter, Anne Jeffers. She didn't think he was important enough. That was why she hadn't put any of her stories about Shawnelle Davis where they belonged. He'd stewed about it for more than an hour, his anger growing steadily.

A little before nine the idea had come to him.

He had to get Anne Jeffers's full attention.

And he knew exactly how to get it:

He would find out where she lived, and the next time he did something, he'd leave her a little souvenir.

Something on her doorstep . . .

Picking up the phone book, he flipped through the pages then ran his finger down a column until he found it. He could barely believe it—the bitch reporter lived right up the street from him!

Before he even thought about what he might do when he got there, the man set out, quickly walking north. It wasn't long before he emerged from the district of shabby apartment buildings around Group Health into the slightly less run-down area that bordered the better neighborhood where Anne and Glen Jeffers lived.

He walked past the Jeffers house on the other side of the street, gazing at it almost surreptitiously. It was large, and stood at the top of a slope, well back from the sidewalk.

And it had a large porch.

Large enough so that he could toss something onto it from the curb if he had to. He wouldn't even have to risk approaching the house, which might leave footprints, or something else that could identify him.

The man walked up the street another block, circled around a second block, then started back toward home, still on the opposite side of the street from the Jeffers house.

He was almost abreast of it when someone emerged from the house next door.

A woman, stepping out onto her front porch to pick up the morning paper.

The man stared at her high-piled blond hair, her overbright makeup, and her green and yellow dress.

Cheap.

Just like Shawnelle Davis.

Now a new idea—an even better idea—was developing in his head.

When the woman disappeared back into her house a moment later, the man remained, rooted to the spot, studying the house, then moved around to view the structure from the alley behind.

Several times the man left the area. But drawn to the house next to Anne Jeffers's like a moth to a flame, he kept coming back.

Finally, in midafternoon, the woman came out again.

She started down the sidewalk, and the man followed her.

He followed her all the way to the Group Health complex and into the emergency room on Thomas Street.

He pushed through the main doors after her, pausing in the foyer just long enough to see her take her place at the reception desk and slip her nameplate into a holder: JOYCE COTTRELL.

The name fixed in his memory, the man pushed deeper into the hospital, moving through the corridors until he came to the main entrance in the new wing facing Sixteenth. Leaving the building, he crossed Sixteenth and was soon back home. He picked up the telephone book again.

There she was, Joyce Cottrell, listed with an address on Sixteenth Avenue North. Right next door to the Jefferses.

The man dialed the number, let it ring twenty times, and hung up.

For the rest of the afternoon and through the evening the man kept calling the number, never getting an answer. Each time he dialed, his confidence grew. By nine-thirty, when he left his apartment to walk the few blocks north for the second time that day, he knew what he would find.

A dark house, totally empty.

But when he got there, the house was not dark at all. Lights glowed in two of the downstairs rooms and one of the upstairs ones.

The man lingered on the sidewalk across the street, watching. And then, at exactly ten, one of the downstairs lights went off, as did the upstairs one, and another light upstairs came on. All at the same instant.

The man smiled. Either three people inside all had thrown light switches at exactly the same moment, or the lights were on a timer.

Walking quickly over to Volunteer Park, the man found a pay phone by the conservatory. He dialed Joyce Cottrell's phone number one final time.

As before, the phone rang on and on but no one picked it up.

Joyce Cottrell lived alone.

Returning to the empty house, he began looking for a way to get inside.

Within less than a minute he'd found it.

Joyce Cottrell had never moved the extra key from the hiding place where her mother had always left it, under the mat on the back porch. Just like his own mother and hundreds of thousands of others.

The man liked Joyce Cottrell's house. It was much bigger than any house he'd ever been in before—big enough that his entire apartment could have been put into just its living room—though it wasn't at all what he'd expected it to be. Shawnelle Davis's apartment had looked just as he would have imagined a whore's place to look—the furniture had been as cheap-looking as Shawnelle herself. But Joyce Cottrell had nice furniture, and everything looked clean and fresh, like it was brand-new.

The man prowled slowly through the house, looking at everything, touching only one thing. Then, as it grew close to the time when Joyce Cottrell would come home from work, he slipped into the master bedroom.

As he waited in her closet for Joyce to come up to her room, his nose was filled with the scent of sachet. The lavender sweetness instantly triggered a memory from when he was a little boy.

His mother's closet had smelled like this.

He inhaled deeply, immediately transported back to a day long ago when he had gone into his mother's closet to play dress-up in her shoes, doing his best to balance on her high heels.

She had caught him.

Caught him, and spanked him, even though he'd been very careful not to touch any of her clothes or hurt the shoes.

He'd been forbidden ever to go into his mother's room again, closed out of her bedroom as coldly as he'd been closed out of the rest of his mother's world.

Now, as the man listened to Joyce Cottrell's footsteps coming up to the second floor, his temples throbbed with rage.

Pressing his eye to the crack in the door he had left slightly ajar, he watched Joyce undress, his anger growing with each passing second.

The fingers of one hand clutched the knife the man had brought up from the kitchen; his other hand unconsciously stroked the hardness that had grown between his legs.

By the time Joyce Cottrell had stripped down to her underwear and moved to the closet to hang up her dress, the man was ready.

Today, Joyce Cottrell had seen a naked man in the backyard next door.

Tonight, she found a fully-clothed one waiting in her closet.

The one in the backyard next door had been holding a broken shaver.

The one in her closet was grasping a knife. But all Joyce saw as she pulled her closet door open was a glint of light reflecting off the long blade that hovered above her, and a pair of eyes, flashing with the pent-up fury the man had been suppressing so long.

"Love me!" he commanded as the knife slashed down to plunge deep into Joyce Cottrell's breast. "Just love me!"

Joyce Cottrell died before the man's words registered in her mind, collapsing to the bedroom floor like a sagging balloon.

Now, fully caught up in his fantasy, seeing his mother's face instead of Joyce's, the man set to work. Laying open Joyce Cottrell's chest, tearing at her heart, his rage poured forth. He talked as he worked, saying all the things to Joyce Cottrell that he had never been able to say to his mother.

Finally, the hardness between his legs no longer to be denied, the man pulled down his pants and mounted Joyce Cottrell's body, barely able to keep from screaming out in ecstasy as for the first time in his life he experienced sexual release.

The Experimenter's eyes bored into the darkness.

The night was silent, yet something had awakened him. Even during the times when most men wouldn't have been able to sleep at all, the Experimenter had always been able to close his eyes to the world beyond his own mind, to retreat within himself to rest undisturbed.

But tonight some outside force—a force over which he had no control—had roused him. With the silence of a phantom, he explored the upper floor, but all he could hear was the slow, steady breathing of the family who lay in their beds, sleeping in peace, blissfully unaware of his presence. At the top of the stairs he paused, not out of any sense of indecision, but to collect data with his acutely honed senses.

Whatever had awakened him was not in the house, for other than the normal creaks and groans of an ancient structure shifting uncomfortably in the night, all was quiet. Satisfied that whatever had roused him from his rest was beyond the protecting walls, he moved down the stairs and through the rooms of the lower floor, gazing out the windows into the comparative light of the urban night, searching for . . . something. If he saw it—even sensed it—he would recognize it at once. But all was quiet beyond the windows; nothing moved; he felt no hidden presence lurking in the shadows.

Yet something had awakened him. He would not rest until he had identified that which had intruded into his sleep.

He moved into the kitchen, then out onto the back porch. The night air was cool against his skin, and unbidden memories of other times when he'd stood naked in the cool of the night flooded into his mind.

Nights when, his experiment finished but the ruined remains of his subject still to be disposed of, he'd stepped out of his laboratory into the refreshing cool of the night, sometimes to vent his frustration at failure in a howl of rage; sometimes simply to wash himself in the river even before beginning the tedious—but very necessary—clean-up process.

Sometimes, though, he'd simply stood naked beneath the eternity of stars sparkling above him, feeling like a newborn child of the universe, his skin glittering darkly with a glowing sheen of blood released only moments earlier from the heart of his latest subject. On those nights he would suck hungrily at the cold night air as if by inhaling deeply enough he might somehow take in enough of the life-sustaining oxygen to support not only himself, but also the ruined body that still lay inside the motor home. But even as he filled his lungs, he'd always known that oxygen was not enough. Without the spark, without the black, invisible lightning that emanated from somewhere deep within the body itself, no amount of air put back into his subject's lungs could restore its body to life. That was when despair always overcame him, when the cool of the night air that had felt like the caress of a lover only a moment earlier became a dark cloak concealing an unseen enemy.

Tonight, though, the darkness was neither lover nor enemy. Tonight it was an enigma, bearing within its folds something that he needed to discover.

He stood still, waiting.

He felt the night, all his senses reaching out, searching for some clue as to exactly what had awakened him. Then, out of the steady drone of insects, frogs and traffic, a new sound emerged.

A latch clicking.

Hinges creaking.

Another latch opening.

A spring stretching, then the soft clack of a screen door striking wood siding.

Next door.

Though no light showed, someone was coming out of the house next door.

The Experimenter stood motionless, the patience of a scientist serving him now. No need to turn, no need to move at all. All he need do was wait, concealed in the dark shadows of the porch.

Soon, the source of his disturbance would reveal itself.

He had not long to wait, for within less than half a minute he heard the heavy tread of thick-soled shoes on wooden steps feeling their way tentatively through the darkness. The mind of the Experimenter automatically began applying the laws of logic. Whoever was descending the steps next door was not familiar with them, had not become accustomed to their width or their height.

Ergo, whoever it was did not belong there.

Perhaps that had been what awakened him; the unexpected sound of someone forcing entry to the house next door. From long experience he knew that it was possible to sleep through any noise, as long as it was an expected norm, while an unexpected sound could banish sleep instantly from an attentive mind. As long as he had existed he had been in possession of an attentive mind. Yet still he did not move, for now his interest was piqued. He hung in the shadows of the night like a phantom, waiting for the intruder to show himself.

A dark figure appeared, carrying a burden which for a moment was nothing more than a gray and shapeless mass barely visible in the blackness that surrounded it. But as the figure moved farther from the house, it came closer to the dim light that glowed above a narrow alley. In this no-man's-land between two rows of opposing backyards, the intruder became more visible.

It was a man. The burden he bore was instantly recognizable to the watcher from the darkness.

A body.

A human body, held clumsily, with no wrappings to prevent blood from dripping to the ground.

As the figure carried the body closer to the alley, closer to the light, every muscle in the Experimenter's body tensed.

The body had been stripped naked, just as he himself had always denuded the bodies of his subjects.

The chest had been laid open, but the surgery had not been neatly done. Rather, the thoracic cavity seemed to have been clumsily hacked open. Even from where he stood, the Experimenter could see that one of the woman's large breasts had been all but cut away.

But the man who bore the naked body was fully clothed, and even in the badly lit alley, the Experimenter could make out the crimson stains of blood spread across the bearer's shirt and oozing down his pants.

The Experimenter watched, and felt contempt, but still his mind worked, and slowly a logic began to form, though it was a logic with so many missing pieces that it could barely be called logic at all.

The body was naked.

The chest torn open.

Very roughly, if viewed through the eye of the ignorant, parallel to the end result of his own experiments.

Today there had been an article in the paper about the dead prostitute—what was her name? Shawnelle Something-or-other—the article written by the woman who lived in this very house, who was even at this moment asleep upstairs.

In her article, Anne Jeffers had suggested the Shawnelle killing might be a copy-cat of his own work.

The police had denied it.

If they were wrong, if the man who was now bearing his handiwork away wanted to draw full attention to what he was doing, how better than to strike next door to the reporter who was recording his deeds? But why was he literally leaving behind a trail of blood? It made no sense, unless the man unconsciously wanted to be caught.

Then, a moment later, the dim light suspended above the alley fell full on the bearer's face, and the Experimenter instantly recognized him.

The pieces of the puzzle fell into place. The Experimenter, fury raging within him, retreated back into the house.

Anne Jeffers's body had a leaden feel to it, as if, despite all evidence to the contrary, she hadn't slept at all. Yet she knew she had, for she clearly remembered that the last time she looked at the clock it had been ten-thirty. She'd been upset, and while not exactly angry at Glen, she'd certainly been worried about him. But in the gray light of the morning, as she gazed down at his sleeping face, nothing seemed amiss. In sleep he looked exactly as he always had, his face clear and unlined, his lips curved into a slight smile at the corners, as if he were enjoying some happy dream. When he stirred a moment later and the faint smile faded away, all Anne's apprehensions from the previous night came flooding back. Instinctively she froze, as if by remaining motionless she could forestall his awakening.

What kind of thought was that?

Always—or at least until his heart attack—early mornings had been among Anne and Glen's favorite times. Even when the kids had been too young to leave alone in the house and they had to jog separately, they still always found a few minutes just to enjoy being alone together, the rest of the world not yet intruding on them. While Glen was in the hospital, it had been the mornings with him she'd missed most. But now, though he was finally home, everything had changed.

Last night she hadn't even wanted him to touch her.

This morning, sensing him awakening, she actually tried to put the moment off. Feeling ashamed, and guilty, Anne leaned over and gently kissed her husband's lips.

Immediately, Glen's arm circled around her, pulling her close, and his lips responded to hers. For just the tiniest instant Anne felt a pang of something that was almost indistinguishable from fear, but she knew that was ridiculous. This was Glen, for God's sake! Still, she had to force herself not to pull away from him, not to withdraw from his touch. She made herself relax, and then, as she felt his tongue gently prodding her lips, she found herself responding to him, and when her body melted against his a moment later, she no longer had to make herself let it happen. This morning, as his fingers slipped under the thin material of her nightgown, his caress felt as it always had—exciting, but at the same time warm and familiar. Now her own arms slipped around him and her lips pressed his, their bodies joining with tiny noises that mixed equal parts of passion and contentment.

Glen made love to Anne with an easy familiarity that both excited and reassured her. The Glen she had loved, the Glen that she had only a few hours ago feared might be gone from her forever, was here again. When it was over, Anne curled up in the crook of his arm, sighing with contentment. "Nice to have you back," she whispered.

Glen's arm tightened around her. "What do you mean? It's not like I just came home this morning."

Anne rolled out of his embrace, then propped herself up on one elbow to look at his face. "But it's the first time I've actually felt as though you were really back," she said.

Glen's eyes clouded, but then he smiled. "I guess maybe I have been acting kind of strange, huh?"

"Kind of?" Anne echoed. "How about off the wall?" Glen's smile disappeared, and Anne wished she could recall her words. But it was already too late—the brief moment of closeness, of feeling as if everything was back the way it should be, was over. "All right, maybe 'off the wall' is a little strong," she offered in an attempt to put things right. "But you have to admit, all that stuff you bought—"

"I don't have to admit anything," Glen cut in, sitting up and swinging his legs off the bed. "All I'm trying to do is what the doctor ordered. Everyone says fishing's a great hobby, so I thought I'd try it. Okay?"

"*Okay,*" Anne agreed, more than willing to drop the whole subject if only she could recapture the closeness she'd felt only a few moments before. But the moment had vanished, replaced with a resurgence of that amorphous anxiety she'd felt when she came home last night—the terrible sensation that something unidentifiable was wrong. She slid off her side of the bed, grabbed her robe from the chair in the corner, and disappeared into the dressing room as Glen went into the bathroom.

By the time he was finished washing his face, she'd pulled on her jogging clothes. As she sat in the chair tying her shoelaces, she felt him watching her. When she looked up, though, his expression was unreadable, and when he offered to go jogging with her, she shook her head. "Gordy said you should be walking. He didn't say anything about running." But what she really meant was, *I'd rather go by myself,* and she could see in his eyes that he'd read her meaning as clearly as if she'd simply spoken those words instead of the excuse she'd come up with. "You're not supposed to rush this, remember?" she added, then tried to take the sting out of her rejection with a kiss. His lack of response told her she'd failed, and for a moment she wondered if she ought to ask him to come along after all.

But she knew what would happen—they'd run in silence, trying to pretend a closeness they weren't feeling right now, and by the time she got to work, she'd be so consumed with worrying about what was happening to them that she wouldn't be able to concentrate. Better just to go alone, she thought, and try again tonight. "Have a cup of coffee ready for me when I get back?" Anne asked. He nodded, and she headed downstairs.

Boots was waiting by the front door, holding his leash in his mouth, looking as though his entire life would be ruined if she didn't take him along. "Oh, all right," she said, snapping the leash onto the little dog's collar and opening the door. "But if you can't keep up, don't expect me to carry you." She bounded off the porch and started up to the corner where she would turn left toward Volunteer Park, then turned back and glanced up at the master bedroom, intending to wave to Glen if he were watching her.

He wasn't.

Tossing her head as if the action might rid her of the dark mood fast enveloping her, she increased her pace to a fast jog. Maybe this morning she'd just take an extra lap or two around the reservoir.

It had rained sometime before dawn. The streets glistened and the early morning air was still heavy with moisture. Anne expanded her lungs exuberantly, sucking in the fresh, cold air, and increased her pace slightly as she crossed Fifteenth Avenue and started into the park, up the gentle incline that led to the greenhouse. From there she could either go straight ahead over the crest, then start down past the tennis courts in the large lower loop that would eventually take her all the way around to the water tower, or she could turn left toward the old Art Museum, jogging easily along the level road that ran south from the greenhouse. Then, when she got close to the reservoir that surmounted the park, she could head off onto the path that led around it, level all the way, where the serious joggers always ran, pacing themselves carefully, monitoring pulse and respiration, some of them spending as much as two hours of every morning in a valiant—if inevitably doomed—effort to keep their bodies in prime condition. Though Anne had only fallen partially prey to the seductive idea that regular exercise could somehow put a stop to the aging process, she knew that after running for half an hour or so she would feel better, if not from the pheromones she only occasionally succeeded in getting high on, then at least from a feeling of virtue, misplaced though it may have been.

How many times had she and Glen observed that the country would be far better off if the population were half as interested in keeping their minds in as good condition as they tried to keep their bodies? And, so far as Anne could see, everyone kept getting older, albeit with ruined knees and ankles which, after years of unnatural abuse, were eventually only marginally capable of propelling them on their morning jogs. The Seattle addiction to coffee, she decided, was a healthy antidote to the overconditioning of the local bodies.

Opting finally for the track around the reservoir because she could do more laps with less effort than if she chose the lower circumference road, Anne started around the north side of the artificial lake, nodding to a few of the regulars she saw out here every morning.

Boots, happily matching her pace with his own near-run, made half-hearted leaps at a couple of people he apparently felt had come too close to his mistress, but generally behaved himself until Anne had made the turn around the northwest corner of the reservoir. Instead of turning with her, he went straight ahead, pulling the leash until, after almost twelve feet had paid out, he was jerked to a stop.

Anne, startled by the sudden tug on the leash, broke stride and wheeled around to reprimand the little animal. But the moment he felt the leash slackening, Boots's stubborn terrier ancestry came to the fore and he pulled the leash taut again, straining, with the stocky body he'd inherited from the bulldog branch of his family tree, toward the thick tangle of vegetation that covered the reservoir's bank. Now he was barking insanely.

"Heel, Boots," Anne commanded.

For just a second the little dog glanced back at her, but then he resumed his struggle against the leash. The two of them stayed in place for nearly a minute, Anne commanding the dog to heel, Boots refusing to budge. In the end, knowing she was ruining whatever minimal training Kevin and Glen might have succeeded in inculcating into the little animal's head, Anne gave in. "Oh, all right. If it's that important to you, pick whatever spot you want."

Letting the dog have his head, she followed, already reaching into her pocket for one of the blue plastic bags she used to clean up after her son's pet. But instead of sniffing madly around until he'd found the perfect place to squat, Boots pulled harder and harder, his body low to the ground as he scrambled toward the brow of the hill. Then he was over the edge of the steep embankment, disappearing from Anne's view for a moment, but at last falling silent, his mad barking dying away as he apparently reached whatever goal he'd set for himself.

When she came to the edge of the lawn where the level area around the reservoir gave way to the slope and a tangle of brush, the dog was nowhere to be seen. Then she spotted him. He'd pushed into the mass of vegetation and was sniffing eagerly at something she couldn't quite see.

Reaching out and pushing a branch aside, Anne looked down.

The dead, empty eyes of Joyce Cottrell gazed back up at her.

Anne's first instinct was to be sick, but she refused to give in to the wave of nausea.

Her next instinct was to try to help the woman whom she'd instantly recognized as her next-door neighbor, but even as the urge rose in her she knew Joyce was far beyond any aid she could give her.

Her third instinct was to scream for help, and that was the instinct she finally acted upon.

"Where's Mom?" The question was issued with a darkly accusatory tone, as if Kevin suspected his mother had been abducted, if not out and out murdered.

"She's just jogging in the park," Glen told him as he poured his son a glass of orange juice, then moved the Grape-Nuts from the cupboard to the kitchen table.

"She's supposed to be back by now," Kevin informed him.

Glen glanced at the blue-green digits on the oven clock. Though he wasn't about to admit it to his son, he realized that Kevin was right. Before his heart attack, their jog had usually lasted no more than half an hour—forty-five minutes at the most. Unless the digital display was wrong, Anne had been gone more than an hour. He was pretty sure he knew why, but he wasn't about to get into that with Kevin. Both he and Anne subscribed to the idea that even if their marriage wasn't perfect—not that it was far short—they had no need to air their dirty laundry in front of the kids. Besides, even if he'd been willing to explain to Kevin what had happened between himself and Anne that morning, he wasn't quite sure he could. The truth was, he wasn't certain himself. When he woke up and found her looking at him, he thought she was still angry at him from the night before. But then they'd made love, and for a few minutes it seemed as though everything was back to normal. Then, when she suggested that he'd been acting "off the wall," he'd flown off the handle. He shook his head. It wasn't as if she was wrong—he knew perfectly well that he hadn't been behaving very much like the man she'd married. Yet instead of confessing to the unaccountable blackouts—

and that they were frightening him—he'd barked that he was just obeying his doctor's orders and that there was nothing wrong at all. It wasn't that he hadn't wanted to tell her. Indeed, in those few quiet minutes after they made love, he'd been rehearsing the words he would say.

Only when it came time to speak, something inside had stopped him, some voice inside his head had whispered to him: *Do you want to go back to the hospital? Do you want her to think you're crazy?* The warning stopped him cold, even knowing he was shutting Anne out, lying to her, refusing to trust her.

Of course she hadn't wanted him to go jogging with her, and of course she had decided to take an extra turn around the reservoir. He could almost hear her telling herself to run her anger out in the park instead of taking it home and dumping it on her family. If she could leave the bad moment in the park, the least he could do was be dressed and have breakfast ready for her by the time she got back, so she'd at least know she wasn't married to an invalid who was planning to lie around in a bathrobe for the rest of his life.

"She'll probably be back by the time you finish your cereal," Glen told Kevin as Heather came into the kitchen. She poured herself a cup of coffee and started working on the crossword puzzle Glen himself had begun only a few minutes earlier. "Do you mind?" he asked his daughter. "I was planning to do that crossword this morning."

Heather shrugged. "So far, you only put in two words, and one of them was wrong. Besides, if you don't do it in ink, it doesn't count."

"Something's happened to Mom," Kevin announced.

Heather looked up, glancing at her brother then turning to her father. "Is she sick?"

Glen sighed exaggeratedly and retrieved the crossword from his daughter. "Nothing's happened to her. She's fine. She just decided to jog a little longer than usual this morning, that's all."

"They had a fight," Heather instantly translated for Kevin.

"We didn't have a fight," Glen told her. "How come nobody around here ever believes anything?"

"Because grown-ups always lie to kids," Kevin informed him. "Justin Reynolds told me so. And how come Mom's allowed to go to the park by herself, when I'm not?"

"Because she's a grown-up," Glen replied, leaning toward Kevin and giving him a mock-fierce glare. "You can tell Justin Reynolds that that's another thing grown-ups do."

Kevin began to giggle, but then Heather spoke again.

"Maybe we better go look for her," she said. "She's never gone this long. What if something *has* happened to her?"

Glen felt the balance of power in the room tilt. In about five more seconds, unless Anne came walking in the door, Kevin would team up with Heather and he might as well give up. Better to offer an instant compromise rather than wind up having them late for school. "I'll tell you what—I'll go take a look, while you two finish your breakfast. But I suspect that your mom will come breezing in ten seconds after I'm gone, and I'll just be on a wild goose chase."

Before Kevin could plead with him to come along, Glen was out the back door and behind the wheel of the ten-year-old Saab he refused to part with despite Kevin's insistence that it was a "dweebmobile."

Minutes later he entered Volunteer Park from the Fifteenth Avenue side, just as Anne had a little more than an hour earlier. Until he reached the greenhouse, everything looked normal, but as he started down the gentle grade past the tennis courts, he saw the first of what turned out to be five police cars. A little farther down he spotted the familiar yellow plastic tape marking a police barricade. The tape ran along the left side of the road, blocking entrance to the shrubbery that covered this flank of the reservoir. Glen slowed to a stop as he came abreast of a cop who was impatiently trying to wave him through.

"Keep it moving, Mac," the cop said as Glen rolled his window down. "Nothing to see here."

"I'm looking for my wife," Glen said, ignoring the policeman's words. "She came out jogging a little over an hour ago, and she hasn't come back yet."

The patrolman's expression changed from impatience to uncertainty, and he unclipped a radio from his belt, speaking into it too quietly for Glen to hear what he was saying. When he'd gotten a reply, he turned his attention back to Glen. "What's your wife's name?"

"Anne Jeffers. She's a report—"

The patrolman's expression shifted again. "She's up there," he said, jerking his thumb toward the crest of the hill. "I can't let you go up this way, but if you want to walk around from the other side, I don't suppose anyone's going to stop you."

"What happened?" Glen asked.

The cop shook his head. "Body. Fact is, I heard your wife found it."

"Gay bashing?" Glen asked, aware that more than one man had been beaten in this part of the park over the last few years.

The cop shook his head. "A woman."

For some reason, an image of Joyce Cottrell flashed into Glen's mind, then was gone almost as quickly as it had come. As another police car pulled up behind, briefly flashing its lights, Glen moved on, completing the circuit around the reservoir and the water tower, then pulling the Saab into an empty space near the huge black granite doughnut that stood across the street from the Art Museum.

Locking the car despite the fact that there were half a dozen more police cruisers within the surrounding fifty yards of roadway, Glen crossed the sidewalk and loped down the short slope. A well-worn path followed the chain-link fence that kept swimmers out of the reservoir. Halfway around, another police tape blocked his way, but before he could decide what to do next, he spotted Anne. Boots was sitting at her feet. As he approached, the little dog caught his scent, barked happily and dashed toward him, only to do a complete back flip as he came to the end of the leash. Unfazed by the mishap, the terrier scrambled back to its feet, straining at the leash, his tail wagging furiously. Anne turned to quiet the dog, caught sight of Glen, and waved him over. Scooping Boots up and cradling him in the crook of one arm, Glen slipped the other protectively around his wife. "What's going on?" he asked.

For a moment Anne said nothing at all. Suddenly Glen realized how pale she was—every drop of blood seemed to have drained from her face. But Anne had seen corpses before—accident victims, even the butchered remains of the brutal Kraven killings; she'd even wondered out loud from time to time if she wasn't becoming insensitive to the violence of the city. Then she spoke, and with a rush of horror, he understood. "It's Joyce, Glen," she said, her voice barely above a whisper. Glen felt a cold knot form in his stomach as he remembered the image that had inexplicably come to him the moment the patrolman at the foot of the hill had told him the body of a woman had been found. But it was crazy—what would Joyce Cottrell have been doing in the park? She rarely even left her house except to go to work!

"Oh, God, Glen, it's horrible. She was naked, and her chest was all torn open, just like Shawnelle Davis's. But they say it didn't happen here. It looks like whoever killed her dumped her here after she was already dead. So it must have happened in her house, Glen." Anne's voice was shaking now, her body shivering. "Right next door to us, while we were sleeping. Oh, God . . ."

Glen's arm tightened around his wife, partly to offer her support, but as much to support himself. For now another image had flashed into his mind.

He saw a figure carrying a body through the dark.

Light was spilling onto the face of the figure so it was clear in his mind, as vivid as if he were staring at a clearly focused black-and-white photograph. But he didn't recognize the face.

It was the face of a stranger, and the stranger was carrying Joyce Cottrell's body.

Though the image was nearly perfect, there was no familiarity to go with it, no sense of recollection. Was it possible he had witnessed a murder but had no memory of it?

Now he remembered the blackouts he'd had, the time that seemed forever lost from his consciousness.

Glen stood mutely listening to Anne as she brokenly described how Boots had led her to their next-door neighbor's corpse, how she hadn't been certain what the object in the bushes was at first, how she'd finally seen the face and recognized it.

Joyce Cottrell.

Someone who had no friends. No enemies.

Someone no one even knew.

Why had Joyce been killed?

Neither of them could answer that question. Still, though neither of them spoke the thought aloud, Anne and Glen each had a terrible feeling: somehow, in a way neither of them had yet begun to understand, this murder had something to do with *them*.

The man called in sick for the second day in a row. He'd intended to go to work this morning, for even though they didn't appreciate him at Boeing, he still took his job seriously.

Just as he took everything seriously.

But when he got home last night, he'd been far too excited to go to sleep right away. Instead of going to bed, he'd stayed up, reliving the event in his memory over and over again.

Relishing the memory of being in Joyce Cottrell's house.

Of waiting for her.

Of watching her undress.

Of killing her, and possessing her.

And finally, he'd relished the memory of the feeling he'd had as he carried her through the night. Bearing her out of her house and up to the park, the man had felt a freedom and exhilaration he'd never experienced before. He'd *known* no one was going to see him as he carried her body through the darkness to the park, known it as surely as he knew he was going to kill Joyce Cottrell from the first moment he saw her. It was in those last moments when he'd held her in his arms in the darkness that the man finally felt complete. For the first time—much more than with Shawnelle Davis—he'd experienced the sheer sense of power and ecstasy that came with extinguishing another life. Joyce Cottrell had truly belonged to him, taken like a trophy, dying at his hands like the prey of a hunter.

He hadn't even tried to hide her body.

Indeed, that was why he'd taken it to the park, to make certain it was discovered early in the morning, when the joggers came out to run the path around the reservoir.

He'd left the park from the south side, walking down Twelfth Avenue to Aloha, then cutting over to Fourteenth. He'd stayed away from the bright lights of Fifteenth Avenue. After he'd deposited the body in the shrubs, he lost the feeling of power, of invincibility, and from then on ducked from one deeply shadowed area to another, feeling as if the light of the streetlamps were trying to expose him. The thick red stains on his clothes had gleamed brightly, and when it started to rain while he was still two blocks from home, he slowed his pace, letting the water wash the blood from his face and hands. Coming at last to the corner of Sixteenth and Thomas, he had to resist the temptation to step into the emergency room and see who had replaced Joyce Cottrell at the reception desk. But resist it he had, knowing that if the person even looked up, the sight of his soaked hair and bloodstained clothing would not be forgotten within a minute or two. In the morning, when the body was discovered, the first place the police would come would be here, to question whoever had relieved Joyce Cottrell, and the person would remember him.

So he passed the emergency room by, slipping instead into the musty, deserted lobby of the building in which he lived, making his way silently to his studio on the second floor.

In the morning, someone would find the body, and Anne Jeffers would report it in the *Herald*. This time it was her next-door neighbor he'd killed. This time, the bitch would put it on the front page.

The front page, where he belonged.

He'd stayed up all night, reveling in the remembered ecstasy of the killing. By dawn he knew he would be too tired to go to work. Too tired, and too excited. He waited until precisely six, the time he normally got up, and then called the plant, telling them he was feeling better than yesterday but that he wasn't well enough yet to come to work. They told him to take as much time as he needed. And why wouldn't they? After all, he wasn't like some of the others at work who called in sick every time they wanted to take an extra day off. This was only the second time he'd ever called in sick at all.

The call finished, he left his apartment and went over to the

7-Eleven on Fifteenth to get a cup of coffee and the first edition of the *Herald*. After all, it was possible that someone—perhaps one of the perverts who hung out in certain parts of the park at night—had found the body even before the joggers were out. He scanned the front page, assuaging his disappointment by telling himself that even if the body had been found right away, they might not have had time to get a story in the earliest edition. Still, he paged quickly through the whole paper, scanning each page.

Nothing.

But by the time he got back to his apartment, he wondered if he might have missed something, so he went through the paper again, this time studying each page carefully. When he turned to the last page, he felt a kind of relief. If he wasn't going to be on the front page, it was better not to be in the paper at all.

He turned on the television, thinking there might be a story on the morning news, then shut it off, afraid one of his neighbors might hear it and wonder why he was watching the news so early.

He began pacing nervously around the apartment. How soon would the next edition of the paper be out?

What if no one had found the body? If someone had found it and called the police, wouldn't there have been sirens when the cops went up to the park?

He hadn't heard any sirens.

When his cheap digital watch—his mother's lousy Christmas present last year—finally told him it was eight, he turned on the radio, tuning it to KIRO.

Endless talk about a press conference the President was going to be holding later that day.

The man went back to pacing the stained avocado carpeting that covered his floor, and wondered if anybody had found the body yet.

Maybe he should call the police himself.

He reached for the phone, then changed his mind. If he was going to do that, he'd better use a pay phone.

And not one near his house.

Maybe one over on Broadway. Or maybe he should even go downtown.

That was it. A phone down on First Avenue, where no one ever looked at anyone else. He was just about to leave, was just reaching out to switch off the radio, when he finally heard it:

> This report just in. A body has been found in the brush near the reservoir in Volunteer Park. In a bizarre coincidence, the nude and mutilated corpse was discovered by *Seattle Herald* reporter Anne Jeffers, well-known nationally for her coverage of the series of killings reputed to have been committed by Seattleite Richard Kraven. Police are withholding identification of the woman pending notification of relatives. More details at the top of the hour. In other stories . . .

The man was no longer listening. It was even better than he'd hoped for—Anne Jeffers herself had found the body! Now there was no question it would make the front page. Soon—very soon—he'd be famous. But of course for a while he wouldn't be able to enjoy seeing his name in the paper. After all, they didn't yet know who had killed Joyce Cottrell. And for a while—he wasn't sure yet exactly how long—he'd make sure they didn't find out who did.

Not until he'd killed at least two more people.

Maybe even three.

The newscaster's words still echoing in his head, the man thought feverishly.

How soon should he strike again?

A month?

A week?

Once again he felt the rush he experienced as he'd ravaged Joyce Cottrell's body, and now he shivered in anticipation. Perhaps he wouldn't wait even a week. Perhaps, now that he understood the pure joy and power of the act of killing, he'd strike again within a few days.

If he could find the right victim.

The man was still savoring the feeling, still reveling in the exaltation of what he'd done, when the phone rang. His hand trembling, he picked it up.

"Is that you?" he heard his mother's voice demand. "Why aren't you at work?"

The man felt his exhilaration begin to fade. "I called in sick, Mama."

"Well, I know *that*," his mother told him.

Why couldn't she use his name? Why couldn't she *ever* use his name, unless she was criticizing him to someone else?

"They told me that at Boeing," she went on. "Did you hear the radio this morning? That reporter found a body in Volunteer Park."

As the man listened numbly, his mother talked on and on. She was talking about *his* body, the woman *he'd* killed, but she wasn't talking about *him*!

Well, maybe one of these days he'd just stop her from talking about anything at all.

CHAPTER 36

Glen hadn't intended to waste two hours of the morning gossip-ing with his neighbors about Joyce Cottrell's death, but that was the way it turned out. When the first police car arrived to set up the yellow tape around Joyce's property, only a couple of people crossed the street to watch. Within ten minutes, though—and not merely coincidentally with the arrival of two more blue-and-whites and one unmarked sedan whose very plainness proclaimed it a police vehicle—a dozen people were clustered on the sidewalk. One of them finally came up and knocked on the Jefferses' front door. It was Marge Hurley, whose family had moved in across the street and three doors down four years ago. Marge had been unsuccessfully at-tempting to organize block parties ever since, as though operating under the illusion that Capitol Hill was the same kind of cozy cul-de-sac which she claimed to be fleeing when she left the great sub-urban morass of Lake Washington's Eastside.

Refusing to accept a simple statement that Anne had found Joyce Cottrell's body in Volunteer Park that morning, Marge drew Glen first out onto the porch, then into the midst of the crowd on the sidewalk. There, he found himself repeating the tale while his neigh-bors, having received no information from the police inside the house, proceeded to speculate about what might have happened. That Joyce Cottrell had been the neighborhood's best-known eccen-tric for years did not stand her in good stead now that she had been murdered. Her neighbors disassembled her character bit by bit, until soon someone suggested that she'd been dealing in drugs (perhaps stolen from the pharmacy at Group Health?) or perhaps even in pornography—now, *that* would certainly explain why she kept people out of her house! Once all the permutations of Joyce's possible venality had been thoroughly explored, speculation turned to the matter of who might have killed her. Immediate neighbors were instantly dismissed: "We all *know* each other in this neighborhood," Marge Hurley insisted after introducing herself to the dozen people she'd never met before.

At last, tired of the gossip and guesswork, Glen retreated to the quiet of his house, only to hear the doorbell ring a few minutes later. He ignored it at first, assuming it was Marge Hurley wanting him to repeat his tale of the body's discovery one more time, but the ringing was insistent. Finally he opened the door. A man with a police badge stood on the porch.

The man smiled. "So we meet at last." When Glen only looked at him blankly, the smile faltered and the man reddened slightly. "You *are* Glen Jeffers?" Glen nodded, but still said nothing. "I'm Detective Blakemoor. Mark Blakemoor?"

Finally, Glen got it. Pulling the door open, he gestured the detective into the foyer. "Anne's friend," he said. His eyes flicked toward the house next door and the crowd of onlookers, smaller now, whose attention had momentarily shifted from Joyce Cottrell's house to the Jefferses'. "But I assume this isn't a social call."

"I wish it were." Mark Blakemoor sighed. "I'm afraid I have to ask you a few questions about last night."

Glen nodded, and led the detective to the kitchen, where he poured them each a cup of coffee. "I'm not supposed to be drinking this, and I'm counting on you not to tell Anne. Deal?"

Mark Blakemoor felt himself blush, but Glen seemed not to notice. "Deal," he agreed, accepting the coffee. "Basically, I just need to know if you heard anything last night."

Glen hesitated. Instead of answering the question directly, he asked one of his own. "What time?"

Blakemoor shrugged. "No particular time," he said. "But we know the Cottrell woman left work at eleven, and walked home. Even if she stopped for coffee, she would have gotten home by midnight, probably a half hour earlier. So let's say any time after eleven-fifteen."

Still Glen hesitated, remembering the image of Joyce Cottrell that had come into his mind as soon as he'd heard a woman's body had been found in the park. Then he shook his head. "I wish I could help you, but I don't think I can. Was she killed in the house?"

"Upstairs, in her bedroom," Blakemoor told him. "There aren't any signs of a forced entry, but that doesn't mean much. A lot of people hide keys around their houses, and a whole lot of creeps know exactly where to look for them. What about friends? Did she have many?"

"None at all, that I know of," Glen replied. "If you talked to any of the people out on the sidewalk, you must already know that Joyce was an odd bird."

Mark Blakemoor's expression gave no clue to his thoughts. "Odd?" he asked blandly. "How do you mean?"

"Just—well, *odd.*" Glen floundered, wishing he hadn't used the word. "She was the kind of woman you assumed was living in a house full of trash. You know—saving everything, letting stuff pile up. She never seemed to go anywhere except work, and she sure never invited anyone into the house." He shrugged helplessly. "I guess we just assumed . . ." he began again, but his voice trailed off.

"Well, you assumed wrong," Blakemoor said, remembering the pristine condition of the interior of the house.

Pristine, anyway, except for the bloodstains. He had found them not only in the bedroom, where it was obvious that Joyce Cottrell had been killed and partially disemboweled, but through most of the rest of the house as well. The killer had made no attempt to keep her body from dripping blood as he carried her from the bedroom down the stairs, through the dining room and kitchen to the utility room, then out the back door. From there on, the rain had washed the trail away. "If anything, she was a neat freak."

"So much for Anne's and my judgment of character, huh?"

"A lot of people aren't what they seem to be," Mark Blakemoor observed. "But you still haven't told me if you heard or saw anything last night." Still Glen hesitated. This time Blakemoor picked up on it. "*Did* you hear something last night?" he pressed.

Glen started to shake his head, then changed his mind. Why not just tell the detective exactly what had happened? "I'm not sure," he said. "I don't think so, but on the other hand, something weird happened when I went up to the park to look for Anne this morning." As clearly as he could, he told Blakemoor exactly why he'd gone to the park, and about the strange image of Joyce Cottrell that had come into his mind the moment he heard that a woman's body had been found in the bushes.

"Any reason why you might have thought of her?" Blakemoor asked with studied casualness.

There was no way to keep from telling the detective the rest of the story. "Well, she *did* tell Anne she saw me out in the backyard yesterday," he said. "She claimed I was naked."

Blakemoor gazed steadily at him. "Your backyard, or hers?"

"Mine," Glen assured him. "But I wasn't naked."

The detective shrugged dismissively. "So what if you were? It's your backyard, isn't it?"

"But I *wasn't* naked," Glen insisted, though even as he uttered the words he knew they might not be true.

The detective let just the tiniest hint of a smile—a congenial smile—play around the corners of his lips. "So I guess you must have been pretty pissed at her, huh?" Glen opened his mouth to reply, then saw the direction the conversation was going. Abruptly he closed his mouth, and at the same time saw the faint smile disappear from Blakemoor's lips. "Weren't you pissed at her?" the detective repeated. "I know if someone accused me of something like that, I'd sure be mad as hell."

"Mad enough to kill her?" Glen asked. "Is that what you're suggesting?"

Blakemoor's expression hardened. "I'm not suggesting anything," he said. "I'm just asking questions."

"And I'm just answering them," Glen said. "And yes, I suppose I *was* pissed off at Joyce. But certainly not enough to have killed her."

"But you instantly thought of her this morning when you heard a body'd been found," Blakemoor reminded him. "Why?"

"That's what I'm trying to figure out," Glen said angrily. "But now I'm wondering if maybe I shouldn't call my lawyer. If you're going to accuse me of killing Joyce Cottrell—"

Blakemoor held up his hands as if to fend off the torrent of angry words. "Hey, slow down! I'm not accusing you of anything. And if you want to call your lawyer, go right ahead. We can call this talk off right now, if that's what you want. All I'm doing is looking for information. I'm not accusing anybody of anything."

Glen's lips twisted into a wry parody of a smile. " 'But anything I say can and will be used against me in a court of law'?" he asked, parroting the phrase he'd heard used on television so often it had become a cliché.

Blakemoor seemed to back off even further. "We only do a Miranda when we're arresting someone," he said tersely. "But you still have a right to have a lawyer present."

Glen thought it over quickly, and sensed that things were about to get out of hand. If he insisted on calling a lawyer, wouldn't that make him look guilty? But he *wasn't* guilty. He'd neither heard nor seen anything, let alone *done* anything!

But what about the blackouts?

What about yesterday, when he'd obviously gone out and dumped the shaver into the trash, although he had no memory of it?

If he'd done that—

He cut the thought off, seeing where it was going and not wanting to follow it.

Finally he made up his mind: he'd done nothing, and he didn't need a lawyer.

"All I was thinking was that there must have been some reason why I thought of Joyce this morning, and the only thing I can come up with is that maybe I *did* hear something last night, but just don't remember it. I mean, if I was sound asleep and I heard something, maybe in my subconscious I remembered it and put it together when I heard about the body. I mean, if I heard a noise when I was half asleep . . ." Once again Glen's words trailed off, and once again he wished he'd said nothing.

The two men's eyes met, and though neither of them said anything, the unspoken question hung between them: What if it wasn't just a noise that Glen didn't remember hearing? What if it was a scream?

What if it was a *killing*?

When Mark Blakemoor left the house a few minutes later, those questions had still not been asked.

But both men were wondering what the answers might be.

Body Found In Volunteer Park

Latest in New Series of Killings?

The nude and mutilated body of a woman was found in Volunteer Park early this morning. According to police, the victim, Joyce Cottrell, was slain in her Capitol Hill home sometime between 11:00 P.M. and 4:00 A.M. Though police are so far denying it, there appears to be a connection between last night's slaying and that of Shawnelle Davis . . .

"Oh, for God's sake," Vivian Andrews groaned, flopping back in her chair. She looked up from the monitor on her desk to glare impatiently through the window at the gray afternoon outside. Taking the kind of deep breath her mother used to tell her would help keep her temper under control, she grabbed the phone and stabbed the digits of Anne Jeffers's extension. Her fingers were already drumming impatiently on her desktop when Anne picked it up on the second ring. "My office," Vivian snapped. "Now." Dropping the phone back on the cradle, she shifted her attention to the monitor and the offending article she had pulled up from the file server only a few seconds before summoning Anne. By the time Anne appeared in her office, the editor had read through the entire article three times.

An equal number of deep breaths had done nothing for her temper, despite what her mother had taught her.

"What the hell is this?" Vivian demanded as Anne came into the small office and shut the door behind her.

Anne edged just far enough around the desk to catch a glimpse of the headline glowing on the editor's computer screen. "My story on—"

"I know what it is!" Vivian Andrews interrupted sharply. "What I want to know is what you *think* it is!"

Anne felt her temper rising at Vivian's tone, but she bit back the first reply that came to mind. For the moment, Vivian would tolerate no sarcasm but her own. "I intended it to be a simple report of the body I found this morning—" she began, but once again the editor cut her off. This time, though, Vivian softened her interruption of Anne's words by gesturing to a chair.

"Sit down, Anne."

Warily, knowing that Vivian often invited people to sit down only so that they would have a slight cushioning against the blast they were about to receive, Anne dropped onto the edge of the single uncomfortable chair the editor provided for visitors to her office.

Placing the tips of her fingers together in an unconscious gesture that invariably signaled trouble to whomever sat opposite her, Vivian glanced briefly at the offending article hovering on the screen, then sighed and dropped her hands onto the desktop. Though Anne gave no outward sign of it, she relaxed slightly; the change in her boss's body language was a sure sign that Vivian had decided on a softer approach than she'd originally planned. Vivian's next words, though, made Anne wish her editor had stuck with Plan A.

"You look terrible," she said. "Maybe you should take some time off."

"It hasn't been the easiest day," Anne replied. "Most of us don't really look forward to finding a body on their morning run, let alone having to write a story about it." As Vivian's eyes flicked toward the computer screen, Anne decided that while her editor might have chosen to avoid a direct approach, she wouldn't. And she would also risk a touch of sarcasm of her own. "I gather from your typically loquacious phone call that there's a problem?"

Vivian shrugged. "Maybe I ought to assign the story to someone else—"

This time it was Anne who interrupted. "On the same theory that
a lawyer who represents himself has a fool for a client?"

"You don't agree?" Vivian countered.

"I don't see the parallel."

Vivian leaned forward and her fingertips came ominously together
again. "Then let me elucidate for you," she said, putting just enough
emphasis on the word "elucidate" to make it sting like the tip of a
flicking whip. "It seems to me that your proper function in this particular story is interviewee rather than interviewer. As for the story itself, it reads far more like an editorial than even your usual stuff
does, and unless you have a lot more backup material than I suspect
you do, the whole thing reeks of supposition. You're supposed to
be a reporter, Anne. When I want opinion pieces from you, I'll let
you know."

Anne felt a vein in her forehead throbbing, and hoped it
didn't show. "Would you like to tell me exactly where the problems are?"

"The whole tenor bothers me. To begin with, I don't think you
should be suggesting this is a serial killing. Until the police see some
parallels between this Cottrell woman and—"

"This 'Cottrell woman' was my next door neighbor," Anne interjected, her voice rising in anger.

Vivian Andrews blinked. "Your neighbor?" she echoed. "Good
God, Anne, what are you doing? You found your neighbor dead in
Volunteer Park this morning, and you not only came to work, but
you wrote about it, too?"

"Writing about things like this is my job," Anne replied. "And as
for parallels between this and Shawnelle Davis, I think there are
plenty. For one thing, neither place seemed to be broken into—"

"Which proves nothing," Vivian cut in. "You know as well as I do
that half the people in the city still leave keys hidden all over the
place."

Anne dipped her head in acknowledgment of the criticism. "So
they do. But it goes a lot further than that. Both women were butchered in the same way. Their chests were cut open and their hearts

were cut out. Furthermore, they both lived on Capitol Hill, only a few blocks apart."

"And one of them was a hooker and the other worked at Group Health. One was in her thirties, the other in her fifties. You know as well as I do that serial killers stick to a type—"

"Richard Kraven didn't."

"And nothing was ever proven against him in this state," Vivian reminded her.

"Whether Richard Kraven was proven guilty in Washington State or not, he was a killer, and you know it as well as I do," Anne flared. "And I'm just as sure that whoever killed Shawnelle Davis also killed Joyce Cottrell."

"You were also sure that Shawnelle Davis's death was somehow connected to Richard Kraven," Vivian Andrews retorted. "I don't get it, Anne. What are you trying to prove here? It seems as though you want to have it every way possible. If the Davis and Cottrell murders are connected to the ones you claim Richard Kraven committed, where does that leave Kraven? You claim he was guilty, but now it sounds as if you think someone else did it."

"If he had an accomplice—"

"If he had an accomplice, don't you think he'd have cut a deal? Call me cynical if you want to, but I've been around long enough to know that the first thing most of these creeps do who get hit with a murder charge, is blow the whistle on their friends! And if that doesn't work, you pull a Menendez and blame the victims."

Anne sank back into the chair as if the air had just been let out of her. "I know." She sighed. "That's what makes me so crazy. I don't really believe Kraven had an accomplice. But I still think there's some kind of connection." Her eyes fixed on Vivian. "You haven't seen the bodies, Viv. And I'll admit I didn't see Shawnelle Davis's, but I saw pictures. It's weird—they're not like what Kraven did. They don't have that surgical quality about them, as if they'd been dissected, but the mutilation is basically the same. It's as if whoever killed Shawnelle and Joyce is trying to pick up where Kraven left off."

Vivian Andrews's lips pursed sourly. "That's not reporting, Anne. That's editorializing. And I don't think I can let it go on any longer."

She rummaged around on the cluttered surface of her desk, found what she was looking for and handed it to Anne. "I'll clean up your story and run it," she said, "but that's it. We run this paper on facts, not on speculation. So until something *real* happens that turns these two deaths into genuine serial killings, I want you to go to work on that."

Anne looked down at the piece of paper in her hand. It was a notice of a planning meeting for a proposed regional light-rail system that would stretch from Everett to Tacoma, a proposal that had been endlessly kicked around among various governmental agencies for most of a decade. Anne looked at Vivian with utter disbelief. "This?" she asked. "You're asking me to cover *this*?"

"I'm not asking at all," Vivian calmly replied. "I'm ordering you to."

CHAPTER 38

The house was quiet.

Glen was asleep.

The Experimenter was not.

He explored the house in a more leisurely fashion than he had before; yesterday, and in the days before that, he had felt a sense of urgency, a need to make preparations. But yesterday, much of what he required had been procured, purchased, and brought into the house while Glen slept, stored carefully away in the basement, ready for his use when the time was ripe.

But not yet.

He was out of practice, and until he could once again perform his experiments perfectly, he wouldn't perform them at all.

He had, after all, certain standards to maintain. Standards that had certainly not been maintained by the man he'd watched last night, the man who had carried a clumsily butchered victim through the darkness as if the simple absence of light would be enough to protect him from the consequences of what he had done.

It would not, of course. Soon—perhaps very soon—the Experimenter would administer a fitting punishment to the blundering imitator he had seen last night.

Today, though, he had other things to do. Today, while Glen slept and the house was quiet, he would begin brushing up on his skills, begin reacquiring the perfect manual dexterity he had lost in the years since events had required him to suspend his research. Thrilling to a growing sense of anticipation, the Experimenter finished his examination of the house, lingering only when he came to Anne

Jeffers's dresser. Opening each of the drawers, he ran his fingers over the soft satiny fabric of her lingerie.

In his mind he touched her skin.

A sigh built in the depths of his chest, and was finally expelled in a sound reminiscent of bellows fanning coals into fire. His fingers tightened for an instant, crushing the silk into a shapeless mass, but he quickly regained control of himself. Closing the drawer, the Experimenter left the room and went to the basement.

The purchases he'd made the day before—with the exception of the fishing rod Kevin had found—were hidden away in a battered footlocker he'd found supporting two boxes of dust-laden books. Moving the two boxes aside, taking care not to disturb the layer of dust that covered their tops, the Experimenter opened the trunk and took out several items: some nylon line, a spool of strong silken thread, some fishhooks, and a book. Carrying the items to the long workbench that stood against one of the basement's walls, he set the items down and pulled the string that hung from the fixture suspended from the joists above. The light flickered for a second or two, then a bright fluorescent glow swept away the cellar's shadowy gloom.

The Experimenter opened the book. It was a manual on fly-fishing, the hobby he had so often used to soothe the frustration that engulfed him when his experiments ended in failure. He began leafing quickly through the book until he found the section on hand-tied flies, then slowly turned the color plates one at a time. Though it would have appeared to an observer that he was only giving the illustrations cursory glances, the truth was exactly the opposite. In the second or two it took him to scan a page, his eyes took in every detail of the two dozen flies each plate displayed.

The fly he was looking for was on the twelfth plate, the second photograph from the left in the third row.

On the page opposite the illustration was a brief paragraph describing how each fly had been made. The fly that caught his attention had been constructed from the feathers of a parakeet, augmented with a small tuft of cat fur, giving it the look of a winged caterpillarlike creature.

The Experimenter knew precisely where he could obtain the materials he would need to duplicate the fly.

Leaving the basement, he went upstairs to the second floor. Boots, growling softly as he passed through the kitchen, followed after him. In Kevin's room the parrot was in the process of removing the shell from a sunflower seed. Kumquat was sitting on Kevin's small desk, her tail wrapped around her feet as she gazed longingly at the parrot.

As the Experimentor came into the room, the bird paused in his eating, bobbing his head menacingly, as if to guard his food from the unexpected visitor.

The Experimenter's eyes fixed on the cat. "What do you think?" he asked. "Are you willing to volunteer a bit of that coat for a fishing fly?" The cat's ears pricked and her nose twitched. The Experimenter smiled. "Suppose we make a bargain: If the bird gives up a feather, then you ought to be willing to contribute a little fuzz, right?"

Moving closer to the parrot's cage, the Experimenter saw a feather lying on its floor. He opened the door and reached inside, but just as his fingers grasped the feather, Hector's beak closed on his thumb. Wincing at the pain, the Experimenter jerked his hand from the cage, shutting the door just in time to thwart Hector's second attack. "A little slow," the Experimenter observed while the bird ruffled its feathers and glared at him through the bars of the cage. "And after all, you pulled it out yourself, didn't you?" Turning to the cat, the Experimenter held the bright green feather high. "The bird has made his offering," he said. "And so shall you." Picking Kumquat up, he started back to the cellar.

Boots, whining nervously, followed.

At the far end of the workbench was a partially completed—and obviously abandoned—model of a three-masted schooner, a picture of which was still pinned to the wall above the hull. Around the hull, covered with dust, were various miniature tools that had been bought for the model ship, only to be forgotten along with the rest of the project. Gathering the tools together, the Experimenter moved them to an open area of the bench in preparation for his task. The book, propped open to display the fly he intended to duplicate, leaned against the wall.

Inserting a bare hook into a small device equipped with infinitely adjustable alligator clamps, the Experimenter set to work, appropriating glue from the model ship supplies to facilitate the attachment of fragments of Hector's feather to the fishhook.

Picking up an X-Acto knife, the Experimenter held it over the bright green feather. How long had it been since he'd tested his skill? But his hand was steady and the knife felt familiar. The fingers of his left hand held the feather flat on the workbench while his right hand expertly manipulated the X-Acto knife. In only a few minutes he had cut out four perfectly shaped pieces of feather, Each of them cut into a graceful contour identical to those shown in the book.

Barely pausing to admire what he'd done, the Experimenter continued working, his fingers deftly wrapping thread around the tiny stems of the scraps of feather, binding them to the shank of the hook with perfect dexterity.

Only when the feathers had been flawlessly placed on the hook did the Experimenter finally step back to gaze at the object he'd created. Though he'd applied a tiny bit of glue to the hook before fastening the feathers, none of it showed; not a single drop had oozed through the perfectly wound and knotted thread whose ends had magically disappeared beneath their own turns. Like the wings of a tiny butterfly, the fragments of Hector's plumage glittered in the bright fluorescent light, and already the Experimenter could see the finished fly flitting above the surface of a stream, floating on its tiny wings, luring a trout from the water's depths.

All that remained was to tie a tuft of Kumquat's fur to the hook, forming a nearly weightless body for the fanciful insect he'd constructed. Reaching down, the Experimenter picked up the cat once more and held it against his chest, turning so the cat's eyes would see the tiny object held in the alligator clamps. "Look at that," he crooned softly. "Isn't that pretty? You don't mind giving up a little fur just to finish it with, do you?"

Kumquat, as if sensing that something unpleasant was about to happen, stirred in the Experimenter's arms, and he tightened his grip. The cat, feeling the pressure of his fingers, struggled against the constraining force, and its heart began to beat faster.

The Experimenter's fingers began to tingle. He could feel energy flowing into him, an energy that was almost electric.

Life. He was feeling the energy of life itself, experiencing the force that transformed the animal in his hands from nothing more than a vastly intricate construction of elemental molecules into a living entity. And once again the question rose in his mind: *How does it work?*

The Experimenter gazed down at Kumquat. The cat struggled in his arms, trying to wriggle free from his grip, but the Experimenter's hands only closed more tightly.

Deep in his soul, the Experimenter knew it was time to begin his research again. It was almost as if the cat had been fated to come into his hands as a harbinger of his renascent career.

Scanning the basement, he spotted a cardboard box, its lid still intact. Placing Kumquat into the box, he moved through the basement, finding all the things he needed.

Some carbon tetrachloride. If he soaked a rag in the toxic chemical, and put the rag in the box with the cat, it would be almost as effective as the ether he'd sometimes used in the past.

A plastic drop cloth, apparently left over from some paint job. Spread out on the workbench, it would contain whatever blood the cat might spill.

The Experimenter took off his clothes, packing them carefully away in the footlocker until he was done.

When all the preparations were finally made, and the cat lay unconscious on the workbench, the Experimenter picked up the X-Acto knife. The soul of the Experimenter swelled with joy. Finally, he was taking up his work once more.

He worked slowly at first, relishing every movement, the techniques of dissection coming back to him as if it had been no more than a day since his last experiment, rather than years.

Deftly, he sliced through the skin of the cat's breast, stanching the flow of blood as best he could with the materials he had found.

He made a pair of transverse cuts, then laid the skin back, exposing the thin layer of tissue that covered the sternum and the rib cage. He pressed the trigger of the small Makita saw he'd purchased yesterday, its keening whine sounding to him as sweet as the familiar strains of a favorite symphony. With a steady hand, he lowered the blade, and savored the change in the saw's pitch as it sank into the cartilage and bone of the cat's breast. In no more than a few seconds the saw had sundered the rib cage, providing the Experimenter free access to the organ that had fascinated him for years.

Laying the saw aside, he spread the rib cage open and slipped his fingers between the lungs to touch the cat's heart. Gently, he worked the pulsing organ loose, lifting it up just enough to cup it in his palm. He watched its throbbing contractions, thrilling to the energy he could feel flowing through his skin.

At last he was working again.

And it felt good. So good.

Then an image came into his mind, an image of Anne Jeffers. Her face seemed to be suspended before him, and as he gazed into her eyes, the Experimenter's fingers closed around the still-throbbing heart in his hand. Just as when he'd held Anne's lingerie a little while ago, the Experimenter's grip on Kumquat's heart tightened.

As with the lingerie, he crushed the heart into a shapeless mass.

Shapeless, and lifeless.

CHAPTER 39

Being the center of attention wasn't all it was cracked up to be. When Heather first arrived at school, it had been great. Everybody already knew that a body had been found in the park early that morning, but only Heather had known who had actually found the body, and whose body it was that her mother had stumbled across.

"Except it wasn't really Mom who found her," she explained at least ten times even before the first class. "It was our dog."

Though she hadn't actually been there, Heather built a highly detailed image of the scene in her imagination. By the third telling she was able to recite it as vividly as if it had been she herself whom Boots had pulled off the trail and led over to Joyce Cottrell's maimed corpse. "He was tugging at the leash and barking like crazy, and finally Mom gave up and went to see what he'd found." Heather felt a delicious shiver as she repeated the story her father told her when he'd gotten back from the park. "And then, when she saw who it was, she nearly *fainted!*" Though her father hadn't actually said that, Heather was sure it must be true, because every time she tried to imagine what it would have been like to find Mrs. Cottrell's body under one of the bushes in the park, she felt a wave of dizziness. Of course, her mom hadn't actually fainted, since that would have prevented her from calmly finding a phone, calling the police, and then guarding the body until the authorities arrived, all of which Heather was pretty sure her mother had done.

"But who *was* it?" someone would invariably ask as soon as Heather let it be known that her mother had recognized the victim.

"Our next door neighbor," Heather would reply. Then she would begin doling out the details of Joyce Cottrell's life.

During first period it had been terrific. Everyone wanted to talk to her, and even hunky Josh Whitman passed her a note asking if she wanted to have lunch with him. But by third period, when Heather was almost five minutes late because people kept asking her questions even after the bell rang, she was starting to tire of telling the story. By lunchtime, when it became totally clear that the only reason Josh Whitman wanted to eat lunch with her was to hear about the murder, she was thoroughly tired of talking about it.

Now, as she and Rayette Hoover left the school at four, Heather was pleased to see that almost everyone else was already gone; at least she wouldn't have to tell the story all over again. "Want to go over to Broadway and get a latte?" she asked Rayette.

"Okay," Rayette agreed.

As they walked across Capitol Hill toward Broadway, Heather could tell right away that Rayette was struggling not to talk about the one thing that everyone in school had been talking about all day. Heather could also tell that Rayette was losing her battle, and silently made a bet that Rayette wouldn't last out the next block. Within half a block Rayette's curiosity got the better of her, but when she spoke, Heather had to give her friend points for trying to be indirect.

"What was it like having lunch with Josh Whitman?"

"He invited me to the prom," Heather replied, injecting just enough excitement into her voice so Rayette actually fell for it, at least for a split second. Then Rayette's lips stretched into a wide grin that exposed the set of braces she usually took care not to reveal to anyone.

"Get out of here, girlfriend!" she hooted. "That big football stud just wanted to know the same thing we all did! Now you just tell me everything you know about that woman who got killed. This is Rayette, honey! Come clean!"

"There isn't anything to come clean about." Heather sighed. "I mean, no one even knew Mrs. Cottrell. She was really weird. She didn't have any friends, and she hardly ever even went out of the house except to go to work. Sometimes you could see her eating all by herself, just sitting at this really huge dining room table all by herself."

Rayette shuddered. She'd always thought there was something spooky about the big house next door to the Jefferses'. Ever since she and Heather had gotten to be friends in sixth grade, she'd known the woman who lived there was kind of weird, but to think of her actually getting murdered ... "What do you think happened?" she asked. "I mean, really?"

Heather shrugged. "How am *I* supposed to know?" she asked. "It's not like I knew her or anything."

"I didn't say you should *know* what happened. I just asked what do you *think* happened. Like, was it someone she knew?"

Heather shrugged. "She didn't know anyone."

They were walking south on Broadway now. As they came to Prospect Street, Rayette stopped. "Let's go up there and see where your mom found her," she said.

Heather's eyes widened. "They're not going to let us do that. They'll have the whole place blocked off."

"No they won't," Rayette insisted. "Some guy got shot down by my uncle's last year, and they didn't have the cops out there more than a couple hours. Come on."

Turning left on Prospect, Rayette started purposefully up the hill toward the park, and a second later Heather followed.

"Where was it?" Rayette asked as they came to the broad swath of lawn that stretched from Prospect up to the road that curved around the base of the hill containing the reservoir.

"I don't think you can see it from here," Heather said, not sure she wanted to go looking for the place where her mother had found Mrs. Cottrell. "Dad said Mom was up by the reservoir."

"Then let's go." Rayette set off once more, cutting diagonally across the lawn to the place where the road came closest to the reservoir. Crossing the road, she scrambled up a steep, well-trod path that led to the flat track around the reservoir.

"Can't we go around by the museum?" Heather complained. "This isn't even a path!"

"It is, too," Rayette retorted. "Besides, why should we go all the way around when we're already here?" Pausing at the top of the slope while Heather caught up, she surveyed the area, immediately spotting a small knot of people who seemed to be staring into a thicket. Now that her goal was within sight, Rayette began having second thoughts. " 'Spose there's gonna be blood all over the ground?" she asked.

Heather grabbed her friend's arm to steady herself; the very thought of finding a pool of Joyce Cottrell's blood was enough to make her dizzy. "Can't we just go over to my house?" she asked. "I mean, if we're not going to go for lattes—" Before she could finish her sentence, she heard her brother's voice calling to her.

"Hey, Heather!" Kevin was shouting, waving frantically. "Look over here! This is where Mom found her!"

She didn't want to see the place at all, but knew that she'd better try to get Kevin home before their parents found out what he was doing. Heather followed Rayette over to where Kevin, together with Justin Reynolds, was regaling half a dozen people with the tale of the discovery of the corpse earlier that morning.

"There was blood all over the place," Kevin was saying. "And she was all torn up. Boots was chewing on her arm, and—"

"Kevin!" Heather shrieked, grabbing her brother and clamping a hand over his mouth to silence him. "Come on! We're going home right now!"

Kevin struggled to get loose from his sister's grip, finally managing to free his mouth. "Help!" he yelled. "She's trying to kidnap me!"

The group of people who had been listening raptly to Kevin only a moment before were grinning now at his attempts to free himself from his sister.

"Did your mom really find the body?" someone asked Heather.

"Oh, God," Heather groaned. "Why did Mom even have to come up here this morning?" Yet even as she uttered the words, Heather was drawn, like iron filings toward a magnet, to the spot where Joyce Cottrell's body had been found. Rayette Hoover, staying close to her best friend, felt all the bravado she had voiced only a few minutes before begin to drain from her, but like Heather, she found herself unable simply to walk away.

Both girls had to see.

Yet when they had finally threaded their way through the knot of people, to stare down at the now empty space beneath the brush where only ten hours earlier Heather's mother came across a disemboweled corpse, there was little left to observe—only a few scraps of yellow plastic tape where the police had cordoned off the area, and an area of earth scraped clean of the fallen leaves and windblown detritus that was scattered through the rest of the thicket.

The very lack of anything to see gave the spot a feeling of loneliness and abandonment. With a shudder, Heather realized that her imagination had not even been close to conjuring what her mother must have seen. Even with all the evidence of Joyce Cottrell's body having been removed, she felt a coldness that penetrated far deeper than the chill of the afternoon. "Come on," she said, unconsciously reaching out and taking Rayette's hand in her own. "Let's go home."

Kevin followed her only a moment later.

Not a word was spoken until the three of them turned the corner onto Sixteenth East, and as they moved down the block toward the Jeffers house, they caught themselves gazing past Heather and Kevin's house to the one just beyond it.

Their paces slowed until at last they came to a stop, all of them staring silently at the house that seemed to loom ominously next door to the Jefferses'. It was Rayette Hoover who finally found her voice: "It . . . it sorta doesn't look the same, does it?"

For a long minute all three peered at the forbidding structure. Until today it had been nothing more than the home of the neighborhood eccentric who had been feared by the smaller children and mocked by the older ones. The fact that there was now a yellow tape strung across its broad porch told them all they needed to know, though they still edged close enough to be able to read the words CRIME SITE—DO NOT CROSS, which were stenciled on the bright plastic.

"Oh, Lord," Rayette breathed. "She must have gotten killed right here." Her eyes wide, she turned to gaze at Heather. "Didn't you hear her scream or something?"

Heather shook her head, unable to tear her eyes away from the house. On the second floor was the room where she was pretty sure Mrs. Cottrell had slept. When she was at work, the lights always went on and off all over the house. Everyone on the block knew they were on a timer. But when she was home, only that one room on the second floor was ever lit.

The one right across from Heather's own bedroom.

Suddenly it became very important to her that she remember exactly what had happened the previous night. She tried to reconstruct the evening. Her parents had had a fight—well, not exactly a fight. But there had been enough tension in the house so that instead of gathering in the living room to read and watch television together the way they usually did, the family split up. She remained in her room even after she finished her homework, and Kevin had stayed in his, and she knew that their mother had gone to bed early while her father had stayed downstairs, reading by himself for a while. But he hadn't stayed up very late: even before she'd gone to bed at ten, he'd knocked at her door, then stuck his head in to say good night to her. It was only a little bit later that she'd gone to bed herself.

Gone to bed, and read for a few minutes, and then gone to sleep.

Mrs. Cottrell hadn't been home yet when she had gone to sleep— she knew that because she'd been sitting at her desk right by the window for almost an hour while she struggled through a geometry proof. The lights next door kept going on and off, practically screaming out that the place was empty.

Heather felt an odd chill as a vague memory came back to her. She hadn't really thought anything about it at the time, but now . . .

Someone on the sidewalk.

Not right in front of the house, but across the street. A man in a dark coat. She hadn't seen him very well. He'd just been walking along the street, but then he stopped, and for a second Heather thought he was looking at her. Then he'd continued up the street. Though she looked out the window a couple of more times, he hadn't come back.

At least she thought he hadn't.

What if she'd actually seen the man who killed Mrs. Cottrell, and hadn't done anything about it? "Oh, God," she breathed out loud. "Maybe I could have saved her."

"What?" Rayette Hoover demanded. "What are you talking about?"

Swallowing the lump that had risen in her throat, Heather told Rayette and Kevin what she'd seen. "What if it was him?" she asked. "What if it was really him? What if he came back later?"

"What if he *saw* you?" Rayette suggested, scanning the block herself, as if half expecting to see a dark-coated stranger eyeing them from somewhere down the street. "Let's go in, okay?" Taking one last glance at the house next door—which had now definitely taken on a scary look that made Rayette glad she lived six blocks away, even if her block wasn't quite as nice as this one—Rayette strode up the walk to the front porch and reached into the planter that stood in the corner farthest from the front door to fish out the key she knew the Jefferses kept there, then stiffened as she realized what she'd done. Again she scanned the block, relieved that there still seemed to be no one observing her. But as she turned back to the front door, Rayette saw Kevin glaring scornfully at her.

"Smooth move, Ex-Lax," he told her. "Why don't you just tell the whole city where we keep the key?"

Heather instantly came to Rayette's defense. "The whole city probably already knows. And we're not going to leave it out here anymore, anyway. Not after what happened to Mrs. Cottrell."

Kevin rolled his eyes. "If that guy saw you, he's gonna get you anyway," he declared, seizing on the opportunity to terrify his sister. "I bet he's been watching you all day."

"Shut up, Kevin," Heather said as she took the key from Rayette and stuck it into the lock. "Just shut up, okay?"

"Don't tell me to shut up," Kevin shot back as they entered the foyer. Heather closed the door behind them and threw the dead bolt. "Scaredy-cat, scaredy-cat," he chanted, dropping down to rub the belly of Boots, who had thrown himself on his master the instant the door had opened and was now lying on his back, his whole body trembling with joy. "Heather is a scaredy-cat!"

"Why don't you just stuff it, Kevin," Heather told her brother, then turned to Rayette as she started toward the kitchen. "Come on. You can open a couple of Cokes while I give Kumquat her food."

Kevin glared at his sister. "I'm gonna tell Dad you told me to stuff it," he threatened. "Dad?" he yelled up the stairs. "Hey, Dad!"

Their father's voice called back from the den behind the living room. "In here!" As the two girls headed through the dining room, Kevin took the opposite direction, Boots scampering after him.

"So what are you gonna do?" Rayette asked as she opened the refrigerator door and pulled two cans of Coke off the bottom shelf.

"About what?" Heather asked, taking a tin of cat food out of the cupboard next to the refrigerator.

"About the man you saw." Rayette popped the tabs on both cans and poured their contents into two large glasses, then dropped into one of the chairs at the big table in the corner of the kitchen. "I mean, what if Kevin's right?"

Heather scooped a lump of Friskies into Kumquat's dish. "He didn't even see me," she said, giving her voice a lot more conviction than she felt.

"But what if he did?" Rayette pressed. "I mean what if—"

"I don't want to talk about it!" Heather set the dish on the floor. Then she frowned as she realized that Kumquat hadn't been rubbing up against her legs the way she always did while her dish was being filled.

"Come *on*, girl," Rayette protested. "If he *did* see you—" But her friend was no longer paying any attention to her.

"Kumquat?" Heather was calling. "Here, kitty, kitty, kitty."

When the cat didn't appear immediately, Heather went back to the foyer. "Dad? Is Kumquat back there?"

"I haven't seen her since this morning," her father called from the den.

Frowning, Heather went upstairs and checked her room. When she didn't find the cat there, she searched the rest of the house, then came back to the kitchen. "She's gone," she reported to Rayette.

"Maybe she got a look at some big tomcat and went out to get her some," Rayette suggested, leering lasciviously.

"She's spayed," Heather replied.

"So's my aunt Tanya, but that doesn't mean she doesn't still like it," Rayette retorted.

"Rayette!" Heather groaned. She opened the back door and once more called out for the missing cat. "Kumquat! Come on, kitty. Supper's ready."

Kevin and Boots came into the kitchen, the dog instantly spotting

the open door and seizing an opportunity to make a break for freedom. Heather moved to slam it closed before the dog could dart
through, but Kevin stopped her.

"It's okay. Dad told me to take him outside."

"Look around for Kumquat, okay?" Heather asked.

"He's your cat—you look for her," Kevin argued, but quickly
changed his mind when he saw the glint in his sister's eye. "Okay,
okay."

"Maybe we all ought to go hunt for her," Heather said.

"Let's just finish our Cokes, and if she still hasn't shown up, *then*
we can go look for her," Rayette countered.

Deciding it would be easier to go along with Rayette than try to
argue with her, Heather sank onto the chair opposite her friend.
Where could the cat have gone? True, she let Kumquat out every
morning and every night, but the cat never stayed outside very long,
and always spent most of the day sleeping on her bed. Then she noticed the door to the basement wasn't shut quite tight. Abandoning
her Coke, she went to the door, pulled it open and looked down the
stairs.

The usual darkness of the cellar was broken by a glow of white
light. Her father must have gone down there sometime during the
day, and if Kumquat found the door open, her curiosity alone would
have made her go through it. "Kumquat?" Heather called again,
starting down the stairs. "Here, kitty, kitty. Come on, Kumquat!"
Coming to the bottom of the stairs, Heather scanned the room for
the cat. Neither seeing or hearing anything, she crossed to the workbench, reaching for the string that would shut off the glaring fluorescent light. Just as her fingers closed on the string, her eyes fell on
something sitting on top of the workbench.

A large, furry bug with bright green wings.

Startled, Heather jumped back, then realized it wasn't a bug after
all. But what was it? Reaching out, she gingerly picked the object up.
Turning it over, she saw the needle-sharp point of the fishhook protruding from the mass of fur, and immediately felt like an idiot for
being frightened by a fishing fly. On the other hand, if it had made
her jump, what would happen if she tossed it at Rayette, who was
terrified of bugs? Taking the fly with her, she turned the light off and

went back up the stairs, closing the door behind her. Approaching the table with an exaggerated nonchalance, she grinned at Rayette. "Want to see what I found?" Without waiting for a reply, she tossed the fly onto the table, eliciting a gratifyingly loud shriek from her friend. Catching on to the joke even as her screech died away, Rayette was about to vent her outrage on Heather when Kevin called from behind the garage.

"Heather? Hey, Heather! Com'ere, quick!"

Responding to the urgency in his voice, both girls ran down the back steps and out into the yard. As they rounded the corner of the garage, they stopped short. Kevin was squatting on the ground, holding a growling Boots in his arms. Hearing them behind him, Kevin turned and looked up at his sister, his face ashen.

"Bootsie found her." He was breathing hard, fighting tears. "Just like he found Mrs. Cottrell this morning."

Her heart pounding, Heather moved closer to her brother, praying she wasn't going to see what she already knew must be there.

Lying half hidden under the wooden decking that supported the trash barrels was Kumquat.

Her fur was matted with blood and her chest was torn open.

Instinctively, Heather started toward her pet, but Rayette stopped her. "Don't, Heather," she whispered. "Don't even touch her. Just leave her where she is, and let's call the police."

Sobbing, unable even to speak, Heather let Rayette lead her back to the house. They came through the back door just as Heather's mother came in the front. While the two girls were still blurting out what they'd found behind the garage, Anne was dialing the police.

Mark Blakemoor was considering whether to knock off at five like a normal human being, or go on working until he'd caught up with the stack of files that seemed to grow on his desk at an inexorable rate. Glancing up at the clock on the wall of the tiny cubicle he and Lois Ackerly shared, he saw that he still had ten minutes before he'd actually have to make a decision. He returned his attention to the open folder in front of him. It was nothing more interesting than a copy of Joyce Cottrell's Group Health personnel record, in which he'd been hunting for something—any little scrap of information that might indicate she'd had an enemy. The problem with Cottrell, though, was that she not only didn't appear to have any enemies, but hadn't appeared to have any friends, either. Even her employment jacket didn't have much to say about her. She'd been working at Group Health for better than twenty years, and in all that time, had accumulated neither praise nor criticism. Apparently she did her job well enough to keep it, but never showed enough initiative to be promoted, either.

Tossing the file aside, he turned his attention to Lois Ackerly, who was already clearing her desk in preparation for an on-time departure, instantly annoying him, though he couldn't have said whether it was the fact that she was leaving on time that irritated him or that she had someone to go home to.

Reflexively, he glanced at the spot where a picture of his ex-wife had once sat. Except, instead of seeing a picture of Patsy Blakemoor in his mind, it was Anne Jeffers's image that popped out of his subconscious. Got to stop that, he told himself. More to get Anne's image out of his mind than because he really wanted to talk about it, he asked Lois Ackerly if she'd had any more luck with her investigation into Joyce Cottrell's background than he'd had with his.

Lois shook her head in a combination of sympathy and disbelief. "That woman lent new meaning to the phrase 'Get a life,' " she said. "Not only can't I find anyone who will admit to being her friend, I can hardly find anyone who even knew her. All I've found out is that she went to work and she went home. At work, she did her job and kept to herself. She didn't have any friends—even took her breaks by herself. It's like she was a complete cipher."

"Same with her personnel jacket," Blakemoor agreed. "Ever seen a record with no pluses and no minuses?" He tossed it across, and Lois Ackerly flipped it open, scanning through the evaluation forms that Blakemoor had already found abnormally dull.

"No friends and no enemies." Ackerly sighed, dropping the file back onto her partner's desk. "No gossip, either. It's like she existed in a void."

"So who killed her?" Blakemoor asked. As he asked the question, another image came into his mind. Glen Jeffers. He had been thinking about Jeffers all afternoon. Though he was sure there was something Anne's husband hadn't told him, he'd finally come to the conclusion that even if he wanted Glen out of the way—and he kept insisting to himself that he didn't, not really—it still didn't add up. Whoever did the Cottrell woman would have been drenched with blood, and if she'd screamed even once, she damned near would have *had* to awaken someone in the house next door. If your whole family was asleep in that house, would you risk that? Mark Blakemoor didn't think so. In fact, he was damned well sure of it. Still, he might just ask Glen Jeffers for a set of prints, if for no other reason than to eliminate him as the person who'd left a few smudged but matchable traces in Cottrell's bathroom, where he'd apparently washed his hands. "Who killed her?" he repeated, sighing in frustration.

"Same creep who did Shawnelle Davis?" Lois Ackerly suggested. "You know Anne Jeffers is going to tie them together, and you know we're going to have to deal with it."

Blakemoor leaned back in his chair, propped his feet up on the desk and clasped his hands behind his head. "So what are you suggesting?" he asked, and it was clear to Ackerly that he was settling in for a long discussion of the case. "Is Anne right? Are you starting to buy her nutty idea that maybe Richard Kraven really didn't do all the others by himself, and that all that shit's starting up again? Or is it just a copycat? Except if it's a copycat, how come he dipped his wick in Cottrell but not in Davis?"

Before Lois Ackerly could answer, the phone on her partner's desk rang. Grateful for the opportunity to stall on Blakemoor's questions, she snatched up the receiver before Mark's feet had dropped back to the floor. As she listened, a frown creased her forehead, and for a moment Blakemoor had a sinking feeling that another corpse had turned up. But then the frown cleared, replaced by a broad smile.

"A cat?" the detective asked. "Come on, Phil—what are you calling us for? We don't do cats. We're homicide, remember? Not—what would it be? *Feli*cide?" Clamping her hand over the mouthpiece, she spoke to Blakemoor. "Would you believe they're calling us about a dead—" But even before she finished the sentence her smile faded and she swore softly. "Oh, Jesus," she said. "Okay, we'll catch it. We're on our way."

Mark Blakemoor stared at her in disbelief as she dropped the receiver back onto the cradle. "A *cat*?" he demanded. "Did I just hear you tell them we'd go out on a dead cat?"

Lois Ackerly nodded unhappily. "It's not just any dead cat," she replied. "It's Anne Jeffers's cat."

"Anne's?" Blakemoor echoed. "And she asked for us?"

Lois Ackerly nodded. "From what Phil said, it sounds like it's cut up the same way Cottrell and Davis were."

Mark Blakemoor swore silently. If it were true—and he hoped it wasn't—he was pretty sure he knew exactly what it meant: they didn't simply have a serial killer loose; they had a serial killer who was going to start playing grisly games.

But playing with whom?

The police, or his next victim?

There was another possibility, of course: it could be someone's idea of a sick joke. After all, Anne's name had been on the radio all day long, with every newscaster in town talking about the oddity of a reporter discovering a body. If someone didn't like Anne, what better way to throw a scare into her than to kill her cat the same way her neighbor had been killed? What else could she think but that she was being warned that she might be the next victim? Christ, she must be falling apart! A wave of fury at whoever had done this to Anne rose within him, and for the briefest of moments Mark wondered if he should take himself off this whole case. But he knew he wouldn't—if anything, he would work even harder to find this particular creep.

It wasn't until they were in the car, headed for Capitol Hill, that Ackerly glanced over at him, her lips curving in an ironic smile. "Well, at least you don't have to go home."

Blakemoor felt himself reddening. "I don't mind going home," he muttered gruffly.

"Which is why you always manage to start a conversation at just a minute or two before five, right?" Lois Ackerly observed, then relented. "Hey, it's okay. Loneliness is a bummer. If I didn't have Jake—"

"Look, can we talk about something else?" Blakemoor broke in.

But they finished the drive in silence. They had pulled up in front of the Jefferses' house when Lois spoke again. "If you want, I can take this one alone," she offered.

Shit! Blakemoor thought. Is it that obvious? "I don't know what you're talking about," he said out loud, getting out of the car and slamming the door harder than necessary. Taking the steep flight of steps up to the porch two at a time, he was about to ring the bell when the door opened and Anne Jeffers let him in, her ashen face making clear just how frightened she was.

"I suppose you think I've really gone around the bend this time," she said with a not very successful attempt to make the words sound bantering.

"I don't even know what happened yet," Mark replied, hoping nothing in his own voice betrayed his urge to put his arms around her. "What happened?" he asked as Lois Ackerly stepped into the foyer. In the living room he could see a teenage girl who he assumed was Anne's daughter huddled on the sofa, crying, while a black girl of about the same age tried to comfort her.

"In back," Anne said quietly, leading the two detectives through the dining room and kitchen, then outside into the backyard. As they crossed the lawn, Mark Blakemoor caught himself glancing over at the house next door and wondering if it were really possible that there was a connection between the brutal murder that had occurred there the previous night and the cat that now lay dead behind Anne Jeffers's house.

Both Glen and Kevin were sitting on the wooden decking that supported the garbage cans. As Anne and the two detectives approached, the little boy jumped to his feet.

"She's right there!" he exclaimed, pointing to the portion of the cat that protruded from beneath the deck. "Boots found her, just like he found Mrs. Cot—"

"That's enough." Anne pulled her son to her and put her arms protectively around his shoulders.

"Has anyone touched it?" Mark asked, squatting down to take a closer look at the cat's corpse.

Kevin shook his head. "I didn't," he reported. "And I wouldn't let Heather or Rayette, either. I told them—"

"Maybe you should go back into the house, honey," Anne suggested.

"Aw, Mom!" Kevin groaned. "Come on! It was me that found her!"

"Go *on*," Anne told him. "If Detective Blakemoor has any questions, we'll come and find you. And be nice to your sister," she warned as Kevin reluctantly started back toward the house.

Easing the dead cat clear of the deck, Blakemoor studied the carnage that had been its chest. The rib cage had been cut open and the lungs pulled out, just as had those of both Shawnelle Davis and Joyce Cottrell. But somehow the mutilation of the cat looked different.

Neater.

The word had come unbidden into his mind, but as he repeated it silently to himself, Blakemoor realized it was the only description that was truly appropriate. Whereas both Davis and Cottrell seemed to have been ripped apart in rage, the animal—at least where the cut up its chest and the opening of its rib cage had been performed— looked almost as if it had been dissected.

"Any idea what might have happened to it?" he asked Glen Jeffers, who was standing now, staring numbly down at the body of his daughter's pet. Blakemoor watched him carefully, but saw nothing in his expression except shock at the mutilation.

Glen shook his head. "I didn't even know she wasn't in the house," he said, his voice dull, his eyes fixed on the bloody corpse. "Christ, I feel like maybe this is my fault."

"Your fault?" Lois Ackerly asked.

For a moment Glen made no reply to the detective's question. Ever since Kevin had yelled out to Heather and Rayette and he'd gone to see what the fuss was about, he'd been trying to remember the last time he'd seen the cat. She'd been there this morning, after he'd gotten back from the park and the kids had left for school. But after that?

He didn't know. But he'd been in and out of the house a lot that morning, and Kumquat could have slipped out any time the door was open. He hadn't bothered to check on her whereabouts when he'd stretched out to take a nap. Nor had he looked for her when he woke up, after sleeping a lot longer than he'd intended to.

As he remembered the care with which Heather checked each morning to make sure there was no way her pet could escape from the house, his sense of guilt increased. All he'd had to do was keep half an eye out.

Instead he'd slept half the day away. "She probably got out this morning," he said finally. His gaze shifted to Mark Blakemoor. "It might even have been when you were leaving."

"You mean you weren't even watching her?" Anne asked. "For God's sake, Glen! You know how careful Heather always is! The least—"

"Hey, look!" Glen protested, suddenly angry. "I said this might be partly my fault, okay? But it's not like I killed her. Jesus!"

"Oh, God, I know," Anne sighed. "I'm sorry. I'm just upset, and—" Leaving the rest of the sentence unspoken, she turned to Blakemoor. "I know I shouldn't have asked for you, but when the kids told me what happened, it just seemed like too much of a coincidence."

"It's okay," Blakemoor assured her. He turned questioningly to his partner. "Think we'd better take it downtown?" he asked, inclining his head toward the body of the cat. "And what about pictures?"

Lois Ackerly shrugged, no more certain than Blakemoor as to proper procedure. One thing she did know—if someone was going to call for a full forensics team, it wasn't going to be her. Not for a dead cat. "I don't think we need them," she said. "We both know where the cat was, right?" She turned to Anne. "Do you have a plastic trash bag?"

Anne, her eyes fixed on the cat, made no reply, and finally her husband spoke again. "I'll get one."

As Glen headed toward the house, Anne glanced up just in time to see Mark Blakemoor watching him, a speculative look in his eyes. "Come on, Mark. You don't think Glen did this, do you?"

"Hey," Mark replied, trying to inject a light note into his tone, which he was very far from feeling. "He was the last person to see the victim alive, right?"

"That's not funny, Mark," Anne said, her voice tight.

Her words stung, and Blakemoor instantly regretted his attempt at humor. "Look, why don't you just let us take the cat down and have someone look it over, all right? I can see exactly why you're so upset, but we don't know that there's any connection at all between this and—"

"Don't we?" Anne interrupted, her shock at the sight of the dismembered cat fading in the face of the detective's obvious attempt to dismiss what had happened. "I didn't see Shawnelle Davis, but I *did* see Joyce Cottrell. I *found* her, remember? And you can't tell me that poor Kumquat wasn't mutilated exactly the same way that she was. So first there was Shawnelle Davis, whom I admit I don't know, but next was my next door neighbor. Now it's my daughter's cat. This is literally in my backyard, Mark. I want some answers." She turned to Lois Ackerly. "I know what you think about what I've been writing—" she began, but Ackerly silenced her with a gesture.

"What we might have thought yesterday doesn't mean a thing today," she said. "We're going to take this seriously. Whether this creep had anything to do with Richard Kraven or not, it sure looks like he's trying to copy his style. If this had been reported from somewhere else in town, we would've sent someone out to take a cruelty report. But after what happened last night, believe me when I tell you that we want to know what happened to this cat just as badly as you do."

Anne's jaw setting and her eyes narrowing, still not positive that Ackerly was doing anything more than placating her, she turned back to Blakemoor.

"We'll call you," he promised. "We're not going to take the cat to the pound. We're going to have the same medical examiner look at it who worked on Davis and Cottrell—"

"Davis *and* Cottrell?" Anne cut in, her reporter's instincts suddenly surging. "Are you saying you *are* treating them as being connected?"

Mark Blakemoor and Lois Ackerly exchanged a look, then Mark sighed. "Off the record, of course we are. The M.O.'s aren't identical, but they're close enough that we aren't about to rule out a serial killer. And very much off the record," he went on, his eyes moving to Kumquat's bloodied corpse, "I'm going to tell you that I'm going to have a very hard look at what happened to your cat. But if you write so much as a single world implying I'm investigating a cat's death as a murder, I swear I'll make sure no cop ever talks to you ever again. About anything. Clear?"

Anne hesitated, then nodded agreement. "Clear." She glanced around, then satisfied that she was still alone with the two detectives, said, "What should we do?" Her gaze fixed on Kumquat's body. "Is this a warning? Does it mean he's coming after me or one of my kids next?" Her eyes were troubled, a mirror of the emotions churning within her. She shifted back to Mark Blakemoor. "I'm scared. I'm really scared."

Again Blakemoor had to resist the impulse to put his arms protectively around her and gently stroke her hair. And again, when he spoke, he was careful to keep his tone perfectly even, the matter-of-fact inflection of any policeman talking to any frightened citizen. "Let's not get too worried until we know what's going on," he told her. "This could be someone's idea of a sick joke, or someone just wants to scare you and figured out the best way to do it. For now, we'll make sure you have a steady parade of cars going by all night, and if anything frightens you—anything at all—call 911. I personally guarantee there'll be someone here in less than a minute."

"But my kids," Anne said, the last of her hard reporter's shell cracking. "What about my kids? What should I tell them?"

"If it were me," Lois Ackerly said, "I think at least for tonight I'd tell them we think a raccoon did it." When Anne started to object, Ackerly pressed on. "Look, there's no sense scaring your kids to death. You'll be worried enough without them having nightmares about it. Tomorrow we should be able to tell you a lot more."

Before Anne could ask anything else, the back door of the house opened and Glen emerged, carrying a white plastic garbage bag.

Though she hated herself for it, and felt utterly disloyal, Anne did nothing to break the silence that fell over the two detectives as her husband approached. Instead, turning finally away from the grisly remains of her daughter's pet, she returned to the house.

As Glen handed Mark Blakemoor the plastic bags he'd finally found in one of the kitchen drawers, he felt the detective's eyes boring into him. Though no words were spoken, none were needed. Desperately, Glen tried to sort out exactly what had happened. Was it really possible that he himself had disemboweled his daughter's pet?

But he had no memory of it.

Except that there was a memory—a vague memory—of a dream.

He'd been in a place of darkness, but there had been a pool of light.

In the middle of the light, something had been happening.

He'd moved closer, wanting to see, but there had been something in the way, something blocking his view. He had a fragmentary recollection of trying to move in the dream. To get away? To see?

He couldn't remember.

Then another fragment of the dream floated up into his consciousness. Red. Bloodred. And with the memory of the color came a strange sensation in his fingers. Warmth. No, more than warmth. Heat. His hands felt hot, and slimy.

Shuddering both at the memory and at the strange feeling in his fingers, Glen slid his hands into his pockets as if to hide them, then quickly pulled them out again. What was wrong? He had nothing to hide—he couldn't even remember what the dream was about.

All that had really happened was that Mark Blakemoor had given him a look that made him feel guilty.

Still, a coldness seized Glen that had nothing to do with the damp chill of the afternoon.

Who was the stranger in the dream?

Could someone have come into the house while he slept? He remembered yesterday, and the inexplicable appearance of the shaver and the fishing rod. He must have bought them, but he couldn't remember!

Could he also have killed Kumquat and not remembered that, either?

It wasn't possible. Surely he hadn't done this to Kumquat. He couldn't have! It had only been a dream!

Or was he losing his mind?

Anne found Heather and Rayette still in the living room, still on the sofa, Heather crying quietly as Rayette did her best to comfort her.

Kevin was nowhere to be seen, but Anne was pretty sure she knew where he was: up in his room, watching from his window as Lois Ackerly and Mark Blakemoor finished their work.

Knowing there was nothing she could say to Heather right now, Anne went into the den, dropping morosely into the chair in front of her computer. For a moment she simply sat there, her eyes focused on nothing, her mind numbly trying to sort out all the events of the day, futilely attempting to make sense of the utterly senseless.

Write it, she finally told herself as her thoughts continued to tumble chaotically. Write it all down. It's the only way to put it in order.

She switched on the computer and waited while it booted up. The orders issued by the autoexec file scrolled by, then the familiar Windows screen appeared. But instead of stopping to await her orders, the computer kept working.

Her word processing program opened, but still the computer didn't stop.

An image appeared, framed in the familiar border of a graphics box. Inside the frame was a note:

> **Too bad about the cat.**
> **Some experiments just don't work.**
> **That's when things die.**
> **I'll try to do better with you.**

By the time the words had registered on Anne's mind, the screen had gone blank. For a moment Anne wondered if she had seen the note at all.

The hard knot of terror in her belly assured her that she had.

There was a fresh stack of the morning *Herald* in the box in front of the 7-Eleven on Broadway, so at least he hadn't had to walk all the way up to the QFC store to find one. But even now, gazing at the box with his heart beginning to race as he thought of the story that was bound to be on the front page, he felt a cold chill of apprehension. What if someone were watching?

He glanced around and instantly regretted the action: even that simple movement would be enough to betray his nervousness to watching eyes.

There had been watching eyes all night long. How many times had he gotten up from his bed to peer out into the street below, only to see a police car cruising by?

Were they just looking because there had now been two murders on Capitol Hill?

Or were they looking for him?

Looking for the Butcher.

The Butcher.

The name had come to him sometime during the night, when he'd been thinking about what Anne Jeffers might have written about him. He'd committed two murders now, so they would be giving him a nickname. There had been the Son of Sam, and the Boston Strangler, and the Green River Killer. Of course, Richard Kraven had never had a nickname, but that was good.

Having a nickname himself would mean he was even more famous than Richard Kraven.

He was the Butcher.

The name had a strength he liked. Maybe he should send a note to Anne Jeffers tomorrow morning, and sign it that way. Then everyone in Seattle would be using it within a day or two.

The Butcher.

He'd thought about it all night long, savoring it, making it his own as he'd lain awake, waiting for morning to come.

Morning, and the early edition of the *Herald*. He would have gone out long before dawn, but with all the police cars out there, it would have been far too risky. So he'd waited. Waited until the shift at the hospital was changing and he could walk over to the 7-Eleven without being the only one on the street.

But now it was too late to buy a paper here—too late, and too dangerous, especially since he'd slipped, giving away his nervousness to anyone who might have been watching. Now he'd have to walk up Fifteenth the three blocks to the QFC.

Quality Food Center. Queens' Food Center they called it on Broadway, which was why the Butcher never went to the one over there. But the QFC on Fifteenth was all right—he'd been there lots of times, and even if someone asked him why he wasn't at work, he knew he looked pretty bad after the sleepless night. He'd just plead the flu, like he would when he called in sick for the third day in a row.

All he had to do was act normal. Normal and casual. Maybe pick up some magazines and soup, like he would have if he'd really had the flu.

All he had to do was be smart. And he knew he was smart, no matter what his mother thought. All he had to do was be careful and think everything through, and pretty soon he'd be famous.

At least as famous as Richard Kraven. Maybe even as famous as Ted Bundy.

As long as he didn't get caught.

So he couldn't just walk away from the 7-Eleven, either. He had to look like he'd come here for something. Turning casually away from the newspaper box, he went into the convenience store, wandered over to the magazine rack and pretended to be scanning the titles while he checked the store out to see who might be watching him.

Except for the clerk behind the counter, it was empty. Still, someone might be outside, maybe watching from a car.

He abandoned the magazine rack—better to buy them at the
QFC when he got the paper—and went to the counter. He picked
up a roll of Clorets and paid for them. By the time he emerged from
the front door, he was busy unwrapping the cylinder of mints, and
anyone who might be observing him wouldn't know he was actually
checking out every car in the area.

All of them were empty except for one black Cadillac he was
pretty sure belonged to a drug dealer. Anyway, he'd seen it in the
neighborhood a lot, and judging by the people who hung around it,
it sure wasn't a police car. Popping one of the mints into his mouth,
he crossed the street against the light and started up the east side of
Fifteenth to the QFC. He picked up a basket as he went inside, then
found the soup section, where he took three cans of Chunky
Chicken Noodle. Then he headed for the checkout counter. Sure
enough, there was a stack of the *Herald*, and when he picked one up,
his hands weren't trembling much at all. He flopped it down on the
counter along an *Enquirer*, a *Globe*, the *Post-Intelligencer*, and the
three cans of soup. He was just reaching into his pocket for his wallet
when the checker spoke.

"You hear about the murder?"

The man's heart raced. He felt his hands turn cold and clammy.

"Murder?" he echoed. What should he say? Should he already
know about it? But it had been on the radio all day yesterday, and
the TV news last night. "Oh, you mean the body they found up in
Volunteer Park yesterday?" he asked. *That had been good. His voice
had sounded just right—interested, but not too interested.*

"She was in here night before last," the checker said.

The man felt his knees weaken. When he pulled his wallet out, his
trembling fingers lost their grip on it and it fell to the floor. "Aah,
shit," he groaned as he bent down to pick it up. But that was all
right, too. At least it gave him a couple of seconds to try to come up
with a response. Then he had it. When he straightened up again, his
eyes were wide. "You mean here?" he asked. "She was right *here*?"

The checker nodded eagerly. As soon as he spoke again, the man
began to relax—it sounded like the guy had already told the story a

dozen times. "Ms. Cottrell," the checker said. "She came in here practically every night for a latte on her way home."

"You mean you *knew* her?" the Butcher asked, giving just enough emphasis to the word "knew" to let the clerk know he was impressed.

"Well, I didn't really *know* her," the clerk said quickly, his own eyes now darting around the store as if he had suddenly realized that any-one who might have known the murdered woman would now be considered a possible suspect. "I mean, not any better than anybody else here did, you know?"

His own nerves calming as the clerk turned edgy, the Butcher handed him a twenty dollar bill, waited for his change, then picked up the bag into which the checker had put his papers and the cans of soup. Barely able to restrain himself, he started home, willing him-self to leave the *Herald* in the bag until he was safely back in his apartment. But no matter how hard he tried, he couldn't keep his pace at the slow amble he was attempting, and finally he gave it up in favor of a purposeful stride down the street, as if he were late for an appointment. After three minutes that seemed to him like an hour, he at last closed his door behind him and yanked the paper out of the bag, letting the chicken soup cans roll unnoticed to the floor. Unfolding the paper, he scanned the front page, then scanned it again.

It wasn't possible! It *had* to be on the front page.

But there was nothing. Nothing! Nothing but some crap about the park the city wanted to build between downtown and Lake Union.

Who the fuck cared about that?

Moving to the battered Formica-topped table that served as both a desk and a dining table, he flipped through the newspaper, his frus-tration mounting as he turned page after page and found nothing.

Then, on the third page of the second section, he finally found it.

And almost exploded with rage.

They'd buried it!

Bad enough they hadn't put it on the front page, or even the sec-ond page of the first section!

He began reading the article, and with every word his rage increased.

Woman Found Slain Near Volunteer Park Reservoir

The nude body of a woman was found in Volunteer Park early this morning. The victim, identified as Ms. Joyce Cottrell, 57, was a receptionist in the emergency room at the Group Health facility on Capitol Hill.

According to police sources, the victim, who was single and lived alone, was slain in her Capitol Hill home sometime between 11:00 P.M. and 4:00 A.M. yesterday morning. The body appears to have been placed near the reservoir in Volunteer Park shortly before dawn, where it was discovered by jogger Anne Jeffers (a staff reporter for this paper).

While the investigation is not yet complete, police sources stressed that there appears to be no connection between the deaths of Ms. Cottrell and of Shawnelle Davis, whose body was discovered last week in her rented apartment.

As he finished the article, the Butcher's fingers tightened on the flimsy paper until it was crumpled into a wad.

No connection?

How could they say that? Hadn't they even looked at what he'd done?

The two killings had been alike! *Exactly* alike! And he'd done it even better on Joyce Cottrell than he had on Shawnelle Davis!

Well, next time it wouldn't be like this. Next time they would know what they were dealing with.

His anger erupting, he hurled the ruined newspaper to the floor. Maybe he should go out right now and do it again! That would show them—maybe he should just go out and find someone, and follow her home, and—

No!

That wasn't the way to do it at all! He had to be smart! He had to be careful, and calm.

No matter what happened, he couldn't let himself get angry.

Breathing deeply, he struggled to get himself under control. He reached down and picked up the crumpled newspaper. Spreading it out again, he smoothed the pages as best he could, then carefully tore out the article that had so offended him. Taking it to the dresser that served not only to hold his clothes, but to support his television as well, he opened the top drawer and added the article to the folder in which he'd already placed everything that had been written about Shawnelle Davis.

Tomorrow, or maybe even later on today, he'd buy an album and start putting the clippings in order.

And the next time he killed, it wouldn't be a woman, even though murdering Joyce Cottrell had given him more pleasure than he'd ever felt before in his life.

He couldn't let himself give in to the lure of that pleasure.

After all, that wasn't why he was killing.

He was killing to please his mother.

It was the killing that counted, not the pleasure.

So better not to let himself be tempted. Next time he killed, it wouldn't be a woman at all.

It would be some other kind of person.

In fact, from now on he'd kill *all* kinds of people.

Maybe later on, when he went out to buy an album, that wouldn't be all he did.

Maybe he would go hunting, too.

Anne had no memory of having slept at all the night before, though she knew she must have since her eyes didn't have the awful gritty feel that had always resulted from her staying awake all night. But she had clear memories of lying in bed, wide-awake, staring at the ceiling as she tried to figure out the source of the briefly flashing note that had appeared on her computer when she'd turned it on.

The mechanics of it hadn't taken her long to unravel: a simple macro file would have done it, triggered by practically anything:

A line in the autoexec.bat file, for instance.

The macro could easily have brought up a file, displayed it for a few seconds, then closed it, immediately erased it, wiped all traces of it from her hard drive with one of the utilities she herself used to make sure certain files could never be recovered, then erased itself as well.

Or it could have arrived as a virus, coming into her computer through the modem anytime she'd left the machine on, but unattended. It would have sat dormant on her hard drive, set to attack the first time the computer was turned on after a specific date and time.

And attack it had. But not her computer. No, this was much more invidious. This virus had attacked *her*, rising up out of the guts of the machine to lash out at her, filling her with a terror she hadn't been able to talk about at all, lest it spread from her into her whole family.

Bad enough they had been frightened by someone killing their pet and leaving it in their own backyard. How would they cope if they knew the unseen enemy had penetrated into the house itself?

She had searched the house, using the pretext of hunting for a misplaced box of old clippings on Richard Kraven. In both the attic and the basement she had searched for signs of a stranger's presence, but had found nothing.

On the kitchen table she had found the fishing fly, and for a moment thought she recognized fragments of one of Hector's feathers and a tuft of fur that could have come from Kumquat. But who could have made the fly? Certainly not Glen—he was notoriously clumsy with his hands, which was why the ship model downstairs had never been finished; Glen had proved even more awkward than Kevin at attaching the planks to the framework of the hull. Still, just before Glen had turned off the light to go to sleep, she'd asked him about the fly. He'd told her he bought it at the same time he bought the fishing rod, but something in his voice had struck her wrong.

When she'd pressed him, though, his mood had instantly blackened, and they'd almost had a fight.

He had gone to sleep while she stared at the ceiling, remembering the look of suspicion Mark Blakemoor and Lois Ackerly had cast in her husband's direction after they'd pulled poor Kumquat's body from beneath the low deck behind the garage.

No! Glen couldn't have killed Kumquat—he just *couldn't* have!

And so she'd lain awake, stewing, trying to find answers, trying to make sense out of senseless horrors.

In the morning, tired, but knowing she must have slept at least a few hours, she'd gotten up and once again concealed her fear from her family, contenting herself with instructing Heather to make certain she walked Kevin to his school before going on to her own, and extracting a promise from Kevin that he wouldn't leave school until Heather arrived to escort him home.

He argued, but she stood firm.

Then, after reading Vivian Andrews's essentially fictional account of the Joyce Cottrell story with growing anger, she went to the office.

When no silence fell over the city room of the *Herald* as she walked in, Anne felt something that she wasn't willing to admit even to herself: disappointment. But what had she expected? This wasn't a ladies afternoon card club—this was a big city newspaper, whose staff wasn't about to express public shock over much less than mass murder. Still, she would have thought someone would ask her how she was doing and if her family was all right. There wasn't even so much as a momentary drop in the decibel level as she threaded her way toward her desk. Perhaps it was that simple fact—that practiced callousness that she knew perfectly well was not only a tool of a reporter's trade, but practically a badge of honor as well—that stopped her from sitting down at her desk. But it wasn't just that, of course.

It was the note that had appeared on her computer last night. Not telling her family about it was one thing. Not telling Vivian Andrews was another. Picking up all her notes from her research on the rapid transit issue, she headed for Vivian Andrews's office, pushed the door open, stepped through it, and closed it behind her before the editor could possibly object.

"I gather you didn't like my editing?" Vivian asked with studied casualness, barely even glancing away from the monitor on which she was already reviewing stories for tomorrow's edition.

"It wasn't editing, Viv," Anne told her. "It was butchery. It was a good story, and it was an honest story. And I'm taking it back." She dropped the sheaf of notes onto the editor's desk, forcing Vivian to shift her attention from the monitor to the reporter who stood opposite her, pale and drawn.

"Toning down an irresponsible story is one of my primary functions around here," she began. But as she finally took a good look at Anne Jeffers, her words died on her lips. "Anne? Are you okay? You look like you've been up all night."

"I might as well have been, for all the sleep I got," Anne confessed. As quickly as she could, she filled Vivian in.

"Your *cat*?" Vivian asked as Anne described what had been done to Heather's pet. "My God, who would do something like that?"

Anne shook her head. "And what kind of a world do we live in when people react more strongly to what happens to a cat than they do to what happens to other people?"

Vivian Andrews reddened. "I didn't mean—" she began, but then dropped back in her chair. "Oh, God, maybe I did." She sighed. "What did the police say?"

Anne repeated most of what Mark Blakemoor and Lois Ackerly had told her, holding back only the few words that had been spoken—and not spoken—about Glen. "And as for your changing my story to say that the police aren't connecting the Davis and Cottrell killings, that simply isn't true," she finished. "They told me off the record that they're definitely treating them as related, and that they're going to have the same medical examiner who autopsied Davis and Cottrell look at our cat, too."

Vivian Andrews sourly eyed the array of papers that Anne had dropped onto her desk. "May I assume you've decided to take yourself off this particular mess?" she asked, tilting her head toward the transit plan notes.

"It seems to me that there are a lot of people around here who could do that story perfectly well."

"I'm not sure that's the point," Vivian replied. "I can also think of half a dozen people who could deal with these new killings in a more objective fashion than you."

"Maybe. But there's something else—something I haven't told anyone else yet." Struggling not to let her voice betray the extent of the fear she'd felt last night—still felt, she realized as she repeated the story—she told Vivian about the note that had appeared on her computer, then disappeared almost as quickly as it had come. "Look," she finished. "Put someone else on the story with me, if you want to. But you have to let me stay with it." When she saw the editor wavering, she pushed harder. "Vivian, something's going on here. This isn't just a copycat. Whoever's doing this has something going against me personally. Maybe he's trying to scare me off, or maybe he's seen a picture of me and just likes the way I look. For some reason, he's fixated on me, and even if you don't think it's a good idea for me to stay on the story, you know damned well that we can slant it to sell more papers than the *P.I.* and the *Times* combined. Picture the headline, Viv: 'Killer Stalks *Herald* Reporter.' I can write it without getting Blakemoor and Ackerly into trouble—I was *there*, Viv! It was my next door neighbor. My cat. And my computer he left his damned note on!"

She fell momentarily silent, then spoke again, no longer making any attempt to keep her voice steady. "My God, Viv—he's been watching me! He as much as said so!" Her voice rose. " 'See you soon!' That's what he said, Viv: *See you soon.*' He might even have taken Joyce Cottrell up to the park and dumped her there because he *knew* I jog there." She shuddered. "Oh, God, I wonder how long it's been going on—how long he's been out there." Again she fell silent, for now a memory was stirring. A faint memory, of having felt as though she were being watched. But where . . . ?

Misreading Anne's silence as a demand for a decision, Vivian Andrews made up her mind. Even as she committed herself, she knew she was doing it for the wrong reasons. Every instinct within her told her to assign someone else to this story. But she also knew that she was no more immune to the lure that Anne had held out than anyone else would be. How often did any reporter anywhere get a chance to go after a murder story where she herself might be one of the intended victims? They would, indeed, sell a lot of papers. "All right," she said. "Keep on it. But be very careful, and keep in mind that I'm going to be going over every word you write with a fine-tooth comb. Keep it fair, keep it objective, and you can keep the story. Agreed?"

Anne stood up. "Agreed." She started out of the editor's office, already composing a mental list of the phone calls she needed to make. But then she turned back, and her eyes met her boss's. "Thanks," she said quietly.

Vivian Andrews gazed steadily at her. "Anne, I hope you're smart enough to realize that all this should be scaring you to death."

"I am," Anne replied. "Right now, I'm more scared than I've ever been in my life. And I don't even know why this guy's mad at me. What could I ever have done to him?"

"What makes you think you did anything to him at all?" Vivian Andrews asked. "It's probably not even about you, Anne. It could still all be just a coincidence. But even if it isn't, don't start thinking it has anything to do with something you did, or even didn't do. It's just him, Anne. It's just some nut."

Anne left the editor's office and returned to her desk, where she riffled through the short stack of messages that had come in over-

night, then checked her E-mail, half expecting to find a duplicate of
the note that had been left on her computer at home. She wasn't
sure whether she felt relief or disappointment when she found
nothing.

Nothing in the way of a note, and nothing pertaining to the murders of either Shawnelle Davis or Joyce Cottrell.

Lots pertaining to the rapid transit mess, which she rerouted to
Vivian Andrews for reassignment.

She was about to reach for the phone to call Mark Blakemoor
when she changed her mind: it had long been her experience that
people found it far easier to lie over the phone than in person, a phenomenon she attributed more to her own ability to read people's
facial expressions and body language than to any peculiar compunctions on the part of those she was interviewing.

Face-to-face, she could reel in practically any fish. On the phone,
they could wriggle off the hook.

Retrieving her coat from the rack that served her own and half a
dozen other desks, she scooped up her gritchel, slung the strap over
her shoulder, left the office, and headed downtown.

Twenty minutes later—her car maybe-not-quite-completely-illegally parked in a passenger zone whose white paint was sufficiently worn away for her to think she might be able to argue the
case—she entered the Public Safety Building and strode directly to
the cramped office Mark Blakemoor and Lois Ackerly shared.

"They're not here," a detective whose name Anne couldn't remember said as she was about to knock on the closed door. He
grinned at her, his eyes glinting with malicious humor. "Would you
believe they're down at the M.E.'s office, checking out a dead cat?"
Not bothering to reply, Anne turned on her heel and walked out of
the Homicide Division. She did, however, make a mental note to
find out the detective's name, just in case she ever got the opportunity to make fun of him in the paper.

She arrived at the medical examiner's office, only to be told there
was no more chance of her attending the autopsy of her cat than
there would be of her attending that of a human being.

"But it's a cat!" Anne protested. "And it's my cat! Doesn't that
make any difference at all?"

The young man behind the desk, whose name was David Smith according to a chipped plastic plaque propped up against a pen holder, shook his head. "Not around here. The rules are the rules. Only our staff and other authorized personnel can attend an autopsy."

"Come on," Anne began, using the her best wheedling and subservient tones. "Surely just this once you could let me—"

"No exceptions," David Smith told her in a voice filled with the kind of smug self-satisfaction that only career bureaucrats seem capable of producing.

Frustrated, but certain that there would be no changing David Smith's mind, Anne dropped onto a hard bench, prepared to wait for the rest of the morning if that's what it took. It turned out to be only forty-five minutes before Mark Blakemoor and Lois Ackerly emerged from the double doors that led to the labs from which Anne had been denied admittance.

There was an uncomfortable moment as the reporter and the two detectives regarded each other uncertainly, their long-standing professional relationship having suddenly taken on a new aspect.

"Why don't I meet you back at the shop," Mark Blakemoor told his partner, breaking the silence. "I'll have a cup of coffee with Anne and fill her in." Lois Ackerly gave him a strange look, started to say something, then seemed to change her mind.

"See you when you get there," she said. Nodding a greeting to Anne, she disappeared out the main door.

Mark led Anne to a small room equipped with two Formica-topped tables, a half-dozen chairs, and a counter on which sat a grease-splattered microwave oven and a crusted coffeepot. Fishing two mugs out of a badly stained sink, the detective rinsed them out, filled them with coffee, and handed one to Anne. "Not exactly a latte, but so far no one's been able to convince Starbucks to take over this space. Sit?"

Anne settled onto a flimsy vinyl chair; Blakemoor leaned against the counter.

"So what's the deal?" Anne asked. "What did you find out?"

"Nothing conclusive," the detective replied. "In fact, no one's even willing to say the same person who did the women did the cat, too."

Anne's brows arched as she recognized what she suspected was only the first of a series of noncommittal statements. Before she could begin questioning him, Mark Blakemoor went on.

"Here's how it lays out," he told her. "We're pretty sure the same guy did both women. We're pretty sure Shawnelle Davis let him into her apartment voluntarily—probably she picked him up thinking he was going to be a score. As for Cottrell, we found a key with a thumbprint on it, and the print isn't Cottrell's. So either she gave him the key or, more likely, he found it hidden in one of the usual places—the doormat, a planter. Everyone knows where to look, right?" Without waiting for Anne to reply, he went on. "Anyway, the only thing we really have to go on are the cuts, and they're pretty much alike on both women. He used knives he found in their own kitchens, so the wounds aren't exactly alike. But they're close enough that Cosmo—that's the M.E. who's working this for us—is willing to say it's the same perp in both homicides."

"And my cat?" Anne asked as Blakemoor finished.

"That's another story." The detective's expression tightened. "There are similarities to both the women. But the cut is—" He hesitated, then used the same word that had come into his mind the previous day, when he'd first examined the cat. "It's a neater cut. Cosmo says it was done with a sharper instrument—a razor blade, possibly a scalpel. And he says the incision is straighter." He paused again, his eyes avoiding Anne's when he finally went on. "He says it could be the same guy, and that by the time he got to the cat he'd had more practice."

"I see." Anne felt numb.

"Or someone else could have done the cat," Blakemoor finished. There was something in his voice that made Anne look up.

"Someone else, like my husband?" she asked, still remembering the silence that had fallen over Blakemoor and Ackerly as Glen had returned from the house with the plastic bag. When Blakemoor made no reply, Anne decided it was time to tell him about the note on her computer. "Whoever killed poor Kumquat put the note there," she finished. "And whoever put the note on my computer knew a lot more about programming than Glen does. He can operate a couple of programs, but he doesn't know the difference between an autoexec.bat and a config.sys. At our house, I even install the programs."

"But you thought of him," Blakemoor pointed out.

Anne almost wished she hadn't told the detective about the note at all. But it was too important to keep from him. "How could I not have?" she countered. "He was there by himself all day." A dark and hollow sound that wasn't quite a chuckle emerged from her throat. "I even searched the house, looking for signs that someone else had been there."

"And you didn't find anything," Blakemoor surmised.

Anne shook her head. "So what's next?" she asked.

"The same thing that's always next in a case like this," Blakemoor told her. Though she'd heard the words before—practically knew them by heart—this time they made Anne's blood run cold. "We keep looking, even though we don't have much of anything to go on." He stopped speaking, and it was Anne herself who finished the recitation.

"And we wait for him to kill someone else, and hope that next time he makes a mistake."

Blakemoor nodded, but said nothing. The silence between them stretched on until finally Anne could take it no longer.

"What if it's me?" she asked, rising to her feet. "What if it's me he kills, or one of my family?"

Without even thinking about what he was doing, Mark Blakemoor put his arms around Anne. "It won't be you," he said. "I won't let it be."

Struggling against an almost overpowering urge to cling to the big detective—even if just for a moment—Anne pulled away from him and picked up her coat and her large leather satchel. They left the medical examiner's office in silence.

Neither of them could think of anything else to say.

Glen Jeffers knew something was wrong the moment he woke up that morning. It was a feeling that flooded not only his brain, but his body as well—a feeling that although he was wide-awake, his mind was only half conscious; that although he'd slept through the night, his body was still exhausted. How could he possibly be so tired when he hadn't done much of anything except rest since coming home from the hospital?

The reality was that he was just plain bored. He'd spent his life being active, rising early for his morning jogs with Anne, putting in long days at the office—days that were often broken only by a fierce lunchtime game of racquetball with Alan Cline—then coming home to work in the evening at the drafting table in the den, or, if it was summer and the evenings long, going up to the park to throw a ball around with Kevin.

What he wasn't used to was inactivity, and this morning, after Anne and the kids had finally left, the house had begun to close in around him. Part of it, he reflected as he set about cleaning up the kitchen, was simply cabin fever. But there was more to it than that. It seemed to him that everything was getting tangled up in his mind. Just before he'd come fully awake this morning, he'd had a dream— one of those half-waking dreams in which you are unpleasantly aware that you're dreaming, but are powerless to stop the unwelcome images parading before you.

This one had been a jumble of scenes: Joyce Cottrell, and Kumquat, and Mark Blakemoor staring at him as though the detective thought he'd killed not only his daughter's cat, but his next door neighbor as well. By the time Glen came fully awake, he felt as surrounded by death and violence as he had when Anne was spending so much of her time on the Richard Kraven story.

That was another thing that was starting to get to him. The whole Kraven thing should have ended when the killer was executed, but it seemed to be rising up all over again. Anne was already looking for a connection between Kraven and the two new killings, and if he knew Anne, she'd find one, no matter how implausible it might seem.

Finished in the kitchen, Glen wandered into the den: maybe he'd just spend a few minutes at the drawing board, not working, really, but just sketching and thinking, seeing if any new ideas came to him. Before he even reached his drafting table, however, his eye was caught by the thick file on Anne's desk.

The Richard Kraven file—the one he'd made Kevin bring to him when he was still in the hospital.

Why had he done that? Now, he couldn't even remember having read the stuff. He leafed through a few pages of the file, but none of the articles struck him as something he'd read recently. And he certainly wasn't interested in reading the pieces this morning.

The mood of restless boredom that had been gathering around him since the moment he'd awakened coalesced into an oppressive claustrophobia. Suddenly he had to get out of the house, had to escape the confines of walls that suddenly seemed to be closing in on him. But where should he go?

A walk?

Forget it. Despite his promise to Gordy Farber, he'd always hated walking just for the sake of walking. What he needed was a destination to give the exercise purpose.

The office?

Forget that, too. If he so much as showed up there, Rita Alvarez would not only send him home, but call Anne, too.

But what about the Jeffers Building? He hadn't been to the construction site since his heart attack. A quick look at its progress, he thought now, would be the perfect antidote for his mood, and unless Alan happened to be there, no one on the job would even know about Farber's orders that he stay away from work. His mind made up, Glen pulled on a jacket against the chill of the overcast morning, locked the house, and set out.

A little less than an hour later he was standing on the sidewalk across the street from the soaring skeleton of the Jeffers Building. Even the quickest glance told him that the work was on schedule despite his not being there to supervise it. He felt a twinge of insecurity that they seemed not to need him at all, but then decided the signs of progress were actually something of a tribute—obviously, he and the huge design team working under him had done a good enough job that Jim Dover hadn't needed to call him.

The building—his building—drew him like a magnet. Crossing the street, he let himself through the door in the fence around the site, and headed for the office, a large trailer that would become unnecessary as soon as the ground floor had been enclosed and could be properly lit and heated. The young woman behind the desk, whose name was Janie Berkey, glanced up from the purchase orders she was working on, looked puzzled for a moment, then smiled.

"Mr. Jeffers!"

"Back among the land of the living," Glen said. "Thought I'd have a look around. Jim here?"

"Mr. Dover won't be on site until after lunch today," Janie told him. "If you want to wait for him—"

"Actually, I'd just as soon poke around on my own a little." Glen gave her a conspiratorial wink. "How can I find out what he's doing wrong if I only see what he wants to show me?"

Janie's eyes darkened. "Mr. Dover doesn't have anything to hide," she began, in a voice that made Glen wonder exactly how close a relationship the receptionist had with her boss. "He's the most—"

"Joke!" Glen interrupted. "It was just a joke."

Janie looked uncertain, then uttered a small laugh. Glen seized the opportunity to pick up a hard hat, put it on, and slip out of the office before she could insist on calling someone to escort him.

He spent a few minutes touring the ground floor, then climbed the temporary stairs to the mezzanine level. But even as he began inspecting the structure, he found himself being drawn toward the elevator.

What would happen if he went up?

Would the acrophobia that had overcome him the day he'd had his heart attack engulf him for a second time, or had his unexpected panic just been some kind of crazy fluke? As he stood in front of the metal cage considering the wisdom of going higher up in the structure, the elevator clanged to a stop and one of the workmen looked at him inquiringly.

"Great to have you back, Mr. Jeffers," he said, with a wide smile. "You going up?"

Glen hesitated, then made up his mind. It was like falling off a horse, he decided. If he didn't get on the elevator right now, and conquer the fear that had nailed him a couple of weeks ago, he might never be able to overcome it at all. "Thanks," Glen said. He stepped into the cage, the man closed the door, and a second later the machine came to life, rattling upward.

Instantly, Glen felt the first stirrings of apprehension in the pit of his belly. But he said nothing, determined that today the acrophobia would not get the better of him. As the machine continued to rise, Glen forced himself to look straight down, through the heavy grating of the elevator's floor, to the steadily receding mass of concrete upon which the steel skeleton of the skyscraper stood.

With every floor they passed, with every twelve feet added to the distance of the drop, the queasiness in his stomach increased. Suddenly the elevator jerked to a stop, and Glen felt a moment of pure terror.

Stuck! They were stuck! Trapped. A wild desperation seized him, blood pounding in his ears. He heard the workman's voice distantly.

"Utility floor," the man announced. "This is where I get out."

The utility floor. Only thirteen stories up, Glen realized, on the floor he'd set aside to hold part of the mass of equipment that would run the huge building's systems. Only a second ago he would have sworn they were much higher.

This was ridiculous!

"I think I'll go on up to the top," he said, forcing himself to sound matter-of-fact, hoping his nervousness wasn't reflected in his voice.

The hard hat hesitated, and Glen instinctively knew the man was remembering what had happened the last time the architect had visited the site. "You want me to go up with you?" he asked.

Glen shook his head. "I'll be fine." But as the construction worker got out of the elevator and it began creaking upward, he wondered if he'd told the truth. When the elevator finally rattled to a stop a few minutes later, he knew he hadn't.

Determined to overcome the fear that was congealing in his gut, Glen opened the door and got out. The platform around the open shaft of the elevator had been expanded since the day he'd had his heart attack. A wide path of rough-cut four-by-twelves extended all the way to the edge of the framework. If he stayed in the center of that path, he would be perfectly safe.

Taking a deep breath, Glen moved forward, telling himself it didn't matter that there were no handrails, that there was, indeed, nothing at all to steady himself with. When he was still five feet short of the edge, he stopped.

His stomach felt queasy, and he was finding it a little difficult to breathe.

His heart was beating quickly, but not quite pounding, and there was none of the pain he'd felt in his chest and left arm before the heart attack.

All he had to do was take a few more steps.

Fixing his eyes on one of the steel girders that would soon support the outer skin of the building, knowing that if he could just get to it—touch it—he would be all right, he started forward.

One step, then another, and another.

Reaching out, his fingers touched the cold steel, then closed on one of the thick ridges of the I beam. He edged closer to the girder.

And to the edge.

Now he was starting to feel dizzy, but he struggled against it, determined not to give in to the panic that was threatening to overwhelm him.

All he had to do was look down. Just one look, down to the sidewalk forty stories below, and he would have done it.

He edged closer and looked down.

Instantly, the chasm yawned open, drawing him outward, pulling him down. He felt himself leaning over, and an insane urge to jump blossomed inside him. Now he could feel it, feel the wind rushing past him as he dropped, feel the weightlessness of the fall. If he just let go . . .

He felt his fingers loosen on the girder, felt himself begin to lean out over the precipice, felt the dizziness take control of him.

No!

The single barked command came out of nowhere, slashing through the panic that had fogged his mind. Instinctively spinning around, Glen swept the platform with his eyes, searching for the person whose voice had broken the terrible trance of the acrophobia.

He saw no one.

But the voice spoke again: *Down. Now.*

Obeying the command, Glen started back toward the elevator. But as he crossed the platform this time, there was no trace of uncertainty in his step, no feeling of dizziness in his head, no hard knot of fear in his stomach.

And no consciousness of what he was doing.

The Experimenter felt good this morning. For the first time, he felt truly strong, strong enough that he would no longer have to put him to sleep.

Even yesterday, when Glen had begun to wake up while the Experimenter was working on the cat, he hadn't really tried to stop the Experimenter's work. He'd merely watched at first, but the Experimenter had been certain that, in a way, Glen had actually enjoyed it. After all, the Experimenter had experienced every emotion Glen had felt as, together, they'd carried out the work on the cat.

First there had been resistance, manifested by a faintly sick feeling in the pit of his belly. But the Experimenter had known that wouldn't last long—perhaps if he'd tried to work with the dog, or even the bird, it would have been more difficult. But the Experimenter had known that Glen didn't really like the cat.

Didn't like her any more than the Experimenter himself did. And that made things even simpler, for with their mutual antipathy toward the animal, their two minds were already working in a primitive synchronicity.

All the Experimenter had to do was reinforce that synchronicity, strengthen that tenuous bond that the cat herself had established between them. He'd worked slowly, letting Glen watch, letting him get used to what they were going to be doing. "It's all right," he'd whispered. "We're not going to kill her. We're only going to see what makes her live."

He'd felt Glen relax slightly, felt him begin to shed that peculiar sense of guilt that kept so many people from accomplishing all that they were able.

The Experimenter had thought about guilt as he waited for the cat to fall into unconsciousness. It was a concept he understood in the abstract, but could not remember ever having experienced. For him, guilt was not something to be overcome, or cast off.

It simply had never existed.

Occasionally he'd wondered if his lack of guilt could be construed as a character flaw, and—again in the abstract—he'd supposed it could be, at least by people of far less intelligence than he. For himself, it was nothing of the sort; indeed, it offered him freedom. His studies—his experiments—were never hindered by any feelings that perhaps he shouldn't be doing what interested him the most.

And what interested him most—the only thing that had ever interested him at all—was the study of life.

Not the meaning of life—he'd lost interest in that when he was still a boy and had come to conclusion that life had no meaning.

Life simply was.

Ergo, since there was no "why," the only important thing was "how."

Logic had long ago made it clear to him that his freedom from the restrictions that guilt imposed on other men allowed him to investigate the phenomenon of life with the use of methods that were unavailable to those selfsame others.

Unfettered, he had pursued his studies.

Yesterday he had begun to teach Glen Jeffers to find the same joy in knowledge that he himself had.

By the time the cat had fallen unconscious, he'd explained to Glen that its death was not their intention. Thus, when he began running the X-Acto knife from the cat's belly up to its neck and Glen had not tried to stop him, the Experimenter knew that Glen had experienced the same thrill as a medical student witnessing his first surgery.

Throughout the procedure, the Experimenter felt Glen's interest grow. Even better, he had been able to experience for himself Glen's own wonder when at last the living creature's beating heart was exposed.

"Touch it," he'd whispered.

Together, they'd touched the animal's throbbing organ, and a surge of joy had gone through the Experimenter, transporting him with an exhilaration he hadn't known in years, for this time he wasn't merely savoring the experience himself, but reveling in Glen's experience of it as well.

The heat of life had poured into him.

The power of the constantly working muscle infused his spirit.

The tingling sensation on his skin thrilled him as he touched the innermost sanctum of life itself.

Together, they had continued the experiment, finally squeezing the creature's heart to the point where it stopped. The Experimenter had prepared a primitive defibrillator, stripping the insulation from the cut end of an extension cord he found hanging from a nail in the wall, but it hadn't worked.

Once again his experiment had ended in failure, as the cat's body refused to respond to his efforts to bring it back to life. He'd worked frantically, inflating the cat's lungs with his own breath. Twice, the heart had begun to flutter, but the uncontrolled energy of the makeshift defibrillator had done no good. Instead of shocking the organ into a steady rhythm, it had only put the animal into convulsions.

Glen had begun to pull away as the Experimenter's fury mounted. When at last the cat died, too abused, too mutilated to survive any longer, the Experimenter had felt Glen's revulsion.

The Experimenter had sent Glen back to sleep, wiping his memory almost clean of what he'd seen, but then his own rage had erupted. He'd dug his fingers deep into the cat, ripping its lifeless heart and lungs loose from their bloodied nest, lifting them out to expose the empty cavity.

Snatching up the X-Acto knife, the Experimenter had slashed at the cat's interior, the blade glinting in the fluorescent light that flickered above the workbench. At last, the experiment over, he'd cleaned up after himself, first disposing of the cat in the alley, shoving it partway under the deck where the garbage cans stood, leaving it where it would quickly be found. Then he had set about cleaning up the basement, carefully erasing every sign of what had happened there.

Finally, he left the note for Anne, setting up her computer so his message would appear just long enough for her to read, then disappear forever.

Only then had he let himself rest, sinking deep beneath Glen's consciousness, not stirring until a few moments ago, when the man's acrophobia had threatened to kill them both.

The Experimenter did not intend to die.

Not ever.

Thus, he had stepped in instantly, seizing control, pulling Glen back from the precipice.

He entered the elevator, studied the controls for a moment, then pressed the button that should take him downward. The machinery came to life and the cage began rattling down the shaft. The Experimenter glanced idly through the grating of the floor, wondering what it was about heights that bothered some people.

To him, they meant nothing.

Nodding a greeting to each of the men who spoke to him, the Experimenter left the construction site. As he paused at the corner, his eyes fell on a newspaper box. Fishing in Glen's pocket for the right change, he bought a copy of the *Herald*, then looked around for a coffee shop. Spotting a Starbucks less than a block away, he strode down the street, bought a latte, and began paging through the newspaper. He found Anne's story on page three in the second section.

Except it wasn't Anne's story: there was no mention of a copycat, let alone of himself. And no byline.

Someone else must have written it.

Why?

What were they afraid of?

A copycat?

But a copycat was nothing but a nuisance.

Particularly this copycat.

The Experimenter dropped the newspaper into a wastebasket.

The police might well spend weeks trying to figure out who had killed the whore over near Broadway, and the woman next door.

The Experimenter knew who had done it.

He even knew why the murders had been committed.

And that was all they had been—murders, pure and simple.

Nothing had been accomplished, no new bit of knowledge gained, no basic truth uncovered. It had been killing for the sake of killing.

Worse, it had been killing for no other purpose than to gain attention.

The Experimenter had been thinking about it since the moment he recognized the man who carried Joyce Cottrell's butchered corpse through her backyard and out into the alley. Reluctantly, he'd come to a decision about what he must do.

Unless he acted, other people would die for no better reason than to gain attention for a fool. That was wasteful.

Any way he looked at it, it was wasteful.

But there was another reason for him to carry out the work of the police, the courts, and the executioner. A reason that appealed to the Experimenter's sense of irony, his sense of style, even his sense of humor. Justice would be served, and Anne—finally—would understand exactly what game was truly afoot.

Dropping a quarter in the pay phone at the back of the coffee shop, the Experimenter dialed a number from memory. On the third ring, a familiar voice answered.

"Hello?" The voice sounded nervous.

The Experimenter said nothing.

"Hello?" the voice said again, and now the Experimenter could clearly hear the terror in it.

The Experimenter knew why the voice sounded nervous.

And he knew more than that—he knew where the man lived, and he knew he hadn't gone to work.

The Experimenter would pay him a visit.

First, though, he would need certain supplies.

Leaving the coffee shop, the Experimenter found a cab and took it to the Broadway Market.

He began picking up the things he would need.

A pen, the kind you could buy anywhere.

A box of notepaper, again the kind you could buy anywhere.

Gloves—cheap knitted ones, nondescript, the kind everyone had.

A roll of transparent plastic.

Paying for it all with cash from Glen Jeffers's wallet, he left the market and started south, walking at a steady pace, neither too fast nor too slow, doing nothing that would attract unwanted attention. Anonymity, he had discovered years ago, was by far the best protection.

He came finally to John Street, turned left, and started toward Fifteenth East. Less than ten minutes later he was across the street from the building in which lived the man he had come to kill. Gazing up at the second floor, he saw the man peering out of the window.

The man looked nervous.

The man was staring right at him.

The man did not, of course, recognize him.

The Experimenter smiled to himself, crossed the street, and entered the building. . . .

The plans the Butcher began making after reading the story in that morning's *Herald* had grown, until he'd finally shaped a perfect structure for his next killing.

It would be a man—he'd definitely made up his mind on that. And he knew where he could find the perfect prey: there were plenty of them over on Broadway, shopping in the QFC, or hanging around the Broadway Market, or just sitting drinking coffee at one of the small espresso bars scattered along both sides of the street. Even better, they were always watching each other, playing their endless mating game. He even knew how they did it, because he'd watched them operate practically every time he'd gone over there. One would be walking toward another on the street, and often, after the two men passed, one would turn around to look at the other. If the second man had turned around, too, they might strike up a conversation and, after a few minutes, head off together. Sometimes one of them only glanced back and smiled, but kept walking. When that happened, the other would pause, watching. If the first one glanced back again, or stopped to look in a window, the watcher would follow him.

Twice, the Butcher had trailed behind to see what would happen, always making sure no one knew what he was doing, so he knew the pattern of pursuit and surrender well.

Once or twice he himself had been followed, but both times he'd gone into the magazine store, or Bartell's drugstore, and browsed through the shelves until his admirer finally got the message that he just wasn't interested and disappeared.

So that was what he would do today.

When he went out to buy the photo album, he would watch the men on the sidewalk, and when he found the right one, he would follow him. The person he chose would not be too big—certainly no taller than himself—and he'd try to select someone who didn't look too strong, either. But it would be easy—even easier than picking up Shawnelle Davis had been. And when they got to the guy's apartment and his quarry made a pass at him, he would act.

The Butcher's reputation would grow.

Just thinking about it excited him. With sudden inspiration, he thought maybe he'd do to the guy he followed home what he'd done to Joyce Cottrell the night before last. That thought excited him even more. He was starting to feel a tingling in his crotch when the phone jangled, the unexpected sound startling him so badly that he almost dropped the Coke he'd been drinking.

"Is that you?" his mother demanded when he picked up the phone on the third ring, her voice carrying an inculpatory tone that made his stomach churn. Could she already know what he'd done? But how could she? Then she spoke again, and his fears eased somewhat. "I called over to Boeing's," she said. "They told me you weren't there again today. Are you all right?"

"I'm fine, Ma," the man replied, the words already out of his mouth before he remembered he was supposed to be sick. "I mean, I was feeling kinda sick earlier, but I'm better now."

"You weren't home when I called earlier," his mother accused. "Did you go to the doctor?"

"No, Ma," he replied, feeling the way he had when he was ten years old and his mother had accused him of faking an illness so he wouldn't have to go to school, in spite of the fact that his temperature had been 102. "I went to the QFC and bought some soup. Chunky Chicken."

"Well, don't ask me to come and fix it for you," his mother told him. "Did you see the paper this morning?"

The man's heart began to pound. "What about it?"

"That woman. The one that got killed up by you the other night. Did you know her?"

The Butcher's chest tightened as if a band of metal had been wound around it. "Why would I have known her?" he asked, his voice catching despite his effort to keep it steady.

"She worked across the street from you, didn't she? And she lived up the street from you, didn't she?"

His head started throbbing. "I didn't know her, Ma. And I didn't do anything to her! I swear I didn't! Why don't you just leave me alone?" A sob closing his throat, he slammed the receiver down, the bravado he'd felt only a few minutes before evaporating. How could she have found out? Was she going to tell the police?

Of course she would—she didn't love him! She'd never loved him. The only one she'd ever loved was his brother!

He paced back and forth in the apartment, trying to figure out what to do. When the phone rang a second time, he froze where he was, across the room from the loudly jangling instrument. He broke into a sweat—an icy sweat that made him feel as if a freezing slime were covering his body. His legs threatened to give out on him.

Should he answer the phone, or just let it keep ringing?

What if it was his mother again?

Worse, what if it was the police? What if she'd called them, and now they were calling him? But they wouldn't, would they? If they wanted him, they'd just come and arrest him, wouldn't they?

So if it wasn't the police, it *had* to be his mother—no one else ever called him!

His legs still threatening to buckle beneath him, he went to the phone and picked it up. "Hello?"

No answer.

"Hello?"

There was a soft click as whoever had called him hung up.

His terror rose another notch. His first instinct was to get out of his apartment, to run to his car, get in, and drive away. Away from Capitol Hill, away from the police, away from his mother, away from Seattle. But where? There was nowhere for him to run to.

Besides, the police were probably already outside, surrounding the building, waiting for him to come out. He went to the window and peered out, his heart pounding so hard he could hear it thumping in his ears.

The street looked normal.

But that's the way they would do it, wasn't it? They wouldn't be right out in plain sight, would they? Their cars would be parked around the corner where he couldn't see them, and the cops themselves would be hiding.

Breathing hard, he turned away from the window. He had to think—had to figure out what to do! What could his mother have told them?

He began pacing the apartment again, the room shrinking with each step. He felt the walls closing in on him, and the air seemed stuffy.

He sat down in his chair—an old La-Z-Boy with stained velour upholstery that he'd found in a used furniture store ten years ago. He tried to calm himself.

He went back over everything he'd done, first with Shawnelle Davis, then with Joyce Cottrell. He'd been careful—as careful as he knew how. But what if he'd left fingerprints?

He'd been cautious in Joyce Cottrell's house—he hadn't touched anything. Or had he? Oh, God, he couldn't remember! But he *had* to remember.

His skin felt itchy now, and he couldn't sit still any longer. Abandoning the chair, he went back to the window and gazed out.

There was a man across the street! A man who was looking up at him! Staring right at him, as if he knew him!

As the stranger started across the street toward his building, he backed away from the window.

The band he'd felt around his chest when his mother had called seized him again, tighter than ever. He could feel cold rivulets of sweat running down his back and trickling from his armpits down his sides.

The nausea was back in his belly, and now his guts were aching as he felt the first pangs of diarrhea grip his intestines.

Hunched against the pain, he had started for the bathroom when he heard the knock at the door. He froze.

Images flashed through his mind, remembered images from things he'd seen on television.

Would they break his door down?

Would they shoot him through it?

A strangled whimper escaped his lips as he imagined a .45 slug ripping through the door, then slashing through his flesh, tearing his guts open. He staggered as the pain of the imagined bullet ripped at his mind, and he lurched toward the door. Better to open it willingly than to have them break in on him.

Pulling the door open, he found himself looking at the man he'd seen gazing up at him from across the street only moments before. A pleasant enough face, with even features.

Not the face of a cop.

His lips worked; he tried to speak and failed.

The stranger was looking at him, his eyes boring into him, and suddenly he had the feeling that he did know this man after all, that he had, indeed, seen him somewhere before. . . .

Moments passed in deadly silence as the Butcher stared at the stranger who had come to his door. Then he knew. It was Anne Jeffers's husband! He had seen him the day before yesterday, when he'd been casing Joyce Cottrell's house. But Jeffers hadn't seen him—he was sure of it!

Then something in Jeffers's face changed, and the man gasped, for he suddenly recognized the eyes he was looking into.

They were his brother's eyes!

But that was crazy—Jeffers didn't look anything like his brother! And besides, his brother was dead!

Then Glen Jeffers spoke, and the man's terror peaked. "Hello, Little Man," he heard his brother's voice say, using the name he'd hated all his life. "You've been bad, Little Man, and I've come to punish you."

His mind reeled, then cracked. It was impossible! This man couldn't possibly be his brother—he was the wrong age, and he had the wrong face, and he wasn't even the same size.

But it *was* his brother!

The voice was his brother's, and the coldness of the eyes was his brother's.

And the words were definitely his brother's.

Rory Kraven, cowering with terror, backed away from the impossible presence of his older brother.

Richard Kraven—the Experimenter—stepped into his younger brother's shabby apartment and silently closed the door behind him.

Edna Kraven let the telephone ring twenty times before she hung up. When he was in one of his moods, Rory sometimes wouldn't answer until he realized she simply wasn't going to give up. But this was the fifth time she'd called him, and she was starting to worry. After all, he *had* said he was sick when she'd talked to him earlier, and although he hadn't sounded that bad (and had always been the kind of boy who malingered—not like Richard at all!) she supposed it was just possible he'd taken a turn for the worse.

Either that or he really wasn't at home, in which case he'd have to answer not only to the nice people at Boeing's who were decent enough to give him steady work, but to her as well. If she trekked all the way up to Capitol Hill only to find that he was out gallivanting somewhere, she would have a lot to say to him. Still, she had always been a good mother, Edna Kraven told herself, no matter what people might have said behind her back, so what choice did she really have? Rory wasn't much, but he was all she had left.

She left her house at one o'clock, climbed off the bus in front of Group Health at a little after two, and trudged the block to Rory's apartment building, her annoyance with her younger son growing with every step she took. Why couldn't he have been more like Richard, who had never caused her a day of grief in his entire life?

A martyr, that's what Richard was. Just a Christian martyr!

Edna had prayed about Richard many times, and over and over the same message came to her: Richard had been an innocent lamb, unjustly led to slaughter. Only his own mother had believed in him. Well, someday they'd find out. After all, weren't those terrible murders happening again right now? Just a week or so ago there had been that woman over on Boylston. Not that Edna felt very sorry for her; after all, she *was* a whore. But then just the night before last there had been that poor woman who lived up the street from Rory. And both of them killed just the way those others had been, the ones they blamed poor Richard for. If only they hadn't killed Richard, they'd know the truth now, and he'd be able to come home to his mother where he belonged. But it was too late. Sighing heavily under the burden of her sorrows, Edna Kraven pulled the front door of Rory's building open, went in, and climbed the steep flight of stairs to the second floor.

Pausing on the landing to catch her breath, she peered with distaste around the dimly lit corridor. The paint on the walls was peeling and the strip of threadbare carpet that ran down the cramped hallway was curling back at the edges. What had she done to deserve a son who would live in a place like this? She'd told him before that it wasn't a fit place for her to visit; today she would put her foot down. If he didn't move, he needn't expect her to visit him again.

She plodded down the hall to Rory's door, lifted her hand to knock, then realized that the door wasn't quite closed. Just like Rory to go out somewhere and not even bother to lock his door—anyone could rob him blind! Pushing the door wider, Edna stepped inside.

"Rory?"

There was no answer, but Edna suddenly felt uneasy. The place just didn't *feel* empty. Scowling, she moved toward the open bathroom door, but before she'd gone more than a step or two, she stopped short.

The walls—the grubby beige walls she'd never been able to get Rory to paint—were streaked with red.

Bright red.

Bloodred.

"Rory?" Edna Kraven said again, but this time the name of her younger son was uttered softly, almost inaudibly, as if she already understood what had happened here. "Rory?" she repeated. "It's Mommy, Rory, come to take care of you."

As if guided by an unseen force, Edna edged toward the bathroom door, terrified of what she might find there, but unable to keep herself from looking. When she was finally able to see exactly what lay in the bathtub, Edna Kraven's stomach heaved. She lurched into the bathroom, bent over, and threw up into the sink. Only when her stomach had completely emptied itself was she finally able to creep back out to the single room in which her younger son had died and call the police.

CHAPTER 47

"Holy Jesus," Mark Blakemoor swore as he gazed at the ruined body of Rory Kraven. "What the hell is going on?"

He and Lois Ackerly had been reviewing the files on Shawnelle Davis and Joyce Cottrell, searching without success for anything that might link the two women together—a friend in common, a distant relative, even a casual acquaintance—when the call came in.

Now, lying naked in his bathtub in a crappy apartment, was Rory Kraven, the kid brother of the man whose crimes had been copycatted by whoever had killed Davis and Cottrell.

Just like Davis and Cottrell, Rory Kraven's chest had been cut open, and his lungs and heart had been torn out. But unlike the mayhem to which the two women had been subjected, what had been done to Rory Kraven appeared to have been carried out with almost surgical precision.

Also unlike either Shawnelle Davis or Joyce Cottrell, Rory Kraven's throat had been slashed. There was blood everywhere—pools of it on the carpet, dark stains on the furniture, even reddish smears on the walls. It was obvious that Rory Kraven hadn't died instantly. From what they could see, it was clear that even after he was injured, he'd still been able to move around the apartment. Yet there didn't seem to be much sign of a fight—none of the furniture was overturned, nothing was broken. From the appearance of the room, it looked as if Rory Kraven's assailant had slashed his throat, then stood aside and let the mortally injured man lurch around the apartment until he finally bled to death. Still, given the victim's hideous wounds, it seemed as if someone, somewhere, surely must have heard something.

As the team from the lab set to work photographing the scene and sifting for evidence that might have been left by Rory's killer, Mark Blakemoor began the laborious job of checking the other apartments. Granted, most of the people in the building would have been at work, but all these buildings seemed to have at least a few tenants who rarely went out except to buy food. Lois Ackerly sat gingerly on the edge of the couch where Edna Kraven still huddled, her heavy breasts heaving as she tried to deal with what she'd seen in the bathroom.

"Do you need a doctor?" Lois Ackerly asked. Edna Kraven's face was pallid, but Lois recalled that Richard Kraven's mother, whom she'd interviewed at least four times in the past few years, always looked rather pale.

"What can a doctor do for a mother's grief?" Edna asked, dabbing at her eyes with a crumpled handkerchief she'd found deep in the bottom of her purse.

"Can you tell me what happened?"

Edna shrugged helplessly. "He was sick this morning. Then I kept calling him, and when he didn't answer his telephone, I thought I'd better come over. He's my son," she added in a tone that struck Lois Ackerly as almost defensive. "What else could I do?"

Lois led Edna through her recitation of the day's events twice more, but as she expected, the minor details never varied. Edna was uncertain exactly what time she'd gotten on the bus, or which bus she'd taken up Fifteenth, but Ackerly had long ago discovered that people too well-equipped with details are often the ones who are lying. She was just finishing when Mark Blakemoor beckoned to her from the door. Leaving Edna on the sofa, she joined him in the corridor.

"No one heard anything," he told her. "I found two people who haven't been out of their apartments all day, and neither of them seems to be deaf. If Kraven put up a struggle, why didn't anyone hear it? And believe me, if the woman in 2B had heard a fight, she would have called the police. It just doesn't jibe: if there wasn't any struggle, how come there's such a mess?"

Lois Ackerly had barely begun to think about her partner's question when one of the techs stepped out into the hall. "Well, at least this one's going to be pretty simple," he said as he handed Blakemoor a transparent Ziplock bag. It contained a piece of yellow paper that Ackerly instantly recognized as a large Post-it Note on which someone had handwritten a message. "It was stuck on the refrigerator door, as if it were a shopping list. We got pictures of it in place, and we'll check it for prints." Blakemoor read the note, then wordlessly passed it to Lois Ackerly.

> **I hate a copycat.**
> **I especially hate an inept copycat.**
> **Killing for the reasons Rory killed is not simply immoral; it's wasteful. Loathing waste, I have therefore put an end to Rory's carnage. I doubt anyone will be too upset that Rory is gone. After all, he could never be me, no matter how hard he tried.**

"Does this say what I think it does?" Ackerly asked as she finished reading the note. "It sounds like whoever whacked Kraven thinks Rory killed Davis and Cottrell. But how could he know? There isn't even any absolute proof both of them were murdered by the same creep. So far, it's all just speculation."

"It'll be easy enough to check now," Blakemoor observed. "We've got a pretty good set of right-hand fingerprints from the knife at Cottrell's, and there were a couple of smudges of a palm print from Davis's kitchen. If they all match Rory, then it looks like we'll have a bingo." Blakemoor shook his head in disgust. "Some crappy world, huh? One creep thinks another creep did something, so he comes in and whacks him."

"Except he didn't just whack him," Lois said almost distractedly, her eyes fixing on the note. "Something hinky's going on here, Mark.

What does this mean, 'I hate a copycat'? Even if it turns out Rory Kraven did kill Davis and Cottrell, what's this new guy's beef with Rory? I mean, here's this new perp doing the same thing to Rory that he claims Rory did to Davis and Cottrell. So who's the copycat? Rory Kraven, or this guy?" She started back into the apartment, but the sound of footsteps coming quickly up the stairs stopped her. Turning, she saw Anne Jeffers, with a photographer in tow, emerge from the stairwell, only to stop short as she recognized the two detectives.

"Oh, God, I was right," Anne said, paling. "Even after I heard the dispatch on the scanner, I hoped maybe . . ." Her words trailed off, and she tried to cover her fear by putting on her reporter's dispassionate mien. She couldn't do it. "It's another one, isn't it?" she whispered. "Like Shawnelle Davis and Joyce Cottrell?"

Mark Blakemoor and Lois Ackerly glanced at each other, wordlessly agreeing that at least where this case was concerned, Anne Jeffers was more than simply a reporter.

"It's Rory Kraven," Mark Blakemoor told her. "Richard's kid brother."

Rory Kraven? Anne thought. But that was crazy. He was nothing but— And then, in a sudden flash of clarity, she remembered exactly where she'd been when she left the hospital after visiting Glen and felt someone watching her. Her gaze shifted from Mark Blakemoor to the open door to Rory Kraven's apartment. Through the window in the opposite wall she could see the looming bulk of the hospital across the street.

"He was watching me one night," she said, her voice so low that neither detective was certain whether she was talking to them or to herself. "I'd been visiting Glen in the hospital, and I was on my way home. I felt someone watching me. It must have been him." She fell silent for a moment, then turned back to the two detectives. "What happened?" she asked.

Wordlessly, Blakemoor handed Anne the note.

She read it through, then looked up at Blakemoor. "He's dead? Rory Kraven's dead?"

The detective nodded. "He's in the bathtub. Naked, just like Cottrell."

Anne suddenly felt numb. Rory Kraven had killed her next door

neighbor? But Rory had been nothing—the kind of man who plodded through life, using all his resources just to get by. She could still
remember interviewing him years ago, when suspicion had first begun focusing on his brother. Rory hadn't wanted to talk about
Richard—all he'd said was that they didn't get along very well, they
weren't close, they weren't very much alike.

Which had certainly been the truth.

Where Richard's features had been strong, even handsome, Rory's
face had been a study in weakness and ineffectuality. He'd had a
low-level job at Boeing, if she remembered correctly, and he seemed
to her the kind who never missed a day, never created a problem for
anyone, could always be counted on to do his work steadily, if never
brilliantly. But dull, uninspired Rory had also been the little brother
of Richard Kraven. Richard, who was brilliant. Richard, who was everything Rory wasn't.

Richard, who was the apple of his mother's eye.

And that, she well knew, hadn't stopped even after Richard had
been executed. Even after her son's trial, failed appeals, and execution, Edna Kraven still insisted that Richard had been innocent.

Innocent, and perfect.

Richard must have been eating at Rory all his life, even if he'd
never shown it. Richard, who had remained newsworthy even after
he'd been executed. She herself—

And suddenly it made sense.

"He wanted the attention," she whispered, barely even aware that
she was speaking out loud. "All his life, everything was focused on
Richard. And even after Richard was dead, it didn't stop."

Her eyes went back to the note she still held in her hand.

*I hate a copycat . . . an inept copycat . . . I doubt anyone will be too
upset that Rory is gone. After all, he could never be me . . .*

She read the words again and again—read them so many times
she was sure she could recite them in her sleep—staring all the while
at the note.

It was the handwriting.

She kept staring at it, knowing she recognized it, but not wanting
to admit it. Not without an explanation.

And there could be no explanation for this.

She had seen Richard Kraven die in the electric chair. She had
watched as his body stiffened, his face contorted, and his eyes rolled
back into his head.

It was impossible that Richard Kraven could have written the note
that was now in her hand.

And yet there was no question.

The handwriting was his.

*B*lood.
   There was blood everywhere, but this time it wasn't the blood of a cat.

This time it was human blood.

Glen Jeffers knew it was human blood, although he had no idea where it had come from. The blood was all over him—on his hands, on his face, smeared down the whole length of his naked body.

Naked?

Why was he naked?

Tearing his eyes away from the stains on his hands and torso, Glen scanned the walls that surrounded him. He was in a room he didn't recognize—a shabby room, the kind he'd lived in years ago when he was a student in the architecture school at the university. But even that apartment, up in the University District just off Roosevelt, had been nicer than this one. Its walls had been cracked, and there'd been a hole in one of them where the previous tenant had let the closet door slam against the plaster every time he opened it. But at least the walls of that apartment had been white—a good, clean white that Glen had put on himself.

The walls surrounding him now were beige—the kind of drab, dirty beige that covers the walls of most cheap apartments. He could see a Murphy bed in one wall, and a sagging recliner, its upholstery so stained it was hard even to tell what color it might once have been.

A rickety-looking table with a couple of badly nicked painted metal chairs.

And more blood.

The walls were covered with it, and so was the furniture.

Blood everywhere.

He wanted to run from the room, but as he turned from one wall to another—and now they seemed to loom over him, imprisoning him—he couldn't find a door.

Only more blood, dripping down the grimy walls, puddling on the floor.

Glen could feel it under his bare feet now, warm and sticky, and he tried to move away from it but his feet felt heavy, immobile, almost as if they were encased in concrete.

The walls seemed to be closing around him, and he reached out to push them away, but succeeded only in smearing their bloody surface. Blood, glistening scarlet, covered his fingertips, and he opened his mouth to vent his terror in a scream.

Nothing came out.

His throat constricted, and now he could barely even breathe, let alone howl out in terror.

He turned again, and finally there was a door.

An open door, leading into another room.

He worked his way toward it, his feet dragging, resisting him every step of the way. There was light flooding through the doorway, and inside he could see the shiny surface of white enamel on the other room's ceiling, and a darkly mildewed grid of uncleaned grout surrounding the tile on the walls.

A bathroom.

There would be a shower there, and at least he could wash the blood from his body, get it off his face, out of his hair. A whimper bubbled out of his throat as he reached the door, but even that whimper died away as he gazed at the carnage in the bathtub.

It was a body—a man's body, stripped as naked as Glen himself—its eyes gazing sightlessly up at the ceiling. The man's throat had been slashed and his chest laid open to expose the heart and lungs.

And although Glen was certain the man was dead, he watched, transfixed with unbelieving horror, as the heart beat steadily and the lungs rose and fell with the slow, deep, even rhythm of sleep.

As another scream was born in Glen's throat, he lurched forward, tripped, and found himself plunging headlong toward the body. In-

stinctively, he threw his hands out to break the fall, only to watch in helpless disgust as first his fingers, then his entire hands, disappeared deep into the corpse's vital organs. Glen gagged, felt his stomach constrict, and knew he was going to throw up. He collapsed into the tub, sprawling on top of the body, the cold clamminess of its skin sending an icy chill through him. Now the corpse seemed to come fully alive, its arms wrapping around him, pulling him closer.

The head moved then, and the eyes blinked.

The mouth began to work, and Glen felt lips against his neck.

Lips, then teeth.

As terror and revulsion built inside him, Glen gathered his strength to jerk himself loose from the macabre embrace.

"No!" he screamed, finally finding his voice. "No!"

"No!" Glen bellowed once more, and this time he sat bolt upright. The nightmare fled as Glen came awake, but the dark image of the corpse in the bathtub was already burned indelibly into his memory.

For a few seconds he wasn't sure where he was. He sat still, gasping to catch his breath, shaking, waiting for the horror of the blood-soaked dream to release him from its grip. He felt his heart pound, and terror seized him. Another heart attack! But then, as he came fully awake, his pounding heart slowly settled back into its normal rhythm.

As his panting, too, began to ease, he gazed around. The blood-smeared beige walls of the room in which he'd been trapped were gone. He was on the temporary platform fronting the construction elevator at the Jeffers Building. Slowly, it began to come back to him. He'd come downtown to take a look at the building, and come up here to the top.

He'd made himself go out to the edge, forced himself to look down.

He'd panicked! A wave of dizziness had come over him, and he'd felt that awful sensation of the abyss enticing him, drawing him in, almost sucking him over the edge. He'd felt himself leaning outward, ready to fall, when . . .

Something—some*one*—had stopped him.

After that, nothing.

Nothing except the nightmare.

Glen glanced at his watch. Almost four. But it had only been ten-thirty when he'd come up here! How could he have lain on the platform most of the day with nobody noticing him? Wouldn't the construction worker who'd ridden partway up with him have wondered why he'd never come back down? Or the girl in the office? Wouldn't she have wondered what had happened when he didn't show up to return the hard hat? Getting to his feet, Glen pulled open the door of the elevator and hit the button to take him back to the bottom of the long shaft.

On the way down he was careful to keep his eyes focused on the door of the cage, never looking down, unwilling to risk another attack of the terrible acrophobia that had almost killed him earlier in the day. The elevator clanged to a stop and Glen sighed in relief. But in the site office, his worry came flooding back: Janie Berkey smiled at him brightly, then said, "That didn't take long! You must have found your pen as soon as you got off the elevator!"

Unable to do more than offer her a quick nod, Glen put the hard hat on the shelf with the others and made his escape from the office.

Once again he'd blacked out.

Once again he'd lost hours out of the day.

Obviously, he'd gone somewhere.

But where?

And what had he done?

The blood-soaked nightmare rose out of his memory. . . .

CHAPTER 49

The story would run on the front page. Anne knew that, even knew she should have been pleased. Instead she was terrified.

It was four-thirty, and she'd finished her account of Rory Kraven's death. She'd talked to Mark Blakemoor one last time, half hoping he'd be able to tell her there had been a mistake, that Rory Kraven's fingerprints hadn't matched the ones lifted from the knife with which Joyce Cottrell had been killed.

He not only confirmed Rory Kraven as Joyce Cottrell's killer, he told her that the lab had now matched parts of Rory's right palm print to one of the smeared prints found in Shawnelle Davis's kitchen.

Finally, Anne had dropped a note in Vivian Andrews's E-mail suggesting they run only the bare bones of the story until they could penetrate at least part of the thick fog of questions that still cloaked the morning's events in the drab apartment on Sixteenth Avenue.

Who?

And why?

Who could have known that Richard Kraven's brother had killed Shawnelle Davis and Joyce Cottrell when the police hadn't yet been willing to state unequivocally even that the same person had committed both those murders?

The questions were still tumbling through her mind as Anne walked out of the Herald Building into the gray afternoon and headed up Denny toward Capitol Hill and home. The worst of it—the part that threatened to drive her crazy—was the appearance of the notes. She'd finally told Mark Blakemoor about the message that

had appeared when she'd booted her computer up the previous afternoon. Though he'd listened intently as she described every detail,
in the end he'd had some questions she wasn't prepared to answer:

He'd still been in her backyard when it had occurred yesterday afternoon. Why hadn't she told him about it then?

She hadn't mentioned the fishing fly to Blakemoor, either.

Why not?

Her fingers tightened on the steering wheel. *Because it didn't mean
anything, that's why. And it didn't have anything to do with the note
on her computer screen, or Kumquat being killed, or anything else!
Glen had explained to her where it had come from, hadn't he? He'd
bought it! It was nothing but a coincidence that it happened to be
made out of feathers and fur that could have come from her children's
pets. For God's sake, what was she thinking? That someone—some
stranger who was pretending to be Richard Kraven—had come sneak-
ing into her house, made a fishing fly, killed her cat, and then left a
note on her computer?*

Anne decided the whole idea was insane; she was starting to sound
paranoid even to herself. Two blocks from home she cut over to Sixteenth and cursed out loud as she crept past the big motor home
somebody had parked on her block, taking up the parking spot she
normally used, and another one as well. Finally finding an empty
spot in the next block, she walked back to the house, glaring at the
motor home one more time before going inside.

"Hello?" she called out. "Anybody home?"

"Back here," Glen called from the den.

Anne dropped her gritchel under the table by the stairs and went
into the den. Glen was sitting at the drafting table, and he looked up
almost guiltily as she came in. "I'm not working," he assured her.
"I'm just doodling."

Moving around the table, she kissed him. "Is that what you've
been doing all day? Doodling?"

She felt him stiffen, but then he nodded.

"Pretty much," he said. "What about you?"

Dropping into her desk chair, Anne told Glen about Rory Kraven's
murder.

And as he listened to his wife, an image came into Glen's mind.

An image from the dream he'd had this afternoon.

An image that was, in every detail, a perfect portrayal of Anne's description of Rory Kraven's body when it had been found in his bathtub that afternoon.

But he had only dreamed it, Glen thought. Surely, he had only dreamed it.

Serial Killer's Younger Brother Found Dead

Rory Kraven Linked to New Series of Capitol Hill Deaths

The body of Rory Kraven, 41, brother of recently executed serial killer, Richard Kraven, was found in his Capitol Hill apartment yesterday afternoon. The victim of a thus-far-unknown assailant, the younger Kraven suffered multiple stab wounds. His unclothed body, mutilated in a manner that police sources concede was similar to the mutilations inflicted on victims of Richard Kraven, was found in the bathtub of the apartment by his mother, Edna Kraven, 66.

As part of their investigation into this most recent Capitol Hill slaying, police have found evidence conclusively linking Rory Kraven to the killings of both Shawnelle Davis and Joyce Cottrell. Detective Mark Blakemoor confirms that Rory Kraven's fingerprints match those found . . .

Edna Kraven glared at the article on the front page of the morning *Herald*. She had sat up all night long, afraid even to go to bed, so certain was she that she would be robbed of her sleep by the image of poor Rory. It was a vision she knew would stay with her for the rest of her life. Even now it was almost more than she could bear just to think about it—the way his eyes had stared at her, and the terrible slashes in his throat and chest! If only she hadn't pushed the door to his apartment open! She'd known something was wrong, had felt it from the moment she came up those stairs. And she'd told Anne Jeffers about it, too.

Not that the woman had printed anything she'd said! Edna thought angrily. She'd only written more lies. And as though it wasn't enough to hash over the falsehoods about Richard again— now the bitch was making up things about poor Rory, too!

The very idea of Rory killing those two women!

It was ridiculous—Rory could barely even bring himself to speak to women.

Edna had seen the photographs of those women on television. Cheap, both of them.

One of them had been a whore, and the other some kind of recluse. What would Rory have had to do with women like them?

Wasn't it obvious that whoever had killed them had killed Rory, too?

Incompetence, that's what it was, Edna told herself. The police couldn't find the killer, so they'd blamed poor, stupid Rory. And then that reporter, who had always been out to get her darling Richard, had gone and printed it! Edna shuddered as she thought of her neighbors reading the slander smeared all over the front page of this morning's paper.

Well, there might not be anything she could do about the police, she decided, but she could certainly give that Jeffers woman a piece of her mind!

Though it wasn't yet seven o'clock, Edna scrabbled through the yellow pages until she found the number for the *Seattle Herald*. She dialed it and demanded to speak to Anne Jeffers. Her lips tightened as she listened to the operator tell her the reporter hadn't come in yet that morning. "No, I certainly do not want to leave a message," Edna said when the girl offered to connect her to the reporter's voice mail. "I want to talk to her!"

Her anger growing steadily, Edna reached for the white pages and began searching through the J's.

> ... on the knife that killed Joyce Cottrell, while a partial palm print taken from the apartment of Shawnelle Davis matches a portion of Kraven's right hand.
>
> An unsigned note was found at the scene of this latest death, but police have so far refused to make its contents public, except to say that neither the note nor the wounds inflicted on the dead man are consistent with a suicide. At the same time, police department sources confirmed that they have no suspects in this killing.
>
> It is, however, believed that his assailant was familiar to Rory Kraven, as no signs of a struggle or of forcible entry were found at the murder scene. Three neighbors, whose names are being withheld at their own request, denied hearing anything unusual yesterday morning. Police are requesting that anyone having any information regarding this murder contact the Homicide Division at ...

As the phone rang, Glen Jeffers looked up from the copy of the *Herald* that lay unfolded on the kitchen table. He waited to see if either Heather or Kevin would answer on the extension in the upstairs hall, then finally reached for the wall phone mounted over the end of the counter.

"Hello?"

"I want to speak to Anne Jeffers." The voice spiking through the phone—a woman's voice—made the hair on the back of Glen's neck stand on end. "Is she there?"

He felt his flesh crawl as goose bumps broke out on his arms. "I— No, she isn't," Glen said. "She went out—" He cut his words short. He had no idea to whom he was speaking, but something about the woman's voice made him feel . . . what?

Frightened? Not quite.

Nervous? Closer, but still not quite right.

Filled with a sense of unease, he decided that until he knew exactly who the caller was and what she wanted with Anne, he wasn't about to tell her that his wife, heedless of recent events, had gone jogging in Volunteer Park. "May I take a message?" he asked.

There was a moment of hesitation, then: "This is Edna Kraven."

A clammy sweat broke out over Glen's body, and he felt a wave of dizziness. He reached out to the counter to steady himself, but as his fingers closed on the hard surface, the dizziness worsened. Blackness began to close around him, as if he were about to faint.

The voice that replied to Edna Kraven's self-identification had changed.

"Oh, Mrs. Kraven," the voice said smoothly into the telephone. "My wife was talking about you only a few minutes ago. I'm sure she'll want to talk to you. Perhaps we can arrange something?"

A buzzing . . . There was a buzzing in Glen's ear, and he felt utterly confused. Then his mind cleared, the last of the dizziness left him, and he began to remember. He'd been drinking a cup of coffee and reading the paper when the phone had rung. He'd answered it, and someone—a woman—had asked for Anne. He frowned, trying to re-member. He'd gotten dizzy then, and now couldn't remember if the woman on the phone had identified herself or not.

"Hello?" he said now, holding the receiver against his ear. But all he heard was the repeated buzz of a phone that's been off the hook too long. He frowned and hung up the receiver.

This morning, he decided, he would definitely call Gordy Farber and tell him what was happening.

The latest blackouts, the steadily worsening nightmares, the mem-ories he was having of things he couldn't possibly have seen . . . If Gordy said he had to go back into the hospital, so be it. Too many strange things were happening to him, and yesterday, when he'd blacked out at the top of the Jeffers Building, he could have killed himself.

But when Anne came back from her morning jog a few minutes later and, seeing the worried look on his face and the sheen of sweat on his skin, asked him how he was, he only shrugged and insisted nothing was wrong. And though he could see the hurt in her eyes when she left for work an hour later after seeing Heather and Kevin off to school, he found himself unable to do or to say anything to soothe her pain.

Nor did he call Gordy Farber.

Anne stared at the terminal screen in front of her. She knew the story she was working on was good—a sidebar piece on the opposite personalities of Rory and Richard Kraven in which she intended to suggest that the brothers might have shared some kind of "killing gene" that had led both of them to become serial murderers. Yet, she was finding it almost impossible to concentrate. It wasn't just her utter confusion about what had happened to Rory Kraven, but everything else in her life, too.

Glen was on her mind, his odd behavior gnawing at her, first Joyce Cottrell's bizarre account of seeing him naked, then the cat. Even something as trivial as the fishing fly bothered her. What's more, the Glen Jeffers she'd fallen in love with wouldn't have sent her off to work this morning without so much as a kiss, let alone a conversation. A gulf was forming between them; every day she could feel it growing wider.

Abandoning her computer, Anne picked up the phone and dialed Gordy Farber's number. Catching him just before his first appointment of the day, she quickly related her fears. "I know you warned me that he'd be different, but I never expected this," she said. A pause, then: "Sometimes I feel like I'm living with a stranger. And it's not just his attitude, Dr. Farber. He's doing some things that—"

"I'll call him," Gordy Farber cut in. In his office, the doctor glanced at the clock; he was already behind schedule, and Anne sounded ready to go on talking for another half hour. "I'll call him right away. Maybe I can squeeze him in this morning."

Anne felt her tension ease a bit. "Thanks, Dr. Farber. I'd appreci-

ate that. And call me back after you talk to him, okay?" Saying good-
bye, she was just hanging up the phone to go back to her story when
the second line rang. She punched the flashing red button. "Anne
Jeffers."

"It's Mark." There was a slight hesitation, then: "Mark
Blakemoor."

Anne smiled at the hesitation. Was he really afraid she wouldn't
recognize his voice after all the years she'd been covering the Kraven
case? Then her smile faded as she realized that a warm glow had
spread through her the moment she'd heard him. The same warm
glow she'd always felt when Glen used to call her. *Used to?* What was
she thinking? Flustered, she covered her nervousness with a busi-
nesslike tone. "I recognize your voice, Mark. What's up?"

"What's your morning look like?"

Anne frowned. It wasn't like the detective to beat around the
bush, and now there was a note in his voice that she'd never heard
before. More than simply uncertain, he sounded downright nervous.
"I'm not sure," she said carefully. "I have a lot to—"

"Cancel it," Blakemoor told her, and now Anne felt a twinge of annoyance. Who did he think he was? Then he went on and her irritation evaporated. "Look, I can't talk about this over the phone—in
fact, I probably shouldn't talk to you about it at all. But I figure with
this one, you have a right to know, at least off-the-record. Get it?"

Anne got it. Whatever he wanted to talk about had to do with
Rory Kraven's murder, and it was definitely not going to be for public
consumption. Then why call her at all? He knew how much she
hated it when sources went off-the-record, encumbering her with information she couldn't use.

"Anne, this is important," Blakemoor said, knowing exactly what
her hesitation meant, and letting her know it. "Believe me, if I didn't
think this was something you need to know right now, I wouldn't be
calling you."

"Where and what time?" Anne asked, making up her mind.

"Red Robin in half an hour?"

"See you there."

When she walked into the restaurant on Fourth Avenue twenty
minutes later, Mark Blakemoor was already waiting for her, his face

expressionless, a manila envelope clutched in his hand. Taking her elbow, he steered her along as the hostess led them to a booth at the back of the room bordered by empty tables on both sides. "Thanks, Millie," he said. "I really need the privacy today."

The hostess smiled. "It's okay, but I can't hold both the tables into lunch."

"Got it." He ordered coffee for both of them, then waited until the hostess had left before fixing his eyes on Anne. "How's your stomach?" he asked.

Anne's eyes automatically shifted to the envelope that lay on the table between them. She felt a slight queasiness in anticipation of what might be in it. "All right, I guess," she countered. "How strong does it have to be?"

The detective tilted his head noncommittally. "I'm going to show you some pictures nobody outside the department has seen," he told her. "They're pictures of some of the people whose deaths have been attributed to Richard Kraven."

" 'Attributed'?" Anne repeated, her antenna instantly rising. "Mark, what's going on?"

The big homicide detective met her gaze. "I need your word that none of what goes on here leaves this table. I didn't show you anything, you didn't see anything, you didn't hear anything, you didn't even infer anything."

"Then why are you talking to me at all?"

Even in the subdued light of the restaurant, Anne could see Mark's face redden. "Because I'm worried about you, and I guess I think you have a right to know what I know."

Anne felt her eyes moisten, and had to restrain herself from reaching out and putting her hand on his. "All right," she agreed. "Let's talk. You have my promise that nothing leaves this table."

The detective opened the envelope and pulled out a photograph, which he slid across to Anne. It was an eight-by-ten glossy, and it was in color.

It was a photograph of a crime scene; a man's body, its nakedness only partially hidden in a clump of rhododendrons, was sprawled on the ground, the arms akimbo, one leg bent underneath the other.

The chest was laid open, the heart and lungs torn out.

"Eugene MacIntyre," Anne said quietly as her stomach threatened to rebel at the carnage committed on the body. "Victim Number Six, wasn't he?"

Mark sighed heavily. "Correct. And this," he said, "is what the medical examiner found when he did the autopsy." He shoved another picture across the table, reflexively glancing around as if to make sure no one was watching them.

Anne reached out and turned the photograph so it was right side up. It was a composite of four shots, showing the thoracic cavity of Eugene MacIntyre—with all the internal organs removed—in successive degrees of enlargement. It was the fourth picture that instantly caught Anne's attention. It showed no more than a few square inches of the inner surface of the dorsal area of MacIntyre's chest.

Etched into the tissue were two perfectly formed marks:

$$\text{\Large ϟ ϟ}$$

Black lightning. They looked exactly like two tiny bolts of black lightning.

As Anne gazed silently at the grotesque monogram, Mark passed her another picture, then another and another. All of them were the same: composite shots, each frame an enlargement of the one before, zooming in on the dorsal area of the thoracic cavity, the last of each series finally focusing on the mark of the man who had presumably killed the person the pictures portrayed. A grotesque signature carved in blood.

"All of them?" Anne asked dully. "He did this to all of them?"

The detective nodded. "It was the one thing we didn't let get outside the task force. It was our ace in the hole, and we kept it that way." His eyes fixed on her. "Tell me the truth, Anne. Did you ever know anything about this? Even hear any rumors of it?"

Anne didn't have to think about her answer. "Never." She could barely breathe.

"Then you'd better look at this," Blakemoor said, taking the last picture out of the envelope. "These were taken last night during the autopsy on Rory Kraven." As he slid the photograph across the table, Anne found herself wishing there were some way she could avoid looking at it, though she knew there wasn't. She turned the picture toward her.

The same composite, but this time the first view was of Rory Kraven's entire body. Then the enlargements began, culminating in the same chilling close-up of Richard Kraven's terrifying lightning monogram.

Except that it was impossible.

"But we saw him die," Anne whispered, her words strangling in her constricting throat. "For God's sake, Mark, we were there! We watched him die!"

"We watched Richard Kraven die," Mark Blakemoor agreed, his voice dull. "But we didn't watch whoever committed these murders die."

Anne sank back against the banquette, trying to grasp what it meant.

But of course the meaning was obvious: she'd been wrong. All of them had been wrong. "What about the notes?" she asked, desperately grasping at the only straw available. "They have to be forgeries. If this guy could forge Richard Kraven's handwriting, surely he could—" She went silent, recognizing the flaw in her own logic.

"The only person who knew about the monogram was the person who did the killings," Mark Blakemoor said, uttering the very thought that had just silenced Anne.

Her mind raced. There had to be an answer—there *had* to be! "An accomplice," she blurted. "If Richard Kraven had an accomplice—"

"It won't wash," Mark interrupted. "I already thought about it. Serial killers just don't have accomplices. It's like masturbation—it's a solitary practice."

"Bonnie and Clyde—" Anne began. "The Manson Family—"

"Not the same thing. Bonnie and Clyde were bank robbers, pure and simple. Violent, but still bank robbers. The Manson outfit was a cult. With cults, nothing ever stays a secret. Sooner or later, someone talks. And with this one, we've never heard a peep out of anyone. No rumors, no anything. Just Richard Kraven's insistence that he never committed a crime."

Anne's gaze fixed on him. "And now it looks like he was telling the truth?" But it was impossible! He'd been convicted! "What about his trial?"

"I talked to the prosecutor. They found the same marks on the bodies in his jurisdiction, and they kept them just as quiet as we did, for exactly the same reason. You have to have something the crazies don't know, or you spend all your time sorting out phony confessions."

Anne felt as if she'd been struck in the stomach with a heavy object. What had she done? How could she have been so completely wrong? She tried to tell herself it hadn't been just her—the whole task force had been certain that Richard Kraven was the man they were after.

But it was she who had latched onto Richard Kraven when he'd first come under suspicion, she who had convicted him in the press long before he'd even been put to trial. She who had insisted over and over again that only the death penalty could protect the public from him.

"What does it mean?" she asked, but even as she uttered the question, she knew the answer: Karma. Divine retribution. Ever since the day of Richard Kraven's execution, her world had begun to come apart. First Glen's heart attack, then the changes in him that had made him a stranger to her.

Now this.

She had no one to blame but herself. She had destroyed an innocent man, and now she had to pay for what she'd done.

"It means that whoever Richard Kraven took the fall for is still out there," Blakemoor replied, sensing Anne's pain and finally reaching out to cover her hand with his own. "And given that he chose to sign Rory's body, I'd say he's planning to resume his career right where he left it while he took a sabbatical to watch Richard Kraven take the rap for him."

Anne heard the words, knew they had to be true, but something inside her still refused to accept them. Something was wrong with the whole thing. Or was she simply incapable of admitting *she'd* been wrong? Was she so consumed with hubris that she couldn't even accept facts?

"Look, let's get out of here, okay?" she heard Mark saying.

Wordlessly, she let him lead her out of the restaurant, and when he slipped his arm protectively around her, she made no move to pull away from him. Unconsciously she moved closer, grateful for any shelter she could find in her suddenly collapsing world.

Glen picked up the phone in the front hall, instantly recognizing Gordy Farber's voice.

"How's it going, Glen?" the heart specialist asked, keeping his voice casual despite the worry he was feeling. Obviously, the fear he'd seen in his patient when Glen had come in the day before yesterday had not been alleviated, since now it had infected Anne Jeffers as well, though he suspected that Anne's fears stemmed much more from the events next door than from what might be happening inside her own home. Still, he'd intended to check on Glen today anyway. "What's happening? Any more of those blackouts?"

Glen suddenly remembered his intention of calling Gordy this morning. Why hadn't he? He glanced at his watch. Almost an hour had passed since he'd finished cleaning up the kitchen and . . .

And what? He couldn't remember! Another hour gone out of his life! Shit!

"Actually, I was going to call you this morning, Gordy," he said. "I'm starting to feel like I have Alzheimer's instead of a heart problem. Yesterday—" Before he could finish the sentence, the doorbell rang. "Hang on, Gord—someone's at the door."

Laying the receiver on the table, Glen crossed to the front door and opened it to a heavyset woman clad in a shapeless dress, who smiled uncertainly at him. In her early sixties, he thought, and wearing too much makeup. Her dyed-black hair was piled up on her head in an attempt at a French twist. Though he was certain he'd never met her, she still looked somehow familiar.

"Mr. Jeffers?" the woman asked. "I'm Edna Kraven."

Even as he stared at her, the same dizziness that had struck him earlier washed over him again. He took a step backward, fighting the blackness that was already closing around him.

He could do nothing, though, to battle the ever-strengthening presence that rose inside him.

The furious presence . . .

"Don't let them, Mama! Please don't let them!"

"Now, you be Mama's brave little boy. They're not going to hurt you. They're going to help you."

But Richard Kraven knew they weren't going to help him. They were going to hurt him, just like they had last time, just like his father had hurt him. Now their hands were reaching out to him, and even though he was trying to hang on to his mother, she was prying his fingers loose, working herself free from his clinging arms.

One of the white-clad figures bent down to pick him up, but Richard shrank away, struggling against the tears that threatened to overwhelm him. He knew all too well what happened if he cried. His father had taught him that long ago.

Despite his attempts to escape, the tall man in the white coat picked him up, pinning his arms to his sides. "Now you just take it easy," he heard the man say. "You don't want us to have to put you in the jacket again, do you?" Richard shook his head, terror filling his heart. Last time his mother had brought him here, when he'd tried to tell her what his father had been doing to him and she hadn't believed him, he'd gotten really angry, and finally they'd put him in a coat with sleeves that tied at the back so he couldn't move his arms at all. He'd been scared then—more scared than he'd ever been before, even when his father took him down to the basement—but the jacket hadn't been the worst part.

Even the ice-cold baths they'd made him lie in hadn't been the worst part.

The worst part was he knew what they were going to do today, because his mother had told him about it. "It's for your own good," she'd explained. "And it doesn't really hurt at all."

But that wasn't true. It hurt more than anything he could ever remember, even more than the shocks his father gave him.

Once again he looked up at his mother, but instead of helping him, she only smiled blandly, as if nothing was wrong at all. "Now you be a good boy, Richard. You be Mama's perfect little boy, just like you always are."

She turned around and walked through the doors, leaving him with the big men in white clothes, never even looking back at him.

That day he didn't cry at all. He didn't cry when they took him into the room where they kept the hard bed with the thick straps they held him down with.

He didn't cry when they attached the wires to his head.

He didn't even cry when he felt the jolts of electricity shoot through him and thought he was going to die.

In fact, he never cried again.

And he always did his best to be his Mama's perfect little boy.

But the anger—the dark, cold fury he always took care to hide—began to build.

Every day, every week, every month it built.

Every year the rage grew larger, more monstrous.

And his mother never knew it was there.

Always, no matter what happened, she kept believing that he was her perfect little boy, who loved her as much as she said she loved him.

But he knew better. No matter what she said, he knew she didn't love him—knew she'd never loved him. If she'd loved him, she would have protected him from his father, and from the men in the white clothes with the terrible machine that was even worse than his father's electric cords.

No, she didn't love him. She hated him, as much as he hated her.

"Won't you come in?" The words issued from Glen Jeffers's mouth, but it was Richard Kraven who asked the question, holding the door wider to let his mother step into the foyer. "I was on the telephone, but if you'll just give me half a second?"

Courtly, Edna Kraven thought as she nodded her agreement to Mr. Jeffers's question. Courtly, just like Richard was. "I do hope I'm not bothering you?"

He held up a gently dismissive hand. "Of course not," he said. Picking up the phone, he spoke briefly into the receiver. "Gordy? I'm afraid something's come up. I'll call you later." Without waiting for a reply from the doctor, he placed the receiver back on the hook, then gently took his mother's elbow and steered her into the living room. "How nice of you to come," he said.

Edna lowered herself nervously onto the edge of the sofa, surreptitiously eyeing the furniture in the room. Some of it, she decided, was almost as nice as the things Richard had had. Probably those were things Mr. Jeffers had chosen. Surely that terrible woman he was married to couldn't have such good taste. Now, as her eyes returned to her host, she felt her heart flutter. Though he didn't look anything like Richard, there was so much about him that reminded her of her son. His voice, of course. The wonderful, gentle way he spoke. And his eyes, too. They weren't really the same color as Richard's had been, but they had the same depth—that quality of looking right inside someone—that Richard's had.

"I just got to thinking," she said, her fingers twisting at one of the large buttons on her dress. "You were so nice to me on the phone this morning, I just thought maybe I should talk to you instead of your wife. If I could just make you understand about Richard. You just don't know how it hurts me when your wife writes those terrible things about him."

He smiled. "But I do understand," he said gently. "Believe me, I understand exactly how you feel."

Edna Kraven brightened. "Oh, I just knew I was right about you. I just *knew* it! Do you know, you remind me of Richard. It happened the minute I heard your voice this morning. And I just had to come and meet you."

"I'm so glad you did," he said softly.

He studied his mother carefully. She was four years older than she'd been the last time he'd seen her, but she hadn't changed much. The same cheap polyester clothes she'd always worn, her hair still done in that silly style she wrongly thought was so sophisticated. In combination with her heavily made-up face, it gave her the look of those over-the-hill entertainers who scraped out livings in the seedier bars in downtown Las Vegas. With the perfect analytical detachment to which he'd long ago disciplined his mind, Richard Kraven tried to analyze what it could have been about this numbingly boring woman that had inspired such love—even adoration—in his brother.

Perhaps, he thought, it was because they were so much alike.

Or perhaps it was something else entirely—perhaps there was some emotion that people of the inferior intellectual status of Rory and Edna felt that was simply foreign to someone at his own level.

"You have no idea how much it means to me that you've come," he said now. "The pain you must be feeling . . ."

Edna reached out with doughy fingers to take the hand of this wonderful man. "You have no idea," she breathed, her voice breaking. "You just have no idea at all. I miss my Richard so much. We used to do things together, just the two of us." Her eyes went briefly to the front window. "That wouldn't be your motor home out there, would it?" she asked on a wistful note. "My Richard had one, you know. He used to take me up to the mountains sometimes. Just the two of us."

A tiny smile played around the corner of his lips. "Did he?" he asked. "Well, as it happens, that *is* my motor home out there. And just before you arrived, I was just thinking it might be fun to go up to the mountains and do a little fishing. Perhaps you'd like to go along?"

Edna Kraven flushed scarlet. "Oh, no, I didn't mean— Well, I couldn't possibly impose on you that way. I just—"

"But of course you'll come with me. I wouldn't have it any other way." He stood up. "I only have a few more things to put in, and we'll be off. We can make a picnic of it."

While Edna Kraven waited nervously in the living room, the man who had become Richard Kraven went down to the basement. He picked up the last of the boxes he'd been transferring to the motor home.

The motor home he'd rented yesterday afternoon, using Glen Jeffers's driver's license and credit card.

The box already contained a gas can and a box of matches, and now he added a few more objects to it.

The Makita saw.

The electrical cord with the stripped ends, with which he'd attempted to defibrillate Heather Jeffers's cat.

The roll of plastic he'd bought yesterday morning, just before he'd visited Rory.

With the box now packed full with everything he would need, he started back up the basement stairs. How many years had he thought about using his mother as the subject for one of his experiments? But of course it had been out of the question.

After all, he only experimented on strangers.

Circumstances, though, had changed.

Now he could see no reason not to make her his subject.

"Ready?" he asked as he paused in the foyer.

Edna Kraven, thrilled at the prospect of spending the day with this charming man who was so very much like her eldest son, heaved herself off the sofa. "One of these days, I've just got to lose some weight," she trilled as she moved toward the front door.

"Not at all," he said. "I think you're perfect the way you are. Just perfect."

As she walked ahead of him down the steps to the motor home waiting on the street, Richard Kraven was already planning the first cut he would make.

It was mid-afternoon when Anne finally returned to her office. She felt utterly worn out, as if she'd had no sleep for at least a week, but she knew that sleeplessness had nothing to do with the exhaustion consuming her. Flopping down into her chair, she sat, head in hands, for almost a full minute, before reaching out to switch her monitor on and erase the sidebar she'd been writing when Mark Blakemoor called. The empty screen seemed to mock her after the story disappeared.

It was not just a single story that had disappeared; it was years out of her life.

She tapped at the keyboard for a few seconds and a directory scrolled down the screen, listing all the articles she had written about Richard Kraven over the years.

Richard Kraven, who was now dead and buried.

Richard Kraven, who, if Mark Blakemoor was right, had not been the man they should have been looking for.

Not been the man they tried.

Not been the man they executed.

She called up one piece after another, reading snatches of what she'd written, starting from the very beginning, when the first mutilated body had been found down in Seward Park.

The next body had turned up below Snoqualmie Falls a month later, and another one had been found near Lake Sammamish within a week. Even then there had been no particular "type" that had seemed to attract the killer, no common trait that might have triggered his urge to kill.

The path that had led to Richard Kraven was tortuous. At the time—even now—there was no direct evidence to link him to any of the murders.

No witnesses.

No bloodstains.

No murder weapon.

Slowly, though, a fuzzy image had emerged.

People reported having seen some of the victims talking to someone.

A man.

And as more and more bodies were discovered, a faint pattern did finally start to appear: most of the victims had spent considerable time in the University District. Some lived there. Some worked there. Some actually went to the university.

Then a sharper picture began to emerge, a picture of a man who had been seen talking with some of the victims.

A man whose Identikit sketch, when it was finally put together, looked a great deal like Richard Kraven.

A few people had mentioned having seen a motor home near some of the places where bodies were found.

Richard Kraven had owned a motor home, which he'd used—

Anne felt her stomach tighten as she remembered, even without reading it, what Richard Kraven had used his motor home for.

Fishing trips!

Sheila Harrar had mentioned it just a few days ago. When her son had left their apartment in Yesler Terrace the day he disappeared, he'd told his mother he was going fishing. Fishing with Richard Kraven!

Was that why she'd had such an angry reaction yesterday when she'd seen that motor home parked on their block?

Because she associated motor homes with Richard Kraven?

And was that why she'd been so negative when Glen had said he was going to take up fishing? Just because it had been Richard Kraven's hobby?

But that was ridiculous. Thousands of people—hundreds of thousands of people—loved to go fishing. There was even a guy over at the *Times*—was it the book editor?—who had suddenly taken up fly fishing. If that guy could do it, why shouldn't Glen?

Her thoughts tumbled over each other, and suddenly she remembered that day while he was still in the hospital when Glen had asked Kevin to bring him her file on Richard Kraven.

Why?

Glen had always thought her own fascination with the serial killer was morbid; why had he suddenly become interested in Kraven?

So interested in him that he'd even taken up his hobby?

Easy, Anne, she told herself. *This is the way people go crazy. No matter what Mark Blakemoor might think, Glen's only taking up a new hobby, just like the doctor ordered.*

But then a new thought popped into her mind, a thought so ludicrous it made her laugh out loud.

Which of Richard Kraven's hobbies is Glen taking up? Fly fishing, or killing? There was a brief lull in the constant racket of the newsroom as everyone within earshot of Anne glanced over at her. The brittle burst of laughter dying on her lips, Anne stared at her computer screen as if she were deeply involved in writing a story.

A moment later the normal hubbub of the room resumed as Anne, oblivious, sat at her desk thinking. Somewhere at the edge of her mind an idea was taking form, but it was so nebulous she couldn't yet bring it into focus.

There was something she was forgetting—something she'd once known, or heard about.

A rumor?

A theory?

Some piece of information that had to be buried somewhere in her computer files, or in the depths of her own mind.

She knew of only one way to retrieve it—to search through the files of everything she'd ever written about Richard Kraven. And not just the story files, either. All her note files were there as well, from verbatim transcripts of every interview she'd ever conducted about him, right down to the complete transcript of his trial and the appeals that had followed. Thousands of pages neatly organized into directories and subdirectories.

Fighting off the terrible exhaustion that threatened to overwhelm her, she tried to face up to the task of rereading it all. It would take days, possibly weeks, but somewhere in those files she knew she would find something—some tiny fact—that would provide her with the key to who had killed Rory Kraven. For despite everything Mark Blakemoor had shown her, despite everything he had told her, Anne Jeffers was still sure of one thing.

She had not been wrong about Richard Kraven.

He had been a killer. He'd been convicted of being a killer, and he'd been executed for being a killer.

He was dead, and Anne did not believe in ghosts. Therefore, someone was playing some kind of terrible game.

Coldly, analytically, Anne began to think.

An accomplice.

There had to be an accomplice, no matter what Mark Blakemoor had said about serial killers working alone. After all, Richard Kraven had never been typical.

So there was someone who was still alive. Someone to whom Richard Kraven had confided his secrets.

Someone whom he had taught to mimic his handwriting perfectly.

That much, she knew, was possible.

But who would have been willing to wait until Richard Kraven was executed, and then take up his own grisly work, simply to make the world think Richard Kraven had been innocent?

Could anyone be that devoted to a monster like Richard Kraven?

She couldn't even imagine it. Yet, there was no other possible answer. And if that person existed, she would find him.

Unless he found her first.

Richard Kraven's last words rushed back to her. *"That's my regret, Anne. That I won't get to watch you die the way you're going to watch me!"*

Was it possible he'd meant something more by those words than she'd thought on the day he was executed? Was it possible he'd already made arrangements for her to die, too?

Abruptly, she realized there was only one way Rory Kraven's killer could have known it was Rory who killed Joyce Cottrell. He must have been there that night. There, not because he'd been watching Joyce's house.

He would have been watching hers.

The icy touch of fear stroked her skin as she imagined someone lurking in the darkness outside her house that night.

Had he been waiting to kill her? Or her family?

Had he been preparing to enter their house while they slept?

And where was he now? Right now?

Was he watching her house?

Watching her children?

Her eyes flicked to the clock—it was already a quarter after three! If Heather hadn't left school yet, she could tell her to find Kevin and stay with him. If both kids were together, they might be safe, but if Kevin was wandering around by himself . . .

Panic seizing her, she snatched up the telephone to call Heather's school. Five minutes later, after what seemed an eternity of waiting, the assistant principal came back on the line.

"I'm sorry, Mrs. Jeffers," Sheila Jones said in a tone she reserved for parents whom she thought were needlessly overwrought. "I've paged your daughter, but she hasn't responded. I think she must already have left the school. Is it something I can help you with? Or one of her teachers?"

Anne hesitated. Should she tell Ms. Jones she was afraid someone might be stalking her or her children? But what if she was wrong? What if she was completely wrong about everything? She didn't know. She didn't know anything! "I—I'm not sure," she stammered. "I guess not. I'm sure there's not really a problem."

Hanging up, she dialed her own number, cursing softly when the answering machine picked up. She waited it out, then said, "Glen? If you're there, pick up. It's me, and I'm worried about the kids. If you're not there and you get home in the next few minutes, could you take your car and drive over to Kevin's school? Something else has happened, and I'm—oh, hell, I don't have time to explain right now. Just do it for me, okay? Thanks, hon. See you later."

Putting the receiver back on the hook, she sat still for a moment, willing her rising panic away. Where was Glen? Why wasn't he at home? Had something happened to him?

Stop it! she told herself. *Just get hold of yourself. You can either do something constructive, or fall apart. Take your choice.*

She had to find the man who had killed Rory Kraven.

The man who might be stalking her.

Somewhere in her files some clue to him would exist. It had to. To be that close to Richard Kraven, to be that devoted to him, the person who was now perfectly imitating him would surely have been mentioned somewhere, by someone.

Indeed, she herself might very possibly have interviewed him back in the days when she'd systematically sought out practically everyone Richard Kraven ever met.

It struck her, then, that not only was it *possible* she'd spoken to the nameless, faceless man she was now consumed with finding. It was almost impossible that she *hadn't* talked to him!

Her exhaustion evaporating, she brought up the index that listed all the interviews she'd conducted over the years, but her momentary excitement faded as she gazed at its statistics.

There were 1,326 files in five subdirectories.

Even those would take days to review.

But she could break them down. No need to go through the interviews with friends and families of the victims.

Only the ones with Richard Kraven's associates were important now. Her fingers tapped on the keys, bringing up a new subdirectory.

The 1,326 files had been culled down to only 127.

Pulling up the first file, Anne set to work.

She would find it. Sooner or later, she would find it.

But until she did, how many more people would die?

And who would they be?

A dim point of light, so faint as to be barely visible at all, slowly began to penetrate the darkness that had closed around Glen Jeffers's mind. Feeling as if he were emerging from a deep sleep, Glen focused on the light, willing it to brighten and wash away the blackness that surrounded him.

Now he could hear a faint sound as well—a high-pitched keening.

The inky black fog in his mind slowly faded into gray, and the point of light spread.

The sound grew clearer.

A drill. A dentist's drill?

Glen struggled to remember what had happened. He'd been at home. In the kitchen, reading the paper. The phone! That was it— the phone had rung.

Gordy Farber. It had been Gordy, calling to find out how he was doing. They'd talked for a moment, and then something had interrupted him.

The doorbell.

Someone had come to the door, and he'd gone to answer it, and . . .

The blackness had closed around him.

The sound grew louder, and the light spread further. It was brightening more quickly now.

You're awake. The voice wasn't loud, but although the keening sound was growing steadily more insistent as the blackness continued to fade, Glen could hear the words perfectly. It was almost as if they emanated from somewhere within his own head. *It was I who woke you,* the voice went on. *Just as it was I who put you to sleep.*

Why? The question formed soundlessly in Glen's mind, but even before he could form it into an audible word, the voice answered it.

I needed our body.

Our body. The words stripped away the last of the fog that had gathered around Glen's mind. *Our body.* What the hell was going on? With the question still half formed in his mind, pieces of the puzzle began to fall into place.

The hours he had lost.

The broken shaver about which he'd made up a story—a story that had then turned out to be at least partly true.

The things that had appeared in the house—objects that he assumed he'd bought, even though he had no memory of doing so: the fishing rod Kevin found, the new shaver he himself found. The fishing fly that could have been made of a feather from Hector and some fur from Kumquat.

Kumquat!

Now he remembered the dream. But it had only been a dream! It hadn't been real—it couldn't have been.

Once again the words the voice had spoken echoed in his head: *Our body.*

Not *our* body, Glen thought desperately. It's *my* body. There wasn't anyone else—couldn't be anyone else. Whatever was happening had to be in his own mind. That was it—he was still waking up, and his mind was playing tricks on him! But now more memories were coming back to him. Making love to Anne the day he'd come home from the hospital. Something had happened that afternoon. He'd felt . . . what? Something odd, almost like another presence inside him.

Waking up in the hospital to find all of Anne's files on Richard Kraven piled on the table beside his bed.

The blackouts . . .

Now he remembered something he'd watched on television—a woman who'd claimed to have eighteen different personalities living inside her. Multiple personality syndrome. The woman had first begun to worry because she was having blackouts. And then she heard about things she'd done. Things she couldn't remember. Things she knew she never would have done—

The keening sound was louder than ever, and now that he could hear it clearly, Glen knew it wasn't a drill at all.

It was a saw.

He could see the blade now. It was right in front of him. He could see his hand holding the blue-green plastic handle of a Makita saw. And beyond the saw was something else.

The upper part of a woman's torso. A heavy woman, whose large, pendulous breasts drooped toward either side, pulling away from each other under no more impetus than their own weight.

Between the woman's breasts, running from a few inches above her navel all the way up to the base of her throat, there was a cut.

A clean, fresh incision, perfectly straight.

The woman's chest expanded as she drew a deep breath of air into her lungs.

The keening whine subsided as the saw stopped.

Glen watched in disbelief as his hand put the saw down and picked up a knife. A sharp X-Acto knife, like the one Kevin had used when he was working on the model ship.

The one he'd used when he was tying the fishing fly.

Glen watched numbly as his hands moved as if under their own volition. The knife traced a line across the woman's torso, intersecting the existing incision at its base. As the knife slid easily through the woman's skin, a line of red appeared in its wake, a line that thickened, then began to lose its shape as the blood welled from the cut and covered her body.

Transfixed, Glen gazed helplessly at what he was doing.

His hands moved again, and a third incision appeared, this one nearly spanning the space between her shoulders.

No! Glen thought. *This can't be happening!* But even as his mind formulated the thought, dark, mocking laughter echoed in his head. Trying to stifle the taunting sound, Glen willed himself not to move his hands again, struggled to halt their inexorable motion. But now he felt something else—a terrible paralysis, robbing him of will, erasing his power over his own body. As he watched helplessly, his fingers went to work, deftly laying back the folds of skin as easily as they might have opened a pair of double doors.

Beneath the skin, clearly visible now, was the woman's sternum.

Even as his hands reached for it, Glen's mind grasped the purpose of the Makita. His fingers squeezed the switch and instantly his ears were filled with the keening whine of the whirling blade.

As the blade, no more than a silvery blur now, moved closer to the woman's sternum, Glen struggled to wrest control of his body from the force that seemed to have seized it. Powerless, he saw the blade descend. Then the teeth dug into the mass of bone and cartilage that formed the ventral support of the woman's rib cage.

Glen tried to scream out against the carnage he was witnessing, but his voice would obey him no more than his fingers and hands. *No,* he whimpered silently to himself. *Oh, God, no. Don't let this happen.*

But even as he made his plea, the spinning blade dug deeper and his hand inexorably laid the woman's torso open, splitting her sternum, ripping through the pleural membrane.

As his eyes focused on the mass of tissue that were the woman's lungs, the darkness closed in on Glen once more.

This time he welcomed it.

"I'm sorry, Mr. Jeffers, but Dr. Farber is with a patient."

The nurse's tone over the phone made Glen wonder if he was being deliberately punished for hanging up on the doctor earlier. "Can't you at least tell him who it is?"

"Doctor does not like to be interrupted," the nurse replied in a voice that made it crystal clear she was annoyed with him. "And you don't have to shout, Mr. Jeffers. I'm not deaf, you know."

"I'm sorry," Glen said. Once again he tried to remember what had happened when he'd been talking to Gordy Farber this morning. They'd been in the middle of setting up an appointment when suddenly he'd had another of his blackouts. This one had come on him fast, and when he'd awakened this time, he found himself on the living room sofa. Though he hadn't felt ill, he hadn't felt rested, either. Certainly not as rested as he should have felt if he'd slept through all the hours that were missing from his day.

There were the usual memories of dreams, too, but unlike yesterday, these weren't merely fragments. They were great cohesive chunks, and as vivid as normal memories.

"Is it an emergency?" the nurse asked, sounding only somewhat mollified.

Glen hesitated. He was scared, more scared than he wanted to admit, at least to the nurse. But was it really an emergency? He wasn't sure.

The memory of the dream flashed back into his mind, as clear now as when he'd awakened a few minutes ago. In the dream, he'd "awakened," too, opening his eyes to discover he was no longer in his own house or any other familiar surrounding, but standing in a stream, stark naked, with a fly rod in his hands and no memory at all of how he'd gotten there.

Like a dream within a dream.

The only memory he had—if it even was a genuine memory—was of cutting open a woman's chest. And that image had been vivid, too, not at all like the fuzzy half-obscured flashes he'd had before.

In the dream, he'd reeled in the fish line and scrambled out of the stream, hurrying to a motor home parked in the middle of a flat grassy area a couple of hundred feet from the stream's edge.

Though he had no memory of where the vehicle had come from, it nevertheless seemed familiar. His heart had begun pounding as he neared the van, but when he went inside, nothing was amiss. There certainly was no sign of anything like the hideous butchery he could also clearly remember. In one of the compartments in the vehicle's undercarriage, he found a Makita saw, its blade removed. In one of the galley drawers he found a handle for an X-Acto blade, but again there was no blade attached to it. He could find no signs of blood anywhere in the motor home, but after putting on his clothes—the same clothes he was wearing now, as he talked to Gordy Farber's nurse—he'd searched the woods surrounding the grassy clearing.

He'd found nothing.

He'd been on his way back to the motor home when he blacked out again.

"Mr. Jeffers?" the nurse asked. "Are you still there?"

"Yes," Glen replied. "And it is an emergency. I really need to talk to Gordy."

The nurse hesitated, as if trying to decide if he was lying, then apparently decided to let her employer make the decision for himself. "I'll see if doctor can be disturbed."

Tinny Muzak dribbled from the speaker for a moment, then Gordy Farber's voice came on the line. "Glen? Where are you? What's going on? How come you hung up on me?"

"Can I come in and see you?" Glen asked. "I can be there as soon as you have some time open."

"I'll make the time," Gordy Farber told him, reading the fear in Glen's voice. "Can you get here in fifteen minutes?"

"I'll be there," Glen replied.

It was actually only ten minutes later that Glen walked into the doctor's office. It would have been less, but as he set off to walk the eight blocks down to the hospital complex, he'd seen a motor home just like the one in the dream. He peered into its windows, and his heart had raced as he recognized what little of the interior he could see. He tried the doors, found them locked, and only then continued on to Group Health and Farber's office.

The heart specialist insisted on a thorough examination despite Glen's protests, then, satisfied that his patient wasn't on the verge of a second attack, he gestured Glen to a chair and rested his own weight against his big walnut desk, arms crossed, eyeing the seated man carefully. Whatever had occasioned Glen's worried phone call, it didn't appear to be a medical emergency; in fact, from all signs, it appeared as if Glen's physical recovery was proceeding satisfactorily. "So," he asked, "what is this all about, Glen?"

"I don't know," Glen replied.

Gordy Farber stared at him. "You don't know?" he echoed. "What the hell kind of answer is that? You were making an appointment. The doorbell rang, and then you came back, were barely civil to me, and hung up. So don't tell me you don't know. Who was at the door?"

Glen shook his head helplessly. "I don't know," he repeated. "I remember talking to you, and I remember the doorbell ringing. After that, the whole day is a mess. I woke up on the sofa twenty minutes ago, but I don't think I was there all day. But it's all crazy. I have this memory of waking up earlier, but that time I wasn't even in the house. I was standing in a stream up in the mountains. I was fishing." He reddened and his eyes shifted away from the doctor. "And I was stark naked." Slowly and carefully, Glen repeated everything he remembered. When he was finally finished, he looked up at the doctor, fear blazing in his eyes. "The thing is, I'm starting to wonder what's real and what's a dream. My God, Gordy, what's happening to me? And don't try to tell me this is something that normally happens after a heart attack."

The specialist moved around his desk and dropped into his chair. "You don't have any memory of driving up to the mountains, or driving back?"

Glen shook his head. "I don't even have a motor home. But the weird thing is, the one in my dream, or whatever it was, is parked half a block from my house. I just have the two memories—cutting up the woman, and then looking for her body in the motor home."

"Obviously, you didn't do either of those things," Farber told him.

"What if I *did?*" Glen countered.

Farber frowned, then switched on the intercom. "Could you bring in this morning's *Herald*, please?" he asked his nurse. "The front page." A moment later the door opened and the woman appeared, a folded newspaper in her hand. When Farber nodded toward Glen, she handed it to him.

"Will that be all?"

"Yes, thanks," Farber replied. As the nurse closed the door behind her, he turned back to Glen. "Take a look at the front page." Glen unfolded the paper to see Anne's story on the murder of Rory Kraven spread across the lower half of page one. "Did you read that this morning?" the doctor asked. Glen nodded. "Then I think we can identify the source of that dream," Farber observed, a thin smile curving his lips. "Come on, Glen—that story doesn't just talk about what happened to the guy they found across the street. It describes what he did to those two women, too. And one thing you can say for your wife—when she draws you a verbal picture, it's vivid. So if you read that article this morning, and dreamed about cutting open a woman's chest this afternoon, I don't think it's rocket science to find a connection between the two events."

Glen shook his head doggedly. "But it doesn't account for the blackouts. And what was I doing fishing in the nude?"

Gordy Farber grinned. "It was only a dream, Glen, remember? Hell, if it had been my dream, I might have been tempted to try it myself." When his attempt to lighten Glen's mood was only met by a dark look, Farber's smile faded. "All right, I admit it's a weird dream. But it's also way out of my field. The kind of stuff you're talking about, you need a shrink for. Want me to call someone?"

Glen hesitated. The image of the woman's torso—and his own

hands cutting into it, first with the X-Acto knife, then with the Makita—filled his mind. "Do you know someone good?" When the heart specialist nodded, he made up his mind. "Set me up."

Jake Jacobson was ten years younger than Glen, five inches shorter, and forty pounds heavier. By the time Glen arrived in Jacobson's office, the psychiatrist had already pulled his medical history from the central computer, and as his new patient came in the door, the doctor looked at him critically. "Well, at least you don't look crazy," he offered in an attempt to put Glen at his ease.

"Is that supposed to make me feel better?" Glen asked.

"If you don't want me to make you feel better, why did you come?" Jacobson countered.

For the next half hour he listened while Glen related as much as he could remember about his state of mind since he'd had the heart attack, and especially the strange, surreal experiences of the past few days. The psychiatrist took some notes, but didn't interrupt Glen's story until he had finished.

"The human mind is a very complex organ," Jacobson observed when Glen at last fell silent. "We already know that a very simple suggestion can implant false memories that are every bit as vivid as genuine ones. We're seeing it all the time in alleged child sex-abuse cases. I don't question your belief that what you remember about this afternoon is real. All I question is the *validity* of that belief." He leaned back in his chair, folding his hands across his ample belly. "For the sake of argument, let's assume the experience in the river was real. You yourself were unable to find any evidence of what you think you did." He smiled. "A saw and a knife, neither of them with a blade?"

"I could have thrown them away anywhere," Glen said, his voice obstinate. "I didn't even look for them."

"But you did look for a body, and didn't find one. Nor did you find any blood, or any sign of a struggle, or anything else that might rationally lead you to believe you'd actually killed someone. It was all a dream, Glen. As for the motor home, obviously you saw it at some point this morning. You probably even looked in the windows earlier, so when you had the dream, the images were already in your mind."

He began ticking points off on his fingers. "Your next door neighbor
was murdered in a manner not unlike what you dreamed. There is a
motor home like the one you dreamed of, sitting almost in front of
your house. Your wife has been writing about Richard Kraven for
years, and one of the things I remember about him is that he liked
to go on fishing trips in a motor home. I can't believe that little fact
isn't buried somewhere in your subconscious, too. What you've done
is put all that material together into a single vivid, pseudomemory of
an event for which you admit you could find no physical evidence
whatsoever."

"What about the blackouts?" Glen pressed.

Jacobson spread his hands in a dismissive gesture. "I can think of
at least one possibility right off the top of my head: you may have
suffered a minor stroke."

"A stroke?" Glen echoed hollowly. "But if I'd had a stroke—"

"People have strokes every day," the psychiatrist cut in. "Most of
them go unnoticed. A stroke doesn't have to be a huge event, you
know. Even the tiniest, most insignificant hemorrhage in the brain
falls into the category. And it's quite possible you've had one." He
picked up the phone and spoke into it. "Ellie, could you set up for
an EEG, please. We'll be in in a couple of minutes." Hanging up the
phone, he turned his attention back to Glen. "An electroencephalo-
gram will tell us if you have any major problems, and we'll schedule
an MRI, just to be sure." He tapped at the keyboard of his computer,
pulling up his scheduling program. "Is Monday all right?"

Glen nodded, feeling the terror begin to retreat. Maybe, after all,
there was a rational explanation for his bizarre and frustrating experiences. The psychiatrist led him through a door into an examining
room, explaining the procedure while Glen rolled up his sleeve so
the nurse could take his blood pressure and pulse.

"It's pretty simple, really," Jacobson told him. "I'm going to attach
some electrodes to your head, and then we'll measure the electrical
activity in your brain." He smiled reassuringly as he saw an expression of panic cross Glen's face. "Believe me, you won't feel a thing."

The nurse unwrapped the cuff of the sphygmomanometer from
Glen's left arm, then began attaching the electrodes to his scalp.
Glen could feel the contacts being attached to his skin.

"All set?" the psychiatrist asked a few moments later.

"Ready," the nurse replied.

The doctor turned a switch on the console of the EEG, and though Glen felt no physical pain whatsoever, a wave of panic swept over him.

And then a howl filled his head. A howl of both terror and agony, it was a sound of such unutterable horror that for a moment Glen was afraid his mind would shatter.

But where was it coming from? His eyes darted from the doctor to the nurse, then back again. Obviously neither of them was hearing the mind-rending scream, so it had to be coming from inside his own brain.

As the doctor adjusted the dials, the tenor of the shriek changed, and when Jacobson finally turned the machine off, it abruptly died away—and left no memory of having happened at all.

"That's it," the psychiatrist said. "And you didn't feel a thing, did you?"

Glen shook his head, his eyes fixed on the sheet of paper that had fed out of the machine. "Is that it?"

"That's it," Jacobson replied, tearing off the sheet. "Let's have a look." He studied the paper for a moment, then showed it to Glen.

All Glen could see were three lines, rising and falling in three distinct, different patterns. "Well?" he asked. "What does it mean?"

Jake Jacobson smiled at him reassuringly. "It means that so far your brain looks very normal. You're not showing any major abnormalities, and unless the MRI turns up something different, I suspect you're mostly simply suffering from stress. Which shouldn't come as a shock, given the severity of your heart attack. Your whole life's changed, and that is traumatic. But it's not fatal." He scribbled on a prescription form, tore the sheet off the pad, and handed it to Glen. "You can get this on your way home. It's a tranquilizer you can use if you need it." He led Glen back into his office. "The main thing is to just try to take it easy," he said. "Tell you what—you dreamed about fishing, so *go* fishing! Then on Monday, we'll take a look at the MRI, and I suspect we'll have all the answers. All right?"

A sense of relief flooded over Glen. "Great." He grinned weakly. "I was afraid you were going to want to put me back in the hospital."

"Not likely," Jacobson replied. "Whatever you may think, I don't see you as a danger to yourself or anyone else. Just go home, relax, and have a good weekend. See you on Monday."

Glen Jeffers left Jake Jacobson's office intending to go directly to the pharmacy to fill the prescription.

Instead he started homeward, the very existence of the prescription obliterated from his memory.

Obliterated as completely as the memory of that terrible scream of agony he'd heard inside his skull when the electrodes attached to his scalp had been activated. . . .

CHAPTER 56

Anne came home to an empty house, and searched in vain for a note telling her where Glen might have gone. There was nothing: no Post-it on the refrigerator, no message on the answering machine. So she was pretty sure he hadn't gone too far, especially since his Saab was parked in its usual spot. At least the damn motor home hadn't been able to displace *both* their cars! Then the front door slammed, and a moment later Kevin came through the dining room into the kitchen. Alone.

"Isn't Heather with you?" Anne asked.

Kevin shook his head. "She's over on Broadway, hangin' with Rayette."

Anne felt a stab of the same fear that had made her call the school that afternoon. She'd distinctly told Heather not to let Kevin walk home alone. Had Heather assumed she'd only meant yesterday? "Why didn't you go with her?" she asked, trying not to let Kevin see how upset she was.

Her son, who was now poking around in the refrigerator, shrugged. "I did, but they weren't doing anything, so I came home." Then, with far more aplomb than Anne would have expected, he added, "That guy that killed Mrs. Cottrell is dead, isn't he? So what's the big deal if I was walking by myself?"

For a moment Anne wasn't sure what to say. But then she wondered why she was surprised at Kevin's composure—after all, for years her children had been dealing with kids who brought knives and guns to school, and she probably knew even better than most parents just how much violence and crime city kids were exposed to every day of their lives. "I think you and I better have a little talk," she said.

Kevin rolled his eyes, but gave up his search for something to eat, and perched on the edge of one of the kitchen chairs.

"Just because the man who killed Mrs. Cottrell is dead doesn't mean it's safe for you to be wandering around by yourself. Until they find out who killed him—"

"Aw, Mom, come on," Kevin groaned. "What are you gonna do, lock me up? What about that kid that got shot down by Garfield? You didn't make me start hangin' with Heather all the time then!"

Anne shuddered as she remembered the girl who'd been killed on the sidewalk in front of Garfield High. She had covered the case—a teenage hazing that up until a few years ago would never have resulted in anything more serious than hurt feelings.

Now kids got killed.

No one could even guarantee Kevin's safety at school anymore— how could she expect to keep him safe simply by making him walk home with his sister every day? The ugly reality was that if someone was truly determined to kill—whether the intended victim was a total stranger, one of her kids, or even herself—there was virtually nothing she could do about it. Furthermore, Kevin was right—she certainly couldn't just lock him up until whoever had killed Rory Kraven was caught. And if, through some bizarre circumstances she couldn't even begin to understand, it turned out that Rory Kraven's killer had actually committed all the crimes Richard Kraven had been accused of, then he'd already eluded identification for years; what made her think he wouldn't be able to keep on doing it? She thought about the five transcripts of interviews she'd read that afternoon. Five out of 127. And she didn't even know what she was looking for.

The sound of the front door opening and closing interrupted her thoughts, then Glen appeared in the kitchen doorway. The second she saw him, Anne felt her anger rising. Her anger, and her defenses, too. He'd known how frightened she was, how worried, since Kumquat had been found dead in the alley, but he'd just taken off somewhere without so much as a note or a message on the answering machine. She found herself looking at him in a way she never had before—searching his face for some clue as to what had gone wrong, what had changed him.

And whether he'd killed Kumquat?

The thought flashed unbidden into her mind; she banished it instantly, furious at herself for allowing Mark Blakemoor to have planted the seed of such an idea. And Glen looked all right—he was smiling; smiling the way he used to, before his heart attack. As he leaned over to kiss her, she felt her guard lowering a little.

"Hey, guy," he said, straightening up from the kiss and rumpling Kevin's hair. "Why the long faces? You two having a fight?"

"Mom thinks I should have to come home with Heather every day," Kevin grumbled.

"I didn't say that," Anne began, then realized it was almost exactly what she had said, or at least implied. "All right, maybe I did. But just promise me you'll be careful, okay? Stay away from strangers, and if you see anyone even looking at you, just walk away. Promise?" Kevin's eyes rolled heavenward once more. "Promise?" Anne repeated.

"Do what your mom says, and I'll take you fishing on Saturday."

Instantly Kevin's face lit up. "Really?"

"Really. I promise, if you promise."

"I promise!" Kevin sang out. "Where?" he demanded. "Are we going to be gone all night? Can Justin go, too?"

"No, Justin can't go." Glen laughed. "It's gonna be just you and me. And I don't know where we'll go. And maybe we'll spend the night somewhere, and maybe we won't, depending on what your mom thinks."

As Kevin dashed out of the room to call Justin Reynolds and tell him how he was going to spend the weekend, Anne tamped down her irritation with her husband. What was going on? When had he decided to take Kevin fishing for the weekend? He certainly hadn't mentioned anything about it to her, and until now they'd always discussed everything concerning the kids. Even before Heather was born, they'd resolved to make all the decisions together. "Don't I have anything to say about this fishing trip?" she asked, abandoning the attempt to conceal her feelings. "And while you're at it, you might tell me why you didn't bother to leave me a note. After what's been happening—"

"Hey," Glen broke in, holding up his hands as if to fend off an attack of swarming bees. "Look, I'm really sorry I didn't leave a note. I went down to see Gordy Farber, and it took a little longer than I thought it would."

Anne's anger instantly dissolved into concern. "What did he say?" she asked, hoping the doctor hadn't told Glen he'd called him at her own urging.

"He said I'm doing just fine," Glen replied, seeing no reason to worry her. Besides, both Farber and Jake Jacobson had told him to stop worrying, hadn't they? "If I'd gotten home five minutes earlier, you wouldn't even have known I'd been gone, would you?" He moved closer to her and drew her to her feet. "Come on, it wasn't more than five minutes, was it?"

His arms drew her close to his chest, and Anne's determination wavered. "It was closer to ten minutes," she said, struggling to keep some kind of control over the situation. "And you still haven't answered my question about this little trip with Kevin. We always talk about these things, remember?"

"How could I remember?" Glen asked. "I've never even considered taking Kevin fishing before."

Now his lips were nuzzling at her neck, and part of Anne wanted to push him away, while the other part wanted to snuggle closer. "Glen, wait," she protested, but his embrace only tightened. "Oh, God, what am I going to do with you?" she sighed, her anger collapsing under a wave of affection for the man she'd married.

Anne was still in Glen's arms when Boots trotted into the room. The little dog started toward Glen but stopped abruptly, one foreleg hovering off the floor. A tiny growl emerged from his throat and his hackles rose.

Then, his eyes still fixed on Glen, he slowly backed away.

Rolph Gustafson and Lars Gunderson had been fishing buddies for more than seven decades, ever since they'd grown up next door to each other in Ballard, where they'd thrown their first lines into the ship canal that separated their neighborhood from the main part of Seattle just to the south. Back then they'd dreamed about all the places they would go to when they grew up, but it turned out that they both still lived in Ballard—a block apart now, but not more than two blocks from the houses in which they'd grown up. They were both widowers, both still talked about going to Norway to look up cousins they'd never met, and both still loved to fish. The main thing that had changed over the seven decades was that they now preferred to cast their lines in the mountain streams to the east of the city rather than in the canal that bisected it. This morning—as on practically every Saturday morning since Lars's wife had died three years earlier—they set out before dawn, their fishing gear stowed in the backseat of Rolph's old Dodge, coffee and dough-nuts balanced on Lars's knees. By the time they had crossed the I-90 bridge and began the climb up toward Snoqualmie Pass, they were already arguing about where to try their luck today.

As on every other Saturday morning, Rolph turned off at the Sno-qualmie exit while Lars grumbled that they really ought to go farther on, and then as they made their way through the town, past the power plant and falls, and started down the road that wound along the river, they launched into their discussion of the merits of trying out a few of the holes they'd heard of over the years but never quite gotten around to fishing. The debate was still going strong as Rolf pulled into the same campground they'd been fishing out of for years, parked the car, and got out. He began extracting fishing equipment from the tangle of possessions that had been filling the backseat since his own wife had died, only two months before Lars's Greta had gone to her reward. "Hildie'd kill me if she saw this," Rolf sighed, eying the accumulation of junk that now completely filled the floor of the backseat.

"Yeah, sure," Lars replied. "But that don't mean you wouldn't want her back, huh?"

Grunting under the weight of their equipment, the two old men started along the trail that wound down from the picnic area where they'd parked Rolf's Dodge to the edge of the river. There was a wide bend at the foot of the trail, and even at the peak of the spring floods there was still a narrow rocky beach. The snowpack had been light this year, though, and the thaw early, so today the beach would be wide.

They were halfway down when Lars stopped short, his eyes fixing on something that lay half concealed in the thick underbrush. "Oh, boy," he said, whistling softly. "Would you look at that. Don't think there's going to be much fishing today."

He moved off to the right as Rolf edged up next to him. For a long moment the two old men stared at the nude body that lay sprawled in the bushes, arms akimbo, empty eye sockets gaping grotesquely.

The body was still recognizable as that of a woman, but already it appeared to have provided meals for several kinds of wildlife. The chest had been torn open, and it looked as though something had been gnawing at one of the arms and the legs. Insects were swarming over the corpse, and even as they watched, something skittered out from under the body and disappeared into the underbrush. As Lars took a step toward the body, Rolf's gnarled hand closed on his friend's elbow. "Don't think we ought to be touchin' nothin'," he said. "Seems to me like we ought to just be calling the police."

Lars, who had enough experience with dead bodies back in World War II to last him whatever years he had left, nodded his agreement. The two men returned to the campground, found a phone, and dialed 911. Then they sat in the front seat of the Dodge to wait for the sheriff to arrive. Lars uncapped the thermos and split the last of the coffee between them.

Sipping their coffee, the two old men quietly reflected on the impermanence of life and the myriad ways there were to die. It was Rolf who finally broke the silence. "When my time comes," he said, "I think I'd just as soon drown in the river with a big fish on my line."

"Yeah, sure," Lars agreed. "You bet'cha!"

By the time the first police car pulled into the parking lot ten minutes later, neither Lars nor Rolf had been able to think of much else to say.

For the next few hours cars continued to stream into the campground, first from the local sheriff's office in Snoqualmie, then from the State Patrol, finally from the Homicide Department of the Seattle Police Department. Neither Mark Blakemoor nor Lois Ackerly were in the best of moods. Blakemoor had been up most of the night—and the night before—combing through the police records in exactly the same kind of search Anne Jeffers was conducting through her files at the *Herald*. Lois Ackerly, on the other hand, had been getting ready for her son's soccer game when she'd gotten the message that a body had been found in one of the campgrounds along the Snoqualmie River.

"Well, we've been here before," Blakemoor observed darkly as they started down the trail toward the site Lars Gunderson and Rolf Gustafson had stumbled upon as the sun was rising that morning.

"And the locals are doing their usual terrific job of securing the site," Ackerly agreed. "Do you suppose anyone thought of looking for footprints before they started tramping up and down the path?"

Blakemoor shrugged. "If it's what we both think it is, there aren't going to be any footprints anyway. Or anything else."

As the two detectives drew closer, they could see that the area had been marked off with yellow plastic crime scene tape. One of the State Patrol officers glanced over, recognized them, and nodded a terse greeting. "I thought we were done with this stuff," he said, tilting his head toward the body. Blakemoor followed his gaze and noted with relief that it did not appear to have been moved yet.

"We all did," Blakemoor replied. He moved closer to the body, squatting down to get a clear look at it. "Anyone have any idea how long it's been here?" he asked of no one in particular.

"Offhand, it looks like a day or two. Maybe since yesterday morning, or the day before. It's not too badly decomposed yet, but it's been getting chewed on. Fulla bugs, too."

Mark Blakemoor's gaze was instantly drawn to the mutilation done to the corpse's chest. There were the familiar cuts, the skin having been laid neatly back after being incised by a scalpel or something equally as sharp.

The sternum cut with a saw.

The rib cage spread wide to expose the lungs and heart.

The heart torn away, as always, and, in this case, missing entirely. Kept by the killer as a souvenir? Or taken by some foraging animal? More likely the latter—if this fit what had been called the Kraven pattern up until now, the killer wasn't interested in souvenirs.

He was, however, interested in leaving signatures.

"Photo guys through?" he asked.

"They burned enough film to make a movie," someone said.

Carefully, Blakemoor moved one of the lungs enough to get a look at the interior of the dorsal surface of the thoracic cavity.

The moment he saw the familiar form of the lightning bolts that had been etched into the pleura, he glanced up at Lois Ackerly and nodded almost imperceptibly. Easing the lung back into the position in which he'd found it, he forced himself to look at the victim's face.

A woman; at least in her sixties, maybe older. In death her skin, already sagging, had gone slack, and the thick layer of makeup she'd worn when she died had been reduced by the elements to dark streaks of mascara under her empty eye sockets; a stain of rouge still clung to one of her cheeks.

Her hair, the too-dark black of someone desperately pretending that the date on her birth certificate was a grotesque error, had broken out of its prison of hairpins and holding spray and was spread around her face in a mud-and-blood-spattered halo. But despite the depredations of the elements, the animals, and time, Mark Blakemoor recognized her almost immediately.

Getting to his feet, he turned to Lois Ackerly. "This is getting weirder and weirder. First he kills Richard Kraven's brother, now he kills his mother. What the hell is going on?"

Lois Ackerly gazed expressionlessly at the body. "I don't get it— first he sets up Richard Kraven, then waits until he's executed, and goes after the brother and the mother. How come?"

Mark Blakemoor's lips curved into a dark smile. "I don't know, either, but at least he's giving us a pattern this time," he said. "And with a pattern, we can find him. Let's get to work." He began issuing orders, organizing a systematic search of the entire area, although he was pretty sure that, as ever, the killer had cleaned up after himself, leaving nothing in the area that would lead anyone back to him. Still, the search had to be made. Sooner or later even this killer would make a mistake.

And when he did, Mark Blakemoor intended to be the one to find it.

"Dad? Hey, Dad, is something wrong?"

The words hovered on the fringes of Glen Jeffers's mind, not quite penetrating. From his place in the Saab's passenger seat, Kevin looked worriedly at his father. Then, just as Kevin was about to speak again, the words sank in, and Glen glanced over at his son.

"No, everything's fine. We're almost there." He sounded confident enough, he knew, but Glen wondered how much truth there was to what he'd said. The fact was, he wasn't really fine; hadn't been since he'd gotten up this morning. Almost as soon as he awakened he had a feeling that something was wrong, that maybe he shouldn't take Kevin fishing after all. But when he'd suggested postponing the trip until the following weekend, the look of devastation on his son's face had quickly changed his mind. Besides, when Anne had asked him what was bothering him, he hadn't been able to tell her—indeed, he hadn't even been quite able to figure it out himself. All day yesterday he'd been feeling fine. There were no repeats of the blackout he'd experienced on Thursday, and finally he'd decided the vague sense of unease he was feeling wasn't worth disappointing Kevin over. By the time the two of them had actually gotten into the car and headed east across the Evergreen Point bridge, he'd felt much better. But as they'd moved farther east, passing through Redmond, then continuing on out toward Carnation and Fall City, he'd started to experience a strange sense of déjà vu—strange because it wasn't exactly that eerie feeling that what was happening right at the moment was a perfect repeat of something that had occurred before. Rather, the experience Glen was having this morning was something else, not a flash of familiarity, as though something was being repeated, but a stroke of anticipation, a feeling that he was *about* to repeat something.

Something that had given him great pleasure, and that even now, even when he couldn't quite grasp what it was, still sent a shiver of excitement through him.

He glanced over at Kevin, and an image flashed through his mind, disappearing so quickly he was almost unaware that it had happened at all.

Yet the memory of it held.

A heart.

A human heart, which he was holding in his hand.

Where had it come from?

Then he remembered the experience he'd had two days before, when he imagined himself staring down at the naked torso of a woman, then watching helplessly as he cut her chest open.

Her heart? Had he taken her heart out? His stomach twisted with revulsion merely at the thought, and he felt a burning sensation as bile rose in his throat.

But it hadn't happened! None of it had happened! It had only been a horrible nightmare, or a trick of his imagination. Hadn't the psychiatrist told him it couldn't possibly have been real?

He shut his mind to the terrible image, and when his eyes threatened to turn toward Kevin once more, he forced them to stay on the road ahead. Now they were starting up into the mountains. To their right the river cascaded down its rocky channel, frothing white as it roared over broad rapids.

"Where are we going, Dad?" Kevin asked, gazing anxiously at the tumbling waters. What would happen if he slipped while they were fishing? He could swim, but not really very well. "We're not going down there, are we?"

"Another couple of miles," Glen said. "There's a campground. We can park there." A campground? he thought. What campground? He didn't know of any campground. But a few minutes later, as he came around a bend in the road, he saw a sign with the familiar graphics of a tent, a picnic table, and a hiker, with the phrase 1 MILE emblazoned below them. Glen felt his hands turn clammy. How had he known it was there? Was it possible that somehow, in some way he couldn't fathom, the dream had been real? No! It had to be some old memory from one of the drives he, Anne, and the kids had taken over the years. That must be it—although he had no conscious memory of it, the campground must have registered on his mind long ago. He slowed the car, ready to turn in when the side road became visible, but as he rounded the next turn in the road, he saw a police car blocking the entrance, and a State Patrolman waving him on by. As they passed, he was barely able to catch a glimpse of several other police cars parked in the lot at the end of the narrow lane.

"What's happening, Dad?" Kevin asked, twisting around to stare out of the back window. "Can we stop and find out? Maybe a bear got someone!"

"We're not stopping," Glen told Kevin as the boy faced forward again in his seat. "And fasten your seat belt, okay?" He glanced over at Kevin, and as his eyes fixed on his son, he heard a voice in his head:

Remember the cat?

Glen tensed, his fingers tightening on the wheel.

We could do it, the voice whispered. *We could do it, and no one would ever know.*

Suddenly Glen's eyelids felt heavy and the road ahead blurred. A fogginess began to settle over his mind, and he felt sleepy. If he could just close his eyes for a—

No!

He jerked his eyes open, sitting straight up in the seat. No blackouts! Not today! Not with Kevin here with him. He pictured the car careening off the road, hurtling through the guardrail to plunge into the river a hundred feet below, and just the image was enough to send a shot of adrenaline into his bloodstream. As the heat of the hormone spread through his system, his heart began to pound and the strange lassitude that had settled over him while the voice whispered inside his head evaporated.

A new sign appeared ahead. Even before Glen saw it clearly, he knew what it was—a sign indicating a side road a quarter mile farther up.

He would turn there.

A few moments later, as he came closer to the narrow track leading off to the right, he once again experienced a strong sense of déjà vu; this looked exactly like the place where he'd dreamed he was fishing.

Fishing nude, with a vague memory of having killed a woman, of having opened her chest, of having—

No! It had only been a dream, and Dr. Jacobson had found rational sources for every image in it! It wasn't real—none of it! Braking harder than he'd intended, Glen turned the car onto a steep road that wound so closely through the trees that branches scraped against both its sides.

"What if we can't turn around?" Kevin asked, instinctively ducking as a branch slapped against the windshield in front of his face.

"Don't worry about it," he heard his father reply. "I've been here before. Lots of times."

Something in his father's voice caught the boy's attention. Kevin's gaze shifted away from the trees.

The eyes of the man and the boy locked for a moment, and then Kevin looked away.

There was something in his father's eyes he'd never seen before.

Something that scared him.

Anne heard the sound of the mail dropping through the slot in the front door and seized the opportunity to shift her eyes away from the monitor, relax the muscles of her neck, then stand up to stretch her whole body. Could it really be almost three hours since she'd sat down at the computer in the den to review a few of the interview files? Now that her concentration had finally been broken, she realized that it felt like even longer—her legs were stiff, and her right shoulder was sore from manipulating the mouse she'd been using to navigate through the files. So far she'd gotten nothing for her very literal pains. Only a long and tedious review of information that was already so familiar to her that she felt she could have repeated it in her sleep.

Richard Kraven, whether or not he was the serial killer she'd made him out to be, had been a man of many parts. He'd mastered both biology and electrical engineering, and had studied religion and metaphysics as well. He'd loved the arts, especially dance, contributing at least a thousand dollars each year to the ballet.

Dozens—hundreds—of people had known him.

And no one had thought of him as a friend.

Over and over the people she'd interviewed had used the same words. A lot of them had been complimentary: "Charming . . . Fascinating . . . Well-read . . . Genius . . ."

But other words kept recurring as well: "Cold . . . Distant . . . Detached . . . Remote . . ."

Sighing, her certainty fading that she would find something in the files she'd overlooked before, Anne moved through the living room into the foyer.

She saw it even before she bent over to pick up the mail strewn across the floor. A plain white envelope—the kind you could buy anywhere—with her name and address written across it in the same spiky script she'd seen only a few days ago when she followed up the police call to Rory Kraven's apartment. Leaving the rest of the mail where it lay, Anne snatched up the envelope and tore it open. She was about to pull the single sheet of paper out when she stopped herself.

Fingerprints! Maybe, just maybe, whoever had written the note had gotten careless. Her hands trembling, she brought the letter to the kitchen, found a pair of tongs, and carefully pulled the neatly folded sheet out of the envelope. Her heart pounding, she spread it open so she could read it.

> **Dearest Anne,**
> **An explanation: As I'm sure you're**
> **aware, I had no opportunity to hone my**
> **surgical skills during my recent**
> **incarceration. Hence, the incident with**
> **your daughter's cat; I simply needed**
> **something to practice on. Perhaps I**
> **should have left my signature on it, but it**
> **was only a cat, and not truly**
> **representative of my best endeavors. By**
> **the way, no one let the cat out. I came**
> **in and got it, just as I came in and left**
> **the note on your computer. I can come**
> **into your house any time, you know.**
> **Any time at all.**

An icy numbness spreading through her, she read the note a second time, then a third. She felt panic rising in her, felt an insane urge to run through the house locking the doors and windows and pulling the curtains. But it was broad daylight outside—eleven o'clock on Saturday morning. What could happen to her? Besides, if Richard Kraven—

No! Not Richard Kraven! Richard Kraven was dead!

She took a deep breath. If whoever had written the note really intended to come into her house, why would he warn her?

He was only trying to scare her.

Her panic of a moment before now yielding to anger, Anne carefully reinserted the note into the envelope, then picked up the telephone and dialed the number Mark Blakemoor had given her after their last meeting. "Call me any time," he'd told her. "If anything happens, or you find something, or you even think of something, call me."

She let the phone ring a dozen times—didn't he even have a machine? What kind of cop was he? Finally, she hung up, and dialed his office number from memory. On the fourth ring someone picked it up.

"Homicide. McCarty."

Jack McCarty? What would the chief of Homicide be doing in the office on a Saturday? "I'm looking for Mark Blakemoor," Anne said. "This is Anne Jeffers." When there was no immediate reply, she added, "It's important. It's about the Richard Kraven killings." She hesitated, then took a gamble: "The new ones."

"What did Mark tell you about them?" McCarty growled suspiciously.

"He didn't tell me anything," Anne said quickly, remembering Mark's warning not to repeat anything he'd told her. "But I have something to tell him. He gave me his home number, but he's not there."

"He damn well better not be," McCarty replied. "He'd better be up on the Snoqualmie, doing his job."

"The Snoqualmie?" Anne echoed, feeling a chill of apprehension creep over her skin. "What's going on up there?"

There was another silence, then McCarty spoke again, his voice dripping with the contempt he held for every member of the press. "You're a reporter, Jeffers. Why don't you go find out?"

The phone went dead in her hand. "I'll do that, Jack," she said out loud. "I'll just do that." Leaving a message for Heather, although her daughter had said she'd be gone until five, Anne shut off the computer, locked the house, and went out to get into her car. But, stepping onto the front porch, she found herself remembering the note she'd stuffed into the depths of her gritchel.

I can come into your house any time, you know. Any time at all.

Though she fought against the impulse, furious that anyone who might actually be watching her would know how well he'd succeeded in terrifying her, she couldn't resist scanning the street.

Empty, except for a few kids playing on the sidewalk a couple of houses down.

And the motor home.

Its massive form squatted near the end of the block, the sight of it sending a chill through her.

Who owned it? Where had it come from?

Why was it here?

Could someone be inside it even now, watching her? Instead of going directly to her car, parked in front of the house, Anne walked down the sidewalk toward the suddenly ominous vehicle. She circled it slowly, finally venturing close enough to peer into its windows.

Empty.

But for how long?

As her memory of Richard Kraven's love for his motor home rose in her mind, she dug into her gritchel for her dog-eared notebook and a pen. Jotting down the license number of the big van, she wondered if she should go back into the house right now, and start the mechanics of putting a trace on it.

Later, she told herself. Plenty of time for that later. Right now she had to find out what sent Mark Blakemoor up to the Snoqualmie River. She slid behind the wheel of the Volvo and twisted the key in the ignition, already knowing the reason. Only one thing would have sent Mark up there this morning.

A body.

They had to have found another body.

The river was fairly shallow as it made its way around the wide bend, deepening only on the far side, where the force of the current had cut the bottom deep into the granite bed. The fly rod, just as it had in his dream the day before yesterday, felt familiar in Glen's hand. On his very first cast, he flicked the fly nearly halfway across the river, then whipped it back and forth a couple of times before letting it settle onto the surface of the water while he reeled the line back in.

"Wow," Kevin breathed. "How'd you do that?"

"It's simple," Glen explained, covering his own amazement at the skill with which he'd cast the fly. "It's all in the wrist."

Laying his own rod on the rocky beach, he went over to Kevin and stood behind him, guiding his son's hands with his own. As soon as he touched Kevin, something happened.

He felt a rush of energy stream into him, as if some kind of electricity were pouring out of his son's body and into his. And something happened inside him, too: The voice began whispering to him again. *You feel it, don't you, Glen? You feel the life inside him. And you want to know where it comes from, don't you?* He jerked his hands away from Kevin as if he'd touched a hot iron, and his son looked up at him, frowning.

"You okay, Dad? You look kinda funny."

"I'm all right," Glen replied, but even to him his voice sounded strained. And the voice was talking to him again, whispering to him: *We could do it. We could do it right now. It's an experiment,* the voice whispered. *It's just an experiment. We won't hurt him. He'll be fine.*

You'll see. The gray fog was drifting around the edge of his consciousness again, and once again fear rose inside of Glen, the same terrible fear he experienced when he'd been afraid he might fall asleep at the wheel. What if he couldn't fight it off again? What if it closed in on him this time? "T-Tell you what," he stammered, the words almost strangling in his throat as he struggled against the softness of the fog and the seductive sound of the words. "Why don't you go downstream a ways, and I'll go up. That way our lines won't get tangled. Okay?"

Kevin, who'd been watching his father out of the corner of his eye, nodded quickly, reeled in his line, and began working his way downriver, jumping from one rock to another. A couple of times he looked back, but his father was going in the other direction, and even when Kevin called out to him, Glen didn't turn around. Kevin felt a twinge of fear. What if his father was sick? What if he had another heart attack? What would he do? "Dad?" he called again, but again his father didn't seem to hear him. Kevin paused. Should he go after his father, in case something really was wrong? Or should he do as his father had told him?

Then he remembered the funny look he'd seen in his father's eyes just now. It had been kind of scary.

Kevin made up his mind. For a while, at least, he'd poke around farther downstream. Maybe see if he could catch a frog, or even a turtle. Because right now, for some reason he didn't understand, he just didn't want to be around his dad.

Right now his father just didn't seem like his father.

He seemed like someone else.

Someone Kevin decided he really didn't like.

As Glen moved farther upstream, the strange sense of déjà vu that he'd experienced on the road upriver came over him again, even stronger than before. Though he was certain he'd never been here— except in the dream, which meant he'd never been here at all—there was still something very familiar about the place. The river curved again farther upstream, but between the two bends there was a straight stretch of perhaps a quarter of a mile where the water ran wide and shallow. The beach was a little narrower across the river, and beyond the rocky strip bordering the stream the bank rose steeply. Perhaps ten feet up above the beach, on what looked like a shelf of the bank, there was a pile of rocks.

A pile that looked familiar to Glen, though he was absolutely sure he hadn't seen it before, even in the dream.

Now that he thought about it, the familiarity it triggered in his mind didn't seem recent, but rather like something he remembered from long ago.

He searched his memory, trying to recall when he might have been here before, but found nothing. He'd been to the falls, a few miles upriver by the power plant, plenty of times. Once, years ago, he and Anne had even climbed down the steep trail to the beach below the falls. And they'd probably driven down the road to Fall City a couple of times, too. But they'd never stopped here, he was sure of it.

Standing on the bank, he cast the fly—the one that looked as though it had been made from a scrap of Hector's feathers and a tuft of Kumquat's fur—out over the river. Instantly, a trout struck, snatching the fly out of the air so quickly Glen almost missed it. The line started to play out from the reel, and Glen, uncertain what to do next, watched it go. Then, inside his head, he heard the voice:

Reel in!

He twisted the crank on the reel. On the first revolution the guide flipped into place and the line began to rewind onto the spool. Abruptly, it went taut and the rod bent. Then there was a buzzing sound as the force on the line exceeded the tension on the reel and the line began to pay out again. The voice in his head directing him, Glen began playing the fish.

The game went on for fifteen minutes, and by the time Glen had finally brought the fish close enough to scoop it out of the water and drop it into the canvas creel he'd slung across his chest, he was halfway across the river. Only a few yards away was the cairn he'd seen from the beach just before the fish had struck. His eyes fixing on it, he waded across the river and the narrow beach that fronted it and climbed the bank until he came to the cairn.

Nothing more than a pile of rocks.

But the sense of familiarity was stronger than ever.

One by one he began removing the rocks.

Finally, when he'd pulled several away, the structure lost its stability; half of the mound fell away, the rounded river cobbles tumbling around Glen's feet.

Something caught his eye. He bent down and picked up a worn pocketknife. Its handle was made from tarnished silver, inlaid with turquoise. Its blade was somewhat rusted, but not so badly that Glen couldn't open it. Its edge, well-protected by the handle, was still wickedly sharp. Glen gazed at the blade for a long moment, then closed it and dropped the knife into his pocket.

Squatting down, he moved another of the rocks.

Now he could see something else.

A bone.

A long bone. Like the leg bone of a deer.

Except that the moment he saw it, Glen knew it wasn't the bone of a deer at all.

It was a human bone.

He reached out and moved more rocks, exposing more bones.

What should he do?

Call the police?

But how would he explain what he'd found? It wasn't as if he'd simply stumbled across it—he'd had to cross the river, climb the bank, then pull the cairn apart stone by stone.

He stood up, still uncertain. Then, from across the river, he heard Kevin calling him.

"Dad! Hey, Dad!"

The boy was still close to the bank, but he was wading into the stream. "Don't!" Glen yelled. "Stay there!"

Kevin kept coming, wading deeper into the swiftly moving water. "What is it? What did you find?" he called.

Even on Glen the water had come up almost to his waist. On Kevin it would be nearly neck deep. "Don't come any farther!" Glen yelled. "It isn't anything! Just a bunch of rocks!" Looking down at the skeleton again, he hesitated for just one more moment, then kicked enough of the stones over it so that it was no longer visible. "Just stay there," he called to Kevin once more. "I'm on my way back." Moving quickly, he scrambled back down the bank, crossed the beach and started back across the river. When he came back to the bank where Kevin was now waiting for him, he opened the creel to show him the fish he'd caught. "What do you say?" he asked. "Shall we have it for lunch?"

Kevin eyed the fish warily. "Can't we just have a hamburger?" he asked.

Glen's eyes shifted back to the stone cairn on the other side of the river, and suddenly he wanted to be somewhere else, somewhere that didn't look familiar, that didn't make strange things happen in his mind. "That's a good idea," he said. "Let's go."

But as they started back toward the car, Glen felt the strange fog closing around him once more, and heard the voice whispering to him yet again.

An experiment, it said. *It will only be an experiment. Use the knife....*

"Maybe this wasn't such a good idea," Anne muttered, gazing dejectedly at the plate of uneaten food on the table. Beyond the window, water was cascading over Snoqualmie Falls, but even that magnificent vista had done nothing to lift her spirits.

"You still have to eat," Mark Blakemoor had told her when he'd suggested they meet here for lunch. "I know you're upset, and I'm not about to say you shouldn't be. But you have to eat, and so do I, and we might as well talk over lunch."

So she'd followed him up the road from the campground to the falls, but so far she'd eaten nothing. Now she gave up entirely on the idea of eating and pushed the plate away. "Edna Kraven," she sighed. An image of the heavy woman with her shoe-polish hair and the clothes that never quite suited her, came into Anne's mind, and with it a discomforting recollection of the woman's hostility as she consistently refused in interview after interview to concede that her eldest son could have been a serial killer. Edna, right up until the end, had maintained her faith in Richard Kraven's perfection, just as she had maintained the utter contempt she had never failed to display toward her younger son.

Even now, as Anne sat in the dining room of the Salish Lodge with Mark Blakemoor, she remembered Edna's scornful clucking when she'd been told that Rory Kraven had killed both Shawnelle Davis and Joyce Cottrell. *"Well, that's just ridiculous! Rory couldn't even talk to a woman, let alone kill one. Now, my Richard—there was a ladies' man. Of course no one could take the place of his mother. But Rory? Don't make me laugh—I was his mother, but I believe in being honest. And Rory just wasn't much of anything. Why, either one of those women could have just barked at Rory, and he'd have run the other way!"*

There'd been more—a lot more—but Anne had tuned it out, not simply because she'd heard most of it before, but because she'd tired years ago of listening to Edna Kraven's version of reality. Anne believed firmly that most, if not all, of Edna's sons' problems could be traced directly to their mother, and had she not known better, both of Edna's sons would have headed her own list of suspects in the woman's murder. But with both sons already dead . . . "My God," she breathed, an idea blooming in her mind. "Mark, what if she knew? What if she knew who killed Rory?"

"Well, I think we can presume she did at the end," the detective observed.

Anne glared at him. "That's sick."

"Cop humor," Blakemoor replied. "It's always sick—goes with the job." Now he, too, pushed his unfinished meal aside. For the last hour he'd been trying to analyze the feelings he'd had when he'd first read the note that arrived in Anne Jeffers's mail that day. He should have been able to take it in stride, to look at it with the detachment of his years of experience with the Homicide Division.

He should have been able to look at it simply as one more scrap of evidence, one piece of the jigsaw puzzle.

Instead, it enraged him. He wanted to grab hold of the creep who'd written it, slam him up against the nearest wall and beat the holy shit out of him.

So much for objectivity, he'd thought wryly as he struggled to keep his rage from showing while he studied the note far longer than he really needed to. For the rest of the morning its ramifications had preyed on him, and now he was worried in a way that went far beyond mere professional concern for a possible victim. Still, when he spoke again, he did his best to keep at least a semblance of a professional patina on his voice. "Look, Anne, have you got someplace you can take your kids until this is all over?"

Anne deliberately shifted her eyes away from him, as if the view beyond the window had finally caught her attention. She'd been thinking about exactly the same thing herself. In fact, she'd already made up her mind that tonight she and Glen would discuss the possibility of temporarily moving out of the house. Mark Blakemoor, though, hadn't made any mention of Glen at all. And she was pretty sure she knew why. Deciding she had to face the issue squarely, she fixed her eyes on his. "Me and the kids," she repeated, her voice flat. "What about Glen?"

Now it was the detective's gaze that wavered, but only for a moment. "What about him?" he asked.

"I believe I asked you first," Anne said, her voice hardening perceptibly. "I didn't miss your implication the other day that he might have killed Heather's cat. Are you now suggesting that he killed Rory Kraven? And Edna?" At least he has the good grace to blush, Anne thought as her words brought a bright flush to the detective's face.

"I don't know what I think," Mark replied. "There's no way I can rule your husband out of what happened to the cat, and you're a good enough reporter that you can't deny that. Not honestly, anyway." Now it was Anne's turn to redden, and Mark had to steel himself against the instinct to apologize for his words. But the fact was, no matter how he felt about her, he still had to tell her exactly what he thought. "As for the other stuff, no, I can't say he did it. And I won't say he did it."

As he saw mollification settle over Anne, he was tempted to leave well enough alone, but once more his job wouldn't let him. "On the other hand, neither one of us can prove he didn't do any of it, or all of it." Anne's eyes darkened and her jaw set angrily, but Blakemoor pushed doggedly on. "Let's assume he's not your husband, okay? Just for the sake of argument. So, we've got a man whose whole personality has changed in the last few weeks." He held up a hand to preclude Anne's interrupting him. "Don't argue that one—you're the one who told me. And you also told me he had Kevin bring your whole Kraven file down to him in the hospital. And if you really want to get down and dirty, try this one on for size—let's just build a scenario, all right? Let's just say that since he's been home, he and Cottrell got a little extra cozy, okay? And don't go all uptight on me—you know this kind of thing goes on all the time. So maybe he and Cottrell have a thing going, and maybe he's awake the night she gets whacked. Maybe he's even thinking of dropping over there."

"That's disgusting," Anne said, fury rising in her.

"Sure it is," Mark agreed, knowing he should just drop the whole thing, but also knowing he couldn't. "So's murder. But it all happens, and we both know it. So he's thinking about going over there. Maybe he's even out on the back porch. And suddenly her back door opens and he sees Rory coming out, carrying his girlfriend's body. What's he do? Call the cops? Hell, no—that means explaining what he was doing snooping around Cottrell's house in the middle of the night. So maybe he just waits. He recognized Rory-boy—hell, his picture's got to be in your files somewhere—and he hatches a plan. He'll kill Rory himself. He's already killed the cat—what's the difference?"

"And Edna?" Anne asked, her voice ice cold. "How does she fit into your little scenario, *Detective*?" She gave the last word just enough emphasis to make it poisonous.

"How about if she was going in when he was coming out?" Mark asked, determined to ignore her tone, and hating what he was doing almost as much as she did. But it had to be dealt with, whether she liked it or not. "How about if she saw him? She wouldn't know Glen from Adam, but she's in your files, too, right? So he knows she's going to visit Rory, and he knows she's seen him. And sooner or later she might be able to identify him."

"So he *whacks* her, too, as you so charmingly put it?" Anne asked, her voice quivering with fury. "And I suppose Glen imitated Richard Kraven's handwriting, too?"

"He's an architect, right?" Blakemoor shot back, unconsciously hunching his body into a defensive position. "That means he can draw, doesn't it?"

Anne stared at him, scarcely able to credit her ears. Had he gone completely crazy? It had been bad enough when he'd only implied that Glen might have killed their cat. Now, apparently, he was determined to wrap this whole case around Glen just the way she'd wrapped a whole case around Richard Kraven! Except there was a difference—Richard Kraven had been guilty, and Glen wasn't! And what Blakemoor had just suggested wasn't merely ludicrous and despicable—it was irresponsible as well. Pushing her chair back from the table, she rose to her feet. "I think this has gone far enough," she said coldly. "I can't imagine how you came up with this scenario, but

I suggest you drop it. Because if I ever hear of you mentioning it to anyone else—anyone at all—I'll have a long talk with Jack McCarty."

"Anne—" Mark began, lurching to his feet, his hand reaching out toward her. But it was too late. She'd already turned and was rushing out of the dining room.

"Ah, *shit*," he muttered, throwing some bills on the table to cover the check, then hurrying after her.

He got to the parking lot just in time to see her Volvo pulling out into the road, heading toward the freeway.

By the time she arrived home, Anne's rage had begun to subside a bit, not because she'd been able to find any merit in Mark Blakemoor's ridiculous theory, but because her anger itself had finally run its course, leaving her drained and as tired emotionally as she was physically. As she turned the corner off Highland onto Sixteenth, she was surprised to see that Glen's Saab was back. But Glen had said they wouldn't be back until late in the afternoon—maybe even tomorrow morning. Sliding her car into a space that was miraculously open right in front of the house, she hurried up the flight of steps to the porch and went inside. "Glen? Kevin? Hello?"

"In the basement!" Glen called, his voice barely audible.

Coming down the stairs a moment later, Anne found her husband standing at the workbench, his back toward her, the bright fluorescent lights casting a harsh glare over everything. "How come you're back so soon?" she asked, moving closer. Glen didn't answer. As Anne approached the workbench she saw what he was doing: in his right hand he held a filleting knife, its thin, razor-sharp blade glimmering in the white light from above. On the wooden workbench, held in place by Glen's left hand, was a large trout. As she watched, Glen jabbed the sharp point of the knife through the skin at the base of the fish's head, then ran it quickly down its spine, laying the flesh open along the dorsal ridge and exposing the innards. Then, the knife flashing so quickly Anne was afraid he might cut himself, Glen cut the meat away from the bones, finally laying the bright pink fillet skin side down on the bench. With a single deft stroke, he peeled the meat from the skin, speared the skin with the tip of the knife, and dropped it into the wastebasket next to his feet. Only then did he turn to her.

"Where'd you learn how to do that?" Anne asked.

Glen shrugged. "I didn't. Turns out it's easy. Want to try?" He offered her the knife, but Anne shook her head.

"Where's Kev?"

"Over at Justin Reynolds's. Where've you been? I thought you said you were going to be glued to your computer all day."

"There was another killing," Anne said. "This time it was Edna Kraven—Richard and Rory's mother. They found her up in a campground on the Snoqualmie." For a split second—a moment so brief she wasn't sure it had happened at all—she thought she saw something in Glen's eyes.

Fear?

Anger?

But it was gone so quickly, she dismissed it a second later.

"So that was it," Glen said. "We passed a campground on the way up that was crawling with cops." He grinned. "Needless to say, Kevin wanted us to stop and find out was going on."

"Thank God you didn't," Anne replied, shuddering. "It was horrible." She hesitated, wondering if she shouldn't tell him about the note that had arrived, while they were alone in the house. But even as she thought about it, Mark Blakemoor's suggestion that Glen himself might have written it popped back into her mind, and she knew if she got started right now, she'd wind up blurting out the whole bizarre scenario the detective had come up with.

That—justifiably—would send Glen into a fury, which was the last thing he needed right now. Better to wait until later, when she was completely calm. Maybe tonight, before they went to bed.

"So how was the fishing?" she asked, deciding to change the subject. "You still haven't told me why you came back so early."

Glen hesitated. An odd look came into his eyes, but then, as before, it cleared almost before Anne was certain she'd seen it. "It was okay," he said at last. He seemed to think it over for a moment, then nodded. "Yeah, it was okay. But I don't think Kevin liked it very much. Next time, I think I'd better go by myself."

A few minutes later Anne headed upstairs. There was something he wasn't telling her. Something had happened—and obviously it had something to do with Kevin—but for some reason he didn't want to talk about it.

She went up to their room, only to find a pile of clothes dumped in the middle of the floor.

Soggy clothes.

Picking them up, she turned and started down the stairs to put them into the washing machine, automatically checking the pockets as she went. In the right front pocket of the sodden khakis she found something.

A knife.

A pocketknife, with a tarnished silver handle that had been inlaid with turquoise.

The flat edge of the folded blade was stained as if it had been lying out in the elements for months, even years.

A knife, with a silver handle inlaid with turquoise.

And then it came to her:

Danny Harrar had had a knife like that—his mother had listed it as something he always carried with him when she'd reported him missing, even told Anne about it.

But that was ridiculous. It couldn't be the same knife.

Could it?

"Glen?" she called as she came back down to the basement to put the wet clothes into the washing machine. He paused in the midst of cleaning up the workbench and looked inquiringly at her. "Where'd this come from?"

He looked at the knife, and once more she thought she saw a flicker of something in his eyes. He shrugged. "I found it by the river," he said. "I was going to give it to Kevin, but I guess I forgot."

As he went back to clearing away the mess from the fish he'd just cleaned, Anne looked at the knife once again.

Then, instead of giving it back to Glen, she slipped it into her own pocket.

Anne had been sitting at the computer for almost two hours, though when she'd first come up from the basement, it was her intention to do no more than reconfirm her memory of Sheila Harrar's description of her son's pocketknife. When it checked out, she considered going down to Pioneer Square to find Sheila Harrar, but the memory of those strange, fleeting looks she'd seen in Glen's eyes stopped her. She hadn't been able to forget those brief glimpses she'd had of— what? Fear? Or something else?

Something, obviously, had happened while Glen and Kevin were fishing. Something that led Glen to cut the trip short.

Or had it been Kevin?

Could something have frightened Kevin and made him demand to be taken home?

As questions—unwelcome, unwanted questions—popped into her mind, all of them springing from the incredible tale Mark Blakemoor had woven over her uneaten lunch, Anne tried to think about other things. But the questions lingered, keeping her from going downtown in search of Danny Harrar's mother. If something *had* happened between Kevin and Glen, she wanted to be there when her son came home. So she forced herself to stay at the computer and concentrate on the transcripts of the interviews she'd conducted years earlier.

The same themes kept coming up over and over again. Biology. Electricity. Metaphysics.

The more she read, the stronger the themes became, until it struck her what Richard Kraven's true fascination had been.

Life!

He had been utterly consumed with analyzing every aspect of life itself! But if he'd been enthralled with life, why had he killed?

Then, her neck aching and her eyes stinging, Anne came across an interview she'd conducted with a former neighbor of the Kravens, a woman named Maybelle Swinney:

A.J.: What about when he was a boy, Mrs. Swinney? Do you have any memories that might have new significance, given what he's been accused of?

M.S.: Well, now, I don't like to speak ill of anyone, and Edna Kraven and I were always good friends. But I always thought his fascination with taking things apart was real strange. Always wanted to find out how things worked, that boy did.

Couldn't ever just enjoy them for what they were—oh, no, not him. He always had to take them apart.

A.J.: What about putting them back together again?

M.S.: Oh, sure, he was always real good at that, too. Why, he could put almost anything back together. Except the things he . . . (Pause) Now what do they call it when they cut animals up in a lab?

A.J.: Dissecting?

M.S.: Dissecting! That's it. Anyway, I don't suppose he ever managed to put the things he dissected back together. (Laughing) Though I daresay he tried. Oh, I bet he tried!

The passage remained on Anne's screen. Staring at it, she thought, What if Maybelle Swinney hadn't laughed years ago before suggesting that Richard Kraven might have tried to put the animals he'd dissected back together again? Would I have thought more about the words then?

Maybe. Maybe not.

But what if that was exactly what he'd been trying to do? Now a new idea began to take shape in her head, an idea so vile she found herself wanting to back away from it even as it was forming. What if—

"Mom?"

Anne jumped, startled by the unexpected interruption, and looked up from the monitor, rubbing at her stinging eyes until she was able to focus on Kevin, who was standing just inside the den door. "Kev! You startled me!"

"What're you doing?" the boy asked, moving closer.

Anne reached out, closed the file with a couple of quick clicks of the mouse. "Nothing much," she said. Then, trying to keep her voice totally neutral: "How was the fishing expedition? Did you have a good time?"

Kevin's open features tightened into a guarded expression. "I guess," he said.

"You guess? What does that mean?" Kevin glanced around, and it took Anne a second to realize what he was doing: looking for his father. So she'd been right—something *had* happened. "Tell you what," she said. "I've got an errand to run in Pioneer Square. How about if you go with me, and you can tell me all about the fishing trip on the way?"

Kevin's expression cleared instantly. "Can we go to the kite store?"

"We'll see," Anne temporized. "Get your jacket while I tell your dad where we're going."

The afternoon light was beginning to fade, giving the broad brick expanse of Pioneer Square a dismal aspect that was only intensified by the chill drizzle falling from the slate clouds gathered overhead. "When can we go home, Mom?" Kevin complained, clutching his newly purchased kite in one hand while trying to pull his other one free from his mother's grasp.

"In a little while," Anne promised. But it was the third time she'd said that, and she could tell Kevin didn't believe her. And why should he? They'd just kept moving around while she asked one person after another where she might find Sheila Harrar. She finally interrupted her search for a stop at the kite shop, but that had only served to shift Kevin's interest from the woman for whom they were searching to the kite he was now impatiently waiting to try out.

The conversation about the fishing trip had gone no better than the search for Sheila Harrar; all Kevin had admitted was that Glen had been "acting funny," but she hadn't been able to find out much more. "I don't know," Kevin kept saying, no matter how she'd phrased her questions. "He kept looking at me funny, that's all. And then he made me go down the river and fish by myself."

"By yourself?" Anne echoed. "He actually sent you off alone?"

Kevin nodded. "Then he went across the river and started messing around in some rocks, but when I wanted to come over and see what he was doing, he wouldn't let me. That's when we came home."

That was all, but it had been enough to make her start worrying all over again.

Now, as the rain fell harder and a bolt of lightning shot across the sky, instantly followed by a crash of thunder, she wondered if maybe she shouldn't give up the search for Sheila Harrar. If she came back tomorrow morning, she might even catch the woman in her room. She was about to head for the parking lot where she'd left the Volvo when a familiar figure rose up off one of the benches and shuffled toward the Grand Central Arcade. Her hand tightening on Kevin's, Anne hurried after the figure.

"Mrs. Harrar?" she called. "Sheila?" The figure paused, turning slowly to gaze at Anne, and for a moment Anne thought she'd made a mistake. Then the woman's lips curved in a smile and she shambled toward them.

It took no more than a second for Anne to realize that Sheila was drunk. Very drunk.

"I know you," Sheila said as she neared Anne and Kevin. Her words were slurred and her eyes were bloodshot. "You came to see me, didn't you? You want to buy me a bottle of wine?"

"How about if I buy you some coffee, Sheila?" Anne countered. "And maybe a cinnamon bun?"

Sheila seemed to consider the possibility of arguing, then shrugged. "Sure. Shouldn't drink anyway. Danny wouldn't like it." Her eyes cleared slightly. "You come to tell me about Danny?" she asked.

"I— Why don't we just get some coffee first?" Anne said. Taking Sheila's elbow, she guided her into the Grand Central Arcade and found a table, ignoring the glares of the people around her. "Wait here," she told Sheila and Kevin. "I'll go get some coffee and buns."

Ten minutes later Sheila had consumed most of the cup of coffee and half of a cinnamon bun. The doughy bun seemed to have soaked up some of the alcohol in her stomach, and her eyes had cleared a bit. At last Anne pulled the knife Glen had found out of her pocket and laid it on the table. "Do you recognize this, Sheila?"

Sheila Harrar stared at the turquoise-inlaid knife for a long time, then reached out with trembling fingers and picked it up. She turned it over and over, gazing at it. "Danny's," she finally breathed. "It's Danny's." She looked up at Anne. "Where? Where'd you get it?"

"Are you absolutely sure it's Danny's?" Anne asked, ignoring Sheila's questions.

Sheila nodded, then tried to pry the blade open. "It's his," she insisted. "I can show you—" Her trembling fingers lost their grip on the knife and it clattered to the floor. Kevin slid off his seat, retrieved the knife and opened it.

"There," Sheila said, touching the blade with her finger. "His initials. See?"

Anne leaned forward, peering at the knife. At first she saw nothing, but then she was able to make out two barely visible letters etched into the metal of the blade: DH.

"See?" Sheila asked. "It's his!" Now she looked at Anne once more, her eyes pleading. "Please—where did you get it? How did you find it?"

"I didn't," Anne said. "My husband did. He went fishing up on the Snoqualmie and found it." A pile of rocks, Kevin had said. Glen was digging in a pile of rocks on the other side of the river. "I—I'm not sure exactly where," she said.

Then Kevin spoke. "I can tell you," he said. "I know exactly where it was."

For the first time in almost two decades, the workbench area in the basement was completely clean. The bench, along with the rows of narrow shelves that had been built into the wall above it, had been there when he and Anne had bought the house. The previous owner, moving to a nursing home, had left everything in place, and there it had remained. Even during the total restoration of the main floors, the basement had never been touched. A tool had occasionally been located and used, an area had now and then been cleared to make way for a new project. But the clutter had always remained.

Until today, when, for some reason he didn't comprehend, Glen hadn't stopped with cleaning up the mess left from the filleting of the trout, but had kept on working, methodically going through the myriad plastic containers filled with nuts, bolts, nails, tacks, rivets, washers, and other assorted hardware, labeling each one of them, then sorting them first by contents, then by size, until, when he was done, the ranks of shelves offered an almost artistically elegant orderliness to the eye. The shelves finished, he'd gone on to clean out the area under the workbench, sweeping and vacuuming the floor until even the most recalcitrant speck of dust had succumbed. Then he'd set about rendering the same kind of order to the tools that had lain scattered on the table and bench, and when he was finally finished, the whole area had taken on a new look. Clean and bright under the fluorescent lights, with a place for everything and everything in its place.

As perfectly kept as any laboratory. Glen stood gazing at it for a few minutes, reveling in the satisfaction the cleanup had given him, then started up the steep flight of stairs to the kitchen. He was half-way up when the headache struck.

A stab of pain shot through his head, so intense it made him stagger against the wall, then drop to his knees. At the same time the pain struck, an explosion of light burst inside his head, blinding him.

A stroke! He was having a stroke. Out of nowhere, Franklin Roosevelt's last words flashed into his mind: "I have a terrific pain in the back of my head." Almost immediately, the president had fallen into a coma and died.

Now it was happening—he felt as though he was sinking into a great dark chasm, falling endlessly into a black, bottomless hole.

He tried to scream, but nothing came out. Then, almost from beyond the edges of his consciousness, he heard laughter.

Dark, scornful laughter.

The laughter of a maniac.

As he sank yet deeper into the lightless abyss, he heard the laughter again, and now he recognized it.

The voice—the voice inside his head, the voice that had whispered to him of evil.

The voice that only today had wanted him to open Kevin's chest and hold his son's heart in his hands.

No!

He couldn't give in to it—he wouldn't! He struggled against the blackness, forcing it back, willing himself not to disappear into the dark pit that yawned around him. Then he heard something else. A low rumble, slowly building, drowning out the mocking laughter. He concentrated on that sound, shutting out the laughter until the blackness began to recede. His vision cleared and slowly he realized the pain had vanished.

Not simply eased—it was completely gone.

But he felt exhausted, as if he'd just run a marathon. His legs felt rubbery, but as he climbed slowly back to his feet, gripping the rail with one hand, resting part of his weight against the wall with the other, they began to feel stronger, and finally he was able to make his way up to the kitchen. As he emerged from the basement door, he saw rain slashing against the window, and then there was a sudden blinding flash of lightning.

Once again pain slashed through Glen's head like a hurled spear, and once again he was dropped to his knees by its blinding force. When the lights in the kitchen dimmed briefly as the lightning died away, Glen didn't see it, for again the black abyss had opened before him. The clap of thunder that burst over the house a second later with enough force to rattle the windows sent him whimpering to the floor while from deep within him the terrible laughter once again erupted.

A visage of evil now appeared before Glen in the darkness, a face whose features radiated such heinous inhumanity that Glen recoiled from it. As the terrible pain in his head grew more intense, Glen cowered into the black shroud closing around him, no longer battling the blackness and the pain, but only seeking refuge from the torture being inflicted upon him.

And as Glen Jeffers's spirit steadily weakened, the spirit of Richard Kraven—seeming to draw strength directly from the electrical storm that raged beyond the confines of the house—burst forth to take total control of the body that until this moment it had been forced to share. Now, seeming to draw more power with every bolt of lightning that flashed across the sky, Richard Kraven drove Glen Jeffers deeper and deeper into the abyss.

So deep that soon there would be no trace of Glen Jeffers left.

Never again would Richard Kraven have to wait for Glen Jeffers to sleep, nor would he have to steal quick moments when rage—the kind of rage only his brother and his mother had been able to inspire—gave him the strength to overcome Glen, at least for a little while.

Now, finally, Richard Kraven was utterly free to do as he pleased.

Rising from the floor, exhilarating in his liberation, Richard Kraven moved leisurely through the house.

Coming to the computer in the den—Anne's computer—he quickly manipulated the mouse to trace the history of the files she had been studying.

Obviously she'd had no trouble figuring out to whom the pocket-knife must have belonged.

Had she figured out how close to the truth Maybelle Swinney had come when she'd tried to make a joke?

Probably: unlike Maybelle Swinney, Anne was smart.

But where had she gone?

To Mark Blakemoor, probably. Even if she wasn't with him right now, she soon would be.

But neither of them could yet suspect the truth, and in the end, when finally he lost this body as surely as he'd lost his own, at least his reputation would be restored.

Glen Jeffers would be convicted of all of it.

For Glen Jeffers, Richard Kraven had decided, would be caught in the act. Indeed, the only thing he'd changed his mind about was whom he would choose to be the subject of his final experiment.

Anne had been his first choice, of course. But now he'd come to a new decision.

An elegant decision.

The kind of decision that was worthy of a man of his intellect.

Anne would stay alive.

And in his own final moment—or at least in the moment before he left this body to find a new one—he would see the expression on her face as she watched her husband clutch her daughter's heart in his hand and tear it from her breast.

For the rest of her life Anne would live with that memory.

Richard Kraven's reputation would be totally restored.

And Anne Jeffers's entire life would be utterly destroyed.

Justice would be served.

Sitting down at Anne's desk, Richard Kraven began writing one last note. And this time he made no effort to keep from leaving Glen Jeffers's fingerprints all over it. Then, leaving the note where Anne would be sure to find it, he left the house. There were preparations to make for his final experiment.

The one he would perform on Heather Jeffers.

The worst of the thunderstorm had moved eastward, and the dismal gray of the rainy afternoon had given way to a glittering darkness. The wet pavement shimmered brightly beneath the streetlights. As Anne turned left from Highland onto Sixteenth, she braked a little too sharply and felt the rear end of the car drift slightly to the right. It wasn't until she'd recovered from the brief skid that Anne noticed the empty spot on the right that had still been occupied by the motor home when she and Kevin had left the house nearly two hours before. At least they wouldn't have to walk too far in the downpour. Locking the car, she followed Kevin up the sidewalk, then climbed the flight of steps to the house, arriving on the porch just as Kevin was opening the door. "Glen?" she called. "Heather? Anybody . . ." Her call died on her lips as she felt the emptiness within the house, the same kind of emptiness she'd experienced while Glen had been in the hospital.

Today, though, something had changed. Always before when she'd been alone in the house, the place was still filled with the vibrancy of her family. This evening that vibrancy was gone; the house had taken on the dead feeling that had pervaded it the first day they had walked in.

Trying to banish her rapidly growing uneasiness, Anne strode quickly through the dining room to the kitchen. No note posted on the refrigerator door; the message light on the answering machine was not flashing. But the door to the basement stairs stood open. Not quite certain why the open door struck her as foreboding, Anne went to the top of the stairs and peered down into the work area below. The white glare of the fluorescent light shone down on the cleared surface of the workbench. Frowning, Anne started slowly down the stairs, her gaze fixed on the workbench. Only when she'd come to the bottom of the stairs did she notice the other things that had been done.

The meticulously sorted containers of hardware.

The perfectly vacuumed floor.

For nearly two decades neither she nor Glen had even bothered to complain about the mess on the workbench, let alone clean it up.

Now it looked as pristine as an operating room.

Turning away from the workbench, Anne remounted the steps, searched the refrigerator door once more for a message from Glen, then went to the den. Maybe he'd left a Post-it on her monitor. But it wasn't a yellow square that she found. It was an envelope with her name written on the outside.

Written in a familiar spiky script.

Recoiling from the envelope as if it were a coiled viper preparing to strike, Anne snatched up the telephone, her fingers punching at the buttons even as her mind tried not to imagine what the message inside the envelope might be, much less the terrifying significance of its presence on her desk. "Can you come over here?" Anne asked, the instant the phone was picked up at the other end. "Something's happened—"

"Five minutes," Mark Blakemoor replied. "Is that soon enough? Do you need me to call 911 for you?"

Anne gazed mutely at the envelope. "No," she breathed. "I— We'll be all right." She laid the phone back on the hook, realizing only then that Kevin was standing in the doorway, his brow creased with worry as he watched her.

"Is something wrong, Mom?" the boy asked, sounding far younger than his ten years. Moving closer to his mother, he put his arms around her, and she, still staring at the envelope on her desk, held him close.

When the doorbell rang five minutes later, Anne had moved to the sofa in the living room, but her arms were still around her son. As the chimes sounded a second time, Anne gently disengaged herself from Kevin and approached the front door. Before she was halfway there, Kevin had scooted around her and pulled the door wide.

Looking up, he gazed quizzically into Mark Blakemoor's face. "I know you," he said. "You came over when I found Kumquat in the alley."

"Pretty good memory," Mark Blakemoor said. He squatted down so his eyes were level with Kevin's. "And now, since I'm a cop, I'm going to ask you a question. How did you know it was me before you opened the door?"

Kevin looked puzzled. "Wh-what do you mean?" he stammered.

"Well, you must have known who it was, or you wouldn't have just opened the door like that, would you? So what was it? Did your mom tell you?" As Kevin glanced nervously at his mother, Blakemoor jerked his head toward one of the curtained windows that flanked the door. "Or did you peek, like I would have done?"

"I peeked," Kevin cried, seizing the opportunity Blakemoor had offered him.

"Good for you," Mark said, tousling Kevin's hair as he rose to his feet. "Always best to know who's outside before you open the door, right?" Finally he turned his attention to Anne. "What happened?" he asked. "On the phone you sounded—" Then, realizing that Kevin was listening to every word he uttered, he made a quick adjustment. "—worried," he finished, feeling inordinately pleased at the glint of appreciation that came into Anne's eyes as she realized that he'd avoided referring to her obvious terror in front of her son. Also, she'd obviously decided to forgive him for the theory he'd expounded at lunch, and the realization had the effect of lifting the depression that had fallen over him as he'd watched her speed out of the parking lot of the Salish Lodge.

"A lot has happened," Anne said. As she led the detective through the living room to the den, she quickly told him about the knife Glen had found, and Sheila Harrar's identification of it as having belonged to her son. "When Kevin and I got home, the motor home was gone, but that was on my desk." She nodded toward the envelope, which Mark Blakemoor gingerly picked up, carefully holding it by its edges.

"You haven't read it?" he asked, his voice betraying nothing of what he might be thinking. When Anne shook her head, he opened the unsealed flap of the envelope and carefully slid the single sheet of paper onto the desk's surface. It was the same kind of paper, he noted, that had been used for the message that had been mailed to Anne. "Got a Baggie?" he asked. "Anything like that?"

"I'll get one," Kevin instantly volunteered. As he darted out of the room, Anne took the opportunity to speak quickly to Blakemoor.

"Everything's crazy," she told him, her voice shaking now. "The basement's cleaned up to the point that it looks like some kind of laboratory, and Kevin said Glen was acting funny up in the mountains today."

"Funny, how?" Mark asked.

Anne shrugged. "All he would say was that Glen kept looking at him in a way that made him nervous, then sent him off to fish all by himself. But he says he can tell us where they were, and he thinks he knows where Glen found the knife. And when I got home from lunch—" She fell silent as Kevin reappeared clutching a box of Baggies in his hand.

The boy watched in fascination as Mark Blakemoor carefully opened the folded note and sealed it inside one of the plastic bags even before reading it. Then, after scanning it himself, he handed it to Anne. Her hand trembling, she focused on the words:

> **Dearest Anne,**
> **Are you ready to face the truth yet? (Only part of it is in the computer, Anne. The rest is in your mind.) You've known it since my release from the hospital. Remember that afternoon, Anne? There was an excitement you'd never felt before, wasn't there? It was electricity, Anne, the kind that filled the theater when Nijinsky leaped. That's the single great sorrow of my life, you know. I never sat in an audience when Nijinsky danced. But at least I know he wasn't mad.**
> **Anyway, it's been fun, but now it's time for the final dance. And I've already chosen my partner.**

She read the note and reread it, her mind struggling to comprehend the words her eyes were seeing.

What did it mean?

Nijinsky? What did a dancer who'd been dead for nearly fifty years have to do with anything?

"Do you have any idea where Glen might have gone?" she heard Mark Blakemoor saying. His voice was gentle, and when she managed to tear her eyes away from the note to look up at him, she saw no trace of the satisfaction of vindication in his expression.

All she saw was sympathy.

"No," she breathed. "His car's out in front, so . . ." Her words died on her lips. She'd been about to say he must have gone for a walk, but it was pouring outside. Even if he'd gone out before the rain started, wouldn't he be back by now?

Suddenly a line from the note popped up in her mind:

It's time for the final dance. And I've already chosen my partner.

Then she remembered a line from the previous note:

I can come into your house any time, you know. Any time at all.

Images tumbled through her mind: the basement, cleaned up for the first time in years.

The motor home that had mysteriously appeared on the street, and remained there, just a couple of houses away.

The motor home that was now gone!

Now the pieces started falling together. Whoever had written the notes had been out there for days, watching them, watching *her*! "I know where he's been," she whispered, turning away from the window, her face drained of color. "Oh, God, Mark, he's been right outside for days. There was a motor home—" Still talking, telling Blakemoor how annoyed she'd been when the big van had appeared down the block, she found her leather carryall and began rummaging through it, searching for her notebook.

Her fingers finally closing on it, she pulled it out, ripped out the page on which she'd scrawled the R.V.'s license number, and handed it to Mark. "He was here, Mark!" she said. "My God, he's taken Glen!" She picked up the note again. "This is wrong. Mark, I know how it looks, and I know what you think, but it's wrong. Glen didn't write this note! Someone else did, and now he's got Glen!" But Mark Blakemoor wasn't listening; he was already on his cellular phone, putting a trace on the motor home's license plate. While he talked, Anne read the note one more time, and slowly her numbed mind began to work again.

The more she studied the note, the more her certainty grew that Glen hadn't written it. One word kept leaping out at her, taunting her. Finally she went to her computer, called up her file manager, and typed the single word into the search utility.

NIJINSKY.

She pressed the return button and waited. A few seconds later a short list of files appeared, all of them transcriptions of interviews she'd had over the years with one man.

Richard Kraven.

She double-clicked on the first file on the list and a second later the transcript appeared on the monitor, the word "Nijinsky" brightly highlighted.

She skipped to the next one, and the next one, her fascination, and her terror, growing as she read.

The truth of Richard Kraven began to emerge.

It was a truth he'd hinted at from the very beginning, offering her a single piece of the puzzle here, another one there. But the pieces had been so small, the hints so oblique, that she'd never recognized them for what they were.

The dance.

Metaphysics.

Electricity.

Life, death, insanity.

And Nijinsky.

Richard Kraven had told her about Vaslav Nijinsky himself. It was right there in one of the earliest interviews:

A.J.: Why the ballet, Mr. Kraven?

R.K.: My interest in ballet doesn't have to do with the dance, per se, Ms. Jeffers. It's the dancers that fascinate me.

A.J.: The dancers?

R.K.: Do you know what it takes to be a ballet dancer? Perfection. Perfection in physical discipline, and perfection in mental discipline. That is what's fascinating. The drive toward perfection.

A.J.: But is it really possible to achieve perfection?

R.K.: There was one. Vaslav Nijinsky. Are you familiar with the name?

A.J.: He died insane, didn't he?

R.K.: So they say, but I'm not at all sure I agree. What he did do was leap higher than anyone else, before or since. But he didn't just leap, Ms. Jeffers. At the zenith of his leaps, he hovered above the stage.

A.J.: I'm not sure I'm following you.

R.K.: Oh, at the time they said he only appeared to hover, but according to Nijinsky himself, he truly did suspend himself above the stage. He said he learned to separate himself from his body, and when he danced, he felt as if he were in the flies above the stage, manipulating his own body as if it were a marionette on strings.

A.J.: And you believe such a thing is possible?

R.K.: Not just possible, Ms. Jeffers. I believe he did it. You see, the reason he stopped dancing was that he began to feel that he might find himself stranded outside of his own body. He said that toward the end of his career he would find the spirit of a stranger inhabiting his body when he came back, and he began to feel the time would come when the invading spirit was stronger than his own and he would not be able to repossess his own body. It is why he stopped dancing, and why he was diagnosed as schizophrenic. But what if he wasn't schizophrenic, Ms. Jeffers? What if he wasn't schizophrenic at all? What would it mean?

The interview had ended there. Anne had made a note to check out the story of Vaslav Nijinsky. At the time, though, it had seemed irrelevant, and she had focused on what she'd then considered more important things.

Now, she realized, there were no more important things. Not if Vaslav Nijinsky—and Richard Kraven—were right.

Her eyes went back to the note one more time, fixing on the last line:

> **. . . I've already chosen my partner.**

If Kraven had been right, it wasn't Glen he'd chosen today, couldn't possibly be Glen, because he already had Glen.

Who, then?

Who might he have chosen? A terrible thought came to her, and she snatched up the phone, dialing Rayette Hoover's number. On the fourth ring, Rayette herself picked up the phone, and Anne, her voice catching in her throat, asked to speak to her daughter. When she hung up the phone a moment later, her face was ashen, her hands trembling. But before she could say anything, Mark Blakemoor spoke as he slid his phone into the pocket of his jacket. "The R.V.'s a rental, Anne," he said quietly. "And Glen rented it a few days ago."

Anne nodded mutely. "But it's not Glen," she said, her voice choked with a sob. "It's really him, Mark. He's taken Heather! Oh, God, he's taken Heather, and he's going to kill her."

Heather Jeffers glanced surreptitiously at her father, doing her best to appear to be staring through the windshield at the storm raging outside. When he'd picked her up at Rayette's, she'd been surprised—usually if either she or Kevin wanted to go somewhere, they walked, took the bus, or rode with friends. She'd been even more surprised when she saw what he was driving.

"Did you and Mom *buy* it?" she'd asked as she gazed at the enormous vehicle.

"I leased it," her father told her. "Your mom doesn't even know about it yet." When he'd told her they were going to meet her mother and brother at the Thai restaurant on Mercer Island, she hadn't questioned it, just as she hadn't questioned him when she asked where the rest of the family was and he'd told her, "They went over to Bellevue Square." He'd grinned at her. "So what do you think of the R.V.?"

As he'd driven down Denny toward the entrance to I-5, she'd explored the big motor home, then returned to the passenger seat. "How can you even drive it?" she asked. "It's so big."

He'd looked at her, and she'd seen something funny in his eyes—they didn't look quite right. "I can do lots of things you don't know about," he said, and his voice, like his eyes, seemed strange. It left her feeling weird—not exactly scared, but a bit worried—and she asked him if he was okay. When he told her—in the kind of voice he'd never let her use on Kevin—that there wasn't anything wrong at all, she'd turned to stare out the window, and hadn't said anything else until they were crossing Mercer Island on I-90 five minutes later.

"You want to get off at Island Crest, don't you?" she finally asked, breaking her silence only because he didn't seem to notice how close to the exit they were.

He hadn't answered her. And he hadn't gotten off at Island Crest, either. Instead he stayed on the freeway, and a minute later they left Mercer Island and were headed across the bridge to Bellevue.

"Dad! What's wrong with you?" Heather demanded as they passed the Factoria exit without even slowing down. "You could have turned around there."

"What makes you think I want to turn around?" her father replied. He'd looked directly at her while speaking, and with a start Heather realized he didn't look anything like her father now. He had a weird look on his face, the kind of look she'd always imagined a crazy person would have, and when he fixed his eyes on her, it made her skin get all crawly.

"Dad, what's going *on* with you?" she demanded. "How come you didn't get off on Mercer Island?"

"Because that's not where we're going," he replied.

"But you said—"

"It doesn't matter what I said. We're not going to Mercer Island."

"Then where are we going?" Heather asked.

"Somewhere else. Somewhere where we can be by ourselves."

It was those last words—*somewhere we can be by ourselves*—that had dissolved Heather's growing anger into sudden fear.

By ourselves.

Why did he want them to be by themselves? But she already knew the answer to that—ever since she'd been a little girl, she'd been warned about not going anywhere with men who said they were going to take her somewhere where they'd be by themselves.

But this was her father!

Then she remembered Jolene Ruyksman, who had been in her class until last year, when she'd tried to kill herself, and it turned out that her father had been getting in bed with her since she was only four, telling her that he'd kill her if she ever told anyone what they'd been doing.

But her own father wasn't like that—he'd never even looked at her funny, or done any of the things the counselors had warned her and her friends to watch out for when they'd talked about what had happened to Jolene.

Now she remembered something else, something her mother told her after her father had come home from the hospital. She had to get used to the idea that her father was going to be different, that he'd almost died, and that it would be a long time before he was completely recovered. But he couldn't have changed this much, could he?

As they passed through Issaquah and started up toward Snoqualmie Pass, she glanced at him again. A bolt of lighting shot across the sky, and for an instant the interior of the motor home was as bright as day. The white light turned her father's face ashen, and when he turned to look at her, his eyes fixed on hers with an intensity that sent a chill through her.

"Can you feel it?" he asked. "Can you feel the electricity?"

Mutely, Heather shook her head.

"You will," he said. "And when you do—"

The rest of his words were cut off by a crash of thunder that struck the motor home with enough force to make it shake.

"D-Dad?" Heather asked as the thunder faded away. "Dad, what are you going to do to me?"

The man who no longer bore any resemblance to her father turned to look at her once again.

He said nothing.

All he did was smile.

And the smile made Heather shudder with pure terror.

Anne and Mark were alone in the car.

When they first left the house, she followed Mark blindly, but even as she and Kevin had gotten into his car—an unmarked sedan with a magnetized set of flashers that could be put onto the top in a couple of seconds—she started to wonder exactly what they could do. With no idea of where the motor home had gone, how were they going to follow it?

"I'd be willing to bet he heads back to the mountains," Mark told her. Picking up the microphone he issued some quick—and to Anne, barely intelligible—orders into the car's radio, alerting every police unit in the county to look for the motor home. Given the weather, though, he knew the odds of it being spotted were next to nil. "Now tell me what you think is going on," he asked Anne, unwilling to let her know just how bad the odds of locating Glen were.

Kevin's presence in the backseat had kept Anne silent, and instead of telling him what she thought had happened, she gave him directions to Alan and Arlene Cline's house. Glen's partner had agreed to keep Kevin for the rest of the evening, even overnight if it became necessary. The look in Anne's eyes as she led Kevin inside had been enough to tell both Alan and Arlene that whatever had happened was serious, and that she didn't have time to explain. It wasn't until she and Mark were back in the car that she finally told him her theory. Even then, she refused to elaborate before calling Gordy Farber, who had pulled Glen's medical records up on the computer he kept at home. Not only had he confirmed what Anne only suspected, but he told her about the blackouts Glen had been having, and the strange dreams. Dreams, Anne instantly understood, that had not been dreams at all. Rather, they were glimpses of what the other entity within him was doing.

"It's not Glen in the motor home," she finally told Mark. "It's Richard Kraven."

"Richard Kraven is dead," Mark said flatly, his eyes staring out the windshield of the car he was guiding toward Highway 520. Kevin had already told him where they'd gone fishing, and how they'd gotten there, and Mark was pretty certain that whatever Glen was doing, he was following a pattern. When the motor home was found, he was sure it would be very close to where Glen had taken Edna Kraven just a few days ago and Kevin only this morning.

"His body's dead," Anne agreed. Then she related the story of Vaslav Nijinsky, the story that Richard Kraven himself had told her years earlier.

"So even if Nijinsky wasn't a nutcase—and I'm not saying he wasn't—how does it relate? Glen isn't into out-of-body experiences, is he?" Mark asked.

"Glen was dead for almost two minutes," Anne said, her voice as flat as the detective's had been a moment earlier. "The morning he had his heart attack, they lost him in the ambulance on the way to Group Health. They had to stop so both of the medics could work on him. It's all in the records, Mark. They used CPR, drugs, and the defibrillator. And it happened at almost exactly nine A.M., Pacific Time."

Mark glanced at her. Pacific Time? What was *that* all about? But before the question was fully formed in his mind, he knew the answer. Nine A.M. Pacific Time was noon Eastern Time.

The exact moment that Richard Kraven had been executed.

Blakemoor remembered the words Anne had uttered only a few moments before, quoting what Richard Kraven had said in one of the interviews she'd reread only a little while earlier: "*Nijinsky stopped dancing because he thought another spirit was entering his body while he was out of it.*" Repeating the words to himself, he still couldn't put them together into anything he could understand. "Anne, it doesn't make any sense," he began, but his voice had lost a little of its confidence.

"Doesn't it? What about all the stories you hear? All the people who have had near-death experiences? They're all the same, Mark. They leave their body, and they float above it. They see what's happening, and they hear what people are saying. Some of them feel like they have a choice about coming back or not. . . ."

Her voice trailed off, but Mark Blakemoor already knew where she was going. "And if Richard Kraven were dying at the same instant," he said, "and wanted to come back badly enough—"

"He hated me," Anne burst out. "I could see it in his eyes, I could hear it in his voice." She kept talking, telling Mark what she'd pieced together from the old interviews, what had finally come to make sense. "He was different from other serial killers," she finally finished. "He wasn't killing them because he wanted them dead, Mark. He was trying to figure out how to bring them back to life after they died."

"That doesn't account for Rory and Edna," Mark countered.

"He was punishing Rory. And I suspect he just plain hated his mother. Besides, his motive is different now. He's finished experimenting. Now he's getting even. With me." She stared out at the storm that was raging around them as they left 520 and started through Redmond, working their way farther east, following the route Kevin had described. "Oh, God," Anne sighed, "why can't they find him?"

"They will," the detective replied. "Or we will. One way or another, we're going to get Heather back." But even as he said the words, Mark Blakemoor wasn't sure he believed them. And he sure didn't believe the weird story Anne had just told him.

At least, he didn't think he did.

The rain slashed out of the sky in a torrent that cascaded off the motor home's windshield in a rippling sheet, distorting everything outside almost to the point of invisibility. Now all that Heather could see were the wavering headlights of oncoming cars, but even those were getting fewer, and farther between. It was as if the night and the storm had conspired to drive everyone but them off the road, and the farther from home they drove, the more frightened Heather became. "Can't we stop?" she pleaded. "Please?"

Richard Kraven let his eyes leave the road ahead just long enough to glance quickly at Heather Jeffers. Her features were barely visible, but as a westbound truck bore down on them from the opposite direction, her face was lit for a quick second.

It was enough: Kraven could clearly see the terror in the child's expression, and even as he shifted his attention back to the road, he savored the fear he had instilled in her.

She knew something was wrong, knew she was in danger.

But she didn't yet know what danger lay ahead, and that uncertainty—and the added terror it produced in Heather—made the moment even sweeter for Richard Kraven. His one regret was that Anne was not here, too.

If only he could talk to her; tell her what he was going to do to her daughter, make her suffer even more from the foreknowledge of what Heather would feel.

If only he could watch Anne's face as he carefully cut Heather's chest open to expose her heart.

If only he could hear Anne scream as he held her daughter's

throbbing heart in his hand, and listen to her pleas as he slowly squeezed that heart to a stop.

If only he could witness her pain and helplessness as he went about his work, just as she'd savored his as she hounded him until finally they'd locked him in a cell and made him sit alone until they'd electrocuted him. He hadn't let her see how much he'd suffered, of course. He'd hidden his terror of the cell, even hidden his terror of the electric chair. But although he'd kept his fears hidden, he knew she'd sensed them, knew she'd pleasured in them.

Tonight, though, she would take her punishment. Tonight, and for the rest of her life.

Lightning blazed across the sky, instantly followed by a thunderclap that shook the motor home, and Richard Kraven felt a thrill of pleasure as a tiny cry escaped Heather Jeffers's lips.

"Please," he heard her beg. "Please can't we stop? We're going to get killed!"

A sign loomed ahead, its face glowing green in the glare of the headlights, and though the water sluicing over the windshield prevented him from reading the letters, he knew what the sign said.

The exit for Snoqualmie Falls was only a little way ahead. Moving his foot off the accelerator, Richard Kraven gently touched the brake, and the motor home slowed.

Heather, her hands clamped tight to the armrests of the passenger seat, tried to catch a glimpse of the sign as they passed under it, but the flash of lightning had momentarily blinded her, and her pupils had not yet readjusted to the darkness of the night.

He hadn't spoken to her for a long time, hadn't even looked her way for so long that she was starting to wonder if he'd forgotten she was even there.

What was wrong? What had happened to her father?

This morning, when he and Kevin had taken off to go fishing, he'd seemed fine. Was it really possible for someone to go crazy in just a few hours? She thought about Kevin. Where was he? Had her father taken her brother home before coming to Rayette's to pick her up?

She stole another glance at the face lit only by the glow of the dash lights. Though the features were still recognizable as those of her father, they had taken on an evil cast that chilled her blood. And when he'd glanced at her a moment ago, she had had the terrible feeling that he was planning what he was going to do to her.

As the motor home left the interstate, Heather leaned forward, searching for something—anything—that would give her a clue as to where they were. If they were coming to a town—even just a gas station—she could make a run for the door before he could stop the van and jump out, even if it was still moving.

"Fasten your seat belt, Heather. And put your hands on the dashboard."

His hard, cold voice—a voice she'd never heard from her father—made her instantly obey the order.

The motor home slowed further, and the man in the driver's seat—the man who looked like her father, but who she knew was not—spoke again.

"Don't think of trying to get out. I'm much stronger than you, and if you try to get to the door, I'll stop you. And I'll make you wish you hadn't tried to get away from me."

Heather's heart pounded. What did he mean? What would he do? As the motor home turned left, and Heather finally recognized the main street of Snoqualmie village, she searched for someone who might be able to help her. But the street was deserted, swept bare of traffic by the ferocity of the storm.

A sob, not just of terror, but of frustration, bubbled out of her throat. If there was no one to help her in the town, she would have no hope at all once they had passed it by and left its lights behind.

As they reached the edge of the village, the man spoke. "You're afraid of me, aren't you, Heather?"

Heather, too numbed even to think, nodded mutely.

"You know I'm not your father, don't you?"

Again Heather could only nod.

"Do you know who I am?"

Now she shook her head, but something in his voice made her turn and look at him.

He was smiling, but it was a smile with no warmth in it.

He was staring at her, his cold eyes boring into her.

"My name is Richard Kraven," he said.

Heather felt a terrible numbness spread through her. What did he mean? Richard Kraven was dead! He'd been executed the day her father had his heart attack! Yet even as her mind tried to deny it, she somehow knew that the words the man had spoken were true. Though this man's flesh and bones were those of her father, his voice and his eyes told her he was not. "What do you want?" she breathed, her voice barely audible.

Richard Kraven's cold smile widened. "I want to touch you, Heather," he said. "I want to touch your heart."

"This is crazy," Anne Jeffers said. She had no idea where they were—they hadn't seen a sign for miles, and except for them, the narrow highway winding along the river was utterly deserted. Beyond the confines of Mark Blakemoor's car a dense blackness seemed to absorb the glow of the headlights, the slashing rain cutting visibility to no more than a few yards. Mark had been forced by the intensity of the storm to slow to little more than a crawl, and Anne's feeling that it was a mistake to have come up here was growing by the second. A flash of lightning burst above them, instantly followed by a crack of thunder so sharp it made Anne jump in her seat. "We've got to go back, Mark! This is insane! We don't even know where we are!"

"We're almost to the campground where they found Edna Kraven this morning," Mark replied. "Kevin said the place they were fishing wasn't very much farther up the road. We'll check those, then—"

The police radio crackled to life, and Mark snatched up the microphone.

"Go ahead."

"Turns out your R.V. has a cell phone, and we got a trace on it," a barely audible voice, almost lost in the static caused by the storm, said.

Anne seemed about to speak, but Mark shook his head, leaning toward the radio's speaker as he strained to catch the crackling words. But only some garbled static came through the speaker.

"Say again!" Mark shouted into the microphone. "We've got a lot of static!"

The radio's speaker crackled again, and from somewhere in the cacophony of background noise a single word emerged.

Snoqualmie.

There was more, but again it was drowned out by static, and when the next transmission came through, nothing was audible at all. "Doesn't matter," Mark muttered. "They're up here." His eyes barely left the road as he quickly told Anne what had happened: "Cellular phones are almost like a homing device—they always stay in contact with the system. You can't pin them down exactly, but you *can* get the general area they're operating out of." Without thinking, he reached out and took Anne's hand, squeezing it gently. "We'll find them. Just hang on. We'll find them."

The car continued creeping up the grade, and finally they came to the campground, but when Mark saw that not only was the police tape still hanging across the road leading into it, but that the gate was closed and locked as well, he didn't even try to turn in. A mile and a half farther up the road, just as he was starting to wonder if Kevin had remembered where he'd been as well as he thought he had, the small sign for the turnoff to the right appeared out of the blackness. When he came to the entrance to the narrow lane a few moments later, he brought the car to a stop. The dirt track, already deeply rutted by a stream of water, was impassable by anything but a four-wheel drive. Mark might get the sedan down, but he would never get it up again, at least not tonight.

But how long had it been like this? What if the motor home was already down there?

He reached into the glove compartment, took out his gun, then got out of the car.

Anne, immediately understanding what he was about to do, scrambled out the passenger door.

"Get back in the car!" Mark shouted over the wind that was screaming through the trees, driving the rain almost horizontally. "You can't—"

"If you can go down there, so can I," Anne shouted back. "It's my daughter, remember?" Before Mark could protest further, she started picking her way down the muddy road, steadying herself against the trunks of trees, grabbing at the shrubbery when she felt her feet skid on the slippery mud.

It wasn't until she was halfway down the twisting lane that she realized she hadn't even thought about the possibility that she might be wrong; that Glen—the real, loving, Glen, might be with Heather, rather than merely the body of her husband, now fully controlled by a monstrous, vengeful, Richard Kraven.

An image of the monogram Kraven had carved into the flesh of each of his victims leapt into her mind, and she visualized Heather, her chest cut open, her lungs and heart—

No!

Not Heather! It couldn't happen to Heather—she wouldn't *let* it happen to Heather!

A strangled sound of fear, fury, and frustration rose in her throat, and she bolted ahead, terrified that even now the motor home might be parked at the foot of the lane.

Terrified that Richard Kraven might already have begun his work.

"It won't hurt, you know."

Heather tried not to look at the man who no longer bore any resemblance at all to her father.

He'd pulled the motor home off the road into a picnic area, a spot so secluded that even if a car passed on the road a few yards away, she knew the van probably wouldn't even be noticed. And if someone did see it, why would they come to see if something was wrong? People parked motor homes everywhere, and nobody ever thought about what might be happening inside them.

The man had pulled all the curtains closed and turned on the generator.

Heather hadn't dared even to move out of the passenger seat.

Part of it was the look in the man's eye. The warmth she'd always seen in her father's eyes, the gentle love she'd always felt when her father looked at her, was gone. The eyes that now stared cruelly from her father's face had a dead look to them, glazed over as if hiding the fact that there was no soul behind them, no human spirit that might show her any kindness. Was it that look of death that had made her slowly come to believe he hadn't lied to her, that he truly was Richard Kraven?

She knew what Kraven had done, knew how many bodies had been found in the area to which this man who was not her father had brought her tonight. She'd read the descriptions of the corpses they'd found, their breasts torn open, their hearts ripped out. It was what he'd meant when he said he wanted to touch her heart, and as the meaning of the words sank in, her terror had inexorably para-lyzed her.

She couldn't run, couldn't bring herself even to try to bolt from the motor home. He would catch her before she even reached the door. And even if she made it out into the raging storm, what would she do? Where would she go?

He was getting something out of one of the cupboards now. A plastic bottle, filled with a liquid. He'd taken a rag out of a drawer, and was soaking it now with the liquid from the bottle.

She could smell it, smell the fumes that were filling the confines of the motor home.

He was moving toward her, holding the rag in his hand, his eyes fixing on her the way those of a rattlesnake fix on its prey in the moments before it strikes. She felt hypnotized by his gaze, and when he reached out to press the rag over her nose and mouth, her fear robbed her even of the power to turn away.

Taking a deep breath, Heather closed her eyes and prayed that Richard Kraven hadn't lied to her, that at least she would feel nothing as he reached inside her body to touch her heart.

Touch her, and kill her.

Anne burst out of the mouth of the dirt road, stumbling as her foot struck a rock hidden by the blackness of the night and the thick grass of the meadow. Mark Blakemoor caught her arm, steadying her, even as he played the brilliant beam of a halogen light over the area. Despite the rain, there were still a pair of curving tracks where the grass had been crushed by the weight of a car driving through it recently. "This is the place Kevin told us about," he said, almost shouting to make himself heard above the howling wind.

"But where are they?" Anne cried. "You said they'd be here—"

"I said we'll find them, and we will!" Mark replied. He moved closer to the river and played his light on the opposite bank. A moment later he found what he was looking for—the pile of stones Kevin said his father had been looking through. Mark started toward the river, keeping the light steady on the rocks, and even before he'd waded into the stream, Anne knew what he was going to do.

"Are you crazy?" she shouted. "You'll never make it—you'll drown!" But he ignored her words, striding into the river, slowing down only enough to make sure of his footing on the rocky bottom. She stood shivering in the rain, her soaked clothes clinging to her skin as the rain sluiced over her, her teeth chattering, her eyes glued to the bobbing beam of the halogen flashlight. After what seemed like an eternity, but couldn't have been more than a few minutes, he was back.

"Come on," he said, his voice taking on a new urgency. "I think we might be running out of time."

"You found him, didn't you?" Anne asked as they started back up the road, half walking, half scrambling through the mud, clinging to each other and whatever else they could find to keep themselves from sliding backward down the slippery track. "You found Danny Harrar."

Blakemoor nodded, seeing no point in trying to keep what he'd found from Anne. He'd been so certain he'd find nothing in the pile of rocks, that even if the knife Glen had found that morning were indeed Danny Harrar's, it meant nothing more than that the boy had dropped it somewhere along the river long ago. What he'd found beneath the rocks, though, had finally convinced him that however bizarre Anne's theory might sound, it was at least an explanation for something he could rationalize no other way. And if it was Richard Kraven that Heather was with instead of her father . . .

Even the veteran homicide detective couldn't bring himself to think about what might be happening to her.

Both of them panting, they finally arrived back at the car. "You drive," Mark told Anne, getting into the passenger seat. "I want to concentrate on the radio. I can't believe that by now this whole area isn't crawling with cops!" As Anne started the car, put it in gear, and headed up the road, Mark Blakemoor grabbed the radio's microphone, attempting to raise the police dispatcher. Another sheet of lightning tore at the darkness, and a roar of thunder drowned out the static that was all that emerged from the radio's speakers.

Anne struggled to see through the rain-streaked windshield. The wipers couldn't even begin to keep up with the wind-driven torrent running down the glass in wide rivulets. Mark suddenly grabbed her arm. "Stop the car!"

Startled by his command, Anne shifted her foot from the accelerator to the brake, hitting it so hard the car lost its traction, the rear end fishtailing wildly before she released the brake, steered into a skid, and felt the tires grab the wet pavement. As the car rolled to a stop, Mark cranked his window down and stuck his head out into the force of the storm. "Back up," he cried, his words all but inaudible, immediately carried away by the wind. Her heart pounding, Anne carefully began backing down the slope. Suddenly the headlights caught a sign with the familiar symbol of a picnic table.

Was it possible? Could Mark have seen the motor home?

Before she could ask him, he was back on the radio, once again desperately trying to make himself heard through the interference of the storm.

CHAPTER 71

Heather felt as if she were drowning.

She could barely breathe, and her mind felt fogged.

But she could hear something.

A steady rumble, as if a train were going past.

Suddenly there was a flash of light, and a terrible crash, and the fog began to disperse.

The motor home.

She was in the motor home with her father—*no, not her father!*—and there was a storm.

Frightened. She was terribly frightened. So frightened she hadn't even been able to move when the man had held the rag over her mouth.

All she'd been able to do was take a single, deep breath, hold it as long as she could, then let herself go limp, as if she'd passed out. But it hadn't worked. The man kept the rag over her face, and finally she had to breathe in the fumes, and she felt herself starting to pass out. Somehow, she'd managed to hold still, not to struggle, not to give any sign at all that she was still even half conscious.

More of the fog lifted, and finally she could open her eyes a tiny bit, just enough to see.

The motor home had changed. Everywhere she looked, everything was blurry, as if covered by some kind of thick not-quite-transparent plastic.

A movement caught her eye, a movement just below her range of vision. She shifted her eyes slightly, and then she saw it: poised above her breast was a hand.

The hand held a knife.

A razor-sharp knife that was moving closer and closer to her.

Her eyes refocused on the face beyond the knife. Her father's face!

A scream rose in her throat and instantly erupted from her mouth. "No! Dad! Oh, God, *no!* Dad, *don't!*"

As Heather's howl of terror crashed against his eardrums, Richard Kraven froze, the knife with which he'd been about to make the first perfect incision into Heather Jeffers's flesh hovering a fraction of an inch above the pale skin of her breast.

Deep within his mind, something stirred.

As the girl on the bed screamed again, the being inside him, the being he thought he'd succeeded in crushing, surged back into consciousness.

For Glen, it was like being jerked out of a deep sleep. One moment there was nothing, and the next he was fully awake. Then, as Heather cried out to him again, all the nightmares he'd had since his heart attack came rushing back to him. All the fleeting images coalesced into a terrible picture of blood, carnage, and death.

And now, in his hand, he held a knife, poised above his daughter's naked breast, and even as he struggled against the terrible force inside him, he felt an almost irresistible urge to use the knife.

To cut Heather's skin and flesh.

To expose the bone beneath.

Do it! Richard Kraven's voice screamed inside his head. *Do it now, before it's too late!* As Richard Kraven recovered from the shock of Heather's sudden scream, Glen felt the power of Kraven's evil begin to take him once again. Gathering himself together, he seized control of his body for a moment, and hurled himself away from the bed into the farthest corner of the tiny bedroom. "Run!" he screamed. "For God's sake, Heather, get away from me!"

Instinctively responding to her father's voice, Heather scrambled off the bed, darted down the narrow passage to the salon, then fumbled with the door for a moment before she managed to yank it open and stumble out into the night. From behind her she heard a great bellow of rage, and then, ahead, a pair of headlights suddenly went on, trapping her in their beam like an insect caught on a pin.

For a split second she felt a wave of panic rise up inside her, but then, over the howling wind, she heard a voice calling to her. "Heather! Oh, God, Heather!" Sobbing with relief, Heather broke into a lurching run, and a second later felt her mother's arms close around her.

Howling with rage, Richard Kraven hurled himself after the fleeing girl, then stopped short in the door to the motor home as the glare of headlights momentarily blinded him. Instinctively ducking away from the light, he retreated back inside, but almost instantly realized his mistake.

The motor home was a trap with no way out except the door he'd just jerked shut!

Leaping back to the door, he shoved it open, then raced out into the blackness of the night, escaping the twin cones of light coming from the automobile just as the first shot was fired, the crack of the exploding shell sharp in his ears, the dull sound of it slamming into the flimsy wall of the motor home almost lost in the wind. "Freeze!" he heard a voice shout, but he ignored the command, racing away into the darkness.

Suddenly another beam of light hit him. He tried to dodge away from it, but it held steady on him no matter which way he turned. Following his instincts, he ran directly away from it, but now was aware of someone following him, chasing him.

He feinted to the right, then cut left, and for just a second he was out of the light. But he was running blind now, his pupils not yet dilated, and then he slammed into something.

His hands groped at it, and just as the white light of the halogen flashlight found him again, he realized what it was. A fence, its wire mesh rising up eight feet from the ground. On the other side was a narrow ledge of rock before the steep bank fell away to the river below.

If he could get over the fence, put it between him and his pursuer, he might still escape. Ignoring the pain as the wire cut into his fingers, Richard Kraven began climbing.

He was at the top, one of his legs already swung over to the other side, when Mark Blakemoor caught up to him, leaping up onto the fence to grab at the one leg that still hung just within his reach. The fingers of both Mark's hands closed on Richard Kraven's ankle, and then a scream of agony erupted from Kraven's mouth as he was jerked down onto the top of the fence, the twisted ends of the wire digging into his testicles, sending spasms of agonizing pain throughout his body. His back went rigid and he thrust his arms toward the sky. Suddenly the night was illuminated by one more bolt of lightning, reaching down from the clouds, searching for the closest point to the ground.

It found Richard Kraven, flashing down to strike his hands, burning its way through his body as it raced down into the fence.

Mark Blakemoor's body went rigid as the voltage shot through him, but as the electricity finally found the ground it sought and faded into the earth, he dropped to the ground and lay still.

As the roll of thunder the lightning had generated faded, a new sound could be heard above the whistling of the wind through the trees. The wail of sirens grew louder, and then, as flashing red and blue lights raced toward the picnic ground, the rain finally began to ease and the wind to die away.

A moment later two police cars pulled to a stop, their headlights illuminating the macabre scene at the fence. As their doors slammed and their occupants raced toward the body that lay on the ground, Anne Jeffers stood next to Heather, holding her daughter close.

She barely heard the questions someone was asking her, was only dimly aware of the men kneeling by the still form of Mark Blakemoor.

Her own eyes were still fixed on the top of the fence where the body of the man who had been her husband still hung. Then, as she watched, the weight of the body tore itself loose from the fence, dropped to the other side, and disappeared over the edge of the bank. If it made any sound as it fell into the river below, Anne didn't hear it.

The last of the rain stopped falling, and the wind finally fell completely still. An eerie quiet came over the night. Her arm still wrapped protectively around Heather, Anne made her way through the crowd of people crouched around Mark Blakemoor. She gazed down at him, and for just a moment she was certain that Mark, too, was dead. But then his eyelids fluttered briefly and opened.

His eyes met hers. Their gaze held for a moment, and for just an instant Anne thought she saw exactly the same kind of twinkle in Mark's eyes that had so often been in Glen's, back before his heart attack. Then the look disappeared and she was once more looking into the eyes of the detective who had just saved her daughter's life.

"He'll live," she heard someone say as Mark managed the tiniest of smiles, then let his eyes close again.

"It's over," Anne murmured into her daughter's ear. "It's over, darling, and we're all right. All of us."

John Saul's first novel, *Suffer the Children*, published in 1977, was an immediate million-copy bestseller. He has since written such *New York Times* bestsellers as *The God Project, Nathaniel, Brainchild, Hellfire, The Unwanted, The Unloved, Creature, Sleepwalk, Second Child, Darkness, Guardian,* and *The Homing,* each a riveting tale of supernatural, technological, or psychological terror. John Saul lives in Seattle, Washington, and Maui, and is at work on his next chilling novel of suspense.

Readers of John Saul now can join the John Saul Fan Club by writing to the address below. Members receive an autographed photo of John, newsletters, and advance information about forthcoming publications. Please send your name and address to:

The John Saul Fan Club
P.O. Box 17035
Seattle, Washington 98107